Lee Wilson Dodd

The Book of Susan

Lee Wilson Dodd

The Book of Susan

1st Edition | ISBN: 978-3-75232-479-2

Place of Publication: Frankfurt am Main, Germany

Year of Publication: 2020

Outlook Verlag GmbH, Germany.

THE
BOOK OF SUSAN

BY

LEE WILSON DODD

THE FIRST CHAPTER

I

I T happens that I twice saw Susan's mother, one of those soiled rags of humanity used by careless husbands for wiping their boots; but Susan does not remember her. John Stuart Mill studied Greek at three, and there is a Russian author who recalls being weaned as the first of his many bitter experiences. Either Susan's mental life did not waken so early or the record has faded. She remembers only the consolate husband, her father; remembers him only too well. The backs of his square, angry-looking hands were covered with an unpleasant growth of reddish bristles; his nostrils were hairy, too, and seemed formed by Nature solely for the purpose of snorting with wrath. It must not be held against Susan that she never loved her father; he was not created to inspire the softer emotions. Nor am I altogether certain just why he was created at all.

Nevertheless, Robert Blake was in his soberer hours—say, from Tuesdays to Fridays—an expert mechanic, thoroughly conversant with the interior lack of economy of most makes of automobiles. He had charge of the repair department of the Eureka Garage, New Haven, where my not-too-robust touring car of those primitive days spent, during the spring of 1907, many weeks of interesting and expensive invalidism. I forget how many major operations it underwent.

It was not at the Eureka Garage, however, that I first met Bob Blake. Nine years before I there found him again, I had defended him in court—as it happens, successfully—on a charge of assault with intent to kill. That was almost my first case, and not far—thank heaven—from my last. Bob's defense, I remember, was assigned to me by a judge who had once borrowed fifty dollars from my father, which he never repaid; at least, not in cash. There are more convenient methods. True, my father was no longer living at the time I was appointed to defend Bob; but that is a detail.

Susan was then four years old. I can't say I recall her, if I even laid eyes on her. But Mrs. Bob appeared as a witness, at my request—it was all but her final appearance, poor woman; she died of an embolism within a week—and I remember she told the court that a kinder husband and father than Bob had never existed. I remember, too, that the court pursed its lips and the gentlemen of the jury grinned approvingly, for Mrs. Bob could not easily conceal something very like the remains of a purple eye, which she attributed to hearing a suspicious noise one night down cellar, a sort of squeaking noise, and to falling over the cat on her tour of investigation—with various circumstantial *minutiæ* of no present importance.

The important thing is, that Bob went scot-free and was as nearly grateful as his temperament permitted. His assault—with an umbrella stand—had been upon a fellow reveller of no proved worth to the community, and perhaps this may have influenced the jury's unexpected verdict.

Of Susan herself my first impression was gained at the Eureka Garage. Bob Blake, just then, was lying beneath my car, near which I hovered listening to his voluble but stereotyped profanity. He had lost the nut from a bolt, and, unduly constricted, sought it vainly, while his tongue followed the line of least resistance. I was marveling at the energy of his wrath and the poverty of his imagination, when I became aware of a small being beside me, in plaid calico. She had eager black eyes—terrier's eyes—in a white, whimsical little face. One very long and very thin black pigtail dangled over her left shoulder and down across her flat chest to her waist, where it was tied with a shoe string and ended lankly, without even the semblance of a curl. In her right hand she bore a full dinner pail, and with her left thumb she pointed toward the surging darkness beneath my car.

"Say, mister, please," said the small being, "if I was to put this down, would you mind telling him his dinner's come?"

"Not a bit," I responded. "Are you Bob's youngster?"

"I'm Susan Blake," she answered; and very softly placed the dinner pail on the step of the car.

"Why don't you wait and see your father?" I suggested. "He'll come up for air in a minute."

"That's why I'm going now," said Susan.

Whereupon she gave a single half skip—the very ghost of a skip—then walked demurely from me and out through the great door.

II

Bob Blake, in those days, lived in a somewhat dilapidated four-room house, off toward the wrong end of Birch Street. His family arrangements were peculiar. He had never married again; but not very long after his wife's death a dull-eyed, rather mussy young woman, with a fondness for rouge pots, had taken up her abode with him—to the scandal and fascination of the neighborhood. It was an outrage, of course! With a child in the house, too!

Something ought to be done about it!

Yet, oddly enough, nothing that much worried Bob ever was done about it, reckoning the various shocked-and-grieved forms of conversation as nothing. As he never tired of asserting, Bob didn't give a damn for the cackle of a lot of hens. He guessed he knew his way about; and so did Pearl. Let the damned hens cackle their heads off; he was satisfied!

And so, eventually, I am forced to believe, were the hens. In the earlier days of the scandal there was much clitter-clatter of having the law on him, serving papers, and the like; but, as hen cackle sometimes will, it came to precisely naught. Nor am I certain that, as the years passed, the neighborhood did not grow a little proud of its one crimson patch of wickedness; I am reasonably certain, indeed, that more than one drab life took on a little borrowed flush of excitement from its proximity.

Of course no decent, God-fearing woman would ever greet either Bob or Pearl; but every time one passed either of them without a nod or a "How's things to-day?" it gave one something to talk about, at home, or over any amicable fence.

As for the men, they too were forbidden to speak; but men, most of them, are unruly creatures if at large. You can't trust them safely five minutes beyond the sound of your voice.

There was even one man, old Heinze, proprietor of the Birch Street grocery store, who now and then cautiously put forth a revolutionary sentiment.

"Dey lifs alvays togedder—like man unt vife—nod? Vere iss der diffurunz, Mrs. Shay?"

"Shame on you for *them* words, Mr. Heinze!"

"*Aber*"—with a slow, wide smile—"vere iss der diffurunz, Mrs. Shay? I leaf id to you?"

That Pearl and Bob lived always together cannot be denied, and perhaps they also lived as some men and their lawful wives are accustomed to live— off toward the wrong end of city streets; and occasionally, no doubt, toward the right end of them as well. Midweek, things wore along dully enough, but over Sunday came drink and ructions. Susan says she has never been able to understand why Sunday happens to be called a day of rest. The day of arrest, she was once guilty of naming it.

Bob's neighbors, I fear, were not half so scandalized by his week-end drunkenness as by what Mrs. Perkins—three doors nearer the right end of

Birch Street—invariably called his "brazen immorality." Intoxication was not a rare vice in that miscellaneous block or two of factory operatives. Nor can it be said that immorality, in the sense of Mrs. Perkins, was so much rare as it was nervously concealed. The unique quality of Bob's sin lay in its brazen element; that was what stamped him peculiarly as a social outlaw.

Bob accepted this position, if sober, with a grim disregard. He had a bitter, lowering nature at best, and when not profane was taciturn. As for Pearl, social outlawry may be said to have been her native element. She had a hazy mind in a lazy body, and liked better than most things just to sit in a rocking-chair and polish her finger nails, as distinguished from cleaning them. Only the guiltless member of this family group really suffered from its low social estate, but she suffered acutely. Little Susan could not abide being a social outlaw.

True, she was not always included in the general condemnation of her family by the grown-ups; but the children were ruthless. They pointed fingers, and there was much conscious giggling behind her back; while some of the daintier little girls—the very little girls whom Susan particularly longed to chum with—had been forbidden to play with "that child," and were not at all averse to telling her so, flatly, with tiny chins in air and a devastating expression of rectitude on their smug little faces. At such times Susan would fight back impending cataracts, stick her own freckled nose toward the firmament, and even, I regret to say, if persistently harassed, thrust forth a rigid pink tongue. This, Susan has since informed me, is the embryonic state of "swearing like anything."

The little boys, on the whole, were better. They often said cruel things, but Susan felt that they said them in a quite different spirit from their instinctively snobbish and Grundyish sisters—said them merely by way of bravado, or just for the fun of seeing whether or not she would cry. And then they often let her join in their games, and on those happy occasions treated her quite as an equal, with an impartial and, to Susan, entirely blissful roughness. Susan early decided that she liked boys much better than girls.

There was, for example, Jimmy Kane, whose widowed mother took in washing, and so never had any time to clean up her huddled flat, over Heinze's grocery store, or her family of four—two boys and two girls. No one ever saw skin, as in itself it really is, on the faces of Mrs. Kane's children, and Jimmy was always, if comparison be possible, the grimiest of the brood. For some reason Jimmy always had a perpetual slight cold, and his funny flat button of a nose wept, winter and summer alike, though never into an unnecessary handkerchief. His coat-sleeve served, even if its ministrations did not add to the tidiness of his countenance.

Susan often wished she might scrub him, just to see what he really looked like; for she idolized Jimmy. Not that Jimmy ever had paid any special attention to her, except on one occasion. It was merely that he accepted her as part of the human scheme of things, which in itself would almost have been enough to win Susan's affectionate admiration. But one day, as I have hinted, he became the god of her idolatry.

The incident is not precisely idyllic. A certain Joe—Giuseppe Gonfarone; *ætat.* 14—whose father peddled fruit and vegetables, had recently come into the neighborhood; a black-curled, brown-eyed little devil, already far too wise in the manifold unseemliness of this sad old planet. Joe was strong, stocky, aggressive, and soon posed as something of a bully among the younger boys along Birch Street. Within less than a month he had infected the minds of many with a new and rich vocabulary of oaths and smutty words. Joe was not of the unconsciously foul-mouthed; he relished his depravity. In fact, youngster as he was, Joe had in him the makings of that slimiest product of our cities—the street pimp, or cadet.

It was one fine spring day, three years or so before I met Susan in the Eureka Garage, that Joe, with a group of Birch Street boys, was playing marbles for keeps, just at the bottom of the long incline which carries Birch Street down to the swamp land and general dump at the base of East Rock. Susan was returning home from Orange Street, after bearing her father his full dinner pail, and as she came up to the boys she halted on one foot, using the toe of her free foot meanwhile to scratch mosquito bites upward along her supporting shin.

"H'lo, Susan!" called Jimmy Kane, with his perfunctory good nature. "What's bitin' you?"

Then it was his turn to knuckle-down. Susan, still balanced cranelike, watched him eager-eyed, and was so delighted when he knocked a fine fat reeler of Joe's out of the ring, jumping up with a yell of triumph to pocket it, that she too gave a shrill cheer: "Oh, goody! I knew you'd win!"

The note of ecstasy in her tone infuriated Joe. "Say!" he shrieked. "You getta hell outta here!"

Susan's smile vanished; her white, even teeth—she had all her front ones, she tells me; she was ten—clicked audibly together.

"It's no business of yours!" she retorted.

"You're right; it ain't!" This from Jimmy, still in high good humor. "You stay here if you want. You're as good as him!"

"Who's as good as me?"

6

"She is!"

"*Her?*" Joe's lips curled back. He turned to the other boys, who had all scrambled to their feet by this time and, instinctively scenting mischief, were standing in a sort of ring. "He says she's good as me!"

Two of the smallest boys tittered, from pure excitement. Susan's nose went up.

"I'm better. I'm not a dago!"

Joe leaped toward Susan and thrust his dense, bull-like head forward, till his eyes were glaring into hers.

"Mebbe I live lika you—eh? Mebbe I live," cried Joe, "with a dirty *whore!*"

There was a gasp from the encircling boys as Susan fell back from this word, which she did not wholly comprehend, but whose vileness she felt, somehow, in her very flesh. Joe, baring gorilla teeth, burst into coarse jubilation.

It was just at this point that Jimmy Kane, younger than Joe by a year or more, and far slighter, jumped on the little ruffian—alas, from behind!—and dealt him as powerful a blow on the head as he could compass; a blow whose effectiveness, I reluctantly admit, was enhanced by the half brick with which Jimmy had first of all prudently provided himself. Joe Gonfarone went to earth, inert, but bleeding profusely.

There was a scuttling of frightened feet in every direction. Susan herself did not stop running until she reached the very top of the Birch Street incline. Then she looked back, her eyes lambent, her heart throbbing, not alone from the rapid ascent. Yes, there was Jimmy—*her* Jimmy!—kneeling in the dust by the still prostrate Joe. Susan could not hear him, but she knew somehow from his attitude that he was scared to death, and that he was asking Joe if he was hurt much. She agonized with her champion, feeling none the less proud of him, and she waited for him at the top of the rise, hoping to thank him, longing to kiss his hands.

But Jimmy, when he did pass her, went by without a glance, at top speed. He was bound for a doctor. So Susan never really managed to thank Jimmy at all. She merely idolized him in secret, a process which proved, however, fairly heart-warming and, in the main, satisfactory.

It took three stitches to mend Joe's head—a fact famous in the junior annals of Birch Street for some years—and soon after he appeared, somewhat broken in spirit, in the street again, his parents moved him, Margharita and the sloe-eyed twins to Bridgeport—very much, be it admitted, to the relief of Jimmy Kane, who had lived for three weeks nursing a lonely fear of dark reprisals.

III

There was one thing about Bob Blake's four-room house—it exactly fitted his family. The floor plan was simple and economically efficient. Between the monolithic door slab—relic of a time when Bob's house had been frankly "in the country"—and the public street lay a walk formed of a single plank supported on chance-set bricks. From the door slab one stepped through the front doorway directly into the parlor. Beyond the parlor lay the kitchen, from which one could pass out through a narrow door to a patch of weed-grown back yard. A ladderlike stair led up from one side of the kitchen, opposite to the single window and the small coal range. At the top of the stair was a slit of unlighted hallway with a door near either end of it. The door toward Birch Street gave upon the bedroom occupied by Bob and Pearl; the rearward door led to Susan's sternly ascetic cubiculum. No one of these four rooms could be described as spacious, but the parlor and Bob's bedroom may have been twelve by fifteen or thereabouts. Susan's quarters were a scant ten by ten.

The solider and more useful pieces of furniture in the house belonged to the régime of Susan's mother—the great black-walnut bed which almost filled the front bedroom; Susan's single iron cot frame; the parlor table with its marble top; the melodeon; the kitchen range; and the deal table in the kitchen, upon which, impartially, food was prepared and meals were served. To these respectable properties Pearl had added from time to time certain other objects of interest or art.

Thus, in the parlor, there was a cane rocking-chair, gilded; and on the wall above the melodeon hung a banjo suspended from a nail by a broad sash of soiled blue ribbon. On the drumhead of the banjo someone had painted a bunch of nondescript flowers, and Pearl always claimed these as her own handiwork, wrought in happier days. This was her one eagerly contested point of pride; for Bob, when in liquor, invariably denied the possibility of her ever having painted "that there bouquet." This flat denial was always the starting point for those more violent Sunday-night quarrels, which had done so much to reduce the furniture of the house to its stouter, more imperishable elements.

During the brief interval between the death of Susan's mother and the arrival of Pearl, Bob had placed his domestic affairs in the hands of an old negro-woman, who came in during the day to clean up, keep an eye on Susan and prepare Bob's dinner. Most of the hours during Bob's absence this poor old creature spent in a rocking-chair, nodding in and out of sleep; and it was rather baby Susan, sprawling about the kitchen floor, who kept an eye on her, than the reverse. Pearl's installation had changed all that. Bob naturally expected any woman he chose to support to work for her board and lodging; and it may be that at first Pearl had been too grateful for any shelter to risk jeopardizing her good luck by shirking. There seems to be no doubt that for a while she did her poor utmost to keep house—but the sloven in her was too deeply rooted not to flower.

By the time Susan was six or seven the interior condition of Bob's house was too crawlingly unpleasant to bear exact description; and even Bob, though callous enough in such matters, began to have serious thoughts of giving Pearl the slip—not to mention his landlord—and of running off with Susan to some other city, where he could make a fresh start and perhaps contrive now and then to get something decent to eat set before him. It never occurred to him to give Susan the slip as well—which would have freed his hands; not because he had a soft spot somewhere for the child, nor because he felt toward her any special sense of moral obligation. Simply, it never occurred to him. Susan was his kid; and if he went she went with him, along with his pipe, his shop tools, and his set of six English razors—his dearest possession, of which he was jealously and irascibly proud.

But, as it happens, Bob never acted upon this slowly forming desire to escape; the desire was quietly checked and insensibly receded; and for this Susan herself was directly responsible.

Very early in life she began to supplement Pearl's feeble housewifery, but it was not until her ninth year that Susan decided to bring about a domestic revolution. Whether or no hatred of dirt be inheritable, I leave to biologists, merely thumbnailing two facts for their consideration: Susan's mother had hated dirt with an unappeasable hatred; her nightly, after-supper, insensate pursuit of imaginary cobwebs had been one of Bob's choicest grievances against her. And little Susan hated dirt, in all its forms, with an almost equal venom, but with a brain at once more active and more unreeling. She had good reason to hate it. She must either have hated it or been subdued to it. For five years, more or less, she had lived in the midst of dirt and suffered. It had seemed to her one of the inexpungable evils of existence, like mosquitoes, or her father's temper, or the smell of Pearl's cheap talcum powder when warmed by the fumes of cooking cabbage. But gradually it came upon her that dirt only accumulated in the absence of a will to removal.

Once her outreaching mind had grasped—without wordily formulating—this physical and moral law, her course was plain. Since the will to removal was dormant or missing in Pearl, she must supply it. Within the scope of her

9

childish strength, she did supply it. Susan insists that it took her two years merely to overcome the handicap of Pearl's neglect. Her self-taught technique was faulty; proper tools were lacking. There was a bucket which, when filled, she could not lift; a broom that tripped her; high corners she could not reach —corners she had to grow up to, even with the aid of a chair. But in the end she triumphed. By the time she was thirteen—she was thirteen when I first saw in the Eureka Garage—Bob's four rooms were spotless six and one-half days out of every seven.

Even Pearl, in her flaccid way, approved the change. "It beats hell," she remarked affably to Bob one night, "how that ugly little monkey likes to scrub things. She's a real help to me, that child is. But no comp'ny. And she's a sight."

"Well," growled Bob, "she comes by that honest. So was the old woman." They were annoyed when Susan, sitting by them, for the first time within their memory burst into flooding, uncontrollable tears.

IV

I should probably, in my own flaccid way, have lost all track of Susan, if it had not been for certain ugly things that befell in Bob's four-room house one breathless evening—June twentieth of the year 1907. It is a date stamped into my consciousness like a notarial seal. For one thing it happened to be my birthday—my thirty-third, which I was not precisely celebrating, since it was also the anniversary of the day my wife had left me, two years before. Nor was I entirely pleased to have become, suddenly, thirty-three. I counted it the threshold of middle-age. Now that eleven years have passed, and with them my health and the world's futile pretense at peace, I am feeling younger.

This book is about Susan, but it will be simpler if you know something, too, concerning her scribe. Fortunately there is not much that it will be needful to tell.

I was—in those bad, grossly comfortable old days—that least happy of Nature's experiments, a man whose inherited income permitted him to be an idler, and whose tastes urged him to write precious little essays about precious little for the more precious reviews. My half-hearted attempt to practice law I had long abandoned. I lived in a commodious, inherited mansion on Hillhouse Avenue—an avenue which in all fairness must be called aristocratic, since it has no wrong end to it. It is right at both ends, so, naturally, though broad, it is not very long. My grandfather, toward the end of a profitably ill-spent life, built this mansion of sad-colored stone in a somewhat mixed Italian style; my father filled it with expensive and unsightly movables—the spoils of a grand

European tour; and I, in my turn, had emptied it of these treasures and refilled it with my own carefully chosen collection of rare furniture, rare Oriental carpets, rare first editions, and costly *objets d'art*. This collection I then anxiously believed, and do still in part believe, to be beautiful—though I am no longer haunted by an earlier fear lest the next generation should repudiate my taste and reverse my opinion. Let the auction rooms of 1960 decide. Neither in flesh nor in spirit shall I attend them.

The tragi-comedy of my luckless marriage I shall not stop here to explain, but its rather mysterious ending had at first largely cut me off from my old family friends and my socially correct acquaintances. When Gertrude left me, their sympathies, or their sense of security, went with her. I can hardly blame them. There had been no glaring scandal, but the fault was inferentially mine. To speak quite brutally, I did not altogether regret their loss. Too many of them had bored me for too many years. I was glad to rely more on the companionship of certain writers and painters which my scribbling had quietly won for me, here and in France. I traveled about a good deal. When at home, I kept my guest rooms filled—often, in the horrid phrase, with "visitors of distinction."

In this way I became a social problem, locally, of some magnitude. Visitors of distinction—even when of eccentric distinction—cannot easily be ignored in a university town. Thus it made it a little awkward, perhaps, that I should so often prove to be their host; a little—less, on the whole, than one would suppose. Within two years—just following Ballou's brief stay with me, on his way to introduce that now forgotten nine-days wonder, Polymorphous Prose, among initiates of the Plymouth Rock Poetry Guild, at Boston—my slight remaining ineligibility was tacitly and finally ignored. The old family friends began to hint that Gertrude, though a splendid woman, had always been a little austere. Possibly there were faults on both sides. One never knew.

And it was just at this hour of social reëstablishment that my birthday swung round again, for the thirty-third time, and brought with it a change in my outer life which was to lead on to even greater changes in all my modes of thinking and feeling. Odd, that a drunken quarrel in a four-room house toward the wrong end of Birch Street could so affect the destiny of a luxurious *dilettante*, living at the very center of bonded respectability, in a mansion of sad-colored stone, on a short broad avenue which is right at both ends!

V

"Never in this (obviously outcast) world!" grumbled Bob Blake, bringing his malletlike fist down on the marble top of the parlor table.

The blow made his half-filled glass jump and clinkle; so he emptied it slowly, then poured in four fingers more, forgetting to add water this time, and sullenly pushed the bottle across to Pearl. But Pearl was fretful. Her watery blue eyes were fixed upon the drumhead of the banjo, where it hung suspended above the melodeon.

"I did so paint them flowers. And well you know it. What's the good of bein' so mean? If you wasn't heeled you'd let me have it my way. Didn't I bring that banjo with me?"

"Hungh! Say you did. What does that prove?"

"I guess it proves somethin', all right."

"Proves you swiped it, likely."

"Me! I ain't that kind, thanks."

"The hell you ain't."

"If you're tryin' to get gay, cut it out!"

"Not me."

"Well, then—quit!"

This was shortly after supper. It was an unusually hot, humid evening; doors and windows stood open to no purpose; and Susan was sitting out on the monolithic door slab, fighting off mosquitoes. She found that this defensive warfare partly distracted her from the witless, interminable bickering within. Moreover, the striated effluvia of whisky, talcum powder, and perspiration had made her head feel a little queer. By comparison, the fetid breath from the exposed mud banks of the salt marsh was almost refreshing.

Possibly it was because her head did feel a little queer that Susan began presently to wonder about things. Between her days at the neighboring public school and her voluntary rounds of housework, Susan had not of late years had much waking time to herself. In younger and less crowded hours, before her father had been informed by the authorities that he must either send his child to school or take the consequences, Susan had put in all her spare moments at wondering. She would see a toad in the back yard, for example, under a plantain leaf, and she would begin to wonder. She would wonder what it felt like to be a toad. And before very long something would happen to her, inside, and she would *be* a toad. She would have toad thoughts and toad feelings.... . There would stretch above her a dim, green, balancing canopy—the plantain leaf. All about her were soaring, translucent fronds—the grass. It was cool there under the plantain leaf; but she was enormously fat and ugly, her brain felt like sooty cobwebs, and nobody loved her.

Still, she didn't care much. She could feel her soft gray throat, like a blown-into glove finger, pulsing slowly—which was almost as soothing a sensation as letting the swing die down. It made her feel as if Someone— some great unhappy cloudlike Being—were making up a song, a song about most everything; chanting it sleepily to himself—or was it *herself?*— somewhere; and as if she were part of this beautiful, unhappy song. But all the time she knew that if that white fluffy restlessness—that moth miller— fluttered only a little nearer among those golden-green fronds, she knew if it reached the cool rim of her plantain shade, she knew, then, that something terrible would happen to her—knew that something swift and blind, that she couldn't help, would coil deep within her like a spring and so launch her forward, open-jawed. It was awful—awful for the moth miller—but she couldn't *not* do it. She was a toad... .

And it was the same with her father. There were things he couldn't not do. She could be—sitting very still in a corner—*be* her father, when he was angry; and she knew he couldn't help it. It was just a dark slow whirling inside, with red sparks flying swiftly out from it. And it hurt while it lasted. Being her father like that always made her sorry for him. But she wished, and she felt he must often wish, that he couldn't be at all. There were lots of live things that would be happier if they weren't live things; and *if* they weren't, Susan felt, the great cloudlike Being would be less unhappy too.

Naturally, I am giving you Susan's later interpretations of her pre-schoolday wonderings; and a number of you would gasp a little, knowing what firm, delicate imaginings all Susan Blake's later interpretations were, if I should give you her pen name as well—which I have promised myself not to do. This is not an official study of a young writer of peculiar distinction; it is merely an unpretending book about a little girl I knew and a young married woman I still know—one and the same person. It is what I have named it— that only: *The Book of Susan.*

Meanwhile, this humid June night—to the sordid accompaniment of Bob and Pearl snarling at each other half-drunkenly within—Susan waits for us on the monolithic door slab; and there is a new wonder in her dizzy little head. I can't do better than let her tell you in her own words what this new wonder was like.

"Ambo, dear"—my name, by the way, is Ambrose Hunt; Captain Hunt, of the American Red Cross, at the present writing, which I could date from a sleepy little village in Southern France—"Ambo, dear, it was the moon, mostly. There was a pink bud of light in the heat mist, way off beyond East Rock, and then the great wild rose of the moon opened slowly through it.

Papa, inside, was sounding just like a dog when he's bullying another dog, walking up on the points of his toes, stiff legged, round him. So I tried to escape, tried to be the moon; tried to feel floaty and shining and beautiful, and —and remote. But I couldn't manage it. I never could make myself be anything not alive. I've tried to be stones, but it's no good. It won't work. I can be trees—a little. But usually I have to be animals, or men and women— and of course they're animals too.

"So I began wondering why I liked the moon, why just looking at it made me feel happy. It couldn't talk to me; or love me. All it could do was to be up there, sometimes, and shine. Then I remembered about mythology. Miss Chisholm, in school, was always telling us about gods and goddesses. She said we were children, so we could recreate the gods for ourselves, because they belonged to the child age of the world. She talked like that a lot, in a faded-leaf voice, and none of us ever understood her. The truth is, Ambo, we never paid any attention to her; she smiled too much and too sadly, without meaning it; and her eyelashes were white. All the same, that night somehow I remembered Artemis, the virgin moon goddess, who slipped silently through dark woods at dusk, hunting with a silvery bow. Being a virgin seemed to mean that you didn't care much for boys. But I did always like boys better than girls, so I decided I could never be a virgin. And yet I loved the thought of Artemis from that moment. I began to think about her—oh, intensely!— always keeping off by herself; cool, and shining, and—and detached. And there was one boy she *had* cared for; I remembered that, too, though I couldn't remember his name. A naked, brown sort of boy, who kept off by himself on blue, distant hills. So Artemis wasn't really a virgin at all. She was just—awfully particular. She liked clean, open places, and the winds, and clear, swift water. What she hated most was *stuffiness!* That's why I decided then and there, Ambo, that Artemis should be my goddess, my own pet goddess; and I made up a prayer to her. I've never forgotten it. I often say it still... .

> *Dearest, dearest Far-Away,*
> *Can you hear me when I pray?*
> *Can you hear me when I cry?*
> *Would you care if I should die?*
> *No, you wouldn't care at all;*
> *But I love you most of all.*

"It isn't very good, Ambo, but it's the first rhyme I ever made up out of my own head. And I just talked it right off to Artemis without any trouble. But I had hardly finished it, when——"

What had happened next was the crash of glassware, followed by Bob's thick voice, bellowing: "C'm ba' here! Damned slut! Tell yeh t' c'm ba' an'—an' 'pol'gize!'"

Susan heard a strangling screech from Pearl, the jar of a heavy piece of furniture overturned. The child's first impulse was to run out into Birch Street and scream for help. She tells me her spine knew all at once that something terrible had happened—or was going to happen. Then, in an odd flash of hallucination, she saw *Artemis* poised the fleetingest second before her—beautiful, a little disdainful, divinely unafraid. So Susan gulped, dug her nails fiercely into her palms, and hurried back through the parlor into the kitchen, where she stumbled across the overturned table and fell, badly bruising her cheek.

As she scrambled to her feet a door slammed to, above. Her father, in a grotesque crouching posture, was mounting the ladderlike stair. On the floor at the stair's foot lay the parchment head of Pearl's banjo, which he had cut from its frame. Susan distinctly caught the smudged pinks and blues of the nondescript flowers. She realized at once that her father was bound on no good errand. And Pearl was trapped. Susan called to her father, daringly, a little wildly. He slued round to her, leaning heavily on the stair rail, his face green-white, his lips held back by some evil reflex in a fixed, appalling grin.

It was the face of a madman... . He raised his right hand, slowly, and a tiny prismatic gleam darted from the blade of an opened razor—one of his precious set of six. He had evidently used it to destroy the banjo head, which he would never have done in his right mind. But now he made a shocking gesture with the blade, significant of other uses; then turned, crouching once more, to continue upward. Susan tried to cry out, tried to follow him, until the room slid from its moorings into a whirlpool of humming blackness....

That is all Susan remembers for some time. It is just as well.

VI

What Susan next recalls is an intense blare of light, rousing her from her nothingness, like trumpets. Her immediate confused notion was that the gates of hell had been flung wide for her; and when a tall black figure presently cut across the merciless rays and towered before her, she thought it must be the devil. But the intense blare came from the head lights of my touring car, and the tall black devil was I. A greatly puzzled and compassionate devil I was too! Maltby Phar—that exquisite anarchist—was staying with me, and we had run down to the shore for dinner, hoping to mitigate the heat by the ride, and my new sensation of frustrate middle-age by broiled live lobsters. It was past eleven. I had just dropped Maltby at the house and had run my car round to the garage where Bob worked, meaning to leave it there overnight so Bob could begin patching at it the first thing in the morning. It had been bucking its way along on three cylinders or less all day.

Bob's garage lay back from the street down a narrow alley. Judge, then, of my astonishment as I nosed my car up to its shut double doors! There, on the concrete incline before the doors, lay a small crumpled figure, half-curled, like an unearthed cut-worm, about a shining dinner pail. I brought the car to a sudden dead stop. The small figure partly uncrumpled, and a white, blinded little face lifted toward me. It was Bob's youngster! What was she up to, lying there on the ribbed concrete at this time of night? And in heaven's name— why the dinner pail? I jumped down to investigate.

"You're Susan Blake, aren't you?"

"Yes"—with a whispered gasp—"your Royal Highness."

Susan says she doesn't know just why she addressed the devil in that way, unless she was trying to flatter him and so get round him.

"I'm not so awfully bad," she went on, "if you don't count thinking things too much!"

The right cheek of her otherwise delicately modeled child's face was a swollen lump of purple and green. I dropped down on one knee beside her.

"Why, you poor little lady! You're hurt!"

Instantly she sprang to her feet, wild-eyed.

"No, no! It's not me—it's Pearl! Oh, quick—please! He had a razor!"

"Razor? *Who* did?" I seized her hands. "I'm Mr. Hunt, dear. Your father often works on my car. Tell me what's wrong!"

She was still half dazed. "I—I can't see why I'm down here—with papa's dinner pail. Pearl was upstairs, and I tried to stop him from going." Then she began to whimper like a whipped puppy. "It's all mixed. I'm scared."

"Of course—of course you are; but it's going to be all right." I led her to the car and lifted her to the front seat. "Hold on a minute, Susan. I'll be back with you in less than no time!"

I sounded my horn impatiently. After an interval, a slow-footed car washer inside the garage began trundling the doors back to admit me. I ran to him.

No. Bob, he left at six, same as usual. He hadn't been round since.... His kid, eh? Mebbe the heat had turned her queer. Nuff to addle most folks, the heat was... .

I saw that he knew nothing, and snapped him off with a sharp request to crank the car for me. As he did so, I jumped in beside Susan.

"Where do you live, Susan? Oh, yes, of course—Birch Street. Bob told me that... . Eh? You don't want to go home?"

"Never, please. Never, never! I *won't!*" Proclaiming this, she flung Bob's dinner pail from her and it bounced and clattered down the asphalt. "It's too late," she added, in a frightened whisper: "I know it is!"

Then she seized my arm—thereby almost wrecking us against a fire hydrant—and clung to me, sobbing. I was puzzled and—yes—alarmed. Bob was a bad customer. The child's bruised face... something she had said about a razor——? And instantly I made up my mind.

"I'll take you to my house, Susan. Mrs. Parrot"—Mrs. Parrot was my housekeeper—"will fix you up for to-night. Then I'll go round and see Bob; see what's wrong." I felt her thin fingers dig into my arm convulsively. "Yes," I reassured her, taking a corner perilously at full speed, "that will be much better. You'll like Mrs. Parrot."

Rather recklessly, I hoped this might prove to be true; for Mrs. Parrot was a little difficult at times... .

It was Maltby Phar who saw me coming up the steps with a limp child in my arms, and who opened the screen door for me. "Aha!" he exclaimed. "Done it this time, eh! Always knew you would, sooner or later. You're too damned absent-minded to drive a car. You——"

"Nonsense!" I struck in. "Tell Mrs. Parrot to ring up Doctor Stevens. Then send her to me." And I continued on upstairs with Susan.

When Mrs. Parrot came, Susan was lying with closed eyes in the middle of a great white embroidered coverlet, upon which her shoes had smeared greasy, permanent-looking stains.

"Mercy," sighed Mrs. Parrot, "if you've killed the poor creature, nobody's sorrier than I am! But why couldn't you have laid her down on the floor? She wouldn't have known."

In certain respects Mrs. Parrot was invaluable to me; but then and there I suspected that Mrs. Parrot would, in the not-too-distant future, have to go.

Within five minutes Doctor Stevens arrived, and, after hurried explanations, Maltby and I left him in charge—and then made twenty-five an hour to Birch Street.

However, Susan's intuitions had been correct. We found Bob's four-room house quite easily. It was the house with the crowd in front of it.... We were an hour too late.

"Cut her throat clean acrost; and his own after," shrilled Mrs. Perkins to us —Mrs. Perkins, who lived three doors nearer the right end of Birch Street. "But it's only what was to be looked for, and I guess it'll be a lesson to some. You can't expect no better end than that," perorated Mrs. Perkins to us and her excited neighbors, while her small gray-green eyes snapped with electric malice, "you can't expect no better end than that to sech *brazen* immorality!"

"My God," groaned Maltby, as we sped away, "How they have enjoyed it all! Why, you almost ruined the evening for them when you told them you'd found the child! They were hoping to discover her body in the cellar or down the well. Ugh! What a world!

"By the way," he added, as we turned once more into the dignified breadth of Hillhouse Avenue, "what'll you do with the homely little brat? Put her in some kind of awful institution?"

The bland tone of his assumption irritated me. I ground on the brakes.

"Certainly not! I like her. If she returns the compliment, and her relatives don't claim her, she'll stay on here with me."

"Hum. Bravo.... About two weeks," said Maltby Phar.

THE SECOND CHAPTER

I

I T was not Susan who left me at the end of two weeks; it was Mrs. Parrot. Maltby had departed within three days, hastening perforce to editorial duties in New York. He then edited, with much furtive groaning to sympathetic friends, the *Garden Exquisite*, a monthly magazine *de luxe*, devoted chiefly to advertising matter, and to photographs taken—by request of far-seeing wives and daughters—at the country clubs and on the country estates of our minor millionaires. For a philosophical anarch, rather a quaint occupation! Yet one must live... . Maltby, however, had threatened a return as soon as possible, "to look over the piteous *débâcle*." There was no probability that Mrs. Parrot would ever return.

"You cannot expect me," maintained Mrs. Parrot, "to wait on the child of a murdering suicide. Especially," she added, "when he was nothing but a common sort of man to begin with. I'm as sorry for that poor little creature as anybody in New Haven; but there are places for such."

That was her ultimatum. My reply was two weeks' notice, and a considerable monetary gift to soften the blow.

Hillhouse Avenue, in general, so far as I could discover, rather sympathized with Mrs. Parrot. She at once obtained an excellent post, becoming housekeeper for the Misses Carstairs, spinster sisters of incredible age, who lived only two doors from me in a respectable mansion whose portico resembled an Egyptian tomb. Wandering freshmen from the Yale campus frequently mistook it for the home office of one of the stealthier secret societies.

There, silently ensconced, Mrs. Parrot burned with a hard, gemlike flame, and awaited my final downfall. So did the Misses Carstairs, who, being cousins of my wife, had remained firmly in opposition. And rumor had it that other members of neighboring families were suffering discomfort from the proximity of Susan. It was as if a tiny, almost negligible speck of coal dust had blown into the calm, watchful eye of the *genius loci*, and was gradually inflaming it—with resultant nervous irritation to all its members.

Susan was happily unconscious of these things. Her gift of intuition had not yet projected itself into that ethereal region which conserves the more tenuous tone and the subtler distinction—denominate "society." For the immediate moment she was bounded in a nutshell, yet seemed to count herself a princess of infinite space—yes, in spite of bad dreams. We—Doctor

19

Stevens and I—had put her to bed in the large, coolly distinguished corner room formerly occupied by Gertrude. This room opened directly into my own. Doctor Stevens counselled bed for a few days, and Susan seemed well content to obey his mandate. Meanwhile, I had requested Mrs. Parrot to buy various necessities for her—toothbrushes, nightdresses, day dresses, petticoats, and so on. Mrs. Parrot had supposed I should want the toilet articles inexpensive, and the clothing plain but good.

"Good, by all means, Mrs. Parrot," I had corrected, "but not plain. As pretty and frilly as possible!"

Mrs. Parrot had been inclined to argue the matter.

"When that poor little creature goes from here," she had maintained, "flimsy, fussy things will be of no service to her. None. She'll need coarse, substantial articles that will bear usage."

"Do you like to wear coarse, substantial articles, Mrs. Parrot?" I had mildly asked. "So far as I am permitted to observe——"

Mrs. Parrot had resented the implication. "I hope in my outer person, Mr. Hunt, that I show a decent respect for my employers, but I've never been one to pamper myself on linjery, if I may use the word—not believing it wholesome. Nor to discuss it with gentlemen. But if I don't know what it's wisest and best to buy in this case, who," she had demanded of heaven, "does?"

"Possibly," heaven not replying, had been my response, "*I* do. At any rate, I can try."

It was fun trying. I ran down on the eight o'clock to New York and strolled up and down Fifth Avenue, shopping here and there as the fancy moved me. Shopping—with a well-filled pocketbook—is not a difficult art. Women exaggerate its difficulties for their own malign purposes. In two hours of the most casual activity I had bought a great number of delightful things—for my little daughter, you know. Her age? . . . Oh, well—I should think about fourteen. Let's call it 'going on fourteen.' Then it's sure to be all right.

It *was* all right—essentially. By which I mean that the parties of the first and second parts—to wit, Susan and I—were entirely and blissfully satisfied.

Susan liked particularly a lacy sort of nightgown all knotted over with little pink ribbony rosebuds; there was a coquettish boudoir cap to match it— suggestive somehow of the caps village maidens used to wear in old-fashioned comic operas; and a pink silk kimono embroidered with white chrysanthemums, to top off the general effect. Needless to say, Mrs. Parrot disapproved of the general effect, deeming it, no doubt with some reason, a thought flamboyant for Gertrude's coolly distinguished corner room.

But Susan, propped straight up by now against pillows, wantoned in this finery. She would stroke the pink silk of the kimono with her thin, sensitive fingers, sigh deeply, happily, then close her eyes.

There was nothing much wrong with her. The green-and-purple bruise on her cheek—a somber note which would not harmonize with the frivolity of the boudoir cap—was no longer painful. But, as Doctor Stevens put it, "The little monkey's all in." She was tired, tired out to the last tiny filament of her tiniest nerve... .

During those first days with me she asked no awkward questions; and few of any kind. Indeed, she rarely spoke at all, except with her always-speaking black eyes. For the time being the restless-terrier-look had gone from them; they were quiet and deep, and said *"Thank you,"* to Doctor Stevens, to Mrs. Parrot, to me, with a hundred modulating shades of expression. In spite of a clear-white, finely drawn face, against which the purple bruise stood out in shocking relief; in spite of entirely straight but gossamery black hair; in spite of a rather short nose and a rather wide mouth—there was a fascination about the child which no one, not even the hostile Mrs. Parrot, wholly escaped.

"That poor, peeny little creature," admitted Mrs. Parrot, on the very morning she left me, "has a way of looking at you—so you can't talk to her like you'd ought to. It's somebody's duty to speak to her in a Christian spirit. She never says her prayers. Nor mentions her father. And don't seem to care what's happened to him, or why she's here, or what's to come to her. And what is to come to her," demanded Mrs. Parrot, "if she stays on in this house, without a God-fearing woman, and one you can't fool most days? Not that I could be persuaded, having made other arrangements. And if I may say a last word, the wild talk I've heard here isn't what I've been used to. Nor to be approved of. No vulgarity. None. I don't accuse. But free with matters better left to the church; or in the dark—where they belong. All I hold is, that some things are sacred, and some unmentionable; and conversation should take cognizance of such!"

I had never known her so moved or so eloquent. I strove to reassure her.

"You are quite right, Mrs. Parrot. I apologize for any painful moments my friends and I have given you. But don't worry too much about Susan. So far as Susan's concerned, I promise to 'take cognizance' in every possible direction."

It was clear to me that I should have to expend a good deal of care upon engaging another housekeeper at once. And, of course, a governess—for lessons and things. And a maid? Yes; Susan would need a maid, if only to do her mending. Obviously, neither the housekeeper, the governess, nor I could be expected to take cognizance of that.

II

But I anticipate. Two weeks before Mrs. Parrot's peroration, on the very evening of the day Maltby Phar had left me, Susan and I had had our first good talk together. My memorable shopping tour had not yet come off, and Susan, having pecked birdlike at a very light supper, was resting—semi-recumbent—in bed, clothed in a suit of canary-yellow pajamas, two sizes too big for her, which I was rather shaken to discover belonged to Nora, my quiet little Irish parlor maid. I had not supposed that Nora indulged in night gear filched from musical comedy. However, Nora had meant to be kind in a good cause; though canary yellow is emphatically a color for the flushed and buxom and should never be selected for peeny, anemic little girls. It did make Susan look middling ghastly, as if quarantined from all access to Hygeia, the goddess! Perhaps that is why, when I perched beside her on the edge of Gertrude's colonial four-poster, I felt an unaccustomed prickling sensation back of my eyes.

"How goes it, canary bird?" I asked, taking the thin, blue-threaded hand that lay nearest to me.

Susan's fingers at once curled trustfully to mine, and there came something very like a momentary glimmer of mischief into her dark eyes.

"If I was an honest-to-God canary, I could sing to you," said Susan. "I'd like to do something for you, Mr. Hunt. Something you'd like, I mean."

"Well, you can, dear. You can stop calling me 'Mr. Hunt'! My first name's pretty awkward, though. It's Ambrose."

For an instant Susan considered my first name, critically, then very slowly shook her head. "It's a nice name. It's *too* nice, isn't it—for every day?"

I laughed. "But it's all I have, Susan. What shall we do about it?"

Then Susan laughed, too; it was the first time I had heard her laugh. "I guess your mother was feeling kind of stuck up when she called you that!"

"Most mothers do feel kind of stuck up over their first babies, Susan."

She considered this, and nodded assent, "But it's silly of them, anyway," she announced. "There are so many babies all the time, everywhere. There's nothing new about babies, Ambo."

"Aha!" I exclaimed. "You knew from the first how to chasten my stuck-up name, didn't you? 'Ambo' is a delightful improvement."

"It's more like you," said Susan, tightening her fingers briefly on mine.

And presently she closed her eyes. When, after a long still interval, she opened them, they were cypress-shaded pools.

"Tell me what happened, Ambo."

"He's dead, Susan. Pearl's dead, too."

She closed her eyes again, and two big tears slipped out from between her lids, wetting her thick eyelashes and staining her bruised and her pallid cheek.

"He couldn't help it. He was made like that, inside. He was no damn good, Ambo. That's what he was always saying to Pearl—'You're no damn good.' She wasn't, either. And he wasn't, much. I guess it's better for him and Pearl to *be* dead."

This—and the two big tears—was her good-by to Bob, to Pearl, to the four-room house; her good-by to Birch Street. It shocked me at the time. I released her hand and stood up to light a cigarette—staring the while at Susan. Where had she found her precocious brains? And had she no heart? Had something of Bob's granitic harshness entered into this uncanny, this unnatural child? Should I live to regret my decision to care for her, to educate her? When I died, would she say—to whom?—"I guess it's better for him to *be* dead. Poor Ambo! He was no damn good."

But even as I shuddered, I smiled. For, after all, she was right; the child was right. She had merely uttered, truthfully, thoughts which a more conventional mind, more conventionally disciplined, would have known how to conceal—yes, to conceal even from itself. Genius was very like that.

"Susan!" I suddenly demanded. "Have you any relatives who will try to claim you?"

"Claim me?"

"Yes. Want to take care of you?"

"Mamma's sister-in-law lives in Hoboken," said Susan. "But she's a widow; and she's got seven already."

"Would you like to stay here with me?"

For all answer she flopped sidelong down from the pillows and hid her bruised face in the counterpane. Her slight, canary-clad shoulders were shaken with stifled weeping.

"That settles it!" I affirmed. "I'll see my lawyer in the morning, and he'll get the court to appoint me your guardian. Come now! If you cry about it, I'll think you don't want me for guardian. Do you?"

She turned a blubbered, wistful face toward me from the counterpane. Her

23

eyes answered me. I leaned over, smoothed a pillow and slipped it beneath her tired head, then kissed her unbruised cheek and walked quietly back into my own room—where I rang for Mrs. Parrot.

When she arrived, "Mrs. Parrot," I suggested, "please make Susan comfortable for the night, will you? And I'll appreciate it if you treat her exactly as you would my own child."

It took Mrs. Parrot at least a minute to hit upon something she quite dared to leave with me.

"Very well, Mr. Hunt. Not having an own child, and not knowing—you can say that. Not that it's the same thing, though you *do* say it! But I'll make her comfortable—and time tells. In darker days, I hope you'll be able to say that poor, peeny little creature has done the same by you."

"Thank you, Mrs. Parrot. Good-night."

"A good night to you, Mr. Hunt," elaborated Mrs. Parrot, not without malice; "many of them, Mr. Hunt; many of them, I'm sure."

III

By the time Mrs. Parrot left us, housekeeper, governess, and maid had been obtained in New York through agencies of the highest respectability.

Miss Goucher, the housekeeper, proved to be a tall, big-framed spinster, rising fifty; a capable, taciturn woman with a positive talent for minding her own affairs. She had bleak, light-gray eyes, a rudderlike nose, and a harsh, positive way of speech that was less disagreeable than it might have been, because she so seldom spoke at all. Having hoped for a more amiable presence, I was of two minds over keeping her; but she took charge of my house so promptly and efficiently, and effaced herself so thoroughly—a difficult feat for so definite a figure—that in the end there was nothing I could complain of; and so she stayed.

Miss Disbrow on the other hand, who came as governess, was all that I had dared to wish for; a graceful, light-footed, soft-voiced girl—she was not yet thirty—with charming manners, a fluent command of the purest convent-taught French, a nice touch on the piano, and apparently some slight acquaintance with the solider branches. Merely to associate with Miss Disbrow would, I felt, do much for Susan.

I was less certain about Sonia, the maid. I had asked for a middle-aged English maid. Sonia was Russian, and she was only twenty-three. But she was sent directly to me from service with Countess Dimbrovitski—formerly, as you know, Maud Hochstetter, of Omaha—and brought with her a most glowing reference for skill, honesty, and unfailing tact. Countess Dimbrovitski did not explain in the reference, dated from Newport, why she had permitted this paragon to slip from her; nor did it occur to me to investigate the point. But Sonia later explained it all, in intimate detail, to Susan—as we shall see.

I had feared that Susan might be at first a little bewildered by the attentions of Sonia and of Miss Disbrow; so I explained the unusual situation to Miss Goucher and Miss Disbrow—with certain reservations—and asked them to make it clear to Sonia. Miss Goucher merely nodded, curtly enough, and said she understood. Miss Disbrow proved more curious and more voluble.

"How wonderful of you, Mr. Hunt!" she exclaimed. "To take in a poor little waif and do all this for her! Personally, I count it a privilege to be allowed some share in so generous an action. Oh, but I do—I do. One likes to feel, even when forced to work for one's living, that one has some little opportunity to do good in the world. Life isn't," asked Miss Disbrow, "all money-grubbing and selfishness, is it?" And as I found no ready answer, she concluded: "But I need hardly ask that of you!"

For the fleetingest second I found myself wondering whether Miss Disbrow, deep down in her hidden heart, might not be a minx. Yet her glance, the happiest mixture of frankness, timidity, and respectful admiration, disarmed me. I dismissed the unworthy suspicion as absurd.

I was a little troubled, though, when Susan that same evening after dinner came to me in the library and seated herself on a low stool facing my easy-chair.

"Ambo," she said, "I've been blind as blind, haven't I?"

"Have you?" I responded. "For a blind girl, it's wonderful how you find your way about!"

"But I'm not joking—and that's just it," said Susan.

"What's wrong, dear?" I asked. "I see something is."

"Yes. I am. The wrongest possible. I've just dumped myself on you, and stayed here; and—and I've no damn business here at all!"

"I thought we were going to forget the damns and hells, Susan?"

"We are," said Susan, coloring sharply and looking as if she wanted to cry. "But when you've heard them, and worse, every minute all your life—it's pretty hard to forget. You must scold me more!" Then with a swift movement she leaned forward and laid her cheek on my knee. "You're too good to me,

Ambo. I oughtn't to be here—wearing wonderful dresses, having a maid to do my hair and—and polish me and button me and mend me. I wasn't meant to have an easy time; I wasn't born for it. First thing you know, Ambo, I'll get to thinking I was—and be mean to you somehow!"

"I'll risk that, Susan."

"Yes, but I oughtn't to let you. I could learn to be somebody's maid like Sonia; and if I study hard—and I'm going to!—some day I could be a governess like Miss Disbrow; only really know things, not just pretend. Or when I'm old enough, a housekeeper like Miss Goucher! That's what you should make me do—work for you! I can clean things better than Nora now; I never skip underneaths. Truly, Ambo, it's all wrong, my having people work for me—at your expense. I know it is! Miss Disbrow made it all clear as clear, right away."

"What! Has Miss Disbrow been stuffing this nonsense into your head!" I was furious.

"Oh, not in words!" cried Susan. "She talks just the other way. She keeps telling me how fortunate I am to have a guardian like you, and how I must be so careful never to annoy you or make you regret what you've done for me. Then she sighs and says life is very hard and unjust to many girls born with more advantages. Of course she means herself, Ambo. You see, she hates having to work at all. She's much nicer to look at and talk to, but she reminds me of Pearl. She's no damn—she's no good, Ambo dear. She's hard where she ought to be soft, and soft where she ought to be hard. She tries to get round people, so she can coax things out of them. But she'll never get round Miss Goucher, Ambo—or me." And Susan hesitated, lifting her head from my knee and looking up at me doubtfully, only to add, "I—I'm not so sure about *you*."

"Indeed. You think, possibly, Miss Disbrow might get round me, eh?"

"Well, she might—if I wasn't here," said Susan. "She might marry you."

My explosion of laughter—I am ordinarily a quiet person—startled Susan. "Have I said something awful again?" she cried.

"Dreadful!" I sputtered, wiping my eyes. "Why, you little goose! Don't you see how I need you? To plumb the depths for me—to protect me? I thought I was your guardian, Susan; but that's just my mannish complacency. I'm not your guardian at all, dear. You're mine."

But I saw at once that my mirth had confused her, had hurt her feelings.... I reached out for her hands and drew her upon my knees.

"Susan," I said, "Miss Disbrow couldn't marry me even if she got round me, and wanted to. You see, I have a wife already."

Susan stared at me with wide, frightened eyes. "You have, Ambo? Where is she?"

"She left me two years ago."

"Left you?" It was evident that she did not understand. "Oh—what will she say when she comes home and finds *me* here? She won't like it; she won't like me!" wailed Susan. "I know she won't."

"Hush, dear. She's not coming home again. She made up her mind that she couldn't live with me any more."

"What's her name?"

"Gertrude."

"Why couldn't she live with you, Ambo?"

"She said I was cruel to her."

"*Weren't* you good to her, Ambo? Why? Didn't you like her?"

The rapid questions were so unexpected, so searching, that I gasped. And my first impulse was to lie to Susan, to put her off with a few conventional phrases—phrases that would lead the child to suppose me a wronged, lonely, broken-hearted man. This would win me a sympathy I had not quite realized that I craved. But Susan's eyes were merciless, and I couldn't manage it. Instead, I surprised myself by blurting out: "That's about it, Susan. I didn't like her—enough. We couldn't hit it off, somehow. I'm afraid I wasn't very kind."

Instantly Susan's thin arms went about my neck, and her cheek was pressed tight to mine.

"Poor Ambo!" she whispered. "I'm so sorry you weren't kind. It must *hurt* you so." Then she jumped from my knees.

"Ambo!" she demanded. "Is my room—*her* room? Is it?"

"Certainly not. It isn't hers any more. She's never coming back, I tell you. She put me out of her life once for all; and God knows I've put her out of mine!"

"If you can't let me have another room, Ambo—I'll have to go."

"Why? Hang it all, Susan, don't be silly! Don't make difficulties where none exist! What an odd, overstrained child you are!" I was a little annoyed.

27

"Yes," nodded Susan gravely, "I see now why Gertrude left you. But she must be awfully stupid not to know it's only your outside that's made like that!"

Next morning, without a permissive word from me, Susan had Miss Goucher move all her things to a small bedroom at the back of the house, overlooking the garden. This silent flitting irritated me not a little, and that afternoon I had a frank little talk with Miss Disbrow—franker, perhaps, than I had intended. Miss Disbrow at once gave me notice, and left for New York within two hours, letting it be known that she expected her trunks to be sent after her.

"Gutter-snipes are not my specialty," was her parting word.

IV

There proved to be little difficulty in getting myself appointed Susan's guardian. No one else wanted the child.

I promised the court to do my best for her; to treat her, in fact, as I would my own flesh and blood. It might well be, I said, that before long I should legally adopt her. In any event, if this for some unforeseen reason proved inadvisable, I assured the court that Susan's future would be provided for. The court benignly replied that, as it stood, I was acting very handsomely in the matter; very handsomely; no doubt about it. But there was a dim glimmer behind the juridic spectacles that seemed to imply: "Handsomely, my dear sir, but whether wisely or no is another question, which, as the official champion of widows and orphans, I am not called upon to decide."

It was with a new sense of responsibility that I opened an account in Susan's name with a local savings bank, and a week later added a short but efficient codicil to my will.

In the meantime—but with alert suspicions—I interviewed several highly recommended applicants for Miss Disbrow's deserted post; only to find them wanting. Poor things! Combined, they could hardly have met all the requirements, æsthetic and intellectual, which I had now set my heart upon finding in one lone governess for Susan! It would have needed, by this, a subtly modernized Hypatia to fulfill my ideal.

I might, of course, have waited for October to send Susan to a select private school in the vicinage, patronized by the little daughters of our more cautious families. It was, by neighborly consent, an excellent school, where carefully sterilized cultures—physical, moral, mental, and social—were painlessly injected into the blue blood streams of our very nicest young girls.

I say that I might have done so, but this is a euphemism. On the one hand, I shrank from exposing Susan to possible snubs; on the other, a little bird whispered that Miss Garnett, principal of the school, would not care to expose her carefully sterilized cultures to an alien contagion. Bearers of contagion—whether physical, moral, mental, or social—were not sympathetic to Miss Garnett's *clientèle*. In Mrs. Parrot's iron phrase, there are places for such.

Public schools, to wit! But in those long-past days—before Susan taught me that there are just two kinds of persons, big and little; those you can do nothing for, because they can do nothing for themselves, and those you can do nothing for, because they can do everything for themselves—in those days, I admit that I had my own finicky fears. Public schools were all very well for the children of men who could afford nothing better. They had, for example, given Bob Blake's daughter a pretty fair preliminary training; but they would never do for Ambrose Hunt's ward. *Noblesse*—or, at any rate, *largesse* —*oblige*.

Yet here was a quandary: Public schools, in my estimation, being too vulgar for Susan; and Susan, in the estimation of Hillhouse Avenue, being too vulgar for private ones; yea, and though I still took cognizance, no subtly modernized Hypatia coming to me highly recommended for a job—how in the name of useless prosperity was I to get poor little Susan properly educated at all!

It was Susan who solved this difficulty for me, as she was destined to solve most of my future difficulties, and all of her own.

She soon turned the public world about her into an extra-select, super-private school. She impressed all who came into contact with her, and made of them her devoted—if often unconscious—instructors. And she began by impressing Miss Goucher and Nora and Sonia, and Philip Farmer, assistant professor of philosophy in Yale University; and Maltby Phar, anarchist editor of *The Garden Exquisite;* and—first and chiefly—me.

The case of Phil Farmer was typical. Phil and I had been classmates in the dark backward and abysm, and we were still, in a manner of speaking, friends. I mean that, though we had few tastes in common, we kept on liking each other a good deal. Phil was a gentle-hearted, stiff-headed sort of man, with a conscience—formed for him and handed on by a long line of Unitarian ministers—a conscience which drove him to incredible labor at altitudes few of us attain, and where even Phil, it seemed to me, found breathing difficult. Not having been thrown with much feminine society on his chosen heights, he had remained a bachelor. The Metaphysical Mountains are said to be infested with women, but they cluster, I am told, below the snow line. Phil did not even meet them by climbing through them; he always ballooned straight up for the Unmelting; and when he occasionally dropped down, his psychic chill seldom wore entirely off before he was ready to ascend again. This protected him; for he was a tall, dark-haired fellow whose features had the clear-cut gravity of an Indian chieftain; his rare, friendly smile was a delight. So he would hardly otherwise have escaped.

Perhaps once a week it was his habit to drop in after dinner and share with me three or four pipes' worth of desultory conversation. We seldom talked shop; since mine did not interest him, nor his me. Mostly we just ambled aimlessly round the outskirts of some chance neutral topic—who would win the big game, for example. It amused neither of us, but it rested us both.

One night, perhaps a month after Susan had come to me, I returned late from a hot day's trip to New York—one more unsuccessful quest after Hypatia Rediviva—and found Phil and Susan sitting together on the screened terrace at the back of my house, overlooking the garden. It was not my custom to spend the muggy midsummer months in town, but this year I had been unwilling to leave until I could capture and carry off Hypatia Rediviva with me. Moreover, I did not know where to go. The cottage at Watch Hill belonged to Gertrude, and was in consequence no longer used by either of us. As a grass widower I had, in summer, just travelled about. Now, with a ward of fourteen to care for, just travelling about no longer seemed the easiest solution; yet I hated camps and summer hotels. I should have to rent a place somewhere, that was certain; but where? With the world to choose from, a choice proved difficult. I was marking time.

My stuffy fruitless trip had decided me to mark time no longer. Hypatia or no Hypatia, Susan must be taken to the hills or the sea. It was this thought that simmered in my brain as I strolled out to the garden terrace and overheard Susan say to Phil: "But I think it's *much* easier to believe in the devil than it is in God! Don't you? The devil isn't all-wise, all-good, all-everything! He's a lot more like *us*."

I stopped short and shamelessly listened.

"That's an interesting concept," responded Phil, with his slow, friendly gravity. "You mean, I suppose, that if we must be anthropomorphic, we ought at least to be consistent."

"Wouldn't it be funny," said Susan, "if I did mean that without knowing it?" There was no flippancy, no irony in her tone. "'*An-thro-po-mor-phic . . .* '" she added, savoring its long-drawn-outness. Susan never missed a strange word; she always pounced on it at once, unerringly, and made it hers.

"That's a Greek word," explained Phil.

"It's a good word," said Susan, "if it has a tremendous lot packed up in it. If it hasn't, it's much too long."

"I agree with you," said Phil; "but it has."

"What?" asked Susan.

"It would take me an hour to tell you."

"Oh, I'm glad!" cried Susan. "It must be a wonderful word! Please go on till Ambo comes!"

I decided to take a bath, and tiptoed softly and undetected away.

V

After that evening Phil began to drop in every two or three nights, and he did not hesitate to tell me that the increasing frequency of his visits was due to his progressive interest in Susan.

"She's a curious child," he explained; which was true in any sense you chose to take it, and all the way back to the Latin *curiosus*, "careful, diligent, thoughtful; from *cura*, care," and so on... .

"I've never seen much of children," Phil continued; "never had many chances, as it happens. My sister has three boys, but she's married to a narrow-gauge missionary, and lives—to call it that—in Ping Lung, or some such place. I've the right address somewhere, I think—in a notebook. Bertha sends me snapshots of the boys from time to time, but I can't say I've ever felt lonely because of their exile. Funny. Perhaps it's because I never liked Bertha much. Bertha has a sloppy mind—you know, with chance scraps of things floating round in it. Nothing coheres. But you take this youngster of yours, now—I call her yours——"

"Do!" I interjected.

"Well, there's the opposite extreme! Susan links everything up, everything she gets hold of—facts, fancies, guesses, feelings; the whole psychic menagerie. Chains them all together somehow, and seems to think they'll get on comfortably in the same tent. Of course they won't—can't—and that's the danger for her! But she's stimulating, Hunt"—Phil always called me Hunt, as if just failing whole-heartedly to accept me—"she's positively stimulating! A mind like that must be trained; thoroughly, I mean. We must do our best for her."

The "we" amused me and—yes, I confess it—nettled me a little.

"Don't worry about that," I said, and more dryly than I had meant to; "I'm combing the country now for a suitable governess."

"Governess!" Phil snorted. "You don't want a governess for Susan. You want, for this job," he insisted, "a male intellect—a vigorous, disciplined male intellect. Music, dancing, water colors—pshaw! Deportment—how to enter a drawing-room! Fiddle-faddle! How to enter the Kingdom of God! That's more Susan's style," cried Phil, with a most unaccustomed heat.

I laughed at him.

"Are you willing to take her on, Phil?" I asked. "I believe it's been done; Epicurus had a female pupil or two."

"I have taken her on," Phil replied, quite without resentment. "Hadn't you noticed it?"

"Yes," I said; "only, it's the other way round."

"I've been appropriated, is that it?"

"Yes; by Susan. We all have, Phil. That vampire child is simply draining us, my dear fellow."

"All right," said Phil, after a second's pause, "if she's a *spiritual* vampire, so much the better. Only, she'll need a firm hand. We must give her suck at regular hours; draw up a plan. You can tackle the languages, if you like— æsthetics, and all that. I'll pin her down to math and logic—teach her to *think* straight. We can safely leave her to pick up history and sociology and such things for herself. You've a middling good library, and she'll browse."

"Oh, she'll browse! She's browsing now."

"Poetry?" demanded Phil, suspicion in his tone, anxiety in his eyes. "If she runs amuck with poetry too soon, there's no hope for her. She'll get to taking sensations for ideas, and that's fatal. A mind like Susan's——"

What further he said I missed; a distant tinkle from the front-door bell had distracted me.

It was Maltby Phar. He came out to us on the garden terrace, unexpected and unannounced.

"Whether you like it or not," he sighed luxuriously, "I'm here for a week. How's the great experiment—eh? Am I too late for the bust-up?" Then he nodded to Phil. "How are you, Mr. Farmer? Delighted to meet an old adversary! Shall it be swords or pistols this time? Or clubs? But I warn you, I'm no fit foe; I'm soft. Making up our mammoth Christmas Number in July always unnerves me. By the time I had looked over a dozen designs for our cover this morning and found Gaspar, Melchior, and Balthazar in every one of them, mounted on fancy camels, and heading for an exaggerated star in the right upper dark-blue corner, I succumbed to heat and profanity, turned 'em all face downward, shuffled 'em, grabbed one at random, and then fled for solace! Solace," he added, dropping into a wicker armchair, "can begin, if you like, by taking a cool, mellow, liquid form."

I rang.

Phil, I saw, was looking annoyed. He disliked Maltby Phar, openly disliked him; so I felt certain—I was perhaps rather hoping—that he would take this opportunity to escape. With Phil I was never then entirely at ease; but in those days I was wholly so with Maltby. Miss Goucher answered my summons in person, and I suggested a sauterne cup for my friends. Phil frowned on the suggestion, but Maltby beamed. The ayes had it, and Miss Goucher, who had remained neutral, withdrew. It was Phil's chance; yet he surprised me by settling back and refilling his pipe.

"When you came, Mr. Phar," he said, his tone withdrawing toward formality, "we were discussing the education of Susan."

"Then I came just in time!" cried Maltby.

"For what?" I queried.

"I may prevent a catastrophe. If you're really going to see this thing through, Boz"—his name for me—"for God's sake do a little clear thinking first! Don't drift. Don't flounder. Don't wallow. Scrap all your musty, inbred prejudices once for all, and see that at least one kid on this filthy old planet gets a plain, honest, unsentimentalized account of what she is and what the world is. If you can bring yourself to do that, Susan will be unique. She will be the first educated woman in America."

"'What she is and what the world is,'" repeated Phil, slowly. "What is the world, may I ask? And what is Susan?"

There was a felt tenseness in the moment; the hush before battle. We leaned forward a little from our easy-chairs, and no one of us noticed that Susan had slipped noiselessly to the window seat by the opened library window which gave upon the terrace. But there, as we later discovered, she was; and there, for the present silently, she remained.

"The world," began Maltby Phar sententiously, "is a pigsty."

"Very well," interrupted Phil; "I'll grant you that to start with. What follows?"

"What we see about us," said Maltby.

"And what do we see?" asked Phil.

At this inopportune moment Miss Goucher reappeared, bearing a Sheffield tray, on which stood three antique Venetian goblets, and a tall pitcher of rare Bohemian glass, filled to the brim with an iced sauterne cup garnished with fresh strawberries and thin disks of pineapple. Nothing less suggestive of the conventional back-lot piggery could have been imagined. By the time a table had been placed, our goblets filled, and Miss Goucher had retired, Maltby had decided to try for a new opening.

"Excellent!" he resumed, having drained and refilled his goblet. "Now, Mr. Farmer, if you really wish to know what the world is, and what Susan is, I am ready. Have with you! And by the way, Boz," he interjected, sipping his wine, "your new housekeeper is one in a thousand. Mrs. Parrot was admirable; I've been absurdly regretting her loss. But Mrs. Parrot never quite rose to *this!*"

Phil's tongue clicked an impatient protest against the roof of his mouth. "I am still unenlightened, Mr. Phar."

"True," said Maltby. "That's the worst of you romantic idealists. It's your permanent condition." He settled back in his chair, and fell to his old trick of slowly caressing the back of his left hand with the palm of his right. "The world, my dear Mr. Farmer," he continued, "the universe, indeed, as we have come gradually to know it, is an infinity of blindly clashing forces. They have always existed, they will always exist; they have always been blind, and they always will be. Anything may happen in such an infinity, and we—this world of men and microbes—are one of the things which has temporarily happened. It's regrettable, but it is so. And though there is nothing final we can do about it, and very little in any sense, still—this curious accident of the human intellect enables us to do something. We can at least admit the plain facts of our horrible case. Here, a self-realizing accident, we briefly are. Death will dissipate us one by one, and the world in due time. That much we know. But while we last, why must we add imaginary evils to our real ones, and torment ourselves with false hopes and ridiculous fears?

"Why can't each one of us learn to say: 'I am an accident of no consequence in a world that means nothing. I might be a stone, but I happen to be a man. Hence, certain things give me pleasure, others pain. And, obviously, in an accidental, meaningless world I can owe no duty to anyone but myself. I owe it to myself to get as much pleasure and to avoid as much pain as possible. Unswerving egotism should be my law.'" He paused to sip again, with a side glance toward Phil.

"Elementary, all this, I admit. I apologize for restating it to a scholar. But such are the facts as science reveals them—are they not? You have to try somehow to go beyond science to get round them. And where do you go—

you romantic idealists? Where *can* you go? Nowhere outside of yourselves, I take it. So you plunge, perforce, down below the threshold of reason into a mad chaos of instinct and desire and dream. And what *there* do you find? Bugaboos, my dear sir, simply bugaboos: divine orders, hells, heavens, purgatories, moral sanctions—all the wild insanity, in two words, that had made our wretched lives even less worth living than they could and should be!"

"*Should?* Why *should?*" asked Phil. "Granting your universe, who gives a negligible damn for a little discomfort more or less?"

"I do!" Maltby asserted. "I want all the comfort I can get; and I could get far more in a world of clear-seeing, secular egotists than I can in this mixed mess of superstitious, sentimental idealists which we choose to call civilized society! Take just one minor practical illustration: Say that some virgin has wakened my desire, and I hers. In a reasonable society we could give each other a certain amount of passing satisfaction. But do we do it? No. The virgin has been taught to believe in a mystical, mischievous something, called Purity! To follow her natural instinct would be a sin. If you sin and get caught on earth, society will punish you; and if you don't get caught here, you'll infallibly get caught hereafter—and then God will punish you. So the virgin tortures herself and tortures me—unless I'm willing to marry her, which would be certain to prove the worst of tortures for us both. And there you are."

It was at this point that Susan spoke from her window.

"Pearl and papa weren't married, Mr. Phar; but they didn't get much fun out of not being."

I confess that I felt a nervous chill start at the base of my spine and shiver up toward my scalp. Even Phil, the man of Indian gravity, looked for an instant perturbed.

"Susan!" I demanded sharply. "Have you been listening?"

"Mustn't I listen?" asked Susan. "Why not? Are you cross, Ambo?"

"The mischief's done," said Phil to me quietly; "better not make a point of it."

"Please don't be cross, Ambo," Susan pleaded, slipping through the window to the terrace and coming straight over to me. "Mr. Phar feels just the way papa did about things; only papa couldn't talk so splendidly. He had a very poor vocabulary"—"Vocabulary!" I gasped—"except nasty words and swearing. But he meant just what Mr. Phar means, *inside*."

Phil, as she ended, began to make strange choking noises and retired suddenly into his handkerchief. Maltby put down his glass and stared at Susan.

"Young person," he finally said, "you ought to be spanked! Don't you know it's an unforgivable sin to spy on your elders!"

"But you don't believe in sin," responded Susan calmly, without the tiniest suspicion of pertness in her tone or bearing. "You believe in doing what you want to. *I* wanted to hear what you were saying, Mr. Phar."

"Of course you did!" Phil struck in. "But next time, Susan, as a concession to good manners, you might let us know you're in the neighborhood—?"

Susan bit her lower lip very hard before she managed to reply.

"Yes. I will next time. I'm sorry, Phil." (*Phil!*) Then she turned to Maltby. "But I wasn't spying! I just didn't know you would any of you mind."

"We don't, really," I said. "Sit down, dear. You're always welcome." I had been doing some stiff, concentrated thinking in the last three minutes, and now I had taken the plunge. "The truth is, Susan," I went on, "that most children who live in good homes, who are what is called 'well brought up,' are carefully sheltered from any facts or words or thoughts which their parents do not consider wholesome or pleasant. Parents try to give their children only what they have found to be best in life; they try to keep them in ignorance of everything else."

"But they can't," said Susan. "At least, they couldn't in Birch Street."

"No. Nor elsewhere. But they try. And they always make believe to themselves that they have succeeded. So it's supposed to be very shocking and dangerous for a girl of your age to listen to the free conversation of men of our age. That's the reason we all felt a little guilty, at first, when we found you'd been overhearing us."

"How funny," said Susan. "Papa never cared."

"Good for him!" exclaimed Maltby. "I didn't feel guilty, for one! I refuse to be convicted of so hypocritically squeamish a reaction!"

"Oh!" Susan sighed, almost with rapture. "You know such a lot of words, Mr. Phar! You can say anything."

"Thanks," said Maltby; "I rather flatter myself that I can."

"And you *do!*" grunted Phil. "But words," he took up the dropped threads rather awkwardly, "are nothing in themselves, Susan. You are too fond of mere words. It isn't words that matter; it's ideas."

"Yes, Phil," said Susan meekly, "but I love words—best of all when they're pictures."

Phil frowned, without visible effect upon Susan. I saw that her mind had gone elsewhere.

"Ambo?"

"Yes, dear?"

"You mustn't ever worry about me, Ambo. My hearing or knowing things —or saying them. I—I guess I'm different."

Maltby's face was a study in suppressed amazement; Phil was still frowning. It was all too much for me, and I laughed—laughed from the lower ribs!

Susan laughed with me, springing from her chair to throw her arms tightly round my neck in one big joyous suffocating hug!

"Oh, Ambo!" she cried, breathless. "Isn't it going to be fun—all of us— together—now we can *talk!*"

VI

The following evening, after dinner, Maltby Phar, still a little ruffled by Susan's unexpected vivacities of the night before, retired to the library with pipe and book, and Susan and I sat alone together on the garden terrace. It was dusk. The heavy air of the past week had been quickened and purified by an afternoon thunderstorm. Little cool puffs came to us across a bed of glimmering white phlox, bearing with them its peculiar, loamy fragrance. Smoke from my excellent cigarette eddied now and then toward Susan.

Silence had stolen upon her as the afterglow faded, revealing the first patient stars. Already I had learned to respect Susan's silences. She was not, in the usual sense of uncertain temper, of nervous irritability, a moody child; yet she had her moods—moods, if I may put it so, of extraordinary definition. There were hours, not too frequent to be disturbing, when she *withdrew;* there is no better word for it. At such times her thin, alert little frame was motionless; she would sit as if holding a pose for a portrait, her chin a trifle lifted, her eyes focusing on no visible object, her hands lying—always with the palms upward—in her lap. I supposed that now, with the veiled yet sharply scented dusk, such a mood had crept upon her. But for once I was mistaken. Susan, this time, had not withdrawn; she was intensely aware.

"Ambo"—the suddenness with which she spoke startled me—"you ought to have lots of children. You ought to have a boy, anyway; not just a girl."

"A boy? Why, dear? Are you lonely?"

"Of course not; with you—and Phil!"

"Then whatever in the world put such a crazy——"

Susan interrupted; a bad habit of hers, never subsequently broken, and due, doubtless, to an instinctive impatience of foreseeable remarks.

"You're so awfully rich, Ambo. You could have dozens and not feel it—except that they'd get in your way sometimes and make your outside cross. But two wouldn't be much more trouble than one. It might seem a little crowded—at first; but after while, Ambo, you'd hardly notice it."

"Possibly. Still—nice boys don't grow on bushes, Susan. Not the kind of brothers I should have to insist upon for you!"

"I'm not so fussy as all that," said Susan. "And it isn't fair that I should have everything. Besides, Ambo, boys are much nicer than girls. Honestly they are."

"Oh, are they! I'm afraid you haven't had much experience with boys! Most of them are disgusting young savages. Really, Susan! Their hands and feet are too big for them, and their voices don't fit. They're always breaking things—irreplaceable things for choice, and raising the devil of a row. Take my word for it, dear, please. I'm an ex-boy myself; I know all about 'em! They were never created for civilized human companionship. Why, I'd rather give you a young grizzly bear and be done with it, than present you with the common-or-garden brother! But if you'd like a nice quiet little sister some day, maybe——"

"I wouldn't," said Susan.

She was silent again for several moments, pondering. I observed her furtively. Nothing was more distant from my desire than any addition, of any age, male or female, to my present family. Heaven, in its great and unwonted kindness, had sent me Susan; she was—to my thinking—perfect; and she was enough. Whether in art or in life I am no lover of an avoidable anticlimax. But Susan's secret purposes were not mine.

"Ambo," she resumed, "I guess if you'd ever lived in Birch Street you'd feel differently about boys."

"I doubt it, Susan."

"I'm sure you'd feel differently about Jimmy."

"Jimmy?"

"Jimmy Kane, Ambo—*my* Jimmy. Haven't I ever told you about him?"

Guilefully, persuasively, she edged her chair nearer to mine.

It was then that I first learned of Jimmy's battle for Susan, of the bloody but righteous downfall of Giuseppe Gonfarone, and of many another incident long treasured in the junior annals of Birch Street. Thus, little by little, though the night deepened about us, my eyes were unsealed. What a small world I had always lived in! For how long had it seemed to me that romance was— approximately—dead! My fingers tightened on Susan's, while the much-interrogated stars hung above us in their mysterious orbits and—— But no, that is the pathetic fallacy. Stars—are they not matter, merely? They could not smile.

"Don't you truly think, Ambo," suggested Susan, "that Jimmy ought to have a better chance? If he doesn't get it, he'll have to work in a factory all his life. And here I am—with you!"

"Yes. But consider, Susan—there are thousands of boys like Jimmy. I can't father them all, you know."

"I don't want you to father them all," said Susan; "and there isn't anybody like Jimmy! You'll see."

It came over me as she spoke that I was, however unwillingly, predestined to see.

Maltby Phar thought otherwise. That night, after Susan had gone up to bed, I talked the thing over with him—trying for an airy, detached tone; the tone of one who discusses an indifferent matter for want of a more urgent. Maltby was not, I fear, deceived.

"My dear Boz," he pleaded, "buck up! Get a fresh grip on your individuality and haul it back from the brink of destruction! If you don't, that little she-demon above-stairs will push it over into the gulf, once for all! You'll be nobody. You'll be her dupe—her slave. How can you smile, man! I'm quite serious, and I warn you. Fight the good fight! Defend the supreme rights of your ego, before it's too late!"

"Why these tragic accents?" I parried. "It's not likely the washlady's kid would want to come; or his mother let him. Susan idealizes him, of course. He's probably quite commonplace and content as he is. No harm, though, if it pleases Susan, in looking him over?"

Maltby took up his book again. He dismissed me. "Whom the gods destroy ——" he muttered, and ostentatiously turned a page.

VII

My feeling that I was predestined to see, with Susan, that there wasn't anybody like Jimmy—that I was further predestined to take him into my heart and home—proved, very much to my own surprise and to the disappointment of Susan, to be unjustified. This was the first bitter defeat that Susan had been called upon to bear since leaving Birch Street. She took it quietly, but deeply, which troubled my private sense of relief, and indeed turned it into something very like regret. The simple fact was that much had happened in Birch Street since the tragedy of the four-room house; life had not stood still there; chance and change—deaths and marriages and births—had altered the circumstances of whole families. In short, that steady flux of mortality, which respects neither the dignity of the Hillhouse Avenues nor the obscurity of the Birch Streets of the world, had in its secret courses already borne Jimmy Kane—elsewhere. Precisely where, even his mother did not know; and first and last it was her entire and passionate ignorance as to Jimmy's present location which foiled us. "West" is a geographical expression certainly, but it is not an address.

Jimmy's mother lived with her unwashed brood, you will remember, above old Heinze's grocery store, and on the following afternoon I ran Susan over there for a tactful reconnaissance. At Susan's request we went slowly along Birch Street from its extreme right end to its ultimate wrong, crossing the waste land and general dump at the base of East Rock—historic ground!—mounting the long incline beyond, and so passing the four-room house, which now seemed to be occupied by at least three families of that hardy, prolific race discourteously known to young America as "wops." Throughout this little tour Susan withdrew, and I respected her silence. She had not yet spoken when we stopped at Heinze's corner and descended.

Here first it was that forebodings of chance and change met us upon the pavement, in the person of old Heinze himself, standing melancholy and pensive before the screened doorway of his domain. Him Susan accosted. He did not at first recognize her, but recollection returned to him as she spoke.

"*Ach*, so!" he exclaimed, peering with mildest surprise above steel-rimmed spectacles. "Id iss you—nod? Leedle Susanna!"

My formal introduction followed; nor was it without a glow of satisfaction that I heard old Heinze assure me that he had read certain of my occasional essays with attention and respect. "Ard for ard—yah! Dot iss your credo," he informed me, with tranquil noddings of his bumpy, oddly shaped skull. "Dot iss der credo of all arisdograds. Id iss nod mine."

But Susan was in no mood for general ideas; she descended at once to particulars, and announced that we were going up to see Mrs. Kane. Then old Heinze snaggily, and I thought rather wearily, smiled.

"*Aber*," he objected, lifting twisted, rheumatic hands, "dere iss no more such a vooman! Alretty, leedle Susanna, I haf peen an oldt fool like oders. I haf made her my vife." And though he continued to smile, he also sighed.

Our ensuing interview with Frau Heinze, formerly the Widow Kane, fully interpreted this sigh. Prosperity, Susan later assured me, had not improved her. She greeted us, above the shop, in her small, shiny, colored lithograph of a parlor, with unveiled suspicion. Her eyes were hostile. She seemed to take it for granted, did Mrs. Heinze, that we could have no kindly purpose in intruding upon her. A dumpy, grumpy little woman, with the parboiled hands and complexion of long years at the wash-tubs, her present state of comparative freedom from bondage had not lightened her heart. Her irritability, I told Susan after our escape, was doubtless due to the fact that she could not share in old Heinze's intellectual and literary tastes. Susan laughed.

"She wouldn't bother much about that; Birch Street's never lonely, and it's only a step to the State Street movies. No; I think it's corsets."

Corsets? The word threw a flood of light. I saw at once that it must be a strain upon any disposition to return after a long and figureless widowhood to the steel, buckram, and rebellious curves of conventional married life. I remembered the harnesslike creaking of Mrs. Heinze's waistline, and forgave her much.

There was really a good deal to forgive. It was neither Susan's fault nor mine that turned our call into a bad quarter of an hour. I had looked for a pretty scene as I mounted the stairs behind Susan. I had pictured the child, in her gay summer frock, bursting like sunshine into Mrs. Heinze's stuffy quarters—and so forth. Nothing of the kind occurred.

"Who is ut?" demanded Mrs. Heinze, peering forth. "Oh, it's you—Bob Blake's girl. What do you want?" Susan explained. "Well, come in then," said Mrs. Heinze.

Susan, less daunted than I by her reception, marched in and asked at once for Jimmy. At the sound of his name Mrs. Heinze's suspicions were sharply focused. If the gentleman knew anything about Jimmy, all right, let him say so! It wouldn't surprise her to hear he'd been gettin' himself into trouble! It would surprise her much more, she implied, if he had not. But if he had, she couldn't be responsible—nor Heinze either, the poor man! Jimmy was sixteen —a man grown, you might say. Let him look after himself, then; and more shame to him for the way he'd acted!

But what way he had acted, and why, Susan at first found it difficult to determine.

"Oh!" she at length protested, following cloudy suggestions of evil courses. "Jimmy couldn't do anything mean! You know he couldn't. It isn't in him!"

"Isn't ut indeed! Me slavin' for him and the childer ever since Kane was took off sudden—and not a cint saved for the livin'—let alone the dead! Slavin' and worritin'—the way you'd think Jimmy'd 'a' jumped wid joy when Heinze offered! And an easier man not to be found—though he's got his notions. What man hasn't? If it's not one thing, it's another. 'Except his beer, he don't drink much,' I says to Jimmy; 'and that's more than I could say for your own father, rest his soul!' 'My father wasn't a Dutchman,' Jimmy says; givin' me his lip to me face. 'He didn't talk out against the Pope,' he says. 'Nor the Pris'dint,' he says. 'He wasn't a stinkin' Socialist,' he says—usin' them very words! 'No,' I says, 'he was a Demycrat—and what's ut to you? All men'll be blatherin' polytics after hours,' I says. 'Heinze manes no harm by ut, no more nor the rest. 'Tis just his talk,' I says. And after that we had more words, and I laid me palm to his head."

"Oh!" cried Susan.

"I'll not take lip from a son of mine, Susan Blake; nor from you, wid all your grand clothes! I've seen you too often lackin' a modest stitch to your back!"

I hastened to intervene.

"We'll not trouble you longer, Mrs. Heinze, if you'll only be good enough to tell me where Jimmy is now. He was very kind to Susan once, and she wants to thank him in some way. I've a proposition to make him—which might be to his advantage."

"Oh—so that's ut at last! Well, Susan Blake, you've had the grand luck for the likes of you! But you're too late. Jimmy's gone."

"Gone?"

"'Tis the gratitude I get for raisin' him! Gone he is, wid what he'd laid by —twenty-sivin dollars—and no word to nobody. There's a son for ye!" "But—

oh, Mrs. Heinze—gone *where?*"

"West. That's all I know," said Mrs. Heinze. "He left a line to say he'd gone West. We've not had a scrap from him since. If he comes to a bad end ———"

"Jimmy won't come to a bad end!" struck in Susan sharply. "He did just right to leave you. Good-by." With that she seized my arm and swept me with her from the room.

"Glory be to God! Susan Blake—the airs of her now!" followed us shrilly, satirically, down the stairs.

VIII

Maltby's visit came to an end, and for the first time I did not regret his departure. For some reason, which perhaps purposely I left unanalyzed, Maltby was beginning to get a trifle on my nerves. But let that pass. Once he was gone, Phil Farmer drew a long breath and plunged with characteristic thoroughness into his comprehensive scheme for the education of Susan. Her enthusiasm for this scheme was no less contagious than his own, and I soon found myself yielding to her wish to stay on in New Haven through the summer, and let in for daily lessons at regular hours—very much to my astonishment, the rôle of schoolmaster being one which I had always flattered myself I was temperamentally unfitted to sustain.

I soon discovered, however, that teaching a mentally alert, whimsically unexpected, stubbornly diligent, and always grateful pupil is among the most stimulating and delightful of human occupations. My own psychic laziness, which had been long creeping upon me, vanished in this new atmosphere of competition—competition, for that is what it came to, with the unwearying Phil. It was a real renascence for me. Forsaken gods! how I studied—off hours and on the sly! My French was excellent, my Italian fair; but my small Latin and less Greek needed endless attention. Yet I rather preen myself upon my success; though Phil has always maintained that I overfed Susan with æsthetic flummery, thus dulling the edge of her appetite for his own more wholesome daily bread.

In one respect, at least, I disagreed fundamentally with Phil, and here—through sheer force of conviction—I triumphed. Phil, who lived exclusively in things of the mind, would have turned this sensitive child into a bemused scholar, a female bookworm. This, simply, I would not and did not permit. If she had a soul, she had a body, too, and I was determined that it should be a vigorous, happy body before all else. For her sake solely—for I am too easily an indolent man—I took up riding again, and tennis, and even pushed myself into golf; with the result that my nervous dyspepsia vanished, and my irritability along with it; with the more excellent result that Susan filled and bloomed and ate (for her) three really astonishing meals a day.

It was a busy life—a wonderful life! Hard work—hard play—fun—travel.... Ah, those years!

But I am leaping ahead——!

Yet I have but one incident left to record of those earliest days with Susan —an incident which had important, though delayed, results—affecting in various ways, for long unforeseen, Susan's career, and the destiny of several other persons, myself among them.

Sonia, Susan's little Russian maid, was at the bottom of it all; and the first hint of the rather sordid affair came to me, all unprepared, from the lips of Miss Goucher. She sought me out in my private study, whither I had retired after dinner to write a letter or two—a most unusual proceeding on her part, and on mine—and she asked at once in her brief, hard, respectful manner for ten minutes of my time. I rose and placed a chair for her, uncomfortably certain that this could be no trivial errand; she seated herself, angularly erect, holding her feelings well in hand.

"Mr. Hunt," she began, "have I your permission to discharge Sonia?"

My face showed my surprise.

"But Susan likes her, doesn't she, Miss Goucher? And she seems efficient?"

"Yes. A little careless perhaps; but then, she's young. It isn't her service I object to."

"What is the trouble?"

"It is a question of character, Mr. Hunt. I have reason to think her lacking in—self-respect."

"You mean—immoral?" I asked, using the word in the restricted sense which I assumed Miss Goucher, like most maiden ladies, exclusively attached to it. To my astonishment Miss Goucher insisted upon more definition.

"No, I shouldn't say that. She tells a good many little fibs, but she's not at heart dishonest. And I'm by no means certain she can be held responsible for her weakness in respect to men." A slight flush just tinged Miss Goucher's prominent cheek bones; but duty was duty, and she persevered. "She has a bad inheritance, I think; and until she came here, Mr. Hunt, her environment was always—unfortunate. If it were not for Susan, I shouldn't have spoken. I should have felt it my duty to try to protect the child and—— However," added Miss Goucher, "I doubt whether much can be done for Sonia. So my first duty is certainly to Miss Susan, and to you."

Susan's quiet admiration for Miss Goucher had more or less puzzled me hitherto, but now my own opinion of Miss Goucher soared heavenward. Why, the woman was remarkable—far more so than I had remotely suspected! She had a mind above her station, respectable though her station might well be held to be.

"My dear Miss Goucher," I exclaimed, "it is perfectly evident to me that my interests are more than safe in your keeping. Do what you think best, by all means!"

"Unfortunately, Mr. Hunt," said Miss Goucher, "that is what I cannot do."

"May I ask why?"

"Society would not permit me," answered Miss Goucher.

"Please explain," I gasped.

"Sonia will cause a great deal of suffering in the world," said Miss Goucher, the color on her cheek bones deepening, while she avoided my glance. "For herself—and others. In my opinion—which I am aware is not widely shared—she should be placed in a lethal chamber and painlessly removed. We are learning to 'swat the fly,'" continued Miss Goucher, "because it benefits no one and spreads many human ills. Some day we shall learn to swat—other things." Calmly she rose to take her leave. Excitedly eager, I sprang up to detain her.

"Don't go, Miss Goucher! Your views are really most interesting—though, as you say, not widely accepted. Certainly not by me. Your plan of a lethal chamber for weak sisters and brothers strikes me as—well, drastic. Do sit down."

Again Miss Goucher perched primly upright on the outer edge of the chair beside my own. "I felt bound to state my views truthfully," she said, "since you asked for them. But I never intrude them upon others. I'm not a social rebel, Mr. Hunt. I lack self-confidence for that. When I differ from the received opinion I always suspect that I am quite wrong. Probably I am in this case. But I think society would agree with me that Sonia is not a fit maid for Susan."

"Beyond a shadow of doubt," I assented. "But may I ask on what grounds you suspect Sonia?"

"It is certainly your right," replied Miss Goucher; "but if you insist upon an answer I shall have to give notice."

"Then I shall certainly not insist."

"Thank you, Mr. Hunt," said Miss Goucher, rising once more. "I appreciate this." And she walked from the room.

It was the next afternoon that Susan burst into my study without knocking —a breach of manners which she had recently learned to conquer, so the irruption surprised me. But I noted instantly that Susan's agitation had carried her far beyond all thought for trifles. Never had I seen her like this. Her whole being was vibrant with emotional stress.

"Ambo!" she cried, all but slamming the door behind her. "Sonia mustn't go! I won't let her go! You and Miss Goucher may think what you please—I won't, Ambo! It's wicked! You don't want Sonia to be like Tilly Jaretski, do you?"

"Like Tilly Jaretski?" My astonishment was so great that I babbled the unfamiliar name merely to gain time, collect my senses.

"Yes!" urged Susan, almost leaping to my side, and seizing my arm with tense fingers. "She'll be just like Tilly was, along State Street—after her baby came. Tilly wasn't a bit like Pearl, Ambo; and Sonia isn't either! But she's going to have a baby, too, Ambo, like Tilly."

With a wrench of my entire nervous system I, in one agonizing second, completely dislocated the prejudices of a lifetime, and rose to the situation confronting me. O Hillhouse Avenue, right at both ends! How little you had prepared me for this precocious knowledge of life—knowledge that utterly degrades or most wonderfully saves—which these children, out toward the wrong end of the Birch Streets of the world, drink in almost with their mothers' milk! How far I, a grown man—a cultured, sophisticated man— must travel, Susan, even to begin to equal your simple acceptance of naked, ugly fact—sheer fact—seen, smelt, heard, tasted! How far—how far!

"Susan," I said gravely, "does Miss Goucher know about Sonia?"

"I don't know. I suppose so. I haven't seen her yet. When Sonia came to me, crying—I ran straight in here!"

"And how long have *you* known?"

"Over a week. Sonia told me all about it, Ambo. Count Dimbrovitski got her in trouble. She loved him, Ambo—her way. She doesn't any more. Sonia can't love anybody long; he can't, either. That's why his wife sent Sonia off. Sonia says she knows her husband's like that, but so long as she can hush things up, she doesn't care. Sonia says she has a lover herself, and Count Dim doesn't care much either. Oh, Ambo—how *stuffy* some people are! I don't mean Sonia. She's just pitiful—like Tilly. But those others—they're different —I can feel it! Oh, how *Artemis* must hate them, Ambo!"

Susan's tense fingers relaxed, slipping from my arm; she slid down to the floor, huddled, and leaning against the padded side of my chair buried her face in her hands.

Very quietly I rose, not to disturb her, and crossing to the interphone requested Miss Goucher's presence. My thoughts raced crazily on. In advance of Miss Goucher's coming I had dramatized my interview with her in seven different and unsatisfactory ways. When she at last entered, my temple pulses were beating and my tongue was stiff and dry. Susan, except for her shaken shoulders, had not stirred.

"Miss Goucher," I managed to begin, "shut the door, please... . You see this poor child——?"

Miss Goucher saw. Over her harsh, positive features fell a sort of transforming veil. It seemed to me suddenly—if for that moment only—that

Miss Goucher was very beautiful.

"If you wouldn't mind," she suggested, "leaving her with me?"

Well, I had not in advance dramatized our meeting in this way. In all the seven scenes that had flashed through me, I had stood, an unquestioned star, at the center of the stage. I had not foreseen an exit. But I most humbly and gratefully accepted one now.

Precisely what took place, what words were said there, in my study, following my humble exit, I have never learned, either from Miss Goucher or from Susan. I know only that from that hour forth the bond between them became what sentimentalists fondly suppose the relationship between mother and daughter must always be—what, alas, it so rarely, but then so beautifully, is.

I date from that hour Miss Goucher's abandonment of her predilection for the lethal chamber; at least, she never spoke of it again. And Sonia stayed with us. Her boy was born in my house, and there for three happy years was nourished and shamelessly spoiled; at the end of which time Sonia found a husband in the person of young Jack Palumbo, unquestionably the pick of all our Hillhouse Avenue chauffeurs. Their marriage caused a brief scandal in the neighborhood, but was soon accepted as an authentic and successful fact.

Chance and change are not always villains, you observe; the temperamental Sonia has grown stout and placid, and has increased the world's legitimate population by three. Nevertheless, it is the consensus of opinion that little Ivan, her first-born, is the golden arrow in her quiver—an opinion in which Jack Palumbo delightedly, if rather surprisingly, concurs.

And so much for Sonia.... Let the curtain quietly descend. When it rises again, six years will have passed; good years—and therefore unrecorded. Your scribe, Susan, is now nearing forty; and you—— Great heavens, is it possible! Can you be "going on"—twenty?

Yes, dear—— You are.

THE THIRD CHAPTER

I

I T was October; the year, 1913. Susan, Miss Goucher and I had just returned from Liverpool on the good ship "Lusitania"—there was a good ship "Lusitania" in those days—after a delightful summer spent in Italy and France. Susan and I entirely agree that the season for Italy is midsummer. Italy is not Italy until she has drunk deep of the sun; until a haze of whitest dust floats up from the slow hoofs of her white oxen along Umbrian or Tuscan roads. You will never get from her churches all they can give unless they have been to you as shadows of great rocks in a weary land. To step from reverberating glare to vast cool dimness—ah, that is to know at last the meaning of sanctuary!

But to step from a North River pier into a cynical taxi, solely energized by our great American principle of "Take a chance!"—to be bumped and slithered by that energizing principle across the main traffic streams of impatient New York—that is to reawaken to all the doubt and distraction, the implacable multiplicity of a scientifically disordered world!

New Haven was better; Hillhouse Avenue preserving especially—through valorous prodigies of rejection—much of its ancient, slightly disdainful, studiously inconspicuous calm.

Phil Farmer was waiting for us at the doorstep. For all his inclusive greeting, his warm, welcoming smile, he looked older, did Phil, leaner somehow, more finely drawn. There was a something hungry about him—something in his eyes. But if Susan, who notices most things, noted it, she did not speak of her impression to me. She almost hugged Phil as she jumped out to greet him and dragged him with her up the steps to the door.

And now, if this portion of Susan's history is to be truthfully recorded, certain facts may as well be set down at once, clearly, in due order, without shame.

1. Phil Farmer was, by this time, hopelessly in love with Susan.

2. So was Maltby Phar.

3. So was I.

It should now be possible for a modest but intelligent reader to follow the approaching pages without undue fatigue.

II

Susan never kept a diary, she tells me, but she had, like most beginning authors, the habit of scribbling things down, which she never intended to keep, and then could seldom bring herself to destroy. To a writer all that his pen leaves behind it seems sacred; it is, I treacherously submit, a private grief to any of us to blot a line. Such is our vanity. However inept the work which we force ourselves or are prevailed upon to destroy, the unhappy doubt always lingers: "If I had only saved it? One can't be sure? Perhaps posterity ——?"

Susan, thank God, was not and probably is not exempt from this folly. It enables me from this time forward to present certain passages—mere scraps and jottings—from her notebooks, which she has not hesitated to turn over to me.

"I don't approve, Ambo," was her comment, "but if you *will* write nonsense about me, I can't help it. What I can help, a little, is your writing nonsense about yourself or Phil or the rest. It's only fair to let me get a word in edgeways, now and then—if only for your sake and theirs."

That is not, however, my own reason for giving you occasional peeps into these notebooks of Susan's.

"I'm beginning to wish that Shelley might have had a sense of humor. 'Epipsychidion' is really too absurd. 'Sweet benediction in the eternal curse!' Imagine, under any condition of sanity, calling any woman that! Or 'Thou star above the storm!'—beautiful as the image is. 'Thou storm upon the star!' would make much worse poetry, but much better sense.... . Isn't it strange that I can't feel this about Wordsworth? He was better off without humor, for all his solemn-donkey spots—and it's better for us that he didn't have it. It's probably better for us, too, that Shelley didn't have it—but it wasn't better for *him*. Diddle-diddle-dumpling—what stuff all this is! Go to bed, Susan."

"There's no use pretending things are different, Susan Blake; you might as well face them and see them through, open-eyed. What does being in love mean?

"I suppose if one is really in love, head over heels, one doesn't care what it means. But I don't like pouncing, overwhelming things—things that crush and blast and scorch and blind. I don't like cyclones and earthquakes and conflagrations—at least, I've never experienced any, but I know I shouldn't like them if I did. But I don't think I'd be so terribly afraid of them—though I might. I think I'd be more—sort of— indignant—disgusted."

Editor's Note: Such English! But pungent stylist as Susan is now acknowledged to be, she is still, in the opinion of academic critics, not sufficiently attentive to formal niceties of diction. She remains too wayward, too impressionistic; in a word, too personal. I am inclined to agree, and yet— am I?

"It's all very well to stamp round declaiming that you're captain of your soul, but if an earthquake—even a tiny one—comes and shakes your house like a dice box and then scatters you and the family out of it like dice—it wouldn't sound very appropriate for your epitaph. 'I am the master of my fate' would always look silly on a tombstone. Why aren't tombstones a good test for poetry—some poetry? I've never seen anything on a tombstone that looked real—not even the names and dates.

"But *does* love have to be like an earthquake? If it does, then it's just a blind force, and I don't like blind forces. It's stupid to be blind oneself; but it's worse to have blind stupid things butting into one and pushing one about.

"Hang it, I don't believe love has to be stupid and blind, and go thrashing through things! Ambo isn't thrashing through things—or Phil either. But, of course, they wouldn't. That's exactly what I mean about love; it can be tamed, civilized. No, not civilized—just tamed. *Cowed?* Then it's still as wild as ever underneath? I'm afraid it is. Oh, dear!

"Phil and Ambo really are captains of their souls though, so far as things in general let them be. *Things in general*—what a funny name for God! But isn't God just a short solemn name for things in general? There I go again. Phil says I'm always taking God's name in vain. He thinks I lack reverence. I don't, really. What I lack is—reticence. That's different—isn't it, Ambo?"

51

The above extracts date back a little. The following were jotted early in November, 1913, not long after our return from overseas.

"This is growing serious, Susan Blake. Phil has asked you to marry him, and says he needs you. Ditto Maltby; only he says he wants you. Which, too obviously, he does. Poor Maltby—imagine his trying to stoop so low as matrimony, even to conquer! As for Ambo—Ambo says nothing, bless him— but I think he wants and needs you most of all. Well, Susan?"

"Jimmy's back. I saw him yesterday. He didn't know me."

"Sex is a miserable nuisance. It muddles things—interferes with honest human values. It's just Nature making fools of us for her own private ends. These are not pretty sentiments for a young girl, Susan Blake!"

"Speak up, Susan—clear the air! You are living here under false pretenses. If you can't manage to feel like Ambo's daughter—you oughtn't to stay."

III

It was perhaps when reticent Phil finally spoke to me of his love for Susan that I first fully realized my own predicament—a most unpleasant discovery; one which I determined should never interfere with Susan's peace of mind or with the possible chances of other, more eligible, men. As Susan's guardian, I could not for a moment countenance her receiving more than friendly attention from a man already married, and no longer young. A grim, confused hour in my study convinced me that I was an impossible, even an absurd, *parti*. This conviction brought with it pain so sharp, so nearly unendurable, that I wondered in my weakness how it was to be unflinchingly borne. Yet borne it must be, and without betrayal. It did not occur to me, in my mature folly, that I was already, and had for long been, self-betrayed.

"Steady, you old fool!" whispered my familiar demon. "This isn't going to

52

be child's play, you know. This is an hour-by-hour torture you've set out to grin and bear and live through. You'll never make the grade, if you don't take cognizance in advance. The road's devilishly steep and icy, and the corners are bad. What's more, there's no end to it; the crest's never in sight. Clamp your chains on and get into low.... Steady!

"But, of course," whispered my familiar demon, "there's probably an easier way round. Why attempt the impossible? Think what you've done for Susan! Gratitude, my dear sir—affectionate gratitude—is a long step in the right direction... if it is the right direction. I don't say it is; I merely suggest, *en passant*, that it may be. Suppose, for example, that Susan——"

"Damn you!" I spat out, jumping from my chair. "You contemptible swine!"

Congested blood whined in my ears like a faint jeering laughter. I paced the room, raging—only to sink down again, exhausted, my face and hands clammy.

"What a hideous exhibition," I said, distinctly addressing a grotesque porcelain Buddha on the mantelpiece. Contrary, I believe, to my expectations, he did not reply. My familiar demon forestalled him.

"If by taking a merely conventional attitude," he murmured, "you defeat the natural flowering of two lives——? Who are you to decide that the voice of Nature is not also the voice of God? Supposing, for the moment, that God is other than a poetic expression. If her eyes didn't haunt you," continued my familiar demon, "or a certain way she has of turning her head, like a poised poppy... ."

As he droned on within me, the mantelpiece blurred and thinned to the blue haze of a distant Tuscan hill, and the little porcelain Buddha sat upon this hill, very far off now and changed oddly to the semblance of a tiny huddled town. We were climbing along a white road toward that far hill, that tiny town.

"Ambo," she was saying, "that isn't East Rock—it's Monte Senario. And this isn't Birch Street—it's the Faenzan Way. How do you do it, Ambo—you wonderful magician! Just with a wave of your wand you change the world for me; you give me—all this!"

A bee droned at my ear: "Gratitude, my dear sir. Affectionate gratitude. A long step."

"Damn you!" I whimpered... . But the grotesque porcelain Buddha was there again, on the mantelshelf. The creases in his little fat belly disgusted me; they were loathsome. I rose. "At least," I said to him, "I can live without *you!*" Then I seized him and shattered him against the fireplace tiles. It was an enormous relief.

Followed a knock at my door that I answered calmly: "Who is it? Come in."

Miss Goucher never came to me without a mission; she had one now.

"Mr. Hunt," she said, "I should like to talk to you very plainly. May I? It's about Susan." I nodded. "Mr. Hunt," she continued resolutely, "Susan is in a very difficult position here. I don't say that she isn't entirely equal to meeting it; but I dread the nervous strain for her—if you understand?"

"Not entirely, Miss Goucher; perhaps, not at all."

"I was afraid of this," she responded unhappily. "But I must go on—for her sake."

Knowing well that Miss Goucher would face death smiling for Susan's sake, her repressed agitation alarmed me. "Good heavens!" I exclaimed. "Is there anything really wrong?"

"A good deal." She paused, her lips whitening as she knit them together, lest any ill-considered word should slip from her. Miss Goucher never loosed her arrows at random; she always tried for the bull's-eye, and usually with success.

"I am speaking in strict confidence—to Susan's protector and legal guardian. Please try to fill in what I leave unsaid. It is very unfortunate for Susan's peace of mind that you should happen to be a married man."

"For *her* peace of mind!"

"Yes."

"Wait! I daren't trust myself to fill in what you leave unsaid. It's too— preposterous. Do you mean—— But you can't mean that you imagine Susan to be in love with—her grandfather?" My heart pounded, suffocating me; with fright, I think.

"No," said Miss Goucher, coldly; "Susan is not in love with her grandfather. She is with you."

I could manage no response but an angry one. "That's a dangerous statement, Miss Goucher! Whether true or not—it ruins everything. You have made our life here together impossible."

"It is impossible," said Miss Goucher. "It became so last summer. I knew then it could not go on much longer."

"But I question this! I deny that Susan feels for me more than—gratitude and affection."

"Gratitude is rare," said Miss Goucher enigmatically, her eyes fixed upon the fragments of Buddha littering my hearth. "True gratitude," she added, "is a strong emotion. When it passes between a man and a woman, it is like flame."

"Very interesting!" I snapped. "But hardly enough to have brought you here to me with this!"

"She feels that you need her," said Miss Goucher.

"I do," was my reply.

"Susan doesn't need *you*," said Miss Goucher. "I don't wish to be brutal; but she doesn't. In spite of this, she can easily stand alone."

"I see. And you think that would be best?"

"Naturally. Don't you?"

"I'm not so sure."

As I muttered this my eyes, too, fixed themselves on the fragments of Buddha. Would the woman never go! I hated her; it seemed to me now that I had always hated her. What was she after all but a superior kind of servant—presuming in this way! The irritation of these thoughts swung me suddenly round to wound her, if I might, with sarcasm, with implied contempt. But it is impossible to wound the air. With her customary economy of explanation Miss Goucher had, pitilessly, left me to myself.

IV

The evening of this already comfortless day I now recall as one of the most exasperating of my life. Maltby Phar arrived for dinner and the week-end—an exasperation foreseen; Phil came in after dinner—another; but what I did not foresee was that Lucette Arthur would bring her malicious self and her unspeakably tedious husband for a formal call. Lucette was an old friend of Gertrude, and I always suspected that her occasional evening visits were followed by a detailed report; in fact, I rather encouraged them, and returned them promptly, hoping that they were. In my harmless way of life even Lucette's talent for snooping could find, I felt, little to feed upon, and it did not wholly displease me that Gertrude should be now and then forced to recognize this.

The coming of Susan had, not unnaturally, for a time, provided Lucette with a wealth of interesting conjecture; she had even gone so far as to intimate that Gertrude felt I was making—the expression is entirely mine—an ass of myself, which neither surprised nor disturbed me, since Gertrude had always had a tendency to feel that my talents lay in that direction. But, on the whole, up to this time—barring the Sonia incident, which had afforded her a good deal of scope, but which, after all, could not be safely misinterpreted— Lucette had found at my house pretty thin pickings for scandal; and I could only wonder at the unwearying patience with which she pursued her quest.

She arrived with poor Doctor Arthur in tow—Dr. Lyman Arthur, who professed Primitive Eschatology in the School of Religion: eschatology being "that branch of theology which treats of the end of the world and man's condition or state after death"—just upon the heels of Phil, who shot me a despairing glance as we rose to greet them.

But Susan, I thought, welcomed them with undisguised relief. She had been surpassing herself before the fire, chatting blithely, wittily, even a little recklessly; but there are gayer evenings conceivable than one spent in the presence of three doleful men, two of whom have proposed marriage to you, and one of whom would have done so if he were not married already. Almost anything, even open espionage and covert eschatology, was better than that.

Lucette—the name suggests Parisian vivacity, but she was really large and physically languid and very blonde, scented at once, I felt, a something faintly brimstoneish in the atmosphere of my model home, and forthwith prepared herself for a protracted and pleasant evening. It so happened that the Arthurs had never met Maltby, and Susan carried through the ceremony of introduction with a fine swinging rhythm which settled us as one group before the fire and for some moments at least kept the conversation animated and general.

But Eschatology, brooding in the background, soon put an end to this somewhat hectic social burst. The mere unnoted presence of Dr. Lyman Arthur, peering nearsightedly in at the doorway on a children's party, has been known, I am told, to slay youngling joy and turn little tots self-conscious, so that they could no longer be induced by agonized mothers to go to Jerusalem, or clap-in clap-out. His presence now, gradually but surely, had much the same effect. Seated at Maltby's elbow, he passed into the silence and drew us, struggling but helpless, after him. For five horrible seconds nothing was heard but the impolite, ironic whispering of little flames on the hearth. Was this man's condition or state after death? Eschatology had conquered.

Susan, in duty bound as hostess, broke the spell, but it cannot be said she rose to the occasion. "Is it a party in a parlor," she murmured wistfully to the flames, "all silent and all—damned?"

Perceiving that Lucette supposed this to be original sin, I laughed much more loudly than cheerfully, exclaiming "Good old Wordsworth!" as I did so.

Then Maltby's evil genius laid hold on him.

"By the way," he snorted, "they tell me one of you academic ghouls has discovered that Wordsworth had an illegitimate daughter—whatever *that* means! Any truth in it? I hope so. It's the humanest thing I ever heard about the old sheep!"

Doctor Arthur cleared his throat, very cautiously; and it was evident that Maltby had not helped us much. Phil, in another vein, helped us little more.

"I wonder," he asked, "if anyone reads Wordsworth now—except Susan?"

No one, not even Susan, seemed interested in this question; and the little flames chuckled quietly once more.

Something had to be done.

"Doctor," I began, turning toward Eschatology, and knowing no more than my Kazak hearthrug what I was going to say, "is it true that——"

"Undoubtedly," intoned Eschatology, thereby saving me from the pit I was digging for myself. My incomplete question must have chimed with Doctor Arthur's private reflections, and he seemed to suppose some controversial matter under discussion. "Undoubtedly," he repeated... . "And what is even more important is this——"

But Lucette silenced him with a "Why is it, dear, that you always let your cigar burn down at one side? It does look so untidy." And she leaned to me. "What delightfully daring discussions you must all of you have here together! You're all so terribly intellectual, aren't you? But do you never talk of anything but books and art and ideas? I'm sure you must," she added, fixing me with impenetrable blue eyes.

"Often," I smiled back; "even the weather has charms for us. Even food."

Her inquisitive upper lip curled and dismissed me.

"Why is it," she demanded, turning suddenly on Susan, "that I don't see you round more with the college boys? They're much more suitable to your age, you know, than Ambrose or Phil. I hope you don't frighten them off, my dear, by mentioning Wordsworth? Boys dislike bluestockings; and you're much too charming to wear them anyway. Oh, but you really are! I must take charge of you—get you out more where you belong, away from these dreadful old fogies!" Lucette laughed her languid, purring, dangerous laughter. "I'm serious, Miss Blake. You musn't let them monopolize you; they will if you're not careful. They're just selfish enough to want to keep you to themselves."

The tone was badinage; but the remark struck home and left us speechless. Lucette shifted the tiller slightly and filled her sails. "Next thing you know, Miss Blake, they'll be asking you to marry them. Individually, of course—not collectively. And, of course—not Ambrose! At least you're safe there," she hastily added; "aren't you?"

Maltby, I saw, was furious; bent on brutalities. Before I could check him, "Why?" he growled. "Why, Mrs. Arthur, do you assume that Susan is safe with Boz?"

"Well," she responded with a slow shrug of her shoulders, "naturally——"

"Unnaturally!" snapped Maltby. "Unless forbidden fruit has ceased to appeal to your sex. I was not aware that it had."

Phil's eyes were signalling honest distress. Susan unexpectedly rose from her chair. Deep spots of color burned on her cheeks, but she spoke with dignity. "I have never disliked any conversation so much, Mrs. Arthur. Good night." She walked from the room. Phil jumped up without a word and hurried after her. Then we all rose.

It seemed, however, that apologies were useless. Doctor Arthur had no need for them, since he had not perceived a slight, and was only too happy to find himself released from bondage; as for Lucette, her assumed frigidity could not conceal her flaming triumph. As a social being, for the sake of the *mores*, she must resent Susan's snub; but I saw that she would not have had things happen otherwise for a string of matched pearls. At last, at last her patience had been rewarded! I could almost have written for her the report to Gertrude—with nothing explicitly stated, and nothing overlooked.

Maltby, after their departure, continued truculent, and having no one else to rough-house decided to rough-house me. The lengthening absence of Susan and Phil had much to do with his irritation, and something no doubt with mine. For men of mature years we presently developed a very pretty little gutter-snipe quarrel.

"Damn it, Boz," he summed his grievances, "it comes precisely to this: You're playing dog in the manger here. By your attitude, by every kind of sneaking suggestion, you poison Susan's mind against me. Hang it, I'm not vain—but at least I'm presentable, and I've been called amusing. Other women have found me so. And to speak quite frankly, it isn't every man in my position who would offer marriage to a girl whose father——"

"I'd stop there, Maltby, if I were you!"

"My dear man, you and I are above such prejudices, of course! But it's only common sense to acknowledge that they exist. Susan's the most infernally seductive accident that ever happened on this middle-class planet! But all the same, there's a family history back of her that not one man in fifty would be able to forget. My point is, that with all her seduction, physical and mental, she's not in the ordinary sense marriageable. And it's the ordinary sense of such things that runs the world."

"Well——"

"Well—there you are! I offer her far more than she could reasonably hope for; or you for her. I'm well fixed, I know everybody worth knowing; I can give her a good time, and I can help her to a career. It strikes me that if you had Susan's good at heart, you'd occasionally suggest these thing's to her—even urge them upon her. As her guardian you must have some slight feeling of responsibility?"

"None whatever."

"What!"

"None whatever—so far as Susan's deeper personal life is concerned. That is her affair, not mine."

"Then you'd be satisfied to have her throw herself away?"

"If she insisted, yes. But Susan's not likely to throw herself away."

"Oh, isn't she! Let me tell you this, Boz, once for all: You're in love with the girl yourself, and though you may not know it, you've no intention of letting anyone else have a chance."

"Well," I flashed, "if you were in my shoes—would *you?*"

The vulgarity of our give and take did not escape me, but in my then state of rage I seemed powerless to escape vulgarity. I revelled in vulgarity. It refreshed me. I could have throttled Maltby, and I am quite certain he was itching to throttle me. We were both longing to throttle Phil. Indeed, we almost leaped at him as he stopped in the hall doorway to toss us an unnaturally gruff good night.

"Where's Susan?" I demanded.

"In your study," Phil mumbled, hunching into his overcoat; "she's waiting to see you." Then he seized his shapeless soft hat and—the good old phrase best describes it—made off.

"She's got to see me first!" Maltby hurled at me, coarsely, savagely, as he started past.

I grabbed his arm and held him. It thrilled me to realize how soft he was for all his bulk, to feel that physically I was the stronger.

"Wait!" I said. "This sort of thing has gone far enough. We'll stop *grovelling*—if you don't mind! If we can't give Susan something better than this, we've been cheating her. It's a pity she ever left Birch Street."

Maltby stared at me with slowly stirring comprehension.

"Yes," he at length muttered, grudgingly enough; "perhaps you're right. It's been an absurd spectacle all round. But then, life is."

"Wait for me here," I responded. "We'll stop butting at each other like stags, and try to talk things over like men. I'm just going to send Susan to bed."

That *was* my intention. I went to her in the study as a big brother might go, meaning good counsel. It was certainly not my intention to let her run into my arms and press her face to my shoulder. She clung to me with passion, but without joy, and her voice came through the tumult of my senses as if from a long way off.

"Ambo, Ambo! You've asked nothing—and you want me most of all. I *must* make somebody happy!"

It was the voice of a child.

V

I could not face Maltby again that evening, as I had promised, for our good sensible man-to-man talk; a lapse in courage which reduced him to rabid speculation and restless fury. So furious was he, indeed, after a long hour alone, that he telephoned for a taxi, grabbed his suitcase, and caught a slow midnight local for New York—from which electric center he hissed back over the wires three ominous words to ruin my solitary breakfast:

"He laughs best——   M. Phar."

While my egg solidified and the toast grew rigid I meditated a humble apologetic reply, but in the end I could not with honesty compose one; though I granted him just cause for anger. With that, for the time being, I dismissed him. There were more immediate problems, threatening, inescapable, that must presently be solved.

Susan, always an early riser, usually had a bite of breakfast at seven o'clock—brought to her by the faithful Miss Goucher—and then remained in her room to work until lunch time. For about a year past I had so far caught the contagion of her example as to write in my study three hours every morning; a regularity I should formerly have despised. Dilettantism always demands a fine frenzy, but now it astounded me to discover how much respectable writing one could do without waiting for the spark from heaven; one could pass beyond the range of an occasional article and even aspire to a book. Only the final pages of my first real book—*Aristocracy and Art*, an essay in æsthetic and social criticism—remained to be written; and Susan had made me swear by the Quanglewangle's Hat, her favorite symbol, to push on with it each morning till the job was done.

Well, *Aristocracy and Art* has since been published and, I am glad to say, forgotten. Conceived in superciliousness and swaddled in preciosity, it is one of the sins I now strive hardest to expiate. But in those days it expressed clearly enough the crusted aridity of my soul. However——

I had hoped, of course, that Susan would break over this morning and breakfast with me. She did not; and from sheer habit I took to my study and found myself in the chair before my desk. It was my purpose to think things out, and perhaps that is what I supposed myself to be doing as I stared dully at an ink blob on my blotter. It looked—and I was idiotically pleased by the resemblance—rather like a shark. All it needed was some teeth and a pair of flukes for its tail. Methodically I opened my fountain pen and supplied these, thereby reducing one fragment of chaos to order; and then my eye fell upon a half-scribbled sheet, marked "Page 224."

The final sentence on the sheet caught at me and annoyed me; it was ill-constructed. Presently it began to rearrange itself in whatever portion of us it is that these shapings and reshapings take place. Something in its rhythm, too, displeased me; it was mannered; it minuetted; it echoed Pater at his worst. It should be simpler, stronger. Why, naturally! I lopped at it, compressed it, pulled it about... .

There! At last the naked idea got the clean expression it deserved; and it led now directly to a brief, clear paragraph of transition. I had been worrying over that transition the morning before when my pen stopped; now it came with a smooth rush, carrying me forward and on.

Incredible, but for one swiftly annihilated hour I forgot all my insoluble life problems! Art, that ancient Circe, had waved her wand; I was happy—and it was enough. I forgot even Susan.

Meanwhile, Susan, busy at her notebook, had all but forgotten me.

"Am I in love with Ambo, or am I just trying to be for his sake? If happiness is a test, then I can't be in love with him, for there is no happiness in me. But what has happiness to do with love? It's just as I told nice old Phil last night. To be in love is to be silly enough to suppose that some other silly can gather manna for you from the meadows of heaven. Meanwhile, the other silly is supposing much the same nonsense about you—or if he isn't, then the sun goes black. What lovers seem to value most in each other is premature softening of the brain. But surely the union of two vain hopes in a single disappointment can never mean joy? No. You might as well get it said, Susan. Love is two broken reeds trying to be a Doric column.

"Still, there must be some test. Is it passion? How can it be?

"When I ran to Ambo last night I was pure rhythm and flame; but this morning I'm the hour before sunrise. No; I'm the outpost star, the one the comets turn—the one that peers off into nowhere.

"Perhaps if Ambo came to me now I should flame again; or perhaps I should only make believe for his sake. Is wanting to make believe for another's sake enough? Why not? I've no patience with lovers who are always rhythm and flame. Even if they exist—outside of *maisons de santé*—what good are they? Poets can rave about them, I suppose—that's something; but imagine coming to the end of life and finding that one had merely furnished good copy for Swinburne! No, thank you, Mrs. Hephæstus—you beautiful, shameless humbug! I prefer Apollo's lonely magic to yours. I'd rather be Swinburne than Iseult. If there's any singing left to be done I shall try to do part of it myself.

"There, you see; already you've forgotten Ambo completely—now you'll have to turn back and hunt for him. And if he's really working on *Aristocracy and Art* this morning, as he should be, then he has almost certainly forgotten you. Oh, dear! but he isn't—and he hasn't! Here he comes——"

Yes, I came; but not to ask for assurances of love. Man is so naïvely egotist, it takes a good deal to convince him, once the idea has been accepted, that he is not the object of an unalterable devotion. Frankly, I took it for granted now that Susan loved me, and would continue to love me till her dying hour.

What I really came to say to her, under the calming and strengthening influence of two or three rather well-written pages, was that our situation had definitely become untenable. I am an emancipated talker, but I am not an emancipated man; the distinction is important; the hold of mere custom upon me is strong. I could not see myself asking Susan to defy the world with me; or if I could just see it for my own sake, I certainly couldn't for hers. Nor could I see it for Gertrude's. Gertrude, after all, was my wife; and though she chose to feel I had driven her from my society, I knew that she did not feel willing to seek divorce for herself or to grant the freedom of it to me. On this point her convictions, having a religious sanction, were permanent. Gentle manners, then, if nothing higher, forbade me to seize the freedom she denied me. Having persuaded Gertrude, in good faith, to enter into an unconditional contract with me for life, I could no more bring myself to break it than I could have forced myself to steal another's money by raising a check.

My New England ancestors had distilled into my blood certain prejudices; only, where my great-grandfather, or even my grandfather, would have said that he refrained from evil because he feared God, I was content merely to feel that there are some things a gentleman doesn't stoop to. With them it was the stern daughter of the voice of God who ruled thoughts and acts; with me it was, if anything, the class obligations of culture, breeding, good form. Just as I wore correct wedding garments at a wedding, and would far rather have cut my throat with a knife than carry food on it from plate to mouth, so, in the face of any of life's moral or emotional crises, I clung to what instinct and cultivation told me were the correct sentiments.

Gertrude, it is true, was not precisely fulfilling her part in our contract, but then—Gertrude was a woman; and the excusable frailties of women should always be regarded as trumpet calls to the chivalry of man. Absurdly primitive, such ideas as these! Seated with Maltby Phar in my study, I had laughed them out of court many a time; for I could talk pure Bernard Shaw— our prophet of those days—with anybody, and even go him one better. But when it came to the pinch of decisive action I had always thrown back to my sources and left the responsibility on them. I did so now.

Yet it was hard to speak of anything but enchantment, witchery, fascination, when, from her desk, Susan looked round to me, faintly puzzled, faintly smiling. She was not a pretty girl, as young America—its taste superbly catered to by popular magazines—understands that phrase; nor was she beautiful by any severe classic standard—unless you are willing to accept certain early Italians as having established classic standards; not such faultless painters as Raphael or Andrea del Sarto, but three or four of the wayward lesser men whose strangely personal vision created new and unexpected types of loveliness. Not that I recall a single head by any one of them that prefigured Susan; not that I am helping you, baffled reader, to see her. Words are a dull medium for portraiture, or I am too dull a dog to catch with them even a phantasmal <u>likeness</u>. It is the mixture of dark and bright in Susan that eludes me; she is all soft shadow and sharpest gleams. But that is nonsense. I give it up.

It was really, then, a triumph for my ancestors that I did not throw myself on my knees beside her chair—the true romantic attitude, when all's said—and draw her dark-bright face down to mine. I halted instead just within the doorway, retaining a deathlike grip on the door-knob.

"Dear," I blurted, "it won't do. It's the end of the road. We can't go on."

"Can we turn back?" asked Susan.

I wonder the solid bronze knob did not shatter like hollow glass in my hand.

"You must help me," I muttered.

"Yes," said Susan, all quiet shadow now, gleamless; "I'll help you."

Half an hour after I left her she telephoned and dispatched the following telegram, signed "Susan Blake," to Gertrude at her New York address:

"Either come back to him or set him free. Urgent."

VI

The reply—a note from Gertrude, the ink hardly dry on it, written from the Egyptian tomb of the Misses Carstairs—came directly to me that evening; and Mrs. Parrot was the messenger. Her expression, as she mutely handed me the note, was ineffable. I read the note with sensations of suffocation; an answer was requested.

"Tell Mrs. Hunt," I said firmly to Mrs. Parrot, "that it was she who left me, and I am stubbornly determined to make no advances. If she cares to see me I shall be glad to see her. She has only to walk a few yards, climb a few easy steps, and ring the bell."

My courtesy was truly elaborate as I conducted Mrs. Parrot to the door. Her response was disturbing.

"It's not for me to make observations," said Mrs. Parrot, "the situation being delicate, and not likely to improve. But if I was you, Mr. Hunt, I'd not be too stiff. No; I'd not be. I would not. No. Not if I valued the young lady's reputation."

Like the Pope's mule, Mrs. Parrot had saved her kick many years. I can testify to its power.

Thirty minutes later this superkick landed me, when I came crashing back to earth, at the door of the Egyptian tomb.

"How hard it is," says Dante, "to climb another's stairs," and he might have added to ring another's bell, under certain conditions of spiritual humiliation and stress. Thank the gods—all of them—it was not Mrs. Parrot who admitted me and took my card!

I waited miserably in the large, ill-lighted reception vault of the tomb, which smelt appropriately of lilies, as if the undertaker had recently done his worst. How well I remembered it, how long I had avoided it! It was here of all places, under the contemptuous eye of old Ephraim Carstairs, grim ancestral founder of this family's fortunes, that Gertrude had at last consented to be my wife. And there he still lorded it above the fireplace, unchanged, glaring down malignantly through the shadows, his stiff neck bandaged like a mummy's, his hard, high cheek bones and cavernous eyes making him the very image of bugaboo death. What an eavesdropper for the approaching reconciliation; for that was what it had come to. That was what it would have to be!

It was not Gertrude who came down to me; it was Lucette. Lucette—all graciousness, all sympathetic understanding, all feline smiles! Dear Gertrude had 'phoned her on arriving, and she had rushed to her at once! Dear Gertrude had such a desperate headache! She couldn't possibly see me to-night. She was really ill, had been growing rapidly worse for an hour. Perhaps to-morrow?

I was in no mood to be tricked by this stale subterfuge.

"See here, Lucette," I said sternly, "I'm not going to fence with you or fool round at cross purposes. Less than an hour ago Gertrude sent over a note, asking me to call."

"To which you returned an insufferable verbal reply."

"A bad-tempered reply, I admit. No insult was intended. And I've come now to apologize for the temper."

"Oh, dear!" sighed Lucette. "Men always do their thinking too late. I wish I could reassure you; but the mischief seems to be done. Poor Gertrude is furious."

"Then the headache is—hypothetical?"

"An excuse, you mean? I wish it were, for her sake!" Lucette's eyes positively caressed me, as a tiger might lick the still-warm muzzle of an antelope, its proximate meal. "If you could see her face, poor creature! She's in torment."

"I'm sorry."

"Isn't that—what you called her headache?"

"No. I'm ashamed of my boorishness. Let me see Gertrude and tell her so."

Lucette smiled, slightly shaking her head. "Impossible—till she's feeling better. And not then—unless she changes her mind. You see, Ambrose, Mrs. Parrot's version of your reply was the last straw."

"No doubt she improved on the original," I muttered.

"Oh, no doubt," agreed Lucette calmly. "She would. It was silly of you not to think of that."

"Yes," I snapped. "Men always underestimate a woman's malice."

"They have so many distractions, poor dears. Men, I mean. And we have so few. You can put that in your next article, Ambrose?" She straightened her languid curves deliberately, as if preparing to rise.

"Please!" I exclaimed. "I'm not ready for dismissal yet. We'll get down to facts, if you don't mind. Why is Gertrude here at all? After years of silence? Did you send for her?"

Lucette's spine slowly relaxed, her shoulders drooped once more. "I? My dear Ambrose, why on earth should I do a thing like that?"

"I don't know. The point is, did you?"

"You think it in character?"

"Oh—be candid! I don't mean directly, of course. But is she here because of anything you may have telephoned her—after your call last night?"

"Really, Ambrose! This is a little too much, even from you."

"Forgive me—I insist! Is she?"

"You must have a very bad conscience," replied Lucette.

"I am more interested in yours."

She laughed luxuriously, "Mine has never been clearer."

Did the woman want me to stop her breath with bare hands? I gripped the mahogany arms of my stiff Chippendale chair.

"Listen to me, Lucette! I know this is all very thrilling and amusing for you. Vivisection must have its charms, of course—for an expert. But I venture to remind you that once upon a time you were not a bad-hearted girl, and you must have some remnants of human sympathy about you somewhere. Am I wrong?"

"You're hideously rude."

"Granted. But I must place you. I won't accept you as an onlooker. Either you'll fight me or help me—or clear out. Is that plain?"

"You're worse than rude," said Lucette; "you're a beast! I always wondered why Gertrude couldn't live with you. Now I know."

"That's better," I hazarded. "We're beginning to understand each other. Now let's lay all our cards face up on the table?"

Lucette stared at me a moment, her lips pursed, dubious, her impenetrable blue eyes holding mine.

"I will, if you will," she said finally. "Let's."

It was dangerous, I knew, to take her at her word; yet I ventured.

"I've a weak hand, Lucette; but there's one honest ace of trumps in it."

"There could hardly be two," smiled Lucette.

"No; I count on that. In a pinch, I shall take the one trick essential, and throw the others away." I leaned to her and spoke slowly: "There is no reason, affecting her honor or rights, why Gertrude may not return to her home—if she so desires. I think you understand me?"

"Perfectly. You wish to protect Miss Blake. You would try to do that in any case, wouldn't you? But I'm rather afraid you're too late. I'm afraid Miss Blake has handicapped you too heavily. If so, it was clever of her—for she must have done it on purpose. You see, Ambrose, it was she who sent for Gertrude."

"Susan!"

"Susan. Telegraphed her—of all things!—either to come home to you or set you free. The implication's transparent. Especially as I had thought it my duty to warn Gertrude in advance—and as Mr. Phar sent her, by messenger, a vague but very disturbing note this morning."

"Maltby?"

"Yes. His note was delivered not five minutes ahead of Susan's wire. Gertrude caught the next train. And there you are."

Well, at least I began to see now, dimly, where Maltby was, where Susan was, where we all were—except, possibly Gertrude. Putting enormous constraint on my leaping nerves, I subdued every trace of anger.

"Two more questions, Lucette. Do you believe me when I say, with all the sincerity I'm capable of, that Susan is slandered by these suspicions?"

"Really," answered Lucette, with a little worried frown, as if anxiously balancing alternatives, "I'm not, am I, in a position to judge?"

I swallowed hard. "All right," I managed to say coldly. "Then I have placed you. You're not an onlooker—you're an open foe."

"And the second question, Ambrose?"

"What, precisely, does Gertrude want from me?"

"I'm not, am I, in a position to judge?" repeated Lucette. "But one supposes it depends a little on what you're expecting—from her?"

"All I humbly plead for," said I, "is a chance to see Gertrude alone and talk things over."

"Don't you mean talk *her* over?" suggested Lucette. "And aren't you," she murmured, "forgetting the last straw?"

VII

My confusion of mind, my consternation, as I left the Egyptian tomb, was pitiable. One thing, one only, I saw with distinctness: The being I loved best was to be harried and smirched, an innocent victim of the folly and malignity of others.

"Never," I muttered, "Never—never—never!"

This was all very grim and virile; yet I knew that I could grit my teeth and mutter Never! from now till the moon blossomed, without in any way affecting the wretched situation. Words, emotional contortions, attitudes—would not help Susan; something sensible must be done—the sooner the better. Something sensible and decisive—but what? There were so many factors involved, human, incalculable factors; my thought staggered among them, fumbling like a drunken man for the one right door that must be found and opened with the one right key. It was no use; I should never be able to manage it alone. To whom could I appeal? Susan, for the time being, was out of the question; Maltby had maliciously betrayed a long friendship. Phil? Why of course, there was always Phil? Why hadn't I thought of him before?

I turned sharply and swung into a rapid stride. With some difficulty I kept myself from running. Phil seemed to me suddenly an intellectual giant, a man of infinite heart and unclouded will. Why had I never appreciated him at his true worth? My whirling perplexities would have no terrors for him; he would at once see through them to the very thing that should at once be undertaken. Singular effect of an overwhelming desire and need! Faith is always born of desperation. We are forced by deep-lying instincts to trust something, someone, when we can no longer trust ourselves. As I hurried down York Street to his door, my sudden faith in Phil was like the faith of a broken-spirited convert in the wisdom and mercy of God.

Phil's quarters were on the top floor of a rooming-house for students; he had the whole top floor to himself and had lived there simply and contentedly many years, with his books, his pipes, his papers, and his small open wood fire. Phil is not destitute of taste, but he is by no means an æsthete. His furniture is of the ordinary college-room type—Morris chair of fumed oak, and so on—picked up as he needed it at the nearest department store; but he has two or three really good framed etchings on the walls of his study; one Seymour Haden in particular—the *Erith Marshes*—which I have often tried to persuade him to part with. There is a blending of austerity and subtlety in the work of the great painter-etchers that could not but appeal to this austere yet finely organized man.

His books are wonderful—not for edition or binding—he is not a bibliophile; they are wonderful because he keeps nothing he has not found it worth while to annotate. There is no volume on his shelves whose inside covers and margins are not filled with criticism or suggestive comment in his neat spiderwebby hand; and Phil's marginal notes are usually far better reading than the original text. Susan warmly maintains that she owes more to the inside covers of Phil's books than to any other source; insists, in fact, that a brief note in his copy of Santayana's *Reason in Common Sense*, at the end of the first chapter, established her belief once for all in mind as a true thing, an indestructible and creative reality, destined after infinite struggle to win its grim fight with chaos. I confess I could never myself see in this note anything to produce so amazing an affirmation; but in these matters I am a worm; I have not the philosophic *flair*. Here it is:

"'We know that life is a dream, and how should thinking be more?' Because, my dear Mr. Santayana, a dream cannot propagate dreams and realize them to be such. The answer is sufficient."

Well, certainly Susan, too, seemed to feel it sufficient; and perhaps I should agree if I better understood the answer... . But I have now breasted four flights to Phil and am knocking impatiently... . He opened to me and welcomed me cordially, all trace of his parting gruffness of the other evening having vanished, though he was still haggard about the eyes. He was not alone. Through the smoke haze of his study I saw a well-built youngster standing near the fireplace, pipe in hand; some college boy, of course, whom

Phil was being kind to. Phil was forever permitting these raw boys to cut in upon his precious hours of privacy; yet he was at the opposite pole from certain faculty members, common to all seats of learning, who toady to the student body for a popularity which they feel to be a good business asset, or which they find the one attainable satisfaction for their tottering self-esteem.

Phil, who had had to struggle for his own education, was genuinely fond of young men who cared enough for education to be willing to struggle for theirs. He had become unobtrusively, by a kind of natural affinity, the elder brother of those undergraduates who were seekers in any sense for the things of the mind. For the rest, the triumphant majority—fine, manly young fellows as they usually were, in official oratory at least—he was as blankly indifferent as they were to him.

"My enthusiasm for humanity is limited, fatally limited," he would pleasantly admit. "For the human turnip, even when it's a prize specimen, I have no spontaneous affection whatever."

On the other hand it was not the brilliant, exceptional boy whom he best loved. It was rather the boy whose interest in life, whose curiosity, was just stirring toward wakefulness after a long prenatal and postnatal sleep. For such boys Phil poured forth treasures of sympathetic understanding; and it was such a youth, I presume, who stood by the fireplace now, awkwardly uncertain whether my coming meant that he should take his leave.

His presence annoyed me. On more than one occasion I had run into this sort of thing at Phil's rooms, had suffered from the curious inability of the undergraduate, even when he longs himself to escape, to end a visit—take his hat, say good-by simply, and go. It doesn't strike one offhand as a social accomplishment of enormous difficulty; yet it must be—it so paralyzes the social resourcefulness of the young.

Phil introduced me to Mr. Kane, and Mr. Kane drooped his right shoulder —the correct attitude for this form of assault—grasped my hand, and shattered my nerves—with the dislocating squeeze which young America has perfected as the high sign of all that is virile and sincere. I sank into a chair to recover, and to my consternation Mr. Kane, too, sat down.

"Jimmy's just come to us," said Phil, relighting his pipe. "He passed his entrance examinations in Detroit last spring, but he had to finish up a job he was on out there before coming East. So he has a good deal of work to make up, first and last. And it's all the harder for him, because he's dependent upon himself for support."

"Oh," said Jimmy, "what I've saved'll last me through this year, I guess."

"Yes," Phil agreed; "but it's a pity to touch what you've saved." He turned to me. "You see, Hunt, we're talking over all the prospects. Aren't we, Jimmy?"

"Yes, sir," answered Jimmy. "Prof. Farmer thinks," he added, "that I may be making a mistake to try it here; he thinks it may be a waste of time. I'm kind of up in the air about it, myself."

"Jimmy's rather a special case," struck in Phil, dropping into a Morris chair and thrusting his legs out. "He's twenty-two now; and he's already made remarkably good as an expert mechanic. He left his home here over six years ago, worked his way to Detroit, applied for a job and got it. Now there's probably no one in New Haven who knows more than this young man about gas engines, steel alloys, shop organization, and all that. The little job that detained him was the working out of some minor but important economy in the manufacture of automobiles. He suggested it by letter to the president of the company himself, readily obtained several interviews with his chief, and was given a chance to try it out.

"It has proved its practical worth already, though you and I are far too ignorant to understand it. As a result, the president of the company offered him a much higher position at an excellent salary. It's open to him still, if he chooses to go back for it. But Jimmy has decided to turn it down for a college education. And I'm wondering, Hunt, whether Yale has anything to give him that will justify such a sacrifice—anything that he couldn't obtain for himself, at much less expense, without three years waste of time and opportunity. How does it strike you, old man? What would you say, offhand, without weighing the matter?"

What I wanted to say was, "Damn it all! I'm not here at this time of night to interest myself in the elementary problems of Jimmy Kane!" In fact, I did say it to myself, with considerable energy—only to stop at the name, to stare at the boy before me, and to exclaim in a swift flash of connection, "Great Scott! Are you *Susan's* Jimmy?"

"'Susan's Jimmy'!" snorted Phil, with a peculiar grin. "Of course he's Susan's Jimmy! I wondered how long it would take you!"

As for Susan's Jimmy, his expression was one of desolated amazement. Either his host and his host's friend, or he himself—had gone suddenly mad! The drop of his jaw was parentheses about a question mark. His blue eyes piteously stared.

"I guess I'm not on, sir," he mumbled to Phil, blushing hotly.

He was really a most attractive youth, considering his origins. I eyed him now shamelessly, and was forced to wonder that the wrong end of Birch Street should have produced not only Susan—who would have proved the phœnix of any environment—but this pleasant-faced, confidence-inspiring boy, whose expression so oddly mingled simplicity, energy, stubborn self-respect, and the cheerfulness of good health, an unspoiled will, and a hopeful heart. He seemed at once too mature for his years and too naïve; concentration had already modelled his forehead, but there was innocence in his eyes. Innocence—I can only call it that. His eyes looked out at the world with the happiest candor; and I found myself predicting of him what I had never yet predicted of mortal woman or man: "He's capable of anything—but sophistication; he'll get on, he'll arrive somewhere—but he will never change."

Phil, meanwhile, had eased his embarrassment with a friendly laugh. "It's all right, Jimmy; we're not the lunatics we sound. Don't you remember Bob Blake's kid on Birch Street?"

"Oh! Her?"

"Mr. Hunt became her guardian, you know, after——"

"Oh!" interrupted Jimmy, beaming on me. "You're the gentleman that ____"

"Yes," I responded; "I'm the unbelievably fortunate man."

"She was a queer little kid," reflected Jimmy. "I haven't thought about her for a long time."

"That's ungrateful of you," said Phil; "but of course you couldn't know that."

Question mark and parentheses formed again.

"Phil means," I explained, "that Susan has never forgotten you. It seems you did battle for her once, down at the bottom of the Birch Street incline?"

"Oh, gee!" grinned Jimmy. "The time I laid out Joe Gonfarone? Maybe I wasn't scared stiff that day! Well, what d'y' think of her remembering that!"

"You'll find it's a peculiarity of Susan," said Phil, "that she doesn't forget anything."

"Why—she must be grown up by this time," surmised Jimmy. "It was mighty fine of you, Mr. Hunt, to do what you did! I'd kind of like to see her again some day. But maybe she'd rather not," he added quickly.

"Why?" asked Phil.

"Well," said Jimmy, "she had a pretty raw deal on Birch Street. Seeing me

—might bring back things?"

"It couldn't," I reassured him. "Susan has never let go of them. She uses all her experience, every part of it, every day."

Jimmy grinned again. "It must keep her hustling! But she always was different, I guess, from the rest of us." With a vague wonder, he addressed us both: "You think a lot of her, don't you?"

For some detached, ironic god this moment must have been exquisite. I envied the god his detachment. The blank that had followed his question puzzled Jimmy and turned him awkward. He fidgeted with his feet.

"Well," he finally achieved, "I guess I'd better be off, professor. I'll think over all you said."

"Do," counselled Phil, rising, "and come to see me to-morrow. We mustn't let you take a false step if we can avoid it."

"It's certainly great of you to show so much interest," said Jimmy, hunching himself at last out of his chair. "I appreciate it a lot." He hesitated, then plunged. "It's been well worth it to me to come East again—just to meet *you*."

"Nonsense!" laughed Phil, shepherding him skillfully toward the door... .

When he turned back to me, it was with the evident intention of discussing further Jimmy's personal and educational problems; but I rebelled.

"Phil," I said, "I know what Susan means to you, and you know—I think —what she means to me. Now, through my weakness, stupidity, or something, Susan's in danger. Sit down please, and let me talk. I'm going to give you all the facts, everything—a full confession. It's bound, for many reasons, to be painful for both of us. I'm sorry, old man—but we'll have to rise to it for Susan's sake; see this thing through together. I feel utterly imbecile and helpless alone."

Half an hour later I had ended my monologue, and we both sat silent, staring at the dulled embers on the hearth... .

At length Phil drew in a slow, involuntary breath.

"Hunt," he said, "it's a humiliating thing for a professional philosopher to admit, but I simply can't trust myself to advise you. I don't know what you ought to do; I don't know what Susan ought to do; or what I should do. I don't even know what your wife should do; though I feel fairly certain that whatever it is, she will try something else. Frankly, I'm too much a part of it all, too heartsick, for honest thought."

He smiled drearily and added, as if at random: "'Physician, heal thyself.' What an abysmal joke! How the fiends of hell must treasure it. They have only one better—'Man is a reasonable being!'" He rose, or rather he seemed to be propelled from his chair. "Hunt! Would you really like to know what all my days and nights of intense study have come to? The kind of man you've turned to for strength? My life has come to just this: I love her, and she doesn't love me!

"Oh!" he cried—"Go home. For God's sake, go home! I'm ashamed... ."

So I departed, like Omar, through the same door wherein I went; but not before I had grasped—as it seemed to me for the first time—Phil's hand.

VIII

There are some verses in Susan's notebook of this period, themselves undated, and never subsequently published, which—from their position on the page—must have been written about this time and may have been during the course of the momentous evening on which I met Jimmy Kane at Phil Farmer's rooms. I give them now, not as a favorable specimen of her work, since she thought best to exclude them from her first volume, but because they throw some light at least on the complicated and rather obscure state of mind that was then hers. They have no title, and need none. If you should feel they need interpretation—"*guarda e passa*"! They are not for you.

> *Though she rose from the sea*
> *There were stains upon her whiteness;*
> *All earth's waters had not sleeked her clean.*
> *For no tides gave her birth,*
> *Nor the salt, glimmering middle depths;*
> *But slime spawned her, the couch of life,*
> *The sunless ooze,*
> *The green bed of Poseidon,*
> *Where with sordid Chaos he mingles obscurely.*
> *Her flanks were of veined marble;*
> *There were stains upon her.*
>
> *But she who passes, lonely,*
> *Through waste places,*
> *Through bog and forest;*
> *Who follows boar and stag*
> *Unwearied;*
> *Who sleeps, fearless, among the hills;*
> *Though she track the wilds,*
> *Though she breast the crags,*
> *Choosing no path—*
> *Her kirtle tears not,*
> *Her ankles gleam,*
> *Her sandals are silver.*

IX

It was midnight when I reached my own door that night, but I was in no mood for lying in bed stark awake in the spiritual isolation of darkness. I went straight to my study, meaning to make up a fire and then hypnotize myself into some form of lethargy by letting my eyes follow the printed lines of a book. If reading in any other sense than physical habit proved beyond me, at least the narcotic monotony of habit might serve.

But I found a fire, already falling to embers, and Susan before it, curled into my big wing chair, her feet beneath her, her hands lying palms upward in her lap. This picture fixed me in the doorway while my throat tightened. Susan did not stir, but she was not sleeping. She had withdrawn.

Presently she spoke, absently—from Saturn's rings; or the moon.

"Ambo? I've been waiting to talk to you; but now I can't or I'll lose it— the whole movement. It's like a symphony—great brasses groaning and cursing—and then violins tearing through the tumult to soar above it."

Her eyes shut for a moment. When she opened them again it was to shake herself free from whatever spell had bound her. She half yawned, and smiled.

"Gone, dear—all gone. It's not your fault. Words wouldn't hold it. Music might—but music doesn't come.... Oh, poor Ambo—you've had a wretched time of it! How tired you look!"

I shut the door quietly and went to her, sitting on the hearth rug at her feet, my knees in my arms.

"Sweetheart," I said, "it seems that in spite of myself I've done you little good and about all the harm possible." And I made a clean breast of all the facts and fears that the evening had developed. "So you see," I ended, "what my guardianship amounts to!"

Susan's hand came to my shoulder and drew me back against her knees; she did not remove her hand.

"Ambo," she protested gently, "I'm just a little angry with you, I think."

"No wonder!"

"Oh!" she exclaimed. "If I am angry it's because you can say stupid things like that! Don't you see, Ambo, the very moment things grow difficult for us you forget to believe in me—begin to act as if I were a common or garden fool? I'm not, though. Surely you must know in your heart that everything you're afraid of for me doesn't matter in the least. What harm could slander or scandal possibly do me, dear? Me, I mean? I shouldn't like it, of course, because I hate everything stodgy and *formidablement bête*. But if it happens, I shan't lose much sleep over it. You're worrying about the wrong things, Ambo; things that don't even touch our real problem. And the real problem may prove to be the real tragedy, too."

"Tragedy?" I mumbled.

"Oh, I hope not—I think not! It all depends on whether you care for freedom; on whether you're really passion's slave. I don't believe you are."

The words wounded me. I shifted, to look up at, to question, her shadowy face. "Susan, what do you mean?"

"I suppose I mean that *I'm* not, Ambo. You're far dearer to me than anybody else on earth; your happiness, your peace, mean everything to me. If you honestly can't find life worth while without me—can't—I'll go with you anywhere; or face the music with you right here. First, though, I must be sincere with you. I can live away from you, and still make a life for myself. Except your day-by-day companionship—I'd be lonely without that, of course—I shouldn't lose anything that seems to me really worth keeping. Above all, I shouldn't really lose you."

"Susan! You're planning to leave me!"

"But, Ambo—it's only what you've felt to be necessary; what you've been planning for me!"

"As a duty—at the bitterest possible cost! How different that is! You not only plan to leave me—I feel that you want to!"

"Yes, I want to. But only if you can understand why."

"I don't understand!"

"Ah, wait, Ambo! You're not speaking for yourself. You're a slave now, speaking for your master. But it's *you* I want to talk to!"

I snarled at this. "Why? When you've discovered your mistake so soon! . . . You don't love me."

She sighed, deeply unhappy; though my thin-skinned self-esteem wrung from her sigh a shade of impatience, too.

"If not, dear," she said, "we had better find it out before it's too late. Perhaps you are right. Perhaps love is something I only guess at and go wrong about. If love means that I should be utterly lost in you and nothing without you—if it means that I would rather die than leave you—well, then I don't love you. But all the same, if love honestly means that to you—I can't and won't go away." She put out her hand again swiftly, and tightened her fingers on mine.

"It's a test, then. Is that it?" I demanded. "You want to go because you're not sure?"

"I'm sure of what I feel," she broke in; "and more than that, I doubt if I'm made so that I can ever feel more. No; that isn't why I want to go. I'll go if you can let me, because—oh, I've got to say it, Ambo!—because at heart I love freedom better than I love love—or you. And there's something else. I'm afraid of—please try to understand this, dear—I'm afraid of stuffiness for us both!"

"Stuffiness?"

"Sex *is* stuffy, Ambo. The more people let it mess up their lives for them, the stuffier they grow. It's really what you've been afraid of for me—though you don't put it that way. But you hate the thought of people saying—with all the muddy little undercurrents they stir up round such things—that you and I have been passion's slaves. We haven't been—but we might be; and suppose we were. It's the truth about us—not the lies—that makes all the difference. You're you—and I'm I. It's because we're worth while to ourselves that we're worth while to each other. Isn't that true? But how long shall we be worth anything to ourselves or to each other if we accept love as slavery, and get to feeling that we can't face life, if it seems best, alone? Ambo, dear, do you see at all what I'm driving at?"

Yes; I was beginning to see. Miss Goucher's desolate words came suddenly back to me: "Susan doesn't need *you*."

X

Next morning, while I supposed her at work in her room, Susan slipped down the back stairs and off through the garden. It was a heavy forenoon for me, perhaps the bleakest and dreariest of my life. But it was a busy forenoon for Susan. She began its activities by a brave intuitive stroke. She entered the Egyptian tomb and demanded an interview with Gertrude. What is stranger, she carried her point—as I was presently to be made aware.

Miss Goucher tapped at the door, entered, and handed me a card. So Gertrude had changed her mind; Gertrude had come. I stared, foolishly blank, at the card between, my fingers, while Miss Goucher by perfect stillness effaced herself, leaving me to my lack of thought.

"Well," I finally muttered, "sooner or later——"

Miss Goucher, perhaps too eagerly, took this for assent. "Shall I say to Mrs. Hunt that you are coming down?"

I forced a smile, fatuously enough, and rose.

"When I'm down already? Surely you can see, Miss Goucher, that I've touched the bottom?" Miss Goucher did not reply. "I'll go myself at once," I added formally. "Thank you, Miss Goucher."

Gertrude was waiting in the small Georgian reception room, whose detailed correctness had been due to her own; waiting without any vulgar pretense at entire composure. She was walking slowly about, her color was high, and it startled me to find her so little altered. Not a day seemed to have added itself; she looked under thirty, though I knew her to be thirty-five; she was even handsomer than I had chosen to remember. Even in her present unusual restlessness, the old distinction, the old patrician authority was hers. Her spirit imposed itself, as always; one could take Gertrude only as she wished to be taken—seriously—humbly grateful if exempted from disdain. Gertrude never spoke for herself alone; she was at all times representative—almost symbolic. Homage met in her not a personal gratitude, but the approval of a high, unbroken tradition. She accepted it graciously, without obvious egotism, not as due to her as a temporal being, but as due—under God—to that timeless entity, her class. I am not satirizing Gertrude; I am praising her. She, more than any person I have ever known, made of her perishing substance the temple of a completely realized ideal.

It was, I am forced to assume, because I had failed in entire respect for and submission to this ideal that she had finally abandoned me. It was not so much incompatibility of temperament as incompatibility of worship. She had removed a hallowed shrine from a felt indifference and a possible contamination. That was all, but it was everything. And as I walked into the reception room I saw that the shrine was still beautiful, faultlessly tended, and ready for any absolute but dignified sacrifice.

"Gertrude," I began, "it's splendid of you to overlook my inexcusable rudeness of yesterday! I'm very grateful."

"I have not forgiven you," she replied, with casual indignation—just enough for sincerity and not a shade too much for art. "Don't imagine it's pleasant for me to be here. I should hardly have risked your misinterpreting it, if any other course had seemed possible."

"You might simply have waited," I said. "It was my intention to call this evening, if only to ask after your health."

"I could not have received you," said Gertrude.

"You find it less difficult here?"

"Less humiliating. I'm not, at least, receiving a husband who wishes to plead for reconciliation—on intolerable grounds."

"May I offer you a chair? Better still—why not come to the study? We're so much less likely to be disturbed."

She accepted my suggestion with a slight nod, and herself led the way.

"Now, Gertrude," I resumed, when she had consented to an easy-chair and had permitted me to close the door, "whatever the situation and misunderstandings between us, can't we discuss them"—and I ventured a smile—"more informally, in a freer spirit?"

She caught me up. "Freer! But I understand—less disciplined. How very like you, Ambrose. How unchanged you are."

"And you, Gertrude! It's a compliment you should easily forgive."

She preferred to ignore it. "Miss Blake," she announced, "has just been with me for an hour."

She waited the effect of this. The effect was considerable, plunging me into dark amazement and conjecture. Not daring to make the tiniest guess as to the result of so fantastic an interview, I was left not merely tongue-tied but brain-tied. Gertrude saw at once that she had beggared me and could now at her leisure dole out the equal humiliation of alms withheld or bestowed.

"Given your curious social astigmatism and her curious mixed charm—so subtle and so deeply uncivilized—I can see, of course, why she has bewitched you," said Gertrude reflectively, and paused. "And I can see," she continued, musing, as if she had adopted the stage convention of soliloquy, "why you have just failed to capture her imagination. For you have failed—but you can hardly be aware how completely."

"Whether or not I'm aware," I snapped, "seems negligible! Susan feels she must leave me, and she'll probably act with her usual promptness. Is that what she called to tell you?"

"Partly," acknowledged Gertrude, resuming then her soliloquy: "You've given her—as you would—a ridiculous education. She seems to have instincts, impulses, which—all things considered—might have bloomed if cultivated. As it is, you found her crude, and, in spite of all the culture you've crammed upon her, you've left her so. She's emancipated—that is, public; she's thrown away the locks and keys of her mind. I grant she has one. But apparently no one has even suggested to her that the essence of being rare, of being fine, is knowing what to omit, what to reject, what to conceal. I find my own people, Ambrose—and they're the *right* people, the only ones worth finding—by feeling secure with them; I can trust them not to go too far. They have decorum, taste. Oh, I admit we're upholding a lost cause! You're a deserter from it—and Miss Blake doesn't even suspect its existence. Still"—with a private smile—"her crudity had certain immediate advantages this morning."

Ignoring rarity, fineness, I sank to the indecorum of a frankly human grin.

"In other words, Gertrude, Susan omitted so little, went so much too far, that she actually forced you for once to get down to brass tacks!"

Gertrude frowned. "She stripped herself naked before a stranger—if that's what you mean."

"With the result, Gertrude?"

"Ah, that's why I'm here—as a duty I owe myself. I'm bound to say my suspicions were unjust—to Miss Blake, at least. I'll even go beyond that ——."

"Careful, Gertrude! Evil communications corrupt good manners."

"Yes," she responded quickly, rising, "they do—always; that's why I'm not here to stay. But all I have left for you, Ambrose, is this: I'm convinced now that in one respect I've been quite wrong. Miss Blake convinced me this morning that her astounding telegram had at least one merit. It happened to be true. I *should* either live with you or set you free. I've felt this myself, from time to time, but divorce, for many reasons... ." She paused, then added: "However, it seems inevitable. If you wish to divorce me, you have legal grounds—desertion; I even advise it, and I shall make no defense. As for your amazing ward—make your mind quite easy about her. If any rumors should annoy you, they'll not come from me. And I shall speak to Lucette." She moved to the door, opening it slowly. "That's all, I think, Ambrose?"

"It's not even a beginning," I cried.

"Think of it, rather, as an ending."

"Impossible! I—I'm abashed, Gertrude! What you propose is out of the question. Why not think better of returning here? The heydey's past for both of us. My dream—always a wild dream—is passing; and I can promise sincere understanding and respect."

"I could not promise so easily," said Gertrude; "nor so much. No; don't come with me," she added. "I know my way perfectly well alone."

Nevertheless, I went with her to the front door, as I ought, in no perfunctory spirit. It was more than a courteous habit; it was a genuine tribute of admiration. I admired her beauty, her impeccable bearing, her frock, her furs, her intellect, the ease and distinction of her triumph. She left me crushed; yet it was a privilege to have known her—to have wooed her, won her, lost her; and now to have received my *coup de grâce* from her competent, disdainful hands. I wished her well, knowing the wish superfluous. In this, if nothing else, she resembled Susan—she did not need me; she could stand alone. It was her tragedy, in the French classic manner, that she must. Would it also in another manner, in a deeper and—I can think of no homelier word—more cosmic sense, prove to be Susan's?

But my own stuffy problem drama, whether tragic or absurd, had now reached a crisis and developed its final question: How in the absence of Susan to stand at all?

XI

From her interview with Gertrude, Susan went straight on to Phil's rooms, not even stopping to consider the possible proprieties involved. But, five minutes before her arrival, Phil had been summoned to the Graduates Club to receive a long-distance call from his Boston publisher; and it was Jimmy Kane who answered her knock and opened the study door. He had been in conference with Phil on his private problems and Phil had asked him to await his return. All this he thought it courteous to explain to the peach of a girl before him, whose presence at the door puzzled him mightily, and whose disturbing eyes held his, he thought, rather too intimately and quizzically for a stranger's.

She could hardly be some graduate student in philosophy; she was too young and too flossy for that. "Flossy," in Jimmy's economical vocabulary, was a symbol for many subtle shades of meaning: it implied, for any maiden it fitted, an elegance not too cold to be alluring; the possession of that something more than the peace of God which a friend told Emerson always entered her heart when she knew herself to be well dressed. Flossy—to generalize—Jimmy had not observed the women graduate students to be, though he bore them no ill will. To be truly flossy was, after all, a privilege reserved for a chosen few, born to a certain circle which Jimmy had never sought to penetrate.

One—and a curiously entrancing specimen—of the chosen evidently stood watching him now, and he wished that her entire self-possession did not so utterly imperil his own. What was she doing alone, anyway, this society girl—in a students' rooming house—at Prof. Farmer's door? Why couldn't she tell him? And why were her eyes making fun of him—or weren't they? His fingers went instinctively to his—perhaps too hastily selected?—cravat.

Then Susan really did laugh, but happily, not unkindly, and walked on in past him, shutting the door behind her as she came.

"Jimmy Kane," she said, "if I weren't so gorgeously glad to see you again, I could beat you for not remembering!"

"Good Lord!" he babbled. "Why—good Lord! You're Susan!"

82

It was all too much for him; concealment was impossible—he was flabbergasted. Sparkling with sheer delight at his *gaucherie*, Susan put out both hands. Her impulsiveness instantly revived him; he seized her hands for a moment as he might have gripped a long-lost boy friend's.

"You never guessed I could look so—presentable, did you?" demanded Susan.

"Presentable!" The word jarred on him, it was so dully inadequate.

"I have a maid," continued Susan demurely. "Everything in Ambo's house —Ambo is my guardian, you know; Mr. Hunt—well, everything in his house is a work of art. So he pays a maid to see that I am—always. I am simply clay in her hands, and it does make a difference. But I didn't have a maid on Birch Street, Jimmy."

Jimmy's blue eyes capered. This was American humor—the kind he was born to and could understand. Happiness and ease returned with it. If Susan could talk like that while looking like that—well, Susan was *there!* She was all right.

Within five minutes he was giving her a brief, comradely chronicle of the missing years, and when Phil got back it was to find them seated together, Susan leaning a little forward from the depths of a Morris chair to follow more attentively Jimmy's minute technical description of the nature of the steel alloys used in the manufacture of automobiles.

They rose at Phil's entrance with a mingling, eager chatter of explanation. Phil later—much later—admitted to me that he had never felt till that moment how damnably he was past forty, and how fatally Susan was not. He further admitted that it was far from the most agreeable discovery of a studious life.

"What do you think, Prof. Farmer," exclaimed Jimmy, "of our meeting again accidentally like this—and me not knowing Susan! You can't beat that much for a small world!"

Phil sought Susan's eye, and was somewhat relieved by the quizzical though delighted gleam in it.

"Well, Jimmy," he responded gravely, "truth compels me to state that I have heard of stranger encounters—less inevitable ones, at least. I really have."

"But you never heard of a nicer one," said Susan. "Haven't I always told you and Ambo that Jimmy would be like this?"

"Sort of foolish?" grinned Jimmy, with reawakening constraint. "I'll bet you have, too."

Susan shook her head, solemn and slow; but the corners of her mouth meant mischief.

"No, Jimmy, not foolish; just—natural. Just—sort of—*you.*"

At this point, Jimmy hastily remembered that he must beat it, pleading what Phil knew to be an imaginary recitation. But he did not escape without finding himself invited to dinner for that very evening, informally of course— Susan suspected the absence of even a dinner coat: Phil would bring him. It was really Phil who accepted for him, while Jimmy was still muddling through his thanks and toiling on to needless apologies.

"If I've been too"—he almost said "fresh," but sank to—"familiar, calling you by your first name, I mean—I wouldn't like you to think—but coming all of a sudden like this, what I mean is——"

"Oh, run along!" called Susan gayly. "Forget it, Jimmy! You're spoiling everything."

"That's what I m-mean," stammered Jimmy, and was gone.

"But he does mean well, Susan," Phil pleaded for him, after closing the door.

It puzzled him to note that Susan's face instantly clouded; there was reproof in her tone. "That was patronizing, Phil. I won't have anybody patronize Jimmy. He's perfect."

Phil was oddly nettled by this reproof and grew stubborn and detached. "He's a nice boy, certainly; and has the makings of a real man. I believe in him. Still—heaven knows!—he's not precisely a subtle soul."

Susan's brow had cleared again. "That's what I m-mean!" she laughed, mimicking Jimmy without satire, as if for the pure pleasure of recollection. "The truth is, Phil, I'm rather fed up on subtlety—especially my own. Sometimes I think it's just a polite term for futility, with a dash of intellectual snobbishness thrown in. It must be saner, cleaner, healthier, to take life straight."

"And now, Phil dear," she said, dismissing the matter, as if settling back solidly to earth after a pleasantly breathless aërial spin, "I need your advice. Can I earn my living as a writer? I'll write anything that pays, so I think I can. Fashion notes—anything! Sister and I"—"Sister" being Susan's pet name for Miss Goucher—"are running away to New York on Monday—to make our fortunes. You mustn't tell Ambo—yet; I'll tell him in my own way. And I must *make* my own way now, Phil. I've been a lazy parasite long enough— too long! So please sit down and write me subtle letters of introduction to any publishers you know. Maltby is bound to help me, of course. You see, I'm feeling ruthless—or shameless; I shall pull every wire in sight. So I'm counting on *The Garden Exquisite* for immediate bread and butter. I did my first article for it in an hour when I first woke up this morning—just the smarty-party piffle its readers and advertisers seem to demand.

"This sort of thing, Phil: 'The poets are wrong, as usual. Wild flowers are not shy and humble, they are exclusive. How to know them is still a social problem in American life, and very few of us have attained this aristocratic distinction.' And so on! Two thousand silly salable words—and I can turn on that soda-water tap at will. Are you listening? Please tell me you don't think poor Sister—she refuses to leave me, and I wouldn't let her anyway—will have to undergo martyrdom in a cheap hall bedroom for the rest of her days?"

Needless to say, Phil did not approve of Susan's plan. He agreed with her that under the given conditions she could not remain with me in New Haven; and he commended her courage, her desire for independence. But Susan would never, he felt, find her true pathway to independence, either material or spiritual, as a journalistic free-lance in New York. He admitted the insatiable public thirst for soda-water, but saw no reason why Susan should waste herself in catering to it. He was by no means certain that she could cater to it if she would.

"You'll too often discover," he warned her, "that your tap is running an unmarketable beverage. The mortal taste for nectar is still undeveloped; it remains the drink of the gods."

"But," Susan objected, "I can't let Ambo pay my bills from now on—I can't! And Sister and I must live decently somehow! I'd like nothing better than to be a perpetual fountain of nectar—supposing, you nice old Phil, that I've ever really had the secret of distilling a single drop of it. But you say yourself there's no market for it this side of heaven, which is where we all happen to be. What do you want me to do?"

"Marry me."

"It wouldn't be fair to you, dear."

There was a momentary pause.

"Then," said Phil earnestly, "I want you to let Hunt—or if you can't bring yourself to do that—to let *me* loan you money enough from time to time to live on simply and comfortably for a few years, while you study and think and write in your own free way—till you've found yourself. My nectar simile was nonsense, just as your soda-water tap was. You have brains and a soul, and the combination means a shining career of some kind—even on earth. Don't

85

fritter your genius away in makeshift activities. Mankind needs the best we have in us; the best's none too good. It's a duty—no, it's more than that—it's a true *religion* to get that expressed somehow—whether in terms of action or thought or beauty. I know, of course, you feel this as I do, and mean to win through to it in the end. But why handicap yourself so cruelly at the start?"

Phil tells me that Susan, while he urged this upon her, quietly withdrew and did not return for some little time after he had ceased to speak. He was not even certain she had fully heard him out until she suddenly leaned to him from her chair and gave his hand an affectionate, grateful squeeze.

"Yes, Phil," she said, "it is a religion—it's perhaps the only religion I shall ever have. But for that very reason I must accept it in my own way. And I'm sure—it's part of my faith—that any coddling now will do me more harm than good. I must meet the struggle, Phil—the hand-to-hand fight. If the ordinary bread-and-butter conditions are too much for me, then I'm no good and must go under. I shan't be frittering anything away if I fail. I shan't fail—in our sense—unless we're both mistaken, and there isn't anything real in me. That's what I must find out first—not sheltered and in silence, but down in the scrimmage and noise of it all. If I'm too delicate for that, then I've nothing to give this world, and the sooner I'm crushed out of it the better! Believe me, Phil dear, I know I'm right; I *know*."

She was pressing clenched hands almost fiercely between her girl's breasts as she ended, as if to deny or repress any natural longing for a special protection, a special graciousness and security, from our common taskmaster, life.

Phil admits that he wanted to whimper like a homesick boy.

XII

Susan's informal dinner for Jimmy that evening was not really a success. The surface of the water sparkled from time to time, but there were grim undercurrents and icy depths. Perhaps it was not so bad as my own impression of it, for I had a sullen headache pulsing its tiresome obbligato above a dull ground base of despair. Despair, I am forced to call it. Never had life seemed to me so little worth the trouble of going on; and I fancy Phil's reasoned conviction of its eternal dignity and import had become, for the present, less of a comfort to him than a curse. Moods of this kind, however ruthlessly kept under, infect the very air about them. They exude a drab fog to deaden spontaneity and choke laughter at its source.

Neither Phil nor I was guilty of deliberate sulking; whether from false pride or native virtue we did our best—but our best was abysmal. Even Susan sank under it to the flat levels of made conversation, and poor Jimmy—who had brought with him many social misgivings—was stricken at table with a muscular rigor; sat stiffly, handled his implements jerkily, and ended by oversetting a glass of claret and blushing till the dusky red of his face matched the spreading stain before him.

At this crisis of gloom, luckily, Susan struggled clear of the drab fog and saved the remnant of the evening—at least for Jimmy, plunging with the happiest effect into the junior annals of Birch Street, till our heavier Hillhouse atmosphere stirred and lightened with *Don't-you-remember's* and *Sure-I-do's*. And shortly after dinner, Phil, tactfully pleading an unprepared lecture, dragged Jimmy off with him before this bright flare-up of youthful reminiscence had even threatened to expire. Their going brought Susan at once to my side, with a stricken face of self-reproach.

"It was so stupid of me, Ambo—this dinner. I've never been more ashamed. How could I have forced it on you to-night! But you were wonderful, dear—wonderful! So was Phil. I'll never forget it." There were tears in her eyes. "Oh, Ambo," she wailed, "do you think I shall ever learn to be a little like either of you? I feel—abject." Before I could prevent it, she had seized my hand in both hers and kissed it. "Homage," she smiled....

It broke me down—utterly... . You will spare me any description of the next ten minutes of childishness. Indeed, you must spare me the details of our later understanding; they are inviolable. It is enough to say that I emerged from it—for the experience had been overwhelming—with a new spirit, a clarified and serener mind. My love for Susan was unchanged—yet wholly changed. The paradox is exact. Life once more seemed to me good, since she was part of it; and my own life rich, since I now knew how truly it had become a portion of hers. She had made me feel, know, that I counted for her —unworthy as I am—in all she had grown to be and would grow to be. We had shaped and would always shape each other's lives. There for the moment it rested. She would leave me, but I was not to be alone.

No; I was not to be alone. For even if she had died, or had quite changed and forsaken me, there would be memories—such as few men have been privileged to recall... .

INTERLUDE

On the rearward and gentler slopes of Mount Carmel, a rough, isolated little mountain, very abrupt on its southerly face, which rises six or seven miles up-country from the New Haven Green, there is an ancient farm, so long abandoned as to be completely overgrown with gray birch—the old field birch of exhausted soils—with dogwood and an aromatic tangle of humbler shrubs, high-bush huckleberry and laurel and sweet fern; while beneath these the dry elastic earth-floor is a deep couch of ghost-gray moss, shining checkerberry and graceful ground pine. The tumbledown farmstead itself lies either unseen at some distance from these abandoned fields or has wholly disappeared along with the neat stone fences that must once have marked them. Yet the boundaries of the fields are now majestically defined through the undergrowth by rows of gigantic red cedars so thickset, so tall, shapely, and dense as to resemble the secular cypresses of Italian gardens more nearly than the poor relations they ordinarily are.

And at the upper edge of one steep-lying field, formerly an apple orchard —though but three or four of the original apple trees remain, hopelessly decrepit and half buried in the new growth—the older cedars of the fence line have seeded capriciously and have thrown out an almost perfect circle of younger, slenderer trees which, standing shoulder to shoulder, inclose the happiest retreat for woodland god or dreaming mortal that the most exacting faun or poet could desire.

That Susan should have happened upon this lonely, this magic circle, I can never regard as a mere accident. Obviously time had slowly and lovingly formed and perfected it for some purpose; it was there waiting for her—and one day she came and possessed it, and the magic circle was complete.

Susan was then seventeen and the season, as it should have been, was early May. Much of the hill country lying northward from the Connecticut coast towns is surprisingly wild, and none of it wilder or lovelier than certain tracts spread within easy reach of the few New Haveners who have not wholly capitulated to business or college politics or golf or social service or the movies, forgetting a deeper and saner lure. A later Wordsworth or Thoreau might still live in midmost New Haven and never feel shut from his heritage, for it neighbors him closely—swamp and upland, hemlock cliff and hardwood forest, precipitous brook or slow-winding meadow stream, where the red-winged blackbirds flute and flash by; the whole year's wonder awaits him; he has but to go forth—alone.

Nature never did betray the heart that loved her, though she so ironically betrays most of us who merely pretend to love her, because we feel, after due instruction, that we ought. For Nature is not easily communicative, nor lightly wooed. She demands a higher devotion than an occasional picnic, and will seldom have much to say to you if she feels that you secretly prefer another society to hers. To her elect she whispers, timelessly, and Susan, in her own way, was of the elect. It was the way—the surest—of solitary communion;

but it was very little, very casually, the way of science. She observed much, but without method; and catalogued not at all. She never counted her warblers and seldom named them—but she loved them, as they slipped northward through young leaves, shyly, with pure flashes of green or russet or gold.

Nature for Susan, in short, was all mood, ranging from cold horror to supernal beauty; she did not sentimentalize the gradations. The cold horror was there and chilled her, but the supernal beauty was there too—and did not leave her cold. And through it all streamed an indefinable awe, a trail one could not follow, a teasing mystery—an unspoken word. It was back of—no rather it interpenetrated the horror no less than the beauty; they were but phases, hints, of that other, that suspected, eerie trail, leading one knew not where.

But surely there, in that magic circle, one might press closer, draw oneself nearer, catch at the faintest hint toward a possible clue? The aromatic space within the cedars became Susan's refuge, her nook from the world, her Port-Royal, her Walden, her Lake Isle of Innisfree. Once found that spring she never spoke of it; she hoarded her treasure, slipping off to it stealthily, through slyest subterfuge or evasion, whenever she could. For was it not hers?

Sometimes she rode out there, tying her horse to a tree in the lowest field back of a great thicket of old-fashioned lilac bushes run wild, where he was completely hidden from the rare passers-by of the rough up-country road or lane. But oftenest, she has since confessed, she would clear her morning or afternoon by some plausible excuse for absence, then board the Waterbury trolley express, descending from it about two miles from her nook, and walking or rather climbing up to it crosslots through neglected woodland and uncropped pasture reverting to the savage.

At one point she had to pass a small swampy meadow through which a mere thread of stream worked its way, half-choked by thick-springing blades of our native wild iris; so infinitely, so capriciously delicate in form and hue. And here, if these were in bloom, she always lingered a while, poised on the harsh hummocks of bent-grass, herself slender as a reed. The pale, softly pencilled iris petals stirred in her a high wonder beyond speech. What supreme, whimsical artistry brought them to being there, in that lonely spot; and for whose joy? No human hand, cunning with enamel and platinum and treated silver, could, after a lifetime of patience, reproduce one petal of these uncounted flowers. Out of the muck they lifted, ethereal, unearthly—yet so soon to die... .

Oh, she knew what the learned had to say of them!—that they were merely sexual devices; painted deceptions for attracting insects and so assuring cross-pollination and the lusty continuance of their race. So far as it went this was unquestionably true; but it went—just how far? Their color and secret manna attracted the necessary insects, which they fed; the form of their petals and perianth tubes, and the arrangement of their organs of sex were cunningly evolved, so that the insect that sought their nectar bore from one flower to the next its fertilizing golden dust——

Astonishing, certainly! But what astonished her far more was that all this ingenious mechanism should in any way affect *her!* It was obviously none of her affair; and yet to come upon these cunning mechanistic devices in this deserted field stirred her, set something ineffable free in her—gave it joy for wings. It was as if these pale blooms of wild iris had been for her, in a less mortal sense, what the unconscious insects were for them—*intermediaries*, whose more ethereal contacts cross-fertilized her very soul. But she could not define for herself or express for others what they did to her. Of one thing only she was certain: These fleeting moments of expansion, of illumination, were brief and vague—moments of pure, uncritical feeling—but they were the best moments of her life; and they were real. They vanished, but not wholly. They left lasting traces. Never to have been visited by them would have condemned her, she knew, to be less than her fullest self, narrower in sympathy, more rigid, more dogmatic, and less complete.

But that first May day of her discovery, when called out to wander lonely as a cloud by the spirit of spring—the day she had happened on her magic circle,—all that rough upland world was burgeoning, and the beauty of those deserted fields hurt the heart. Susan never easily wept, but that day—safely hidden in the magic circle, then newly hers—she threw herself down on the ghost-gray moss among the spicy tufts of sweet fern and enjoyed, as she later told me, the most sensuously abandoned good cry of her life. The dogwood trees were a glory of flushed white about her, shining in on every hand through the black-green cedars, as if the stars had rushed forward toward earth and clustered more thickly in a nearer midnight sky. Life had no right to be so overwhelmingly fair—if these poignant gusts of beauty gave no sanction to all that the bruised heart of man might long for of peace and joy! If life must be accepted as an idiot's tale, signifying nothing, then it was a refinement of that torture that it could suddenly lift—as a sterile wave lifts only to break—to such dizzying, ecstatic heights... . No, no—it was impossible! It was unthinkable! It was absurd!

That year we spent July, August, and early September in France, but late September found us back in New Haven for those autumnal weeks which are the golden, heady wine of our New England cycle. Praise of the New England October, for those who have experienced it, must always seem futile, and for those who have not, exaggerated and false. Summer does not decay in New

England; it first smoulders and then flares out in a clear multicolored glory of flame; it does not sicken to corruption, it shouts and sings and is transfigured. I had suggested to Susan, therefore, a flight to higher hills—to the Berkshires, to be precise—where we might more spaciously watch these smoke-less frost-fires flicker up, spread, consume themselves, and at last leap from the crests, to vanish rather than die. But Susan, pleading a desire to settle down after much wandering, begged off. She did not tell me that she had a private sanctuary, too long unvisited, hidden among nearer and humbler hills.

The rough fields of the old farm were now rich with crimson and gold—bright yellow gold, red gold, green and tarnished gold—or misted over with the horizon blue of wild asters, a needed softening of tone in a world else so vibrant with light, so nakedly clear. This was another and perhaps even a deeper intoxication than that of the flood tide of spring. Unbearably beautiful it grew at its climax of splendor! An unseen organist unloosed all his stops, and Susan, like a little child overpowered by that rocking clamor, was shaken by it and almost whimpered for mercy… .

It was not until the following spring that chance improbably betrayed her guarded secret to me. All during the preceding fall I had wondered at times that I found it so increasingly difficult to arrange for afternoons of tennis or golf or riding with Susan; but I admonished myself that as she grew up she must inevitably find personal interests and younger friends, and it was not for me to limit or question her freedom. And though Susan never lied to me, she was clever enough, and woman enough, to let me mislead myself.

"I've been taking a long walk, Ambo." "I've been riding."

Well, bless her, so she had—and why shouldn't she? Though it came at last with me to a vague, comfortless feeling of shut-outness—of too often missing an undefined something that I had hoped to share.

During a long winter of close companionship in study and socially unsocial life this feeling disappeared, but with the spring it gradually formed again, like a little spreading cloud in an empty sky. And one afternoon, toward middle May, I discovered myself to be unaccountably alone and wishing Susan were round—so we could "do something." The day was a day apart. Mummies that day, in dim museums, ached in their cerements. Middle-aged bank clerks behind grilles knew a sudden unrest, and one or two of them even wondered whether to be always honestly handling the false counters of life were any compensation for never having riotously lived. Little boys along Hillhouse Avenue, ordinarily well-behaved, turned freakishly truculent, delighted in combat, and pummelled each other with ineffective fists. Settled professors in classrooms were seized with irrelevant fancies and, while trying to recover some dropped thread of discourse, openly sighed—haunted by visions of the phœbe bird's nest found under the old bridge by the mill dam, or of the long-forgotten hazel eyes of some twelve-year-old sweetheart. A rebellious day—and a sentimental! [See Lord Tennyson, and the poets, *passim*.] The apple trees must be in full bloom… .

Well then, confound it, why had Susan gone to a public lecture on Masefield? Or had she merely mentioned at lunch that there was a public lecture on Masefield? Oh, damn it! One can't stay indoors on such a day!

Susan and I kept our saddle horses at the local riding academy, where they were well cared for and exercised on the many days when we couldn't or did not wish to take them out. As the academy was convenient and had good locker rooms and showers, we always preferred changing there instead of dressing at home and having the horses sent round. Riding is not one of my passions, and oddly enough is not one of Susan's. That intense sympathy which unites some men and women to horses, and others to dogs or cats, is either born in one or it is not. Susan felt it very strongly for both dogs and cats, and if I have failed to mention Tumps and Togo, that is a lack in myself, not in her. I don't dislike dogs or cats or, for that matter, well-broken horses, but—though I lose your last shreds of sympathy—they all, in comparison with other interests, leave me more than usual calm. Of Tumps and Togo, nevertheless, something must yet be said, though too late for their place in Susan's heart; or indeed, for their own deserving. But they are already an intrusion here.

For Alma, her dainty little single footer, Susan's feeling was rather admiration than love. Just as there are poets whose songs we praise, but whose genius does not seem to knit itself into the very fabric of our being, so it was with Alma and Susan. She said and thought nothing but good of Alma, yet never felt lonely away from her—the infallible test. As for Jessica, my own modest nag, I fear she was very little more to me than an agreeably paced inducement to exercise, and I fear I was little more to her than a possible source of lump sugar and a not-too-fretful hand on the bridle reins. To-day, however, I needed her as a more poetic motor; failing Susan's companionship, I wanted to be carried far out into country byways apart from merely mechanical motors or—ditto—men.

Jessica, well up to it, offered no objections to the plan, and we were soon trotting briskly along the aërial Ridge Road, from which we at length descended to the dark eastern flank of Mount Carmel. It would mean a long pull to go right round the mountain by the steep back road, and I had at first no thought of attempting it; but the swift remembrance of a vast cherry orchard bordering that road made me wonder whether its blossoms had yet fallen. When I determined finally to push on, poor Jessica's earlier fire had cooled; we climbed the rough back road as a slug moves; the cherry orchard proved disappointing; and the sun was barely two hours from the hills when we crossed the divide and turned south down a grass-grown wood road that I had never before traveled. I hoped, and no doubt Jessica hoped, it might prove a shorter cut home.

What it did prove was so fresh an enchantment of young leaf and flashing wing, that I soon ceased to care where it led or how late I might be for dinner. Then a sharp dip in the road brought a new vision of delight; dogwood—cloudy masses of pink dogwood, the largest, deepest-tinted trees of it I had ever seen! It caught at my throat; and I reined in Jessica, whose æsthetic sense was less developed, and stared. But presently the spell was broken. An unseen horse squealed, evidently from behind a great lilac thicket in an old field at the left, and Jessica squealed back, instantly alert and restive. The sharp whinnying was repeated, and Jessica's dancing excitement grew intense; then there was a scuffling commotion back of the lilacs and to my final astonishment Susan's little mare, Alma, having broken her headstall and wrenched herself free of bit and bridle, came trotting amicably forth to join her old friends—which she could easily do, as the ancient cattle bars at the field-gate had long since rotted away.

It was unmistakably dainty Alma with her white forehead star—but where was her mistress? A finger of ice drew slowly along my spine as I urged Jessica into the field and round the lilac thicket. Alma meekly followed us, softly breathing encouragement through pink nostrils, and my alarm quieted when I found nothing more dreadful than the broken bridle still dangling from the branch of a dead cedar. It was plain that Susan had tied Alma there to explore on foot through the higher fields; it was plain, too, that she must have preferred to ride out here alone, and had been at some pains to conceal her purpose.

For a second, so piqued was I, I almost decided to ride on and leave the willful child to her own devices. But the broken bridle shamed me. I dismounted to examine it; it could be held together safely enough for the return, I saw, with a piece of stout twine, and there was certain to be a habitation with a piece of stout twine in it on down the road somewhere. Susan must have come that way and could tell me. But I must find her first… .

"Susan!" I called. "*Oh-ho-o-o! Soo-san!*"

No answer. I called again—vainly. Nothing for it, then, but a search! I tethered Jessica to the cedar stump, convinced that Alma wouldn't wander far from her old friend, and started off through the field past a senile apple tree bearing a few scattered blossoms, beyond which a faintly suggested path seemed to lead upward through a wonder-grove of the pink dogwood, mingled with laurel and birch and towering cedars. That path, I knew, would have tempted Susan.

What there was of it soon disappeared altogether in an under-thicket of high-bush huckleberry, taller than a man's head. Through this I was pushing my way, and had stooped to win past some briers and protect my eyes—when I felt a silk scarf slip across them, muffling my face.

It was swiftly knotted from behind; then my hand was taken, and Susan's voice—on a tone of blended mischief and mystery—quavered at my ear: "Hush! Profane mortal—speak not! This is holy ground."

With not another word spoken she drew me after her, guiding me to freer air and supporting me when I stumbled. We continued thus for some moments, on my part clumsily enough; and then Susan halted me, and turned me solemnly round three times, while she crooned in a weird gypsy-like singsong the following incantation:

Cedar, cedar, birch and fern,
Turn his wits as mine you turn.

If he sees what now I see
Welcome shall this mortal be.

If he sees it not, I'll say
Crick-crack and vanish May!

But I must have seen! My initiation was pronounced successful. From that hour all veils were withdrawn, and I was made free of the magic circle... .

It was a dip in Lethe. Dinner was forgotten—the long miles home and the broken bridle. A powerful enchantment had done its work. For me, only the poised moment of joy was real. Nothing else mattered, nothing else existed, while that poised fragile moment was mine. We talked or were silent—it was all one. And when dusk crept in, and a grateful wood-thrush praised it, we still lingered to join in that praise... . Then a whippoorwill began to call insistently, grievously, from very far off. It was the whippoorwill that shattered my poised crystal moment of perfect joy.

"Those poor horses," I said.

"Oh!" cried Susan, springing up, "how *could* we let them starve! I'm starved, too, Ambo—aren't you? What sillies we are!"

We got home safely, after some trifling difficulties, past ten o'clock... .

When the lamp is shattered
The light in the dust lies dead——

Only it doesn't, always—thank God! Memories... . And this was but one. Oh, no; I was not to be alone. I should never really be alone... .

XIII

The morning after Jimmy had dined with us, Susan, at my request, brought Miss Goucher to my study, and we had a good long talk together. And first of all the problem of Gertrude loomed before us, starting up ghostlike at a chance remark, and then barring all progress with more practical considerations, till laid. Neither Susan's telegram nor her private interview with Gertrude had been discussed between us; I had nervously shied off from both matters in my dread of seeming to question Susan's motives. But now Susan herself, to put it crudely, insisted on a show-down.

"The air needed clearing, Ambo, and I sent the telegram hoping to clear it by raising a storm. But, as Sister reminded me at breakfast, storms don't always clear the air—even good hard ones; they sometimes leave it heavier than ever. I'm afraid that's what my storm has done. Has it, Ambo? What happened when Mrs. Hunt came to see you here? But perhaps I ought to tell you first what happened between us?"

"No," I smiled; "Gertrude made that fairly plain, for once. And your storm did sweep off the worst of the fog! You see, Gertrude has, intensely, the virtues of her defects—a fastidious sense of honor among them. Once she felt her suspicions unjust, she was bound to acknowledge it. I can't say you won a friend, but you did—by some miracle—placate a dangerous foe."

"Is she coming back to you, Ambo?"

"No. She suggests divorce. But that of course is impossible!"

"Why?"

"Is it kind to ask?" said Miss Goucher. "And—forgive me, dear—after your decision, is it necessary for you to know?"

Susan reflected anxiously. "No," she finally responded, "it isn't kind; but it is necessary. I'll tell you why, Ambo. If you had been free, I think there's no doubt I should have married you. Oh, I know, dear, it sounds cold-blooded like that! But the point is, I shouldn't then have questioned things as I do now. My feeling for you—your need of me—they wouldn't have been put to the test. Now they have been—or rather, they're being tested, every minute of every hour. Suppose I should ask you now—meaning every word of it—to divorce Mrs. Hunt so you could marry me? At least you'd know then, wouldn't you, that simply being yours meant more to me than anything else in life? Or suppose I couldn't bring myself to ask it, but couldn't face life without you? Suppose I drowned myself——"

"Good God, dear!"

"I'm not going to, Ambo—and what's equally important, neither are you. Why, you don't even pause over Mrs. Hunt's suggestion! You don't even wait to ask my opinion! You say at once—it's impossible! That proves something, doesn't it—about you and me? It either proves we're not half so much in love as we think we are, or else that love isn't for either of us the only good thing in life—the whole show." She paused, but added: "Why can't you consider divorcing Mrs. Hunt, Ambo? After all, she isn't honestly your wife and doesn't want to be; it would only be common fairness to yourself."

Miss Goucher stirred uneasily in her chair. I stirred uneasily in mine.

"There are so many reasons," I fumbled. "I suppose at bottom it comes to this—a queer feeling of responsibility, of guilt even... ."

"Nonsense!" cried Susan. "You never could have satisfied her, Ambo. You weren't born to be human, but somehow, in spite of everything, you just are! It's your worst fault in Mrs. Hunt's eyes. Mrs. Hunt shouldn't have married a man; she should have married a social tradition; an abstract idea."

"How could she?" asked Miss Goucher.

"Easily," said Susan; "she's one herself, so there must be others. It's hard to believe, but apparently abstractions like that do get themselves incarnated now and then. I never met one before—in the flesh. It gave me a creepy feeling—like shaking hands with the fourth dimension or asking the Holy Roman Empire to dinner. But I don't pretend to make her out, Ambo. Why *did* she leave you? It seems the very thing an incarnate social tradition could never have brought herself to do!"

Before I could check myself I reproved her. "You're not often merely cruel, Susan!" Then, hoping to soften it, I hurried on: "You see, dear, Gertrude isn't greatly to blame. Suppose you had been born and brought up like her, to believe beauty and brains and a certain gracious way of life a family privilege, a class distinction. Don't you see how your inbred worship of class and family would become in the end an intenser form of worshipping yourself? Gertrude was taught to live exclusively, from girlhood, in this disguised worship of her own perfections. We're all egotists of course; but most of us are the common or garden variety, and have an occasional suspicion that we're pretty selfish and intolerant and vain. Gertrude has never suspected it. How could she? A daughter of her house can do no wrong—and she is a daughter of her house." I sighed.

"Unluckily, my power of unreserved admiration has bounds, and my tongue and temper sometimes haven't. So our marriage dissolved in an acid bath compounded of honest irritations and dishonest apologies. *I* made the dishonest apologies. To do Gertrude justice, she never apologized. She knew the initial fault was mine. I shouldn't have joined a church whose creed I couldn't repeat without a sensation of moral nausea. That's just what I did when I married Gertrude. There was no deception on her side, either. I knew her gods, and I knew she assumed that mine were the same as hers, and that I was humbly entering the service of their dedicated priestess. Well, I apostatized—to her frozen amazement. Then a crisis came—insignificant enough... . Gertrude refused to call with me on the bride of an old friend of mine, because she thought it a misalliance. He had no right, she held, under her jealous gods, to bring a former trained nurse home as his wife, and thrust her upon a society that would never otherwise have received her.

"I was furious, and blasphemed her gods. I insisted she should either accompany me, then and there, or I'd go myself and apologize for her—yes, these are the words I used—her 'congenital lunacy.' She left me like a statue walking, and went to her room."

"And you?" asked Susan.

"I made the call."

"Did you make the apology?"

"No; I couldn't."

"Naturally not," assented Miss Goucher.

"Oh, Ambo," protested Susan, "what a coward you are! Well, and then?"

"I returned to a wifeless house. From that hour until yesterday morning there have been no explanations between Gertrude and me. Gertrude is superb."

"I understand her less than ever," said Susan.

"I understand her quite well," said Miss Goucher. "But your long silence, Mr. Hunt—that I can't understand."

"I can," Susan exclaimed. "Ambo's very bones dislike her. So do mine. Do you remember how I used to shock you, Ambo, when I first came here— saying somebody or other was no damn good? Well, I can't help it; it's stronger than I am. Mrs. Hunt's no——"

"Oh, *child!*" struck in Miss Goucher. "How much you have still to learn!" Then she addressed me: "I've never seen a more distinguished person than Mrs. Hunt. I know it's odd, coming from me, but somehow I sympathize with her—greatly. I've always"—hesitated Miss Goucher—"been a proud sort of nobody myself."

Susan reached over and slipped her hand into Miss Goucher's. "Poor Sister! Just as we're going off together you begin to find out how horrid I can be. But I'll make a little true confession to both of you. What I've been saying about Mrs. Hunt isn't in the least what I think about her. The fact is, I'm jealous of her, in so many ways—except in the ordinary way! To make a clean breast of it, when I was with her she brought me to my knees in spite of myself. Oh, I acknowledge her power! It's uncanny. How did you ever find strength to resist it, Ambo? My outbreak was sheer Birch Street bravado—a cheap insult flung in the face of the unattainable! It was all my shortcomings throwing mud at all her disdain. Truly! Why, the least droop of her eyelids taught me that it takes more than quick wits and sensitive nerves and hard study to overcome a false start—or rather, no start at all!

"Birch Street isn't even a beginning, because, so far as Mrs. Hunt's concerned, Birch Street simply doesn't exist! And even Birch Street would have to admit that she gets away with it! I'd say so, too, if I didn't go a step farther and feel that it gets away with her. That's why ridicule can't touch her. You can't laugh at a devotee, a woman possessed, the instrument of a higher power! Mrs. Hunt's a living confession of faith in the absolute rightness of the right people, and a living rebuke to the incurable wrongness of the wrong! Oh, I knew at once what you meant, Ambo, when you called her a dedicated priestess! It's the way I shall always think of her—ritually clothed, and pouring out tea to her gods from sacred vessels of colonial silver! You can smile, Ambo, but I shall; and way down in my common little Birch Street heart, I believe I shall always secretly envy her... . So there!"

For the first time in my remembrance of her, Miss Goucher laughed out loud. Her laugh—in effect, not in resonance—was like cockcrow. We all laughed together, and Gertrude vanished... . But ten minutes later found us with knit brows again, locked in debate. Susan had at length seized courage to tell me that when she left my house she must, once and for all, go it completely alone. She could no longer accept my financial protection. She was to stand on her own feet, for better or worse, richer or poorer, in sickness or in health. This staggering proposal I simply could not listen to calmly, and would not yield to! It was too preposterously absurd.

Yet I made no headway with my objections, until I stumbled upon the one argument that served me and led to a final compromise, "Dear," I had protested, really and deeply hurt by Susan's stubborn stand for absolute independence, "can't you feel how cruelly unkind all this is to me?"

"Oh," she wailed, "unkind? Why did you say that! Surely, Ambo, you don't mean it! Unkind?"

I was quick to press my advantage. "When you ask me to give up even the mere material protection of my family? You *are* my family, Susan—all the family I shall ever have. I don't want to be maudlin about it. I don't wish to interfere with your freedom to develop your own life in your own way. But it's beyond my strength not to plead that all that's good in my life is bound up with yours. Please don't ask me to live in daily and hourly anxiety over your reasonable comfort and health. There's no common sense in it, Susan. It's fantastic! And it is unkind!"

Susan could not long resist this plea, for she felt its wretched sincerity, even if she knew—as she later told me—that I was making the most of it. It was Miss Goucher who suggested our compromise.

"Mr. Hunt," she said, "my own arrangement with Susan is this: We are to pool our resources, and I am to make a home for her, just as if I were her own mother. I've been able to save, during the past twenty-five years, about eight thousand dollars; it's well invested, I think, and brings me in almost five hundred a year. This is what we were to start with; and Susan feels certain she can earn at least two thousand dollars a year by her pen. I know nothing of the literary market, but I haven't counted on her being able to earn so much—for a year or so, at least. On the other hand, I feel certain Susan will finally make her way as a writer. So I'd counted on using part of my capital for a year or two if necessary. We plan to live very simply for the present, of course—but without hardship."

"Still——" I would have protested, if for once Miss Goucher had not waived all deference, sailing calmly on:

"As Susan has told you, she's convinced that she needs the assurance of power and self-respect to be gained by meeting life without fear or favor and making her own career in the face of whatever difficulties arise. There's a good deal to be said for that, Mr. Hunt—more than you could be expected to understand. Situated as you have always been, I mean. But naturally, as Susan's guardian, you can't be expected to stand aside if for any reason we fail in our attempt. I see that; and Susan sees it now, I'm sure. Yet I really feel I must urge you to let us try. And I promise faithfully to keep you informed as to just how we are getting on."

"Please, Ambo," Susan chimed in, "let us try. If things go badly I won't be unreasonable or stubborn—indeed I won't. Please trust me for that. I'll even go a step farther than Sister. I won't let her break into her savings—not one penny. If it ever comes to that, I'll come straight to you. And for the immediate present, I have over five hundred dollars in my bank account; and"—she smiled—"I'll try to feel it's honestly mine. You've spent heaven knows how much on me, Ambo; though it's the least of all you've done for me and been to me! But now, please let me see whether I could ever have made anything of myself if I hadn't been so shamelessly lucky—if life had treated me as it treats most people... . Jimmy, for instance... . *He* hasn't needed help, Ambo; and I simply must know whether he's a better man than I am, Gunga Dhin! Don't you see?"

Yes; I flatter myself that I did, more or less mistily, begin to see. Thus our morning conference drew to its dreary, amicable close.

But from the door Susan turned back to me with tragic eyes: "Ambo—I'm caring. It does—hurt." And since I could not very safely reply, she attempted a smile. "Ambo—what is to become of poor Tumps? Togo will have to come; I can't reduce him to atheism. But Tumps would die in New York; and he never has believed in God anyway! Can you make a martyr of yourself for his surly sake? Can you? Just to see, I mean, that he gets his milk every day and fish heads on Friday? Can you, dear?"

I nodded and turned away... . The door closed so quietly that I first knew when the latch ticked once how fortunately I was alone.

XIV

Maltby Phar was responsible for Togo; he had given him—a little black fluff-ball with shoe-button eyes—to Susan, about six months after she first came to live with me. Togo is a Chow; and a Chow is biologically classified as a dog. But if a Chow is a dog, then a Russian sable muff is a dish rag. Your Chow—black, smoke blue, or red—is a creation apart. He is to dogdom what Hillhouse Avenue is to Birch Street—the wrong end, *bien entendu*. His blood is so blue that his tongue is purple; and, like Susan's conception of Gertrude, he is a living confession of faith in the rightness of the right people, a living rebuke to the wrongness of the wrong; the right people being, of course, that master god or mistress goddess whom he worships, with their immediate *entourage*. No others need apply for even cursory notice, much less respect.

I am told they eat Chows in China, their native land. If they do, it must be from the motive that drove Plutarch's Athenian to vote the banishment of Aristides—ennui, to wit, kindling to rage; he had wearied to madness of hearing him always named "the Just." Back, too, in America—for I write from France—there will one day be proletarian reprisals against the Chow; for in the art of cutting one dead your Chow is supreme. He goes by you casually, on tiptoe, with the glazed eye of indifference. He sees you and does not see you—and will not. You may cluck, you may whistle, you may call; interest will not excite him, nor flattery move him; he passes; he "goes his unremembering way." But let him beware! If Americans are slow to anger, they are terrible when roused. I have frequently explained this to Togo—more for Susan's sake than his own—and been yawned at for my pains.

Personally, I have no complaint to make. In Togo's eyes I am one of the right people. He has always treated me with a certain tact, though with a certain reserve. Only to Susan does he prostrate himself with an almost mystical ecstasy of devotion. Only for her does his feathered tail-arc quiver, do his ears lie back, his calm ebon lips part in an unmistakably adoring smile. But there is much else, I admit, to be said for him; he never barks his deep menacing bark without cause; and as a mere *objet d'art*, when well combed, he is superb. Ming porcelains are nothing to him; he is perhaps the greatest decorative achievement of the unapproachably decorative East... .

But for Tumps, my peculiar legacy, I have nothing good to say and no apologies to offer. Like Calverley's parrot, he still lives—"he will not die." Tumps is a tomcat. And not only is he a tomcat, he is a hate-scarred noctivagant, owning but an ear and a half, and a poor third of tail. His design was botched at birth, and has since been degraded; his color is unpleasant; his expression is ferocious—and utterly sincere. He has no friends in the world but Susan and Sonia, and Sonia cannot safely keep him with her because of the children.

Out of the night he came, shortly after Togo's arrival; starved for once into submission and dragging himself across the garden terrace to Susan's feet. And she accepted this devil's gift, this household scourge. I never did, nor did Togo; but we were finally subdued by fear. Those baleful eyes cursing us from dim corners—Togo, Togo, shall we ever forget them! Separately or together, we have more than once failed to enter a dusky room, toward twilight, where those double phosphors burned from your couch corner or out from beneath my easy-chair.

But nothing would move Susan to give Tumps up so long as he cared to remain; and Tumps cared. Small wonder! Nursed back to health and rampageous vivacity, he soon mastered the neighborhood, peopled it with his ill-favored offspring, and wailed his obscene balladry to the moon. Hillhouse Avenue protested, *en bloc*. The Misses Carstairs, whose slumbers had more than once been postponed, and whose white Persian, Desdemona, had been debauched, threatened traps, poison and the law. Professor Emeritus Gillingwater attempted murder one night with a .22 rifle, but only succeeded in penetrating the glass roof of his neighbor's conservatory.

Susan was unmoved, defending her own; she would not listen to any plea, and she mocked at reprisals. Those were the early days of her coming, when I could not force myself to harsh measures; and happily Tumps, having lost some seven or eight lives, did with the years grow more sedate, though no more amiable. But the point is, he stayed—and, I repeat, lives to this hour on my distant, grudging bounty.

Such was the charge lightly laid upon me... .

Oh, Susan—Susan! For once, resentment will out! May you suffer, shamed to contrition, as you read these lines! Tumps—and I say it now boldly—is "no damn good."

XV

I am clinging to this long chapter as if I were still clinging to Susan's hand on the wind-swept station platform, hoarding time by infinitesimally split seconds, dreading her inevitable escape. Phil—by request, I suspect—did not come down; and Susan forbade me to enter the train with her, having previously forbidden me to accompany her to town. Togo was forward, amid crude surroundings, riling the brakemen with his disgusted disdain. Miss Goucher had already said a decorous but sincerely felt good-by, and had taken her place inside.

"Let's not be silly, Ambo," Susan whispered. "After all, you'll be down soon—won't you? You're always running to New York."

Then, unexpectedly, she snatched her hand from mine, threw her arms tight round my neck, and for a reckless public moment sobbed and kissed me. With that she was gone... . I turned, too, at once, meaning flight from the curious late-comers pressing toward the car steps. One of them distinctly addressed me.

"Good morning, Ambrose. Don't worry about your charming little ward. She'll be quite safe—away from you. I'll keep a friendly eye on her going down."

It was Lucette.

THE FOURTH CHAPTER

I

I HAD a long conference with Phil the day after Susan's departure, and we solemnly agreed that we must, within reasonable limits, give Susan a clear field; her desire to play a lone hand in the cut-throat poker game called life must be, so far as possible, respected. But we sneakingly evaded any definition of our terms. "Within reasonable limits;" "so far as possible"—the vagueness of these phrases will give you the measure of our secret duplicity.

Meanwhile we lived on from mail delivery to mail delivery, and Susan proved a faithful correspondent. There is little doubt, I think, that the length and frequency of her letters constituted a deliberate sacrifice of energy and time, laid—not reluctantly, but not always lightly—on the altar of affection. It was a genuine, yet must often have been an arduous piety. To write full life-giving letters late at night, after long hours of literary labor, is no trifling effort of good will—good will, in this instance, to two of the loneliest, forlornest of men. Putting aside the mere anodyne of work we had but one other effective consolation—Jimmy; our increasing interest and joy in Jimmy. But, for me at least, this was not an immediate consolation; my taste for Jimmy's prosaic companionship was very gradually acquired.

Our first word from Susan was a day letter, telephoned to me from the telegraph office, though I at once demanded the delivery of a verbatim copy by messenger. Here it is:

"At grand central safe so far new york lies roaring just beyond sister and togo tarry with the stuff near cab stand while I send. Love Mrs. Arthur snooped in vain now for it courage Susan whos afraid dont you be alonsen fan."

Phil, the scholar, interpreted the last two verbatim symbols: *"Allons, enfants!"*

II

SUSAN TO ME

"Sister and I are at the nice old mid-Victorian Brevoort House for three or four days. Sister is calmly and courageously hunting rooms for us—or, if not rooms, a room. She hopes for the plural. We like this quarter of town. It's near enough publishers and things for walking, and it's not quite so New Yorky as some others. What Sister is trying to avoid for us is slavery to the Subway, which is awful! But we may have to fly up beyond Columbia, or even to the Bronx, before we're through. The hotel objected to Togo, but I descended to hitherto untried depths of feminine wheedle—and justified them by getting my way. Sister blushed for me—and herself—but has since felt more confident about my chances for success in this wickedly opportunist world.

"Better skip this part if you read extracts to Phil; he'll brood. But perhaps you'd better begin disillusioning him at once, for I'm discovering dreadful possibilities in my nature—now the Hillhouse inhibitions seem remote. New York, one sees overnight, is no place for a romantic idealist—Maltby's phrase, not mine, bless Phil's heart!—but luckily I've never been one. Birch Street is going to stand me in good stead down here. New York *is* Birch Street on a slightly exaggerated scale; Hillhouse Avenue is something entirely different. Finer too, perhaps; but the world's future has its roots in New Birch Street. I began to feel that yesterday during my first hunt for a paying job.

"I've plunged on shop equipment, since Jimmy says, other things being equal, the factory with the best tools wins—that is, I've bought a reliable typewriter, and I tackled my first two-finger exercises last night. The results were dire—mostly interior capitals and extraneous asterisks. I shan't have patience to take proper five-finger lessons. Sister vows she's going to master the wretched thing too, so she can help with copying now and then. There's a gleam in her eye, dear—wonderful! This is to be her great adventure as well as mine. 'Susan, Sister & Co., Unlicensed Hacks—Piffle While You Wait!' Oh, we shall get on—you'll see. Still, I can't truthfully report much progress yesterday or to-day, though a shade more to-day than yesterday. I've been counting callously on Maltby, as Phil disapprovingly knows, and I brought three short manufactured-in-advance articles for the Garden Ex. down with me. So my first step was to stifle my last maidenly scruple and take them straight to Maltby; I hoped they would pay at least for the typewriter. It was a clear ice-bath of a morning, and the walk up Fifth Avenue braced me for anything. I stared at everybody and a good many unattached males stared back; sometimes I rather liked it, and sometimes not. It all depends.

"But I found the right building at last, somewhere between the Waldorf and the Public Library. There's a shop on its avenue front for the sale of false pearls, and judging from the shop they must be more expensive than real ones. Togo dragged me in there at first by mistake; and as I was wearing my bestest tailor-made and your furs, and as Togo was wearing his, plus his haughtiest atmosphere, we seemed between us to be just the sort of thing the languid clerks had been waiting for. There was a hopeful stir as we entered—

no, swept in! I was really sorry to disappoint them; it was horrid to feel that we couldn't live up to their expectations.

"We didn't sweep out nearly so well! But we found the elevator round the corner and were taken up four or five floors, passing a designer of *de luxe* corsets and a distiller of *de luxe* perfumes on the way, and landed in the impressive outer office of the Garden Ex.

"But how stupid of me to describe all this! You've been there twenty times, of course, and remember the apple-green art-crafty furniture and potted palms and things. Several depressed-looking persons were fidgeting about, but my engraved card—score one for Hillhouse!—soon brought Maltby puffing out to me with both hands extended. Togo didn't quite cut him dead, but almost, and he insulted an entire roomful of stenographers on his way to the great man's sanctum. My first *sanctum*, Ambo! I did get a little thrill from that, in spite of Maltby.

"Stop chattering, Susan—stick to facts. Yes, Phil, please. Fact One: Maltby was surprisingly flustered at first. He was, Ambo! He jumped to the conclusion that I was down for shopping or the theaters, and assumed of course you were with me. So you were, dear—our way! But I thought Maltby asked rather gingerly after you. Why?

"Fact Two: I did my best to explain things, but Maltby doesn't believe yet I'm serious—seemingly he can't believe it, because he doesn't want to. That's always true of Maltby. He still thinks this must be a sudden spasm—not of virtue; thinks I've run away for an unholy lark. It suits him to think so. If I'm out on the loose he hopes to manage the whole *Mardi gras*, and he needn't hear what I say about needing work too distinctly. That merely annoyed him. But I did finally make him promise—while he wriggled—to read my three articles and give me a decision on them to-morrow. I had to promise to lunch with him then to make even that much headway.—Oof!

"Meanwhile, I fared slightly better to-day. I took your letter to Mr. Sampson. The sign, Garnett & Co., almost frightened me off, though, Ambo; and you know I'm not easily frightened. But I've read so many of their books —wonderful books! I knew great men had gone before me into those dingy offices and left their precious manuscripts to strengthen and delight the world. Who was I to follow those footsteps? Luckily an undaunted messenger boy whistled on in ahead of me—so I followed his instead! By the time I had won past all the guardians of the *sanctum sanctorum*, my sentimental fit was over. Birch Street was herself again.

"And Mr. Sampson proved all you promised—rather more! The dearest odd old man, full of blunt kindness and sudden whimsy. I think he liked me. I know I liked him. But he didn't like me as I did him—at first sight. Togo's fault, of course. Why didn't you tell me Mr. Sampson has a democratic prejudice against aristocratic dogs? I must learn to leave poor Togo at home— if there ever is such a place!—when I'm looking for work; I may even have to give up your precious soul-and-body-warming furs. Between them, they belie every humble petition I utter. Sister and I may have to eat Togo yet.

"Mr. Sampson only began to relent when I told him a little about Birch Street. I didn't tell him much—just enough to counteract the furs and Togo. And he forgave me everything when I told him of Sister and confessed what we were hoping to do—found a home together and earn our own right to make it a comfy one to live in. He questioned me pretty sharply, too, but not from snifty-snoops like Mrs. Arthur.

"By the way, dear, she was on the train coming down, as luck would have it, in the chair just across from mine. Her questions were masterpieces, but nothing to my replies. I was just wretched enough to scratch without mercy; it relieved my feelings. But you'd better avoid her for a week or two—if you can! I didn't mind any of Mr. Sampson's questions, though I eluded some of them, being young in years but old in guile. I'm to take him my poems to-morrow afternoon, and some bits of prose things—the ones you liked. They're not much more than fragments, I'm afraid. He says he wants to get the hang of me before loading me down with bad advice. I do like him, and— the serpent having trailed its length all over this endless letter—I truly think his offhand friendship may prove far more helpful to me than Maltby's——! *You* can fill in the blank, Ambo. My shamelessness has limits, even now, in darkest New York.

"Good night, dear. Please don't think you are ever far from my me-est thoughts. Now for that —— typewriter!"

III

Susan to Jimmy

"That's a breath-taking decision you've made, but like you; and I'm proud of you for having made it—and prouder that the idea was entirely your own. I suppose we're all bound to be more or less lopsided in a world slightly flattened at the poles and rather wobbly on its axis anyway. But the less lopsided we are the better for us, and the better for us the better for others— and that's one universal law, at least, that doesn't make me long for a universal recall and referendum.

"Oh, you're right to stay on at Yale, but so much righter to have decided on a broad general course instead of a narrow technical one! *Of course* you can carry on your technical studies by yourself! With your brain's natural twist and the practical training you've had, probably carry them much farther by yourself than under direction! And the way you've chosen will open vistas, bring the sky through the jungle to you. It was brave of you to see that and take the first difficult step. *"Il n'y a que le premier pas qui coûte"*—but no wonder you hesitated! Because at your advanced age, Jimmy, and from an efficient point of view, it's a downright silly step, wasteful of time—and time you know's money—and money you know's everything. Only, I'm afraid you *don't* know that intensely enough ever to have a marble mansion on upper Fifth Avenue, a marble villa at Newport, a marble bungalow at Palm Beach, a marble steam yacht—but they don't make those of marble, do they!

"It's so possible for you to collect all these marbles, Jimmy—reelers, every one of them!—if you'll only start now and do nothing else for the next thirty or forty years. You can be a poor boy who became infamous just as easy as pie! Simply forget the world's so full of a number of things, and grab all you can of just one. But I could hug you for wanting to be a man, not an adding-machine! For caring to know why Socrates was richer than Morgan, and why Saint Francis and Sainte-Beuve, each in his own way, have helped more to make life worth living than all the Rothschilds of Europe! Oh, I know it's a paradox for me to preach this, when here am I trying to collect a few small clay marbles—putting every ounce of concentration in me on money making, on material success! Not getting far with it, either—so far.

"But what I'm doing, Jimmy, is just what you've set out to do—I'm trying not to be lopsided. You've met life as it is, already; I never have. And I'd so love to moon along pleasantly on Ambo's inherited money—read books and write verses and look at flowers and cats and stars and trees and children and cows and chickens and funny dogs and donkeys and funnier women and men! I'd so like not to adjust myself to an industrial civilization; not to worry over that sort of thing at all; above everything, not to earn my daily bread. I could cry about having to make up my mind on such bristly beasts as economic or social problems!

"The class struggle bores me to tears—yet here it is, we're up against it; and I *won't* be lopsided! What I want is pure thick cream, daintily fed to me, too, from a hand-beaten spoon. So I mustn't have it unless I can get it. And I don't know that I can—you see, it isn't all conscience that's driving me; curiosity's at work as well! But it's scrumptious to know we're both studying the same thing in a different way—the one great subject, after all: How not to be lopsided! How to be perfectly spherical, like the old man in the nonsense rhyme. Not wobbly on one's axis—not even slightly flattened at the poles!"

"Hurrah for us! Trumpets!

"But I'm gladdest of all that you and Ambo are beginning at last to be friends. You don't either of you say so—it drifts through; and I could sing about it—if I could sing. There isn't anybody in the world like Ambo.

"As for Sister and me, we're getting on, and we're not. Sister thinks I've done marvels; I know she has. Marvels of economy and taste in cozying up our room, marvels of sympathy and canny advice that doesn't sound like advice at all. As one-half of a mutual-admiration syndicate I'm a complete success! But as a professional author—hum, hum. Anyway, I'm beginning to poke my inquisitive nose into a little of everything, and you can't tell— something, some day, may come of this. As the Dickens man said—who was he?—I hope it mayn't be human gore. Meanwhile, one thing hits the most casual eye: We're still in the double-room-with-alcove boarding-house stage, and likely to stay there for some time to come."

IV

SUSAN TO PHIL

"Your short letter answering my long one has been read and reread and read again. I know it by heart. Everything you say's true—and isn't. I'll try to explain that—for I can't bear you to be doubting me. You are, Phil. I don't blame you, but I do blame myself—for complacency. I've taken too much for granted, as I always do with you and Ambo. You see, I know so intensely that you and Ambo are pure gold—incorruptible!—that I couldn't possibly question anything you might say or do—the fineness of the motive, I mean. If you did murder and were hanged for it, and even if I'd no clue as to why you struck—I should know all the time you must have done it because, for some concealed reason, under circumstances dark to the rest of us, your clear eyes marked it as the one possible right thing to do.

"Yes, I trust you like that, Phil; you and Ambo and Sister and Jimmy. Think of trusting four people like that! How rich I am! And you can't know how passionately grateful! For it isn't blind trusting at all. In each one of you I've touched a soul of goodness. There's no other name for it. It's as simple as fresh air. You're good—you four—good from the center. But, Phil dear, a little secret to comfort you—just between us and the stars: So, mostly, am I.

"Truly, Phil, I'm ridiculously good at the center, and most of the way out. There are things I simply can't do, no matter how much I'd like to; and lots of oozy, opally things I simply can't like at all. I'm with you so far, at least— peacock-proud to be! But we're tremendously different, all the same. It's really this, I think: You're a Puritan, by instinct and cultivation; and I'm not. The clever ones down here, you know, spend most of their spare time swearing by turns at Puritanism and the Victorian Era. Their favorite form of exercise is patting themselves on the back, and this is one of their subtler ways of doing it. But they just rampantly rail; they don't—though they think they do—understand. They mix up every *passé* narrowness and bigotry and hypocrisy and sentimental cant in one foul stew, and then rush from it, with held noses, screaming "Puritanism! *Faugh!*" Well, it does, Phil—their stew! So, often, for that matter—and to high heaven—do the clever ones!

"But it isn't Puritanism, the real thing. You see, I know the real thing—for I know you. Ignorance, bigotry, hypocrisy, sentimentalism—such things have no part in your life. And yet you're a Puritan, and I'm not. Something divides us where we are most alike. What is it, Phil?

"May I tell you? I almost dare believe I've puzzled it out.

"You're a simon-Puritan, dear, because you won't trust that central goodness, your own heart; the very thing in you on whose virgin-goldness I would stake my life! You won't trust it in yourself; and when you find it in others, you don't fully trust it in them. You've purged your philosophy of Original Sin, but it still secretly poisons the marrow of your bones. You guard your soul's strength as possible weakness—something that might vanish suddenly, at a pinch. How silly of you! For it's the *you*-est you, the thing you can never change or escape. Instead of worrying over yourself or others—me? —you could safely spread yourself, Phil dear, all over the landscape, lie back in the lap of Mother Earth and twiddle your toes and smile! Walt Whitman's way! He may have overdone it now and then, posed about it; but I'm on his side, not yours. It's heartier—human-er—more fun! Yes, Master Puritan— more fun! That's a life value you've mostly missed. But it's never too late, Phil, for a genuine cosmic spree.

"Now I've done scolding back at you for scolding at me.—But I loved your sermon. I hope you won't shudder over mine?"

V

The above too-cryptic letter badly needs authoritative annotation, which I now proceed to give you—at perilous length. But it will lead us far... .

Though it is positively not true that Phil and I, having covenanted on a hands-off policy, were independently hoping for the worst, so far as Susan's ability to cope unaided with New York was concerned; nevertheless, the ease with which she made her way there, found her feet without us and danced ahead, proved for some reason oddly disturbing to us both. Here was a child, of high talents certainly, perhaps of genius—the like, at least, of whose mental precocity we had never met with in any other daughter—much less, son—of Eve! A woman, for we so loved her, endowed as are few women; yet assuredly a child, for she had but just counted twenty years on earth. And being men of careful maturity, once Susan had left us, our lonely anxieties fastened upon this crying fact of her youth; it was her youth, her inexperience, that made her venture suddenly pathetic and dreadful to us, made us yearn to watch over her, warn her of pitfalls, guide her steps.

True, she was not alone. Miss Goucher was admirable in her way; though a middle-aged spinster, after all, unused to the sharp temptations and fierce competitions of metropolitan life. It was not a house-mother Susan would need; the wolves lurked beyond the door—shrewd, soft-treading wolves, cunningly disguised. How could a child, a charming and too daring child—however gifted—be expected to deal with these creatures? The thought of these subtle, these patient ones, tracking her—tracking her—chilled us to hours-long wakefulness in the night! Then with the morning a letter would come, filled with strange men's names.

We compared notes, consulted together—shaking unhappy heads. We wrote tactful letters to Heywood Sampson, begging him, but always indirectly, to keep an eye. We ran down singly for nights in town, rescued—the verb was ours—Susan and Miss Goucher from their West 10th Street boarding-house, interfered with their work or other plans, haled them—the verb, I fear, was theirs—to dinner, to the opera or theater, or perhaps to call on someone of ribbed respectability who might prove an observant friend. God knows, in spite of all resolutions, we did our poor best to mind Susan's business for her, to brood over her destiny from afar!

And God knows our efforts were superfluous! The traps, stratagems, springes in her path, merely suspected by us and hence the more darkly dreaded, were clearly seen by Susan and laughed at for the ancient, pitiful frauds they were. The dull craft, the stale devices of avarice or lust were no novelties to her; she greeted them, *en passant*, with the old Birch Street terrier-look; just a half-mocking nod of recognition—an amused, half-wistful salute to her gamin past. It was her gamin past we had forgotten, Phil and I, when we agonized over Susan's inexperienced youth. Inexperienced? Bob Blake's kid! If there were things New York could yet teach Bob Blake's kid—and there were many—they were not those that had made her see in it "Birch

Street—on a slightly exaggerated scale"!

But, as the Greeks discovered many generations ago, it is impossible to be high-minded or clear-sighted enough to outwit a secret unreason in the total scheme of things. Else the virtuous, in the Greek sense, would be always the fortunate; and perhaps then would grow too self-regarding. Does the last and austerest beauty of the ideal not flower from this, that it can promise us nothing but itself! You can choose a clear road, yet you shall never walk there in safety: Chance—that secret unreason—lurks in the hedgerows, myriad-formed, to plot against you. *"Hélas!"* as the French heroine might say. "Diddle-diddle-dumpling!" as might say Susan... . Meaning: That strain, Ambo, was of a higher mood, doubtless; but do return to your muttons.

Susan had reached New York late in November, 1913, and the letter to Phil dates from the following January. Barely two months had passed since her first calls upon Maltby and Heywood Sampson, but every day of that period had been made up of crowded hours. Of the three manufactured-in-advance articles for the Garden Ex., Maltby had accepted one, paying thirty dollars for it, half-rate—Susan's first professional earnings; but the manner of his acceptance had convinced Susan it was a mere stroke of personal diplomacy on his part. He did not wish to encourage her as a business associate, for Maltby kept his business activities rigidly separate from what he held to be his life; neither did he wish to offend her. What he wholly desired was to draw her into the immediate circles he frequented as a social being, where he could act as her patron on a scale at once more brilliant and more impressive.

So far as the Garden Ex. was concerned, his attitude from the first had been one of sympathetic discouragement. Susan hit off his manner perfectly in an earlier letter:

"'My dear Susan! You can write very delicate, distinctive verse, no doubt, and all that—and of course there's a fairly active market for verse nowadays, and I can put you in touch with some little magazines, *à côté*, that print such things, and even occasionally pay for them. They're your field, I'm convinced. But, frankly, I can't see you quite as one of our contributors—and I couldn't pay you a higher compliment!

"'You don't suppose, do you, I sit here like an old-fashioned editor, reading voluntary contributions? No, my dear girl; I have a small, well-broken staff of writers, and I tell them what to write. If I find myself, for example, with a lot of parade interiors taken in expensive homes, I select four or five, turn 'em over to Abramovitz, and tell him to do us something on "The More Dignified Dining-Room" or "The Period Salon, a Study in Restfulness." Abramovitz knows exactly what to say, and how to point the snobbish-but-not-too-snobbish captions and feature the best names. I've no need to experiment, you see. I count on Abramovitz. Just so with other matters. Here's an article, now, on "The Flaunting Paeony." Skeat did that, of course. It's signed "Winifred Snow"—all his flower-and-sundial stuff is—and it couldn't be better! I don't even have to read it.

"'Well, there you are! I'm simply a purveyor of standardized goods in standardized packages. Dull work, but it pays.'

"'Exactly!' I struck in. 'It pays! That's why I'm interested. Sister and Togo and I need the money!'"

As for the brilliant, intertwined circles frequented by Maltby as a social being, within which, he hoped to persuade Susan, lay true freedom, while habit slyly bound her with invisible chains—well, they are a little difficult to describe. Taken generally, we may think of them as the Artistic Smart Set. Maltby's acquaintance was wide, penetrating in many directions; but he felt most at home among those iridescent ones of earth whose money is as easy as their morals, and whose ruling passion for amusement is at least directed by æsthetic sensibilities and vivacious brains.

Within Maltby's intersecting circles were to be found, then, many a piquant contrast, many an anomalous combination. There the young, emancipated society matron, of fattest purse and slenderest figure, expressed her sophisticated paganism through interpretative dancing; and there the fashionable painter of portraits, solidly arrived, exhibited her slender figure on a daring canvas—made possible by the fatness of her purse—at one of his peculiarly intimate studio teas. There the reigning *ingénue*, whose graceful *diablerie* in imagined situations on the stage was equalled only by her roguish effrontery in more real, if hardly less public situations off, played up to the affluent *amateur*—patron of all arts that require an unblushing coöperation from pretty young women. There, in short, all were welcome who liked the game and were not hampered in playing it by dull inhibitions, material or immaterial. It was Bohemia *de luxe*—Bohemia in the same sense that Marie Antoinette's dairy-farm was Arcady.

That Susan—given her doting guardian, her furs, her Chow, her shadowy-gleaming, imaginative charm, her sharp audacities of speech—would bring a new and seductive personality to this perpetual carnival was Maltby's dream; she was predestined—he had long suspected the tug of that fate upon her—to shine there by his side. He best could offer the cup, and her gratitude for its heady drafts of life would be merely his due. It was an exciting prospect; it promised much; and it only remained to intoxicate Susan with the wine of an unguessed freedom. This, Maltby fondly assured himself, would prove no difficult task. Life was life, youth was youth, joy was joy; their natural affinities were all on his side and would play into his practiced hands.

Doubtless Phil and I must have agreed with him—from how differently anxious a spirit!—but all three of us would then have proved quite wrong. To intoxicate Susan, Maltby did find a difficult, in the end an impossible, task. He took her—not unwilling to enter and appraise any circle from high heaven to nether hell—to all the right, magical places, exposed her to all the heady influences of his world; and she found them enormously stimulating—to her sense of the ironic. Maltby's sensuous, quick-witted friends simply would not come true for Susan when she first moved among them; they were not serious about anything but refined sensation and she could not take their refined sensations seriously; but for a time they amused her, and she relished them much as Charles Lamb relished the belles and rakes of Restoration Drama: "They are a world of themselves almost as much as fairyland."

To their intimate dinners, their intimate musical evenings, their intimate studio revels—she came on occasion with Maltby as to a play: "altogether a speculative scene of things." She could, in those early weeks, have borrowed Lamb's words for her own comedic detachment: "We are amongst a chaotic people. We are not to judge them by our usages. No reverend institutions are insulted by their proceedings—for they have none among them. No peace of families is violated—for no family ties exist among them… . No deep affections are disquieted, no holy-wedlock bands are snapped asunder—for affection's depth and wedded faith are not the growth of that soil. There is neither right nor wrong… . Of what consequence is it to Virtue or how is she at all concerned? . . . The whole thing is a passing pageant."

It is probable that Maltby at first mistook her interest in the spectacle for the preliminary stirrings of its spell within her; but he must soon have been aware—for he had intelligence—that Susan was not precisely flinging herself among his maskers with the thrilled abandon that would betoken surrender. She was not afraid of these clever, beauty-loving maskers, some of whom bore celebrated names; it was not timidity that restrained her; she, too, loved beauty and lilting wit and could feel joyously at ease among them—for an hour or two—once in a while. But to remain permanently within those twining circles, held to a limited dream, when she was conscious of wilder, freer, more adventurous spaces without——! Why should she narrow her sympathies like that? It never occurred to her as a temptation to do so. She had drunk of a headier cup, and had known a vaster intoxication. From the magic circle of her cedar trees, in that lonely abandoned field back of Mount Carmel, the imagination of her heart had long since streamed outward beyond all such passing pageants, questing after a dream that does not pass... .

No gilded nutshell could bound her now; she could become the slave of no *intersected* ring... . Lesser incantations were powerless.

So much, then, for my own broad annotation of Susan's letter to Phil! But I leave you with generalizations, when your interest is in concrete fact. Patience. In my too fumbling way I am ready for you there, as well.

VI

SUSAN TO JIMMY

"I suppose you'd really like to know what I've lately been up to; but I hardly know myself. It's absurd, of course, but I almost think I'm having a weeny little fit of the blues to-night—not dark-blue devils exactly—say, light-blue gnomes! I hate being pushed about, and things have pushed me about, rather. It's that, I think. There's been too much—of everything—somehow
——

"You see, my social life just now is divided into three parts, like all Gaul, and as my business opportunities—Midas forgive them!—have all come out of my social contacts, I'll have to begin with them. Maltby's the golden key to the first part; Mr. Heywood Sampson, the great old-school publisher and editor-author, is the iron key to the second; and chance—our settling down here on the fringes of Greenwich Village—is the skeleton key to the third.

"I seem to be getting all Gaul mixed up with Bluebeard's closets and things, but I'll try to straighten my kinky metaphors out for you, Jimmy, if it takes me all night. But I assume you're more or less up to date on me, since I find you all most brazenly hand me round, and since I wrote Phil—and got severely scolded in return; deserved it, too—all about Maltby's patiently snubbing me as a starving author and impatiently rushing me as a possible member for his Emancipated Order of Æsthetic May-Flies—I call it his, for he certainly thinks of it that way. Now—Maltby and I have not precisely quarreled, but the north wind doth blow and we've already had snow enough to cool his enthusiasm. The whole thing's unpleasant; but I've learned something. Result—my occasional flutterings among the Æsthetic May-Flies grow beautifully less. They'd cease altogether if I hadn't made friends—to call them that—with a May-Fly or two.

"One of them's the novelist, Clifton Young, a May-Fly at heart—but there's a strain of Honeybee in his blood somewhere. It's an unhappy combination—all the talents and few of the virtues; but I like him in spite of himself. For one thing, he doesn't pose; and he can *write!* He's a lost soul, though—thinks life is a tragic farce. Almost all the May-Flies try to think that; it's a sort of guaranty of the last sophistication; but it's genuine with Clifton, he must have been born thinking it. He doesn't ask for sympathy, either; if he did, I couldn't pity him—and get jeered at wittily for my pains!

"Then there's Mona Leslie, who might have been a true Honeybee if everybody belonging to her hadn't died too soon, leaving her hopeless numbers of millions. Mona, for some reason, has taken a passing fancy to me; all her fancies pass. She sings like an angel, and might have made a career—if it had seemed worth while. It never has. Nothing has, but vivid sensation—from ascetic religion to sloppy love; and, at thirty, she's exhausted the whole show. So she spends her time now in a mad duel with boredom. Poor woman! Luckily the fairies gave her a selfishly kind heart, and there's a piece of it left, I think. It may even win the duel for her in the end. More and more she's the reckless patron of all the arts, almost smothering ennui under her benefactions. She'd smother poor me, too, if I'd let her; but I can't; I'm either not brazen enough or not Christian enough to let her patronize me for her own amusement. And that's her one new sensation for the last three years!

"Still, I've one thing to thank her for, and I wish I could feel grateful. She introduced me, at one of her Arabian-Nightish *soirées musicales*, to Hadow Bury, proprietor of *Whim*, the smarty-party weekly review. In two years it's made a sky-rocketing success, by printing the harum-scarumest possible comment on all the social and æsthetic fads and freaks of the day—just the iris froth of the wave, that and that only. Hadow's a big, black, bleak man-mountain. You'd take him for an undertaker by special appointment to coal-beef-and-iron kings. You'd never suspect him of having capitalized the Frivolous. But he's found it means bagfuls of reelers for him, so he takes it seriously. He's after the *goods*. He gets and delivers the goods, no matter what they cost. He's ready to pay any price now for a new brand of cerebral champagne.

"Well, I didn't know *what* he was when Mona casually dropped me beside him, but he loomed so big and black and bleak he frightened me—till my thoughts chattered! I rattled on—like this, Jimmy—only not because I wanted to, but because having madly started I didn't know how to stop. I made a fool of myself—utter; with the result that he detected a slightly different flavor in my folly, a possibly novel *bouquet*—let's call it the 'Birch Street *bouquet*.' At any rate, he finally silenced me to ask whether I could write as I talked, and I said I hoped not; and he looked bleaker and blacker than ever and said that was the worst of it, so few amusing young women could! It seemed to be one of the more annoying laws of Nature.

"The upshot was, I found out all about him and his ambitions for *Whim;* and the fantastic upshot of *that* was, I'm now doing a nonsense column a week for him—have been for the past five—and getting fifty dollars a week for my nonsense, too! I sign the thing "Dax"—a signature invented by shutting both eyes and punching at my typewriter three times, just to see what would happen. "Dax" happened, and I'm to be allowed to burble on as him—I think Dax is a him—for ten weeks; then, if my stuff goes, catches on, gets over—I'm to have a year's contract. And farewell to double-room-and-alcove for aye! Else, farewell *Whim!* So it *must* get over—I'm determined! I stick at nothing. I even test my burble on poor Sister every week before sending it in. If she smiles sadly, twice, I seal up the envelope and breathe again.

"That's my bird in the hand, Jimmy—a sort of crazily screaming jay—but I mustn't let it escape.

"There's another bird, though. A real bluebird, still in the bush—and oh, so shy! And he lures me into the second and beautifulest part of all Gaul——

"It's no use, I'm dished! Sister says no one ever wrote or read such a monstrous letter, and commands me to stop now and go to bed. There's a look in her eye—she means it. Good-night and good luck—I'll tell you about my other two parts of Gaul as soon as I can, unless you wire me—collect—'Cut it out!' Or unless you run down—you never have—and learn of them that way. Why not—*soon?*"

VII

Jimmy Kane took the hint, or obeyed the open request, in Susan's letter and went down to New York for the week-end; and on the following Monday Miss Goucher wrote her first considerable letter to me. It was a long letter, for her, written—recopied, I fancy—in precise script, though it would have been a mere note for Susan.

My dear Mr. Hunt: I promised to let you know from time to time the exact truth about our experiment. It is already a success financially. Susan is now earning from sixty to seventy dollars a week, with every prospect of earning substantially more in the near future. Her satirical paragraphs and verses in "Whim" are quoted and copied everywhere. They do not seem to me quite the Susan I love, but then, I am not a clever person; and it is undeniable that "Who is Dax?" is being asked now on every hand. If this interest continues, I am assured it can only mean fame and fortune. I am very proud of Susan, as you must be.

But, Mr. Hunt, there is another side to my picture. In alluding to it I feel a sense of guilt toward Susan; I know she would not wish me to do so. Yet I feel that I must. If I may say so to you, Susan has quickened in me many starved affections, and they all center in her. In this, may I not feel without offense that we are of one mind?

If I had Susan's pen I could tell you more clearly why I am troubled. I lack her gift, which is also yours, of expressing what I feel is going on secretly in another's mind. Mr. Phar and a Mr. Young, a writer, have been giving Susan some cause for annoyance lately; but that is not it. Mr. Hunt, she is deeply unhappy. She would deny it, even to you or me; but it is true.

My mind is too commonplace for this task. If my attempt to explain sounds crude, please forgive it and supply what is beyond me.

I can only say now that when I once told you Susan could stand alone, I was mistaken. In a sense she can. If her health does not give way, life will never beat her down. But—there are the needs of women, older than art. They tear at us, Mr. Hunt; at least while we are young. I could not say this to you, but I must manage somehow to write it. I do not refer to passion, taken by itself. I am old enough to be shocked, Mr. Hunt, to find that many brilliant women to-day have advanced beyond certain boundaries so long established. You will understand.

A woman's need is greater than passion, greater even than motherhood. It is so hard for me to express it. But she can only find rest when these things are not lived separately; when, with many other elements, they build up a living whole—what we call a *home*. How badly I put it; for I feel so much more than the conventional sentiments. Will you understand me at all if I say that Susan is homesick—for a home she has never known and may never be privileged to know? With all her insight I think she doesn't realize this yet; but I once suffered acutely in this way, and it perhaps gives me the right to speak. Of course I may be quite wrong. I am more often wrong than right.

I venture to inclose a copy of some lines, rescued last week from our scrap-basket. I'm not a critic, but am I wrong in thinking it would have been a pity to burn them? As they are not in free verse, which I do not appreciate as I should, they affected me very much; and I feel they will tell you, far more than my letter, why I am a little worried about Susan.

Young Mr. Kane informed me, when he was here on Sunday, that you and Professor Farmer are well. He seems a nice boy, though still a little crude perhaps; nothing offensive. I am confined to the room to-day by a slight cold of no consequence; I hope I may not pass it on to Susan. Kindly give my love to Sonia, if you should see her, and to little Ivan. I trust the new housekeeper I obtained for you is reasonably efficient, and that Tumps is not proving too great a burden. I am,

Respectfully yours,

MALVINA GOUCHER.

The inclosed "copy of some lines" affected me quite as much as they had Miss Goucher, and it was inconceivable to me that Susan, having written them, could have tossed them away. As a matter of fact she had not. Like Calais in the queen's heart, they were engraven in her own. They were too deeply hers; she had meant merely to hide them from the world; and it is even now with a curious reluctance that I give them to you here. The lines bore no title, but I have ventured, with Susan's consent, to call them

MENDICANTS

We who are poets beg the gods
Shamelessly for immortal bliss,
While the derisive years with rods
Flay us; nor silvery Artemis
Hearkens, nor Cypris bends, nor she,

The grave Athena with gray eyes.
Were they not heartless would they be
Deaf to the hunger of our cries?

We are the starving ones of clay,
Famished for deathless love, no less.

Oh, but the gods are far and fey,
Shut in their azure palaces!

Oh, but the gods are far and fey,
Blind to the rags of our distress!

We pine on crumbs they flick away;
Brief beauty, and much weariness.

And the night I read these lines a telegram came to me from New York, signed "Lucette Arthur," announcing that Gertrude was suddenly dead... .

THE FIFTH CHAPTER

I

I AM an essayist, if anything, trying to tell Susan's story, and telling it badly, I fear, for lack of narrative skill. So it is with no desire to prolong cheaply a possible point of suspense that I must double back now before I can go forward. My personal interest centers so entirely in Susan herself, in the special qualities of her mind and heart, that I have failed to bring in certain stiff facts—essential, alas, to all further progress. A practiced novelist, handling this purely biographic material—such a man as Clifton Young— would quietly have "planted" these facts in their due order, thus escaping my present embarrassment. But indeed I am approaching a cruel crisis in Susan's life and in the lives of those dearest to her; a period of sheer circumstantial fatality; one of those incursions of mad coincidence, of crass melodrama, which—with a brutal, ironic, improbability, as if stage-managed by an anarchistic fiend of the pit—bursts through some fine-spun, geometrical web of days, leaving chaos behind; and I am ill-equipped to deal with this chance destruction, this haphazard wantonness.

Even could I merely have observed it from the outside, with æsthetic detachment, it would baffle me now; I should find it too crude for art, too arbitrary. It is not in my line. But God knows the victim of what seems an insane break in Nature is in no mood for art; he can do little more than cry out or foolishly rail!

———

Jimmy returned from his excursion to New York on the Sunday evening preceding Miss Goucher's letter. She must have been at work on it the next evening when Phil brought him to dine with me. It was our deliberate purpose to draw him out, track his shy impressions of Susan and of her new life in her new world. But it was hard going at first; for ten minutes or so we bagged little but the ordinary Jimmyesque *clichés*. He had had a great time, *etc.*, *etc.* . . .

Matters improved with the roast. It then appeared that he had lightly explored with Susan the two-thirds of Gaul omitted from her letter. He had called with her on Heywood Sampson, and fathomed Susan's allusion to the shy bluebird. Mr. Sampson, he assured us, was a fine old boy—strong for Susan too! He'd read a lot of her poems and things and was going to bring out the poems for her right away. But the bluebird in the bush had to do with a pet scheme of his for a weekly critical review of a different stamp from Hadow Bury's *Whim*. Solider, Jimmy imagined; safe and sane—the real thing! If Mr. Sampson should decide to launch it—he was still hesitating over the business outlook—Susan was to find a place on his staff.

Mr. Sampson, Jimmy opined, had the right idea about things in general. He didn't like Susan's quick stuff in *Whim;* thought it would cheapen her if she kept at it too long. And Mr. Sampson didn't approve of Susan's remaining third of Gaul, either—her Greenwich Village friends. Not much wonder, Jimmy added; Susan had trotted him round to three or four studios and places, and they were a funny job lot. Too many foreigners among them for him; they talked too much; and they pawed. But some nice young people, too. Most of them were young—and not stuck up. Friendly. Sort of alive—interested in everything—except, maybe, being respectable. Their jokes, come to think of it, were all about being respectable—kidding everyday people who weren't up to the latest ideas. There was a lot of jabber one place about the "Œdipus Complex," for example, but he didn't connect at all. He had his own idea— surely, not of the latest—that a lot of the villagers might feel differently when they began to make good and started their bank accounts. But Susan was on to them, anyway, far more than they were on to her! She liked them, though—in spite of Mr. Sampson; didn't fall for their craziest ways or notions of course, but was keen about their happy-go-lucky side—their pep! Besides, they weren't all alike, naturally. Take the pick of them, the ones that did things instead of posing round and dressing the part, and Jimmy could see they might be there. At least, they were on their way—like Susan.

This was all very well, so far as it went; but we had felt, Phil and I, a dumb undercurrent struggling to press upward into speech, and after dinner before the fire, we did our best to help Jimmy free its course. Gradually it became apparent; it rather trickled than gushed forth. Jimmy was bothered, more than bothered; there was something, perhaps there were several things, on his mind. We did not press him, using subtler methods, biding our time; and little by little Jimmy oozed toward the full revelation of an uneasy spirit.

"Did you see Mr. Phar?" Phil asked.

"No," said Jimmy, his forehead knotting darkly; "I guess it's a good thing I didn't too!"

"Why?"

"Well, that letter I had from Susan—the one I showed you, Mr. Hunt—

mentioned some unpleasantness with Mr. Phar; and all Saturday afternoon while she was trotting me round, I could see she'd been worrying to herself a good deal."

"Worrying?"

"Yes. Whenever she thought I wasn't paying attention her face would go—sort of dead tired and sad—all used up. I can't describe it. And one or two remarks she dropped didn't sound as happy as she meant them to. Then, Sunday morning, she had to get some work done, so I took Miss Goucher to church. I'm supposed to be a Catholic, you know; but I guess I'm not much of anything. I'd just as soon go to one kind of church as another, if the music's good. Anyway, it was a nice morning and Miss Goucher thought I'd like to see the Fifth Avenue parade; so we walked up to some silk-stocking church above Thirty-fourth Street, where they have a dandy choir; and back again afterwards. I stayed at the Brevoort, down near them, you know; and Miss Goucher certainly is a peach. We got along fine. And I found out from her how Mr. Phar's been acting. He's a bad actor, all right. I'm just as glad I didn't run into him. I might have done something foolish."

"What, for instance?" I suggested.

"Well," muttered Jimmy, "there's some things I can't stand. I might have punched his head."

Phil whistled softly.

"He's not what I call a white man," explained Jimmy, dogged and slow, as if to justify his vision of assault. "He's a painted pup."

"Come, Jimmy!" Phil commanded. "Out with it! Hunt and I know he's been annoying Susan, but that's all we know. I supposed he might have been pressing his attentions too publicly. If it's more than that——"

There was an unusual sternness in Phil's eye. Jimmy appealed from it to mine, but in vain.

"Look here, Mr. Hunt," he blurted, "Susan's all right, of course—and so's Miss Goucher! They've got their eyes open. And maybe it's not up to me to say anything. But if I was in your place, I'd feel like giving two or three people down there a piece of my mind! Susan wouldn't thank me for saying so, I guess; she's modern—she likes to be let alone. Why, she laughed at me more than once for getting sort of hot! And I know I've a bunch to learn yet. But all the same," he pounded on, "I do know this: It was a dirty trick of Mr. Phar's not to stand up for Susan!"

"Not stand up for her! What do you mean?" Phil almost barked.

"Jimmy means, Phil," I explained, "that some rather vague rumors began not along ago to spread through Maltby's crowd in regard to Susan—as to why she found it advisable to leave New Haven. Many of his friends know me, of course—or know Gertrude; know all about us, at any rate. It's not very remarkable, then, that Susan's appearance in New York—and so far as Maltby's May-Flies know, in some sense under his wing—has set tongues wagging. I was afraid of it; but I know Maltby's set well enough to know that to-day's rumor, unless it's pretty sharply spiced, is soon forgotten. To-morrow's is so much fresher, you see. The best thing for innocent victims to do is to keep very still. And then, I confess, it seemed to me unlikely that Maltby would permit anything of the sort to go too far."

I saw that Jimmy was following my exposition with the most painful surprise. Phil grunted disgustedly as I ended.

"I don't pretend to much knowledge of that world," he said deliberately, "but common sense tells me Maltby Phar might think it to his advantage to fan the flame instead of stamping it out. I may be unfair to him, but I'm even capable of supposing he touched it off in the first place."

"No, Phil," I objected, "he wouldn't have done that. But you seem to be right about his failing to stamp out the sparks. That's what you meant by his not standing up for Susan, isn't it, Jimmy?"

The boy's face was a study in unhappy perplexity. "I guess I'm like Professor Farmer!" he exclaimed. "I'm not on to people who act like that. But, Mr. Hunt, you're dead wrong—excuse me, sir!"

"Go on, Jimmy."

"Well, I mean—you spoke of vague rumors, didn't you? They're not vague. I guess Susan hasn't wanted to upset you. Miss Goucher told me all about it, and she wouldn't have done it, would she, if she hadn't hoped I'd bring it straight back to you? I guess she promised Susan not to tell you, so she told me. That's the only way I can figure it," concluded Jimmy.

Phil was grim now. "Give us your facts, Jimmy—all of them."

"Yes, sir. There's a Mr. Young; he writes things. He's clever. They're all clever down there. Well, Mr. Young's dead gone on Susan; but then, he's the kind that's always dead gone on somebody. It's women with him, you see, sir. Susan understands. It don't seem right she should, somehow; but—well, Susan's always been different from most girls. At least, I don't know many girls——"

"Never mind that," prompted Phil.

"No, sir. Talking about things like this always rattles me. I can't help it. They kind of stick in my throat. Well, Mr. Young don't want to marry anybody, but he's been making love to Susan—trying to. He had the wrong idea about her, you see; and Susan saw that, too—saw he thought she was playing him for a poor fish. So—her way—out she comes with it to him, flat. And he gets sore and comes back at her with what he'd heard." Jimmy's handkerchief was pulled out at this point; he mopped his brow. "It don't feel right even to speak of lies like this about—any decent girl," he mumbled.

"No," Phil agreed, "it doesn't. But there's nothing for it now. Get it said and done with!"

"Yes, sir. Mr. Young told Susan he wasn't a fool; he knew she'd been—what she shouldn't be—up here."

"Hunt's mistress, you mean?" snapped Phil.

"Yes, sir," whispered Jimmy, his face purple with agonized shame.

"And then?"

"Susan's a wonder," continued Jimmy, taking heart now his Rubicon lay behind him. "Most girls would have thrown a fit. But Susan seems to feel there's a lot to Mr. Young, in spite of all that rotten side of him. She saw right away he believed that about her, and so he couldn't be blamed much for getting sore. Anyway, he must have a white streak in him, for Susan talked to him—the way she can—and he soon realized he was in all wrong. But the *reason* he was in wrong—that's what finished things between Susan and Mr. Phar! I guess you won't blame me for wanting to punch his head."

"No," I threw in; "I shouldn't blame you for wanting to punch mine!"

"Give us the reason, Jimmy," insisted Phil, his grave, Indianlike face stiffened to a mask.

"Mr. Young didn't get that lie from Mr. Phar," admitted Jimmy, "but he did take it straight to him, when he first heard it, thinking he ought to know."

"Good God!" I cried. "Do you mean to tell me Maltby confirmed it?"

"Well," Jimmy hesitated, "it seems he didn't come right out and say, 'Yes, that's so!' But he didn't deny it either. Sort of shrugged his shoulders, I guess, and did things with his eyebrows. Whatever he did or didn't, Mr. Young got it fastened in his head then and there that Susan——"

But this time Jimmy simply couldn't go on; the words stuck in his throat and stayed there.

Phil's eyes met mine and held them, long.

"Hunt," he said quietly at last, "it's a fortunate thing for Susan—for all of us—that I have long years of self-discipline behind me. Otherwise, I should go to New York to-morrow, find Maltby Phar, and shoot him."

Jimmy's blue eyes flashed toward Phil a startled but admiring glance.

"What do *you* propose to do, Hunt?" demanded Phil.

"Think," I replied; "think hard—think things through. Wednesday morning I shall leave for New York."

II

My prophecy was correct. Wednesday, at 12.03 A. M., I left for New York, in response to the shocking telegram from Lucette. I arrived at Gertrude's address, an august apartment house on upper Park Avenue, a little before half-past two, dismissed my taxi at the door, noting as I did so a second taxi standing at the curb just ahead of my own, and was admitted to the dignified public entrance-hall with surprising promptness, considering the hour, by the mature buttons on duty. Buttons was a man nearing sixty, at a guess, of markedly Irish traits, and he was unexpectedly wide-awake. When I gave him my name, and briefly stated the reason for my untimely arrival, his deep-set eyes glittered with excited curiosity, while he drew down deep parallels about his mouth in a grimacing attempt at deepest sympathy and profoundest respect. I questioned him. Several persons had gone up to Mrs. Hunt's apartment, he solemnly informed me, during the past two hours. He believed the police were in charge.

"Police?" I exclaimed, incredulous.

He believed so. He would say no more.

"Take me up at once!" I snapped at him. "Surely there's a mistake. There can be no reason for police interference."

His eyes glittered more shrewdly, the drawn parallels deepened yet further as he shot back the elevator door... .

It was unmistakably a police officer who admitted me for the first and last time to Gertrude's apartment. On hearing my name he nodded, then closed the door firmly in the face of Buttons, who had lingered.

"He's been warned not to tip off the press," said the police officer, "but it's just as well to be cautious."

"The press? What do you mean?" I asked, still incredulous. "Is it a New York custom for police to enter a house of mourning?" I was aware as I spoke of repressed voices murmuring in an adjoining room.

"I'm Sergeant Conlon," he answered, "in charge here till the coroner comes. He should make it by seven. If you're the poor lady's husband, you'll be needed. I'll have to detain you."

As he ended, the murmur ended in the adjoining room, and Lucette walked out from it. She was wearing an evening gown—blue, I think—cut very low, and a twinkling ornament of some kind in her hair. She has fine shoulders and beautiful hair. But her face had gone haggard; she had been weeping; she looked ten years older than when I had last seen her.

"What is it? What is it?" I demanded of her. "I know nothing but your telegram!"

"Looks like murder," said Sergeant Conlon, dry and short. "I wouldn't talk much if I was you, not till the coroner gets here. I'm bound to make notes of what you say."

For the merest hundredth of a second my scalp prickled, my flesh went cold; but sheer incredulity was still strong upon me; it beat back the horror. It was simply not real, all this.

"At least," I managed, "give me facts—something!"

Then unreality deepened to utter nightmare, passing all bounds of reason. Lucette spoke, and life turned for me to sheer prattling madness; to a gibbering grotesque!

"*Susan* did it!" she cried, her voice going high and strident, slipping from all control. "I know it! I know she did! I know it! Wasn't she with her? *Alone* with her? Who else could have done it! Who else! *It's in her blood!*"

Well, of course, when a woman you have played tag with in her girlhood goes mad before you, raves——

How could one act or answer? Then, too, she had vanished; or had I really seen her in the flesh at all? Really heard her voice, crying out.... .

Sergeant Conlon's voice came next; short, dry, businesslike. It compelled belief.

"I've a question or two for you, Mr. Hunt. This way; steady!"

I felt his hand under my elbow.

Gertrude's apartment was evidently a very large one; I had vaguely the sensation of passing down a long hall with an ell in it, and so into a small, simply furnished, but tasteful room—the sitting-room for her maids, as I later decided. Sergeant Conlon shut the door and locked it.

"That's not to keep you in," he said; "it's to keep others out. Sit down, Mr. Hunt. Smoke somethin'. Let's make ourselves comfortable."

The click of the shot bolt in the lock had suddenly, I found, restored my power of coördination. It had been like the sharp handclap which brings home a hypnotized subject to reason and reality. I was now, in a moment, not merely myself again, but peculiarly alert and steady of nerve, and I gave matter-of-fact assent to Sergeant Conlon's suggestions. I lit a cigarette and took possession of the most comfortable chair. Conlon remained standing. He had refused my cigarettes, but he now lighted a long, roughly rolled cigar.

"I get these from a fellow over on First Avenue," he explained affably. "He makes them up himself. They're not so bad."

I attempted a smile and achieved a classic reaction. "They look—efficient," I said. "And now, sergeant, what has happened here? If I've seemed dazed for the past ten minutes, it's little wonder. I hurried down in response to a telegram saying my wife... . You know we've lived apart for years?" He grunted assent... . "Saying she had died suddenly. And I walk in, unprepared, on people who seem to me to be acting parts in a crook melodrama of the crudest type. Be kind enough to tell me what it's all about!"

Sergeant Conlon's gray-blue eyes fixed me as I spoke. He was a big, thickset man, nearing middle age; the bruiser build, physically; but with a solidly intelligent-looking head and trustworthy eyes.

"I'll do that, Mr. Hunt," he assented. "I got Mrs. Arthur to send you that telegram; but I'll say to you first-off, now you've come, I don't suspect you of bein' mixed up in this affair. When I shot that 'It looks like murder' at you, I did it deliberate. Well—that's neither here nor there; but I always go by the way things strike me. I have to." He twirled a light chair round to face me and seated himself, leaning a little forward, his great stubby hands propped on his square knees. "Here's the facts, then—what we know are facts: It seems, Mrs. Arthur—she's been visitin' Mrs. Hunt for two weeks past—she went to the opera to-night with a Mr. Phar; she says you know him well." I nodded. "Durin' the last act of the opera they were located by somebody in the office down there and called out to the 'phone—an accident to Mrs. Hunt—see?—important." Again I nodded. "Mrs. Arthur answered the 'phone, and Doctor Askew—he lives in this house, but he's Mrs. Hunt's reg'lar doctor—well, he was on the wire. He just told her to hurry back as fast as she could—and she and Mr. Phar hopped a taxi and beat it up here. Doctor Askew met them at the door, and a couple of scared maids. The doc's a good man—big rep—one of the best. He'd taken charge and sent on the quiet for us. I got here with a couple of my men soon after Mrs. Arthur——"

"But——"

"I know, *I* know!" he stopped me off. "But I want you to get it all straight. Mrs. Hunt, sir, was killed—somehow—with a long, sharp-pointed brass paper-knife—a reg'lar weapon. I've examined it. And someone drove that thing—and it must'a' took some force, believe *me!*—right through her left eye up to the handle—a full inch of metal plumb into her brain!"

I tried to believe him as he said this; as, seeing my blankness, he repeated it for me in other words. For the moment it was impossible. This sort of thing must have happened in the world, of course—at other times, to other people. But not now, not to Gertrude. Certainly not to Gertrude; a woman so aloof, so exquisite, self-sheltered, class-sheltered, not merely from ugliness, from the harsh and brutal, but from everything in life even verging toward vulgarity, coarse passion, the unrestrained... .

"That's the way she was killed, Mr. Hunt—no mistake. Now—who did it —and why? That's the point."

At my elbow was a table with a reading-lamp on it, a desk-set, a work-basket, belonging, I suppose, to one of the maids, and some magazines. One magazine lay just before me—*The Reel World*—a by-product of the great moving-picture industry. I had been staring—unseeingly, at first—at a flamboyant advertisement on its cover that clamored for my attention, until now, with Conlon's question, it momentarily gained it. The release of a magnificent Superfeature was announced—in no quavering terms. "The Sins of the Fathers" it shrieked at me! "All the thrilling human suspense"; "virile, compelling"; "brimming over with the kind of action and adventure your audiences crave"; "it delivers the wallop!"

Instantly, with a new force, Lucette's outcry swept back upon me. "Susan did it! Wasn't she with her? Alone with her? *It's in her blood!*"

And at once every faculty of my spirit leaped, with an almost supernatural acuteness, to the defense of the one being on earth I wholly loved. All sense of unreality vanished. Now for it—since it must be so! Susan and I, if need be, against the world!

"Go on, sergeant. What's your theory?"

"Never mind my theory! I'd like to get *yours* first—when I've given you all I know."

"All right, then! But be quick about it!"

"Easy, Mr. Hunt! It's not as simple as all that. Well, here it is: Somewhere round ten o'clock, a Miss Blake—a magazine-writer livin' on West 10th

Street—your ward, I understand——"

"Yes."

"Well, she calls here, alone, and asks for Mrs. Arthur. Mrs. Hunt's personal maid—English; she's no chicken either—she lets her in and says Mrs. Arthur isn't here—see—and didn't the door boy tell her so? Yes, says Miss Blake, but she'll wait for her anyway. The maid—name of Iffley—says she thought that was queer, so she put it to Miss Blake that maybe she'd better ask Mrs. Hunt. Oh, says Miss Blake, I thought she was out, too. But it seems Mrs. Hunt was in her private sittin' room; she'd had a slight bilious attack, and she'd got her corsets off and somethin' loose on, the way women do, and was all set for a good read. So the maid didn't think she could see Miss Blake, but anyhow she took in her card—and Mrs. Hunt decided to see her. That maid Iffley's an intelligent woman; she's all broke up, but she ain't hysterical like the cook—who didn't see nothin' anyway. The parlor maid was havin' her night off, but she's back now, too, and I've got 'em all safe where they can't talk to outsiders, yet. I don't want this thing in the papers to-morrow, not if I can help it; I want to keep it dark till I know better where I'm gettin' off."

"Right!" I approved. "What's the maid's story?"

"Well, I've questioned her pretty close, and I think it's to be relied on. It hits me that way. Mrs. Hunt, she says, when she took in Miss Blake's card, was lyin' on her couch in a long trailin' thing—what ladies call a negligee."

"Yes?"

"And she was cuttin' the pages of some new book with that paper-knife I spoke of."

"Yes?"

"And her dog, a runty little French bull, was sleepin' on the rug beside the couch."

"What does that matter?"

"More'n you'd think! He's got a broken leg—provin' some kind of a struggle must'a'——"

"I see. Go on!"

"Well, Mrs. Hunt, the maid says, looked at Miss Blake's card a minute and didn't say anythin' special, but seemed kind of puzzled. Her only words was, 'Yes, I ought to see her.' So the maid goes for Miss Blake and shows her to the door, which she'd left ajar, and taps on it for her, and Mrs. Hunt calls to come in. So Miss Blake goes in and shuts the door after her, and the maid comes back to this room we're in now—it's round the corner of the hall from

Mrs. Hunt's room—see? But she don't much more than get here—just to the door—when she hears the dog give a screech and then go on cryin' like as if he'd been hurt. The cook was in here, too, and she claims she heard a kind of jarrin' sound, like somethin' heavy fallin'; but Iffley—that's the maid, they call her Iffley—says all she noticed was the dog. Anyway she listened a second, then she started for Mrs. Hunt's room—and the cook, bein' nervous, locked herself in here and sat with her eyes tight shut and her fingers in her ears. Fact. She says she can't bear nothin' disagreeable. Too bad about her, ain't it!"

"And then?" I protested, crossly.

"Well, Mr. Hunt, when the Iffley woman turned the hall corner—the door of your poor wife's room opens, and Miss Blake walks out. She had the paper-knife in her right hand, and the knife and her hand was all bloody; her left hand was bloody too; and we've found blood on her clothes since. There was a queer, vacant look about her—that's what the maid says. She didn't seem to see anythin'. Naturally, the maid was scared stiff—but she got one look in at the door anyway—that was enough for her. She was too scared even to yell, she says. Paralyzed—she just flopped back against the wall half faintin'.

"And then she noticed somethin' that kind of brought her to again! Mr. Hunt, that young woman, Miss Blake—she'd gone quiet as you please and curled herself down on a rug in the hallway—that bloody knife in her hand—and she was either dead or fast asleep! And then the doorbell rang, and the Iffley woman says she don't know how she got past that prostrate figger on the rug—her very words, Mr. Hunt—that prostrate figger on the rug—but she did, somehow; got to the door. And when she opened it, there was Doctor Askew and the elevator man. And then she passed out. And I must say I don't much blame her, considerin'.."

"Where's Miss Blake now?" I sharply demanded.

"She's still fast asleep, Mr. Hunt—to call it that. The doc says it's— somethin' or other—due to shock. Same as a trance."

I started up. "Where is Doctor Askew? I must see him at once!"

"We've laid Miss Blake on the bed in Mrs. Arthur's room. He's observin' her."

"Take me there."

"I'll do that, Mr. Hunt. But I'll ask you a question first—straight. Is there any doubt in your mind that that young lady—your ward—killed Mrs. Hunt?"

I met his gray-blue glance directly, pausing a moment before I spoke. "Sergeant Conlon," I replied, while a meteor-shower of speculation shot through me with the rapidity of light waves, "there is no doubt whatever in my mind: Miss Blake could not—and so did not—kill my wife."

"Who did, then?"

"Wait! Let me first ask you a question, sergeant: Who sent for Doctor Askew?"

"That's the queerest part of it; Miss Blake did."

"Ah! *How?*"

"There's a 'phone in Mrs. Hunt's sittin' room. Miss Blake called the house operator, gave her name and location, and said not to waste a moment—to send up a doctor double-quick!"

"Is that *all* she said?"

"No. The operator tells me she said Mrs. Hunt had had a terrible accident and was dyin'."

"You're certain she said 'accident'?"

"The girl who was at the switchboard—name of Joyce—she's sure of it."

I smiled, grimly enough. "Then that is exactly what occurred, sergeant—a terrible accident; hideous. Your question is answered. Nobody killed Mrs. Hunt—unless you are so thoughtless or blasphemous as to call it an act of God!"

"Oh, come on now!" he objected, shaking his head, but not, I felt, with entire conviction. "No," he continued stubbornly, "I been turnin' that over too. But there's no way an accident like that could 'a' happened. It's not possible!"

"Fortunately," I insisted, "nothing else is possible! Are you asking me to believe that a young, sensitive girl, with an extraordinary imaginative sympathy for others—a girl of brains and character, as all her friends have reason to know—asking me to believe that she walked coolly into my wife's room this evening, rushed savagely upon her, wrested a paper knife from her hand, and then found the sheer brute strength of will and arm to thrust it through her eye deep into her brain? Are you further asking me to believe that having done this frightful thing she kept her wits about her, telephoned at once for a doctor—being careful to call her crime an accident—and so passed at once into a trance of some kind and walked from the room with the bloody knife in her hand? What possible motive could be strong enough to drive such a girl to such a deed?"

"Jealousy," said Sergeant Conlon. "She wanted *you*—and your wife stood in her way. That's what I get from Mrs. Arthur."

"I see. But the three or four persons who know Miss Blake and me best will tell you how absurd that is, and you'll find their reasons for thinking so are very convincing. Is Mr. Phar still about?"

"He is. I've detained him."

"What does he think of Mrs. Arthur's nonsensical theory?"

"He's got a theory of his own," said Conlon; "and it happens to be the same as mine."

"Well?"

"Mr. Phar says Miss Blake's own father went mad—all of a sudden; cut some fancy woman's throat, and his own after! He thinks history's repeated itself, that's all. So do I. Only a crazy woman could 'a' done this—just this way. A strong man in his senses couldn't 'a' drove that paper-knife home like that! But when a person goes mad, sir, all rules are off. I seen too many cases. Things happen you can't account for. Take the matter of that dog now—his broken leg, eh? What are you to make of that? And take this queer state she's in. There's no doubt in my mind, Mr. Hunt—the poor girl's gone crazy, somehow. You nor me can't tell how nor why. But it's back of all this—that's sure."

Throughout all this coarse nightmare, this insane break in Nature, as I have called it and must always regard it, let me at least be honest. As Conlon spoke, for the tiniest fraction of a second a desolating fear darted through me, searing every nerve with white-hot pain. Was it true? Might it not conceivably be true? But this single lightning-thrust of doubt passed as it came. No, not as it came, for it blotted all clearness, all power of voluntary thought from my mind; but it left behind it a singular intensity of vision. Even as the lightning-pang vanished, and while time yet stood still, a moving picture that amounted to hallucination began to play itself out before me. It was like

> *. . . that last*
> *Wild pageant of the accumulated past*
> *That clangs and flashes for a drowning man.*

I saw Susan shutting the door of a delicately panelled Georgian room, and every detail of this room—a room I had never entered in the flesh—was distinct to me. Given time, I could have inventoried its every object. I saw Gertrude lying on—not a couch, as Conlon had called it—on a *chaise-longue*, a book with a vivid green cover in her left hand, a bronze paper knife with a thin, pointed blade in her right. She was holding it with the knuckles of her hand upward, her thumb along the handle, and the point of the blade turned to her left, across and a little in toward her body. She was wearing a very lovely *négligé*, a true creation, all in filmy tones of old gold. On a low-set tip-table at her elbow stood a reading-lamp, and a small coal-black French bull lay asleep on a superb Chinese rug—lay close in by the *chaise-longue*, just where a dropped hand might caress him. A light silky-looking coverlet of a peculiar dull blue, harmonizing with certain tones of the rug, was thrown across Gertrude's feet.

As Susan shut the door, the little bull pricked up his bat-ears and started to uncurl, but Gertrude must have spoken to him, for he settled back again—not, however, to sleep. It was all a picture; I heard no sounds. Then I saw Gertrude put down her book on the table and swing her feet from the *chaise-longue*, meaning to rise and greet Susan. But, as she attempted to stand up, the light coverlet entangled her feet and tripped her; she lost her balance, tried with a violent, awkward lurch of her whole body to recover herself, and stamped rather than stepped full on the dog's forepaws. He writhed, springing up between her feet—the whole grotesque catastrophe was, in effect, a single, fatal gesture!—and Gertrude, throwing her hands instinctively before her face, fell heavily forward, the length of her body, prone. I saw Susan rush toward her—— And the psychic reel flickered out, blanked... . I needed to see no more.

"Don't you agree with me, Mr. Hunt?" Conlon was asking.

"No," I said bluntly. "No madwoman would have summoned a doctor. Miss Blake called it a terrible accident. It was. Her present state is due to the horror of it. When she wakes, it will all be explained. Now take me to her."

Conlon's gray-blue glance fixed me once more. "All right," he grunted, "I've no objections. But I'd 'a' thought your first wish would 'a' been to see your wife."

"No," I replied. "Mrs. Hunt separated from me years ago, for reasons of her own. I bore her no ill will; in a sense, I respected her, admired her.

Understand me, Sergeant Conlon. There was nothing vulgar in her life, and her death in this stupid way—oh, it's indecent, damnable! A cheap outrage! I could do nothing for her living, and can do nothing now. But I prefer to remember her as she was. *She* would prefer it, too."

"Come on, then," said Conlon; pretty gruffly, I thought.

He unlocked the door.

III

It was a singular thing, but so convincing had my vision been to me that I felt no immediate desire to verify the details of its setting by an examination of Gertrude's boudoir. It had come to me bearing its own credentials, its own satisfying accent of truth. One question did, however, fasten upon me, as I followed Conlon's bulky form, down the hall to Lucette's bedroom. Whence had this vision, this psychic reel come to me? What was its source? How could the mere fact of it—clearing, as it did, at least, all perplexities from my own mind—have occurred? For the moment I could find no answer; the mystery had happened, had worked, but remained a mystery.

Like most men in this modern world I had taken a vague, mild interest in psychical research, reading more or less casually, and with customary suspension of judgment, anything of the sort that came in my way. I had a bowing acquaintance with its rapidly growing literature; little more; and until now I had had no striking psychical experiences of my own, and had never, as it happened, attended a séance of any kind, either popular or scientific. Nevertheless, I could—to put it so—speak that language. I was familiar with the described phenomena, in a general way, and with the conflicting theories of its leading investigators; but I had—honestly speaking—no pet theories of my own, though always impatient of spiritistic explanations, and rather inclined to doubt, too, the persistent claim that thought transference had been incontrovertibly established. On the whole, I suppose I was inclined to favor common-sense mechanistic explanations of such phenomena, and to regard all others with alert suspicion or wearily amused contempt.

Now at last, in my life's most urgent crisis, I had had news from nowhere; now, furthermore, the being I loved and would protect, *must* protect, had been thrown by psychic shock into that grim borderland, the Abnormal: that land of lost voices, of the fringe of consciousness, of dissociated personalities, of morbid obsession, and wild symbolic dreams. Following on Conlon's heels, then, I entered a softly illumined room—a restrained *Louis Seize* room—a true Gertrude room, with its cool French-gray panelled walls; but entered there as into sinister darkness, as if groping for light. The comfortably accustomed, the predictable, I felt, lay all behind me; I must step warily henceforth among shifting shadows and phosphoric blurs. The issues were too terrifying, too vast, for even one little false move; Susan's future, the very health of her soul, might depend now upon the blundering clumsiness or the instinctive tact with which I attempted to pick and choose my way. It was with a secret shuddering of flesh and spirit that I entered that discreet, faultless room.

Susan was lying on the low single French bed, a coverlet drawn over her; they had removed her trim tailored hat, the jacket of her dark suit, and her walking-boots, leaving them on the couch by the silk-curtained windows, where they had perhaps first placed her. She had not dressed for the evening before coming up to Gertrude's; it was evidently to have been a businesslike call. Her black weblike hair—smoky, I always called it, to tease her; it never fell lank or separated into strings—had been disordered, and a floating weft of it had drifted across her forehead and hung there. Her face was moon-white, her lips pale, the lines of cheek and chin had sharpened, her eyes were closed. It was very like death. My throat tightened and ached.... .

Doctor Askew stood across the bed from us, looking down at her.

"Here's Mr. Hunt," said Conlon, without further introduction. "He wants to see you." Then he stepped back to the door and shut it, remaining over by it, at some distance from the bed. His silence was expressive. "Now show me!" it seemed to say. "This may be a big case for me and it may not. If not, I'm satisfied; I'm ready for anything. Go on, show me!"

Doctor Askew was not, as I had expected to find him, old; nor even middle-aged; an expectation caught, I presume, from Conlon's laconic "One of the best—a big rep"; he was, I now estimated, a year or so younger than I. I had never heard of him and knew nothing about him, but I liked him at once when he glanced humorously up at Conlon's "He wants to see you," nodded to me, and said: "I've been hoping you'd come soon, Mr. Hunt. I've a mind to try something here—if you've no objection to an experiment?"

He was a short man, not fat, but thickset like Conlon; only, with a higher-strung vitality, carrying with it a sense of intellectual eagerness and edge. He had a sandy, freckled complexion, bronzy, crisp-looking hair with reddish gleams in it, and an unmistakably red, aggressive mustache, close-clipped but untamed. Green-blue eyes. A man, I decided, of many intensities; a willful man; but thoughtful, too, and seldom unkind.

"Why did you wait for my permission?" I asked.

"I shouldn't have—much longer," he replied, his eyes returning to Susan's unchanging face. "But I've read one or two of your essays, so I know something of the feel of your mind. It occurred to me you might be useful. And besides, I badly need some information about this"—he paused briefly —"this very lovely child." Again he paused a moment, adding: "This is a singular case, Mr. Hunt—and likely to prove more singular as we see it through. I acted too impulsively in sending for Conlon; I apologize. It's not a police matter, as I at first supposed. However, I hope there's no harm done. Conlon is holding his horses and trying to be discreet. Aren't you, Conlon?"

"What's the idea?" muttered Conlon, from the doorway; Conlon was not used to being treated thus, *de haut en bas*. "Even if that poor little girl's crazy, we'll have to swear out a warrant for her. It's a police matter all right."

"I think *not*," said Doctor Askew, dismissing Conlon from the conversation. "Have you ever," he then asked me, "seen Miss Blake like this before?"

I was about to say "No!" with emphasis, when a sudden memory returned to me—the memory of a queer, crumpled little figure lying on the concrete incline of the Eureka Garage; curled up there, like an unearthed cutworm, round a shining dinner-pail. "Yes," I replied instead; "once—I think."

"You think?"

I sketched the occasion for him and explained all its implications as clearly and briefly as I could; and while I talked thus across her bed Susan's eyes did not open; she did not stir. Doctor Askew heard me out, as I felt, intently, but kept his eye meanwhile—except for a keen glance or two in my direction—on Susan's face.

"All right," he said, when I had concluded; "that throws more or less light. There's nothing to worry us, at least, in Miss Blake's condition. Under psychical trauma—shock—she has a tendency to pass into a trance state— amounting practically to one of the deeper stages of hypnosis. She'll come out of it sooner or later—simply wake up—if we leave her alone. Perhaps, after all, that's the wisest thing for us to do."

On this conclusion he walked away from the bed, as if it ended the matter, and lit a cigarette.

"Well, Conlon," he grinned, "we're making a night of it, eh? Come, let's all sit down and talk things over." He seated himself on the end of the couch as he spoke, lounging back on one elbow and crossing his knees. "I ought to tell you, Mr. Hunt," he added, "that nervous disorders are my specialty; more than that, indeed—my life! I studied under Janet in Paris, and later put in a couple of years as assistant physician in the Clinic of Psychiatry, Zurich. Did some work, too, at Vienna—with Stekel and Freud. So I needn't say a problem of this kind is simply meat and drink to me. I wouldn't have missed it for anything in the world!"

I was a little chilled by his words, by an attitude that seemed to me cold-bloodedly professional; nevertheless, I joined him, drawing up a chair, and Conlon gradually worked his way toward us, though he remained standing.

"What I want to know, doc," demanded Conlon, "is why you've changed your mind?"

"I haven't," Doctor Askew responded. "I can't have, because I haven't yet formed an opinion. I'm just beginning to—and even that may take me some time." He turned to me. "What's your theory, Mr. Hunt?"

I was prepared for this question; my mind had been busying itself foresightedly with every possible turn our conversation was likely to take. All my faculties were sharpened by strain, by my pressing sense that Susan's future, for good or evil, might somehow be linked to my lightest word. I had determined, then, in advance, not to speak in Conlon's presence of my inexplicable vision, not to mention it at all to anyone unless some unexpected turn of the wheel might make it seem expedient. I could use it to Susan's advantage, I believed, more effectively by indirection; I endeavored to do so now.

"My theory?" I queried.

"As to how Mrs. Hunt met her death. However painful, we've got to face that out, sooner or later."

"Naturally. But I have no theory," I replied; "I have an unshakable conviction."

"Ah! Which is——"

"That the whole thing was accidental, of course; just as Miss Blake affirmed it to be over the telephone."

"You believe that *because* she affirmed it?"

"Exactly."

"That won't go down with the coroner," struck in Conlon. "How could it? I'd like to think it, well enough—but it don't with me!"

"Wait, Conlon!" suggested Doctor Askew, sharply. "I'll conduct this inquiry just now, if you don't mind—and if Mr. Hunt will be good enough to answer."

"Why not?" I replied.

"Thank you. Conlon's point is a good one, all the same. Have you been able to form any reasonable notion of how such an accident could have occurred?"

"Yes."

"The hell you have!" exclaimed Conlon excitedly, not meaning, I think, to be sarcastic. "Why, you haven't even been in there"—he referred to Gertrude's boudoir—"or seen the body!"

"No," I responded, "but you and Doctor Askew have, so you can easily put me right. Extraordinary as the whole thing is—the one deadly chance in perhaps a million—there's nothing impossible about it. Merely from the facts you've given me, Sergeant Conlon, I can reconstruct the whole scene—come pretty near it, at any rate. But the strength of my conviction is based on other grounds—don't lose sight of that! Miss Blake didn't kill Mrs. Hunt; she's incapable of such an action; and if she didn't, no one else did. An accident is the only alternative."

"Well, then," grunted Conlon, "tell us about it! It'll take some tellin'!"

"Hold on!" exclaimed Doctor Askew before I could begin. "Sorry, Mr. Hunt—but you remember, perhaps—when you first came in—I had half a mind to try something—an experiment?" I nodded. "Well, I've made up my mind. We'll try it right now, before it's too late. If it succeeds, it may yield us a few facts to go on. Your suppositions can come afterward."

I felt, as he spoke, that something behind his words belied their rudeness, that their rudeness was rather for Conlon's benefit than for mine. He got up briskly and crossed to the bedside. There after a moment he turned and motioned us both to join him.

As we did so, tiptoeing instinctively: "Yes—this is fortunate," he said; "she's at it again. Look."

Susan still lay as I had first seen her, with shut eyes, her arms extended outside the coverlet; but she was no longer entirely motionless. Her left arm lay relaxed, the palm of her left hand upward. I had often seen her hands lie inertly thus in her lap, the palms upward, in those moments of silent withdrawal which I have more than once described. But now her right hand was turned downward, the fingers slightly contracted, as if they held a pen, and the hand was creeping slowly on the coverlet from left to right; it would creep slowly in this way for perhaps eight inches, then draw quickly back to its point of starting and repeat the manœuvre. It was uncanny, this patient repetition—over and over—of a single restricted movement.

"My God," came from Conlon in a husky whisper, "is she dyin'—or

139

what?"

"Far from it!" said Doctor Askew, his abrupt, crisp speech in almost ludicrous contrast to Conlon's sudden awe. "Get me some paper from that desk over there, Conlon. A pad, if possible."

He drew out a pencil from his pocket as he spoke. Conlon hesitated an instant, then obeyed, tiptoeing ponderously, with creaking boots, over to a daintily appointed writing-table, and returning with a block of linen paper. Doctor Askew, meanwhile, holding the pencil between his teeth, had lifted Susan's unresisting shoulders—too roughly, I thought—from the bed.

"Stick that other pillow under her," he ordered me, sharply enough in spite of the impeding pencil. "A little farther down—so!"

Susan now lay, no less limply than before, with her trunk, shoulders, and head somewhat raised. Her right hand had ceased its slow, patient movement.

"What's the idea?" Conlon was muttering. "What's the idea, doc?"

Whatever it was, it was evident that Conlon didn't like it.

"Got the pad?" demanded Doctor Askew. "Oh, good! Here!"

He almost snatched the pad from Conlon and tore the blotter cover from it; then he slipped it beneath Susan's right palm and finally thrust his pencil between her curved fingers, its point resting on the linen block, which he steadied by holding one corner between finger and thumb. For a moment the hand remained quiet; then it began to write. I say "it" advisedly; no least trace of consciousness or purposed control could be detected in Susan's impassive face or heavily relaxed body. *Susan* was not writing; her waking will had no part in this strange automatism; so much, at least, was plain to me and even to Conlon.

"Mother of God," came his throaty whisper again, "it's not *her* that's doin' it. Who's pushin' that hand?"

"It's not *sperits*, Conlon," said Doctor Askew ironically; "you can take my say-so for that." With the words he withdrew the scribbled top sheet from the pad, glanced at it, and handed it to me. The hand journeyed on, covering a second sheet as I read. "That doesn't help us much, does it?" was Doctor Askew's comment, when I had devoured the first sheet.

"No," I replied; "not directly. But I'll keep this if you don't mind."

I folded the sheet and slipped it into my pocket. Doctor Askew removed the second sheet.

"Same sort of stuff," he grunted, passing it over to me. "It needs direction." And he began addressing—not *Susan*, to Conlon's amazement—the *hand!* "What happened in Mrs. Hunt's room to-night?" he demanded firmly of the hand. "Tell us exactly what happened in Mrs. Hunt's room to-night! It's important. What happened in Mrs. Hunt's room to-night?"

Always addressing the hand, his full attention fixed upon it as it moved, he repeated this burden over and over. "We must know exactly what happened in Mrs. Hunt's room to-night! Tell us what happened in Mrs. Hunt's room to-night.... What happened in Mrs. Hunt's room to-night?"

Conlon and I both noted that Susan's breathing, hitherto barely to be detected, gradually grew more labored while Doctor Askew insisted upon and pressed home his monotonous refrain. He had so placed himself now that he could follow the slowly pencilled words. More and more deliberately the hand moved; then it paused....

"What happened in Mrs. Hunt's room to-night?" chanted Doctor Askew.

"This ain't right," muttered Conlon. "It's worse'n the third degree. I don't like it."

He creaked uneasily away. The hand moved again, hesitatingly, briefly.

"Ah," chanted Doctor Askew—always to the hand—"it was an accident, was it? How did it happen? Tell us exactly how it happened—exactly how it happened. *We must know.* . . . How did the accident happen in Mrs. Hunt's room to-night?"

Again the hand moved, more steadily this time, and seemingly in response to his questions.

Doctor Askew glanced up at me with an encouraging smile. "We'll get it now—all of it. Don't worry. The hand's responding to control."

Though sufficiently astonished and disturbed by this performance, I was not, like Conlon, wholly at sea. Sober accounts of automatic writing could be found in all modern psychologies; I had read some of these accounts—given with all the dry detachment of clinical data. They had interested me, not thrilled me. No supernatural power was involved. It was merely the comparative rarity of such phenomena in the ordinary normal course of experience that made them seem awe-inspiring. And yet, the *hand* there, solely animate, patiently writing in entire independence of a consciously directing will——! My spine, too, like Conlon's, registered an authentic shiver of protest and atavistic fear. But, throughout, I kept my tautened wits about me, busily working; and they drove me now on a sudden inspiration to the writing-table, where I seized pen and paper and wrote down with the most collected celerity a condensed account of—for so I phrased it—"what must, from the established facts, be supposed to have taken place in Mrs. Hunt's boudoir, just after Miss Blake had entered it." I put this account deliberately as my theory of the matter, as the one solution of the problem consistent with the given facts and the known characters involved; and I had barely concluded when I was startled to my feet by Doctor Askew's voice—raised cheerily above its monotonous murmur of questions to the hand—calling my name.

"What are you up to, Mr. Hunt? My little experiment's over. It's a complete success."

He was walking toward me with a handful of loose scribbled sheets from the linen block.

"How is she now?" I inquired anxiously, as if she had just been subjected to a dangerous operation.

"All right. Deep under. I shan't try to pull her out yet. Much better for her to come out of it naturally herself. I suggest we darken the room and leave her."

"That suits *me!*" I just caught from Conlon, over by the door.

"She'll be quite safe alone?"

"Absolutely. I want to read this thing to Conlon and Mrs. Arthur and Mr. Phar, before the coroner gets here. I rather think they'll find it convincing."

"Good," I responded. "But, first of all, let me read them this. I've just jotted down my analysis of the whole situation. It's a piece of cold constructive reasoning from the admitted data, and I shall be greatly surprised if it doesn't on the whole agree with what you've been able to obtain."

Doctor Askew stared at me a moment curiously. "And if it doesn't agree?" he asked.

"If it don't," exclaimed Conlon, with obvious relief, "it may help us, all the same! This thing can't be settled by *that* kind of stuff, doc." He gave a would-be contemptuous nod toward Doctor Askew's handful of scrawled pages. "That's no evidence—whatever it says. Where does it come from? Who's givin' it? It can't be sworn to on the Book, that's certain—eh? Let's get outa here and begin to talk sense!" Conlon opened the door eagerly, and creaked off through the hall.

"Go with him," ordered Doctor Askew. "I'll put out the lights." Then he touched my elbow and gave me a slight nod. "I see your point of course. But I hope to God you've hit somewhere near it?"

"Doctor," I replied, "this account of mine is exact. I'll tell you later how I know that."

"Ah!" he grunted, with a green-blue flash of eyes. "What a lucky devil I am! . . . But I've felt all along this would prove a rewarding case."

IV

Up to this point I have been necessarily thus detailed, but I am eager now to win past the cruder melodrama of this insanely disordered night. I am eager to win back from all these damnable and distracting things to Susan. This book is hers, not mine; it is certainly not Sergeant Conlon's or Doctor Askew's. So you will forgive me, and understand, if I present little more than a summary of the immediately following hours.

We found Maltby and Lucette in the drawing-room, worn out with their night-long vigil; Maltby, somnolent and savage; Lucette still keyed high, suffering from exasperated nerves which—perhaps for the first time in her life —she could not control. They were seated as far apart as the room permitted, having long since talked themselves out, and were engaged, I think, in tacitly hating one another. The situation was almost impossible; yet I knew I must dominate it somehow, and begin by dominating myself—and in the end, with Conlon's and Doctor Askew's help, I succeeded. Conlon, I confess, proved to be an unexpected ally all through.

"Now, Mrs. Arthur, and you, Mr. Phar," he stated at once as we entered the drawing-room together, "I've brought Mr. Hunt in here to read you his guess at what happened last evenin'. Doctor Askew'll be with us in a minute, and *he's* got somethin' to lay before you... . No; Miss Blake's not come round yet. The doc'll explain about her. But we'll hear from Mr. Hunt first, see? I've examined him and I'm satisfied he's straight. You've known him long enough to form your own opinions, but that's mine. Oh, here's the doc! Go on, Mr. Hunt."

With this lead, I was at length able to persuade Lucette and Maltby to listen, sullenly enough, to my written analysis. My feeling toward them both, though better concealed, was quite as hostile as theirs toward me, but I saw that I caught their reluctant attention and that Maltby was somewhat impressed by what I had written, and by my interjected amplifications of the more salient points. I had been careful to introduce no facts not given me by Sergeant Conlon, and when I had finished, ignoring Lucette's instant murmur of impatience and incredulity, I turned to him and said: "Sergeant, is there anything known to you and not known to me—any one detail discovered during your examination of Mrs. Hunt's boudoir, say—which makes my deductions impossible or absurd?"

He reflected a moment, then acknowledged: "Well, no, Mr. Hunt. Things might 'a' happened like that; maybe they did. But just sayin' so don't prove they did!"

"May I ask you a few questions?"

"Sure."

"Had Mrs. Hunt's body been moved when you arrived? I mean, from the very spot where it fell?"

"It had and it hadn't. The doc here found her lyin' face down on the floor, right in front of the couch. He had to roll her over on her back to examine her. That's all. The body's there now like that, covered with a sheet. Nothin' else has been disturbed."

"The body was lying face down, you say?"

"Yes," struck in Doctor Askew; "it was."

"At full length?"

"Yes."

"Isn't that rather surprising?"

"Unquestionably."

"How do you account for the position?"

"There's only one possible explanation," replied Doctor Askew, as if giving expert testimony from a witness box; "a sudden and complete loss of balance, pitching the body sharply forward, accompanied by such a binding of the legs and feet as to prevent any instinctive movement toward recovery."

"Thank you. Were there any indications of such binding?"

"Yes. Mrs. Hunt's trailing draperies had somehow wound themselves tightly about her legs below the knee, and I judge her feet were further impeded by a sort of coverlet which I found touselled up on the rug beneath them."

"Grant all that!" growled Maltby. "It points to just the opposite of what we'd all like to think is true. If Mrs. Hunt had risen slowly to greet a caller in the usual way—well, she wouldn't have gotten herself tangled up. She was the last woman in the world to do anything awkwardly. But if she leaped to her feet in terror—what? To defend herself—or try to escape? Don't you see?"

"Of course we see!" cried Lucette. "It proves everything!"

"Hardly," I replied. "Try to imagine the scene, Maltby, as you seem to believe it occurred. I won't speak of the major impossibility—that Susan, a girl you've known and have asked to be your wife, could under any circumstances be the author of such a crime! We'll pass that. Simply try to picture the crime itself. Susan, showing no traces of unnatural excitement, is conducted to my wife's boudoir. She enters, shuts the door, turns, then rushes at her with so hideous an effect of insane fury that Gertrude springs up, terrified. Susan—more slightly built than Gertrude, remember!—grapples with her, tears a paper knife from her hand, and plunges it deep into her eye, penetrating the brain. Suppose, if you will, that madness lent her this force. But, obviously, for the point of the knife to enter the eye in that way, Gertrude must have been fronting Susan, her chin well raised. Obviously, the force of such a blow would have thrown her head, her whole body, backward, not forward; and if her feet were bound, as Doctor Askew says they were, she must have fallen backward or to one side, certainly not forward at full length, on her face."

"You've said somethin' this time, Mr. Hunt!" exclaimed Conlon. "There's a lot to that!"

Maltby was visibly impressed; but not Lucette. "As if," she said, "Susan wouldn't have arranged the body—afterward—in any way she thought to her advantage!"

"There wasn't time!" Doctor Askew objected impatiently. "And," he went on, "it happens that all this is futile! I have proof here, corroborating Mr. Hunt's remarkably acute theories in the most positive way."

But before reading what Susan's hand had written, he turned to Sergeant Conlon, requesting his close attention, and then gave him briefly a popular lecture on the nature of automatic writing as understood by a tough-minded neurologist with no faith in the supernatural. It was really a masterly performance in its way, for he avoided the jargon of science and cut down to essentials.

"Conlon," he said, "you've often forgotten something, tried to recall it, and finally given it up. We all have. And then some day, when you least expected it and were thinking of something else, that forgotten something has popped into your mind again—eh? All right. Where was it in the meantime, when you couldn't put your finger on it? Since it eventually came back, it must have been preserved somewhere. That's plain enough, isn't it? But when you say something you've forgotten 'pops into your mind' again, you're wrong. It's never been out of your mind. What too many of us still don't know is that a man's mind has two parts to it. One part, much the smallest, is consciousness—the part we're using now, the part we're always aware of. The other part is

145

a big dark storehouse, where pretty much everything we've forgotten is kept. We're not aware of the storehouse or the things kept in it, so the ordinary man doesn't know anything about it. You're not aware of your spleen, and wouldn't know you had one if doctors hadn't cut up a lot of people and found spleens in every one of them. You believe you've got a spleen because we doctors tell you so. Well, I'm telling you now that your mind has a big storehouse, where most of the things you've forgotten are preserved. We mind-doctors call it your Unconscious Mind. All clear so far? . . . Good.

"Now then—when a man's hypnotized, it means his conscious mind has been put to sleep, practically, and his unconscious mind has, in a sense, waked up. When a man's hypnotized we can fish all sorts of queer things from his big storehouse, his unconscious mind; things he didn't know were there, things he'd forgotten.... And it's the same with what we call trances. A man in a trance is a man whose conscious mind is asleep and whose unconscious mind is awake.

"That's exactly Miss Blake's condition now. The shock of what she saw last evening threw her into a trance; she doesn't know what's going on round her—but her unconscious mind has a record, a sort of phonograph-record of more or less everything that's ever happened to her, and if she speaks or writes in this trance state she'd simply play one of these stored-up records for us; play it just like a phonograph, automatically. Her will power's out of commission, you see; in this state she's nothing more nor less than a highly complicated instrument. And the record she plays may be of no interest to anybody; some long-forgotten incident or experience of childhood, for example. On the other hand, if we can get the right record going—eh?— we've every chance of finding out exactly what we want to know!" He paused, fixing his already attentive pupil with his peculiarly vivid green-blue glance.

"Now, Conlon, *get* this—it's important! I must ask you to believe one other thing about the Unconscious Mind—simply take it on my say-so, as a proved fact: When the conscious mind is temporarily out of business—as under hypnotism, or in trance—the unconscious mind, like the sensitive instrument it is, will often obey or respond to outside suggestions. I can't go into all this, of course. But what I ask you to believe about Miss Blake is this: In her present state of trance, at my suggestion, *she has played the right record for us!* She has automatically written down for us an account of her experiences last evening. And I assure you this account, obtained in this way, is far more reliable and far more complete than any she could give us in her normal, conscious, waking state. There's nothing marvellous or weird about it, Conlon. We have here"—and he slightly rattled the loose sheets in his hand

—"simply an automatic record of stored-up impressions. Do you see?"

Conlon grunted that he guessed maybe he saw; at any rate, he was willing to be shown.

Then Doctor Askew read us Susan's own story of the strange, idiotically meaningless accident to Gertrude. As it corresponded in every particular with my vision, I shall not repeat it; but it produced an enormous impression on Sergeant Conlon and Maltby, and even on Lucette. Taken in connection with my independent theory of what must have occurred, they found Susan's story entirely convincing; though whether Lucette really found it so or had suddenly decided—because of certain uncomfortable accusations against herself made by Susan's hand—that the whole matter had gone quite far enough and any further publicity would be a mistake, I must leave to your later judgment.

As for the coroner, when at length he arrived, he too—to my astonishment and unspeakable relief—accepted Susan's automatic story without delay or demur. Here was a stroke of sheer good luck, for a grateful change—but quite as senseless in itself, when seriously considered, as the cruel accident to Gertrude. It merely *happened* that the coroner's sister was a professional medium, and that he and his whole family were ardent believers in spiritualism, active missionaries in that cause. He had started life as an East Side street-urchin, had the coroner, and had scrambled up somehow from bondage to influence, fighting his way single-fisted through a hard school that does not often foster illusions; but I have never met a more eagerly credulous mind. He accepted the automatic writing as evidence without a moment's cavil, assuring us at once that it undoubtedly came as a direct message from the dead.

Doctor Askew's preliminary explanations he simply brushed aside. If Miss Blake in her present trance state, which he soon satisfied himself was genuine, had produced this message, then her hand had been controlled by a disembodied spirit—probably Mrs. Hunt's. There was no arguing with the man, and on my part, heaven knows, no desire to oppose him! I listened gratefully for one hour to his wonder tales of spirit revelations, and blessed him when he reluctantly left us—with the assurance that Gertrude's death would be at once reported as due to an unavoidable accident. It was so announced in the noon editions of the evening papers. Sergeant Conlon and his aids departed by the service elevator, and were soon replaced by a shocked and grieved clergyman and a competent undertaker. The funeral—to take place in New Haven—was arranged for; telegrams were sent; one among them to Phil. Even poor Miss Goucher was at last remembered and communicated with—only just in time, I fear, to save her reason. But of her more in its place. And, meanwhile, throughout all this necessary confusion, Susan slept on. Noon was past, and she still slept.... And Doctor Askew and I watched beside her, and talked together.

At precisely seven minutes to three—I was bending over her at the moment, studying her face for any sign of stirring consciousness—she quietly opened her eyes.

"Ambo," were her first words, "I believe in God now; a God, anyway. I believe in *Setebos*———"

V

In my unpracticed, disorderly way—in the hurry of my desire to get back to Susan—I have again overstepped myself and must, after all, pause to make certain necessary matters plain. There is nothing else for it. I have, on reflection, dropped too many threads—the thread of my own vision, the thread of those first two or three pages scrawled by Susan before her hand had fully responded to Doctor Askew's control; other weakly fluttering, loose-ended threads! My respect for the great narrative writers is increasing enormously, as I bungle onward. "Order is heaven's first law," and I wish to heaven it might also more instinctively be mine!

Just after the coroner's departure Maltby left us, but before he left I insisted upon a brief talk with him in Lucette's presence. I was in no mood for tact.

"Maltby," I said, "I can't stop now for anything but the plain statement that you've been a bad friend—to Susan and me. As for you, Lucette, it's perfectly clear now that Susan believes you responsible for spreading a slanderous lie about her. Between you, directly or indirectly, you've managed to get it believed down here that Susan has been my mistress and was forced to leave New Haven because the scandal had grown notorious. That's why Susan came here, determined to see you, Lucette; that's why Gertrude received her. Gertrude was never underhanded, never a sneak. My guess is, that she suspected you of slandering Susan, but wasn't sure; and then Susan's unexpected call on you———"

Lucette flared out at this, interrupting me. "I'm not particularly interested in your guesswork, Ambrose Hunt! We've had a good deal of it, already. Besides, I've a raging headache, and I'm too utterly heartsick even to resent your insults. But I'll say this: I've very strong reasons for thinking that what you call a lying slander is a fact. Mr. Phar can tell you why—if he cares to."

With that, she walked out of the room, and I did not see her again until we met in New Haven at Gertrude's funeral, on which occasion, with nicely calculated publicity, she was pleased to cut me dead.

When she had gone I turned on Maltby.

"Well?" I demanded.

Maltby, I saw, was something more than ill-at-ease.

"Now see here, Boz," he began, "can't we talk this over without quarreling? It's so stupid, I mean—between men of the world." I waited, without responding. "I'll be frank with you," he mumbled at me. "Fact is, old man, that night—the night Phil Farmer said Susan wanted to see you—was waiting for you in your study—remember? You promised to rejoin me shortly and talk things out… . But you didn't come back. Naturally, I've always supposed since then——"

"You have a scoundrelly imagination!" I exclaimed.

His face, green-pale from loss of sleep, slowly mottled with purplish stains.

"Years of friendship," he stumbled, thick-voiced, through broken phrases. "Wouldn't take that from any one else… . Not yourself… . Question of viewpoint, really… . I'd be the last to blame either of you, if—— However ——."

"Maltby," I said, "you're what I never thought you—a common or garden cad. That's my deliberate opinion. I've nothing more to say to you."

For an instant I supposed he was going to strike me. It is one of the major disappointments of my life that he did not. My fingers ached for his throat.

Later, with the undertaker efficiently in charge of all practical arrangements, and while Susan still hid from us behind her mysterious veil, I talked things out with Doctor Askew, giving him the whole story of Susan as clearly and unreservedly as I could. My purpose in doing so was two-fold. I felt that he must know as much as possible about Susan before she woke again to what we call reality. What I feared was that this shock—which had so profoundly and so peculiarly affected her—might, even after the long and lengthening trance had passed, leave some mark upon her spirit, perhaps even some permanent cloud upon her brain. I had read enough of these matters to know that my fear was not groundless, and I could see that Doctor Askew welcomed my information—felt as keenly as I did that he might later be called upon to interpret and deal with some perplexing borderland condition of the mind. It was as well at least to be prepared. That was my major purpose. But connected with it was another, more self-regarding. My own vision, my psychic reel, greatly disturbed me. It was not orthodox. It could not be explained, for example, as something swiftly fabricated from covert memories by my unconscious mind, and forced then sharply into consciousness by some freak of circumstance, some psychic perturbation or strain.

My vision of the accident itself—of the manner of its occurrence—might conceivably have been such a fabrication, subconsciously elaborated from the facts given me by Conlon; not so my vision of its setting. I had seen in vivid detail the interior of a room which I had never entered and had never heard described; and every detail thus seen was minutely accurate, for I had since examined the room and had found nothing in it unfamiliar, nothing that did not correspond with what my mind's eye had already noted and remembered. Take merely one instance—the pattern and color scheme of the Chinese rug beside the *chaise-longue*. As an amateur in such matters I could easily, in advance of physically looking at it, have catalogued that rug and have estimated its value to a collector. How then to account for this astounding clairvoyance? I could not account for it without widening my whole conception of what was psychically possible. Seated with Doctor Askew in the room where Susan lay withdrawn from us, from our normal world of limited concrete perceptions, I was oppressed as never before by the immensity and deluding vagueness of the unknown. What were we, we men and women? Eternal forces, or creatures of an hour? An echo, from days long past returned to me, Phil's quiet, firm voice demanding—of Maltby, wasn't it? Yes, yes, of course—demanding of Maltby: *"What is the world, may I ask? And what is Susan?"*

Doctor Askew cross-questioned me closely as we sat there, a little off from Susan, our eyes seldom leaving her face. "You must have patience," he kept assuring me in the midst of his questioning. "It will be much better for her to come out of this thing tranquilly, by herself. We're not really wasting time." When his cross-questioning was over he sat silent for a long time, biting at his upper lip, tapping one foot—almost irritably, I thought—on the parquet floor.

"I don't like it," he said finally, in his abrupt way. "I don't like it because I believe you're telling the truth. If I could only persuade myself that you are either lying or at least drawing a long bow"—he gave a little disgusted snort of laughter—"it would be a great relief to me!"

"Why?"

"Why? Because you're upsetting my scientific convictions. My mind was all tidied up, everything nicely in order, and now you come raging through it with this ridiculous tale of a sudden hallucinating vision—of seeing things that you'd never seen, never heard described—whose very existence you were completely unaware of! Damn it! I'd give almost anything to think you a cheerful liar—or self-deceived! But I can't."

"Still, you must have met with similar cases?"

"Never, as it happens, with one that I couldn't explain away to my own satisfaction. That's what irritates me now. I can't explain you away, Mr. Hunt. I believe you had that experience just as you describe it. Well, then, if you had —what follows?" He pulled for a moment or two at a stubby end of red mustache.

"What does?" I suggested.

"One of three things," he replied, "all equally impossible. Either your vision—to call it that—was first recorded in the mind of another living person and transferred thence to yours—or it was not. If it wasn't, then it came direct from God or the devil and was purely miraculous! With your kind permission, we'll rule that out. But if it was first recorded in the mind of another living person, then we're forced to accept telepathy—complete thought transference from a distance—accept it as a fact. I never have so accepted it, and hate like hell to do it now! And even if I could bring myself to accept it, my troubles have only begun. From whose mind was this exact vision of the accident to Mrs. Hunt transferred to yours? So far as I can see, the detailed facts of it could have been registered in the minds of only two persons—Miss Blake and your wife. Isn't that so?"

I agreed.

"All right. See where that leaves us! At the time you received this vision, Miss Blake is lying here in a deep trance, unconscious; and your wife is dead. Which of these incredible sources of information do you prefer? It's a matter of indifference to me. Either way my entire reasoned conception of the universe topples in ruins!"

"But surely," I protested, "it might have come to me from Miss Blake, as you suggest, without our having to descend to a belief in spirit communication? Let's rule that out, too!"

"As you please," smiled Doctor Askew, pretty grimly. "If you find it easier to believe your vision came from Miss Blake, do so by all means! Personally, I've no choice. I can accept the one explanation quite as readily as the other. Which means, that as a thinking being I can accept neither! Both are—absurd. So I can go no further—unless by a sheer act of faith. I'm baffled, you see— in my own field; completely baffled. That's what it comes to. And I find it all devilishly annoying and inconvenient. Don't you?"

I did not reply. For a time I mused, drearily enough, turning many comfortless things over in my mind. Then I drew from my pocket the three sheets scribbled by Susan's hand, before it had responded to Doctor Askew's insistent suggestions.

"Doctor," I asked, handing him the scribbled pages, "in view of all I've told you, doesn't what Miss Blake has written here strike you as significant? You see," I added, while he glanced through them, "how strongly her repressed feelings are in revolt against me—against the tyranny of my love for her. Doesn't it seem improbable, then, to say the least of it, that my vision could have come from that direction?"

He was reading the pages through again, more slowly. "Jimmy?" he queried to himself. "Oh, yes—Jimmy's the boy you spoke of. I see—I see." He looked up, and I did my best to smile.

"That's a bitter dose of truth for me, doctor; but thank God it came in this way—came in time!"

Except for the punctuation, which I have roughly supplied, the three pages read as follows:

"A net. No means of escape from it. To escape—somehow. Jimmy—— Only wretchedness for Ambo—for us both. How can he care! Insufferably self-satisfied; childishly blind. I won't—I won't—not after this. No escape from it—my net. But the inner net—Ambo's—binding him, too. Some way out. A dead hand killing things. My own father. How he killed and killed— always—more than he knew. Blind. Never felt that before as part of me—of me. Wrong way round though—it enfolds—smothers. I'm tangled there—part of it—forever and ever. Setebos—God of my father—Setebos knows. Oh, how could I dream myself free of it like others—how could I! A net—all a net —no breaking it. Poor Ambo—and his love too—a net. It shan't hold me. I'll gnaw through—mouselike. I must. Fatal for Ambo now if it holds me. Fatal— Setebos—Jimmy will——"

"Hum," said Doctor Askew quietly.

"That doesn't help me much," I complained.

"No," he responded; "but I can't see that all this has any bearing on the possible source of your vision."

"I only thought that perhaps this revelation of a repressed inner revolt against me——"

"Yes, I see. But there's no reasoning about the unthinkable. I've already said I can make nothing of your vision—nothing I'm yet prepared to believe." He handed the three sheets back to me with these words: "But I'm afraid your interpretation of this thing is correct. It's a little puzzling in spots—curious, eh, the references to Setebos?—still, if I were you, Mr. Hunt, I should quietly withdraw from a lost cause. It'll mean less trouble all round in the end." He shook his head impatiently. "These sexual muddles—it's better to see 'em out frankly! They're always the devil, anyway! What silly mechanisms we are—how Nature makes puppet-fools of us! That lovely child there—she admires you and wants to love you, because you love her. Why shouldn't she? What could be a happier arrangement—now? You've had your share of marital misfortune, I should say. But Nature doesn't give a damn for happy arrangements! God knows what she's after, I don't! But just at present she seems to be loading the dice for Jimmy—for Jimmy, who perhaps isn't even interested in the game! Well, such—for our misery or amusement—is life! And my cigarettes are gone... . How about yours——?"

VI

It did not take Susan long to make it perfectly clear to Doctor Askew and me that she had waked from her trance to complete lucidity, showing no traces of any of the abnormal after-effects we had both been dreading. Her first rather surprising words had been spoken just as she opened her eyes and before she had quite realized anything but my familiar presence beside her. They were soon followed by an entirely natural astonishment and confusion. What had happened? Where was she? She sat up in bed and stared about her, her eyes coming to rest on Doctor Askew's eager, observant face.

"Who are you?" she asked.

"Doctor Askew," he replied quietly. "Don't be alarmed, Miss Blake. Mr. Hunt and I have been looking after you. Not that you've been much trouble," he smiled; "on the contrary. You've been fast asleep for more than twelve hours. We both envy you."

For a long two minutes she did not reply. Then, "Oh, yes," she said. "Oh, yes." Her chin began to quiver, she visibly shuddered through her whole slight frame, and for an instant pressed her palms hard against her eyes. "Ambo," she murmured, "it was cruel—worse than anything! I got to the 'phone all right, didn't I? Yes, I remember that. I gave the message. But I knew I must go back to her. So much blood, Ambo... . I'm a coward—oh, I'm a coward! But I tried, I did try to go back! Where *did* I go, Ambo?"

"You went to sleep like a sensible little woman!" struck in Doctor Askew, briskly. "You'd done all you could, all anyone could—so you went to sleep. I wish to God more women under such circumstances would follow your example! Much better than going all to pieces and making a scene!"

Susan could not respond to his encouraging smile. "To sleep!" she sighed miserably; "just as I did—once before. What a coward I am! When awful things happen, I dodge them—I run away."

"Nonsense, dear. You knew Gertrude was beyond helping, didn't you?"

"Yes; but if she hadn't been?" She shook her head impatiently. "You're both trying to be kind; but you won't be able to make me forgive myself—not this time. I don't rise to a crisis—I slump. Artemis wouldn't have; nor Gertrude. You know that's true, Ambo. Even if I could do nothing for her—there were others to think of. There was you. I ought to have been helping you; not you, me." She put out her hand to me. "You've done everything for me, always—and I make no return. Now, when I might have, I—I've been a quitter!"

Tears of shame and self-reproach poured from her eyes. "Oh," she cried out with a sort of fierce disgust, "how I hate a coward! How I hate myself!"

"Come, come!" protested Doctor Askew. "This won't do, little lady!" He laid a firm hand on her shoulder and almost roughly shook it, as if she had been a boy. "If you're equal to it, I suggest you get up and wash your face in good cold water. Do your hair, too—put yourself to rights! Things never look quite normal to a woman, you know, when her hair's tumbling!" His hand slipped from her shoulder to her upper arm; he drew the coverlet from her, and helped her to rise. "All right? Feel your pins under you? . . . Fine! Need a maid? No? . . . Splendid! Come along, Mr. Hunt, we'll wait for the little lady in the drawing-room. She'll soon pull herself together."

He joined me and walked with me to the door. Susan had not moved as yet from the bedside.

"Ambo," she demanded unexpectedly, "does Sister know?"

"Yes, dear."

"Why isn't she with me then? Is her cold worse?"

"Rather, I'm afraid. I've sent a doctor to her, with instructions to keep her in bed if possible. We'll go right down when you're ready and feel up to it."

"Why didn't I stay with her, Ambo? I should have. If I had, all this wouldn't have happened. It was pure selfishness, my coming here to see Mrs. Arthur. I simply wanted the cheap satisfaction of telling her—oh, no matter! I'll be ready in five minutes or less."

"Ah," laughed Doctor Askew, "then we know just what to expect! I'll order my car round for you in half an hour."

Phil and Jimmy arrived in town that afternoon and I met them at the

Brevoort, where the three of us took rooms, with a sitting-room, for the night. I told them everything that had occurred as fully as I could, with one exception: I did not speak of those first three pages automatically scribbled by Susan's hand. Nor did I mention my impression—which was rapidly becoming a fixed idea—that my love for her had darkened her life. This was my private problem, my private desolation. It would be my private duty to free Susan's spirit from this intolerable strain. No one could help me here, not even Susan. In all that most mattered to me, my isolation must from now on be complete.

All else I told them, not omitting my vision—the whole wild story. And, finally, I had now to add to my devil's list a new misfortune. We had found poor Miss Goucher's condition much more serious than I had supposed. Doctor Askew had taken us down in his car, and we were met in the nondescript lower hall of the boarding-house by his friend, Doctor Carl—the doctor whom I had sent to Miss Goucher on his advice. Miss Goucher's heavy chest cold, he at once informed us, had taken a graver turn; double pneumonia had declared itself. Her fever was high and she had lately grown delirious; he had put a trained nurse in charge. The crisis of the disease would probably be passed during the next twelve hours; he was doing everything possible; he hoped for the best.

Susan, very white, motionless, had heard him out. "If Sister dies," she had said quietly when he ended, "I shall have killed her." Then she had run swiftly up the stairs and the two doctors had followed her. I had remained below and had not again seen her; but Doctor Askew had returned within ten minutes, shaking his head.

"No one can say what will happen," I had finally wrested from him. "One way or the other now, it's the flip of a coin. Carl's doing his best—that is, nothing, since there's nothing to do. I've warned him to keep an eye on the little lady. I'll look in again after dinner. Good-by. Better find a room and get some sleep if you can."

There was little doubt that Miss Goucher's turn for the worse had come as the result of Susan's disturbing all-night absence. Susan had made her comfortable and left her in bed, promising to be home before twelve. Miss Goucher had fallen asleep about eleven and had not waked until two. The light she had left for Susan had not been switched off, and Susan's bed, which stood beside her own, was unoccupied. Feverish from her bronchial cold, she was at once greatly alarmed, and sprang from her bed to go into the sitting-room, half hoping to find Susan there and scold her a little for remaining up so late over her work. She did not even stop to put on a dressing-gown or find her slippers. All this Susan later learned from her red-eyed landlady, Miss

O'Neill, whose own bedroom, as it happened, was just beside their own. Miss O'Neill, a meritorious if tiresome spinster of no particular age, had at last been waked from heavy and well-earned sleep by persistent knocking at her door. She had found Miss Goucher standing in the unheated, draughty hall, bare-footed, in her nightgown, her cheeks flushed with mounting fever while her teeth chattered with cold.

Like a sensible woman she had hurried her instantly back to bed, and would have gone at once for a hot-water bottle, if Miss Goucher had not insisted upon a hearing. Miss O'Neill was abjectly fond of Miss Goucher, who had the rare gift of listening to voluble commonplace without impatience —a form of sympathy so rare and so flattering to Miss O'Neill's so often bruised self-esteem that she would gladly—had there been any necessity— have carried Miss Goucher rent-free for the mere spiritual solace of pouring out her not very romantic troubles to her. She had taken, Susan felt, an almost voluptuous pleasure in this, her one opportunity to do something for Miss Goucher. She had telephoned Gertrude's apartment for her: "no matter if it is late! I won't have you upset like this for nobody! They've got to answer!" And she had talked with some man—"and I didn't like his tone, neither"— who had asked her some rather odd questions, and had then told her Miss Blake was O. K., not to worry about Miss Blake; she'd had a fainting-spell and been put to bed; she'd be all right in the morning; sure; well, he was the doctor, he guessed he ought to know! "Queer kind of doctor for a lady," Miss O'Neill had opined; "he sounded more like a mick!" A shrewd guess, for he was, no doubt, one of Conlon's trusties.

Miss Goucher had then insisted that she was going to dress and go up at once to Susan, and had even begun her preparations in spite of every protest, when she was seized with so stabbing a pain in her chest that she could only collapse groaning on the bed and let Miss O'Neill minister to her as best she might with water bottles and a mustard plaster borrowed from Number Twelve... .

By the time I had tardily remembered to telephone Miss Goucher it was almost nine A. M., and it was Miss O'Neill who had answered the call, receiving my assurances of Susan's well-being, and informing me in turn that poor Miss Goucher was good and sick and no mistake, let alone worrying, and should she send for a doctor? She was a Scientist herself, though she'd tried a mustard plaster, anyway, always liking to be on the safe side; but Miss Goucher wasn't, and so maybe she ought. At this point I had naturally taken charge.

And it was at this point in my long, often interrupted relation to Phil and Jimmy that Phil took charge.

"You're going to bed, Hunt—and you're going now! There's absolutely nothing further you can do this evening, and if anything turns up Jimmy or I can attend to it. You've been living on your nerves all day and you show it, too plainly. We don't want another patient to-morrow. Run out and get some veronal powders, Jimmy. Thanks. No protests, old man. You're going to bed!"

I went; and, drugged with veronal, I slept—slept dreamlessly—for fourteen hours. When I woke, a little past ten, Jimmy was standing beside me.

"Good morning, Mr. Hunt. You look rested up some! How about breakfast?" His greeting went through all the sounds and motions of cheerfulness, but it was counterfeit coin. There was something too obviously wrong with Jimmy's ordinarily fresh healthy-boy face; it had gone sallow and looked pincushiony round the eyes. I stared at him dully, but could not recall anything that might account for this alteration. Only very gradually a faint sense of discomfort began to pervade my consciousness. Hadn't something happened—once—something rather sad—and rather horrible? When was it? Where was I? And then the full gust of recollection came like a stiff physical blow over my heart. I sat up with a sharp gasp for breath... .

"Well!" I demanded. "Miss Goucher! How is she?"

"She's dead, sir," answered Jimmy, turning away.

"And——"

"She's wonderful!" answered Jimmy.

He had not needed Susan's name.

Yes, in a sense, Jimmy was right. He was not a boy to look far beneath the surface effects of life, and throughout the following weeks Susan's surface effect was indeed wonderful. Apparently she stood up to her grief and mastered it, developing an outer stillness, a quietude strangely disquieting to Phil and to me. Gentleness itself in word and deed, for the first time since we had known her she became spiritually reticent, holding from us her deeper thoughts. It was as if she had secretly determined—God knows from what pressure of lonely sorrow—to conventionalize her life, to present the world hereafter nothing but an even surface of unobtrusive conformity. This, we feared, was hereafter to be her wounded soul's protection, her Chinese Wall. It had not somehow the feel of a passing mood; it had rather the feel of a permanent decision or renunciation. And it troubled our hearts....

I spare you Gertrude's funeral, and Miss Goucher's. The latter, held in a small, depressingly official mortuary chapel, provided—at a price—by the undertaker, was attended only by Phil, Jimmy, Susan, Sonia, Miss O'Neill and me. Oh—there was also the Episcopal clergyman, whom I provided. He read the burial service professionally, but well; it is difficult to read it badly. There are a few sequences of words that really are foolproof, carrying their own atmosphere and dignity with them.

Phil and I, at Susan's request, had examined Miss Goucher's effects and had made certain inquiries. She had been for many years, we found, entirely alone in the world—a phrase often, but seldom accurately, used. It is a rare thing, happily, to discover a human being who is absolutely the last member of his or her family line; in Miss Goucher's case this aloneness was complete. But so far as her nonexistent ancestors were concerned, Miss Goucher, we ascertained, had every qualification necessary for a D. A. R.; forebears of hers had lived for generations in an old homestead near Poughkeepsie, and the original Ithiel Goucher had fought as a young officer under Washington. From soldiering, the Gouchers had passed on to farming, to saving souls, to school-teaching, to patent-medicine peddling, and finally to drink and drugs and general desuetude. Miss Goucher herself had been a last flare-up of the primitive family virtues, and with her they were now extinct.

All this we learned from her papers, and from an old lady in Poughkeepsie who remembered her grandfather, and so presumably her mother and father as well—though in reply to my letter of inquiry she forbore to mention them. They were mentioned several times in letters and legal documents preserved by Miss Goucher, but—except to say that they both died before she was sixteen—I shall follow the example of the old lady in Poughkeepsie. She, I feel, and the Roman poet long before her, had what Jimmy calls the "right idea." . . .

Miss Goucher, always methodical, left a brief and characteristic will: "To Susan Blake, ward of Ambrose Hunt, Esq., of New Haven, Conn., and to her heirs and assigns forever, I leave what little personal property I possess. She has been to me more than a daughter. I desire to be cremated, believing that to be the cleanest and least troublesome method of disposing of the dead."

That, with the proper legal additions, was all. Her desire was of course respected, and I had a small earthenware jar containing her ashes placed in my own family vault. On this jar Susan had had the following words inscribed:

MALVINA
GOUCHER
A GENTLE
WOMAN

VII

On one point Susan was from the first determined: Miss Goucher's death should make no difference in her struggle for independence; she would go on as she had begun, and fight things through to a finish alone. Neither Phil nor I could persuade her to take even a few days for a complete change of scene, a period of rest and recuperation. Simply, she would not. She settled down at once to work harder than ever, turning out quotable paragraphs for *Whim*, as daring as they were sprightly; and she resolutely kept her black hours of loneliness to herself. That she had many such hours I then suspected and now know, but on my frequent visits to New York—I had been appointed administrator of Miss Goucher's more than modest estate—she ignored them, and skillfully turned all my inquiries aside. These weeks following on Miss Goucher's death were for many reasons the unhappiest of my life.

Never since I had known Susan, never until now, had our minds met otherwise than candidly and freely. Now, through no crying fault on either side—unless through a lack of imagination on mine—barriers were getting piled up between us, barriers composed of the subtlest, yet stubbornest misunderstandings. Our occasional hours together soon became a drab tissue of evasions and cross purposes and suppressed desires. Only frankness can serve me here or make plain all that was secretly at work to deform the natural development of our lives.

There are plays—we have all attended them to our indignation—in which some unhappy train of events seems to have been irrationally forced upon his puppets by the author; if he would only let them speak out freely and sensibly, all their needless difficulties would vanish! Such plays infuriate the public and are never successful.

"Good Lord!" we exclaim. "Why didn't she *say* she loved him in the first place!"—or, "If he had only told her his reasons for leaving home that night!"

We, the enlightened public, feel that in the shoes of either the hero or the heroine we must have acted more wisely, and we refuse our sympathy to misfortunes that need never have occurred. Our reaction is perhaps inevitable and æsthetically justified; but I am wondering—I am wondering whether two-thirds of the unhappiness of most mortals is not due to their failure clearly to read another's thoughts or clearly to reveal their own? Is not half, at least, of the misery in our hearts born of futile misunderstandings, misunderstandings with which any sane onlooker in full possession of the facts on both sides, can have little patience, since he instinctively feels they ought never to have taken place? But it is only in the theater that we find such an onlooker, the audience, miraculously in possession of the facts on both sides. In active life, we are doing pretty well if we can partly understand our own motives; we are supermen if we divine the concealed, genuine motives of another. Certainly at this period Susan, with all her insight, did not seize my motives, nor was I able to interpret hers. Hence, we could not speak out! What needed to be said between us could not be said. And the best proof that it could not is, after all, that it was not... .

The conversation that ought to have taken place between us might not unreasonably have run something like this:

SUSAN: Ambo dear—what *is* the matter? Heaven knows there's enough!—but I mean between *us?* You've never been more wonderful to me than these past weeks—and never so remote. I can feel you edging farther and farther away. Why, dear?

I: I've been a nuisance to you too long, Susan. Whatever I am from now on, I won't be that.

SUSAN: As if you could be; or ever had been!

I: Don't try to spare my feelings because you like me—because you're grateful to me and sorry for me! I've had a glimpse of fact, you see. It's the great moral antiseptic. My illusions are done for.

SUSAN: What illusions?

I: The illusion that you ever have really loved me. The illusion that you might some day grow to love me. The illusion that you might some day be my wife.

SUSAN: Only the last is illusion, Ambo. I do love you. I'm growing more in love with you every day. But I can't be your wife, ever. If I've seemed changed and sad—apart from Sister's death, and everything else that's happened—it's *that,* dear. It's killing me by half-inches to know I can never be completely part of your life—yours!

I:

[But I can't even imagine what babble of sorrow and joy such words must have wrung from me! Suppose a decent interval, and a partial recovery of verbal control.]

SUSAN: You shouldn't have rescued me from Birch Street, Ambo. Everything's made it plain to me, at last. But I've already ground the mud of it into your life now—in spite of myself. You'll never feel really clean again.

I: What nonsense! Susan, Susan—dearest!

SUSAN: It isn't nonsense. You forget; I'm a specialist in nonsense nowadays. Oh, Ambo, how can you care for me! I've been so insufferably self-satisfied; so childishly blind! My eyes are wide open now. I've had the whole story of what happened that awful night—all of it—from Doctor Askew. He thought he was psycho-analyzing me, while I pumped it out of him, drop by drop. And I've been to Maltby, too; yes, I've been to Maltby, behind your back. Ambo, he isn't really certain yet that I didn't go crazy that night and kill your wife. Neither, I'm sure, is Mrs. Arthur. They've given me the benefit of the doubt simply because they dread being dragged through a horrible scandal, that's all. But they're not convinced. Of course, Maltby didn't say so in so many words, but it was plain as plain! He was afraid of me —afraid! I could feel his fear. He thinks madness is in my blood. Well, he's right. Not just as he means it, but as *Setebos* means it—the cruel, jealous God of this world! . . . No, wait, dear! Let me say it out to you, once for all. My father ended a brutal life by an insanely brutal murder, then killed himself; my own father. And I've never all these years honestly realized that as part of my life—part of *me!* But now I do. It's there, back of me. I can never escape from it. Oh, how could I have imagined myself like others—a woman like others, free to love and marry and have children and a home! How could I!

I: Susan! Is that all? Is it really all that's holding you from me? Good God, dear! Why, I thought you—secretly—perhaps even unknown to yourself— loved Jimmy!

SUSAN: Jimmy? You thought——

I: I think so even now. How can I help it? Look... . [And here you must suppose me to show her those first scrawled sheets, written automatically by her hand.] Perhaps I'm revealing your own heart to you, Susan—dragging to light what you've tried to keep hidden even from yourself. See, dear. "A net. No means of escape from it. To escape—somehow. Jimmy——"

[And then Susan would perhaps have handed back those scrawled pages to me with a pitying and pitiful smile.]

SUSAN:

[*Author's Note:* This carefully written, imaginary speech has been deleted *in toto* by Censor Susan from the page proof—at considerable expense to me —and the following authentic confession substituted for it in her own hand.

But she doesn't know I am making this explanation, which will account to you for the form and manner of her confession, purposely designed to be a continuation of my own imaginary flight. In admitting this, I am risking Susan's displeasure; but conscience forbids me to let you mistake a "genuine human document"—so dear to the modern heart—for a mere effort at interpretation by an amateur psychologist. What follows, then, is veracious, is essentially that solemn thing so dear to a truth-loving generation—sheer *fact*.]

Ambo dear, I can explain that, but not without a long, unhappy confession. Must I? It's a shadowy, inside-of-me story, awfully mixed and muddled; not a nice story at all. Won't it be better, all round, if I simply say again that I love *you*, not Jimmy, with all my heart?

[No doubt I should then have reached for her hands, and she would have drawn away.]

Ah, no, dear, please not! I've never made a clean breast of it all, even to myself. It's got to be done, though, Ambo, sooner or later, for both our sakes. Be patient with me. I'll begin at the beginning.

I'm ridiculously young, Ambo; we all keep forgetting how young I am! I'm an infant prodigy, really; you and Phil—and God first, I suppose—have made me so. And the main point about infant prodigies is that experience hasn't caught up with them. They live in things they've imagined from things they've been told or read, live on intuition and second-hand ideas; and they've no means of testing their real values in a real world. And they're childishly conceited, Ambo! I am. Less now than some months ago; but I'm still pretty bad... .

Well, back in Birch Street, before I came to you, when I was honestly a child, I lived all alone inside of myself. I lived chiefly on stories I made up about myself; and of course my stories were all escapes from reality—from the things that hurt or disgusted me most. There was hardly anything in my life at home that I didn't long to escape from. You can understand that, in a general way. But there's one thing you perhaps haven't thought about; it's such an ugly thing to think about. I know it isn't modern of me, but I do hate to talk about it, even to you. I must, though. You'll never understand—oh, lots of later things—unless I do.

Love, Ambo, human love, as I learned of it there at home—and I saw and heard much too much of it—frightened and sickened me. It was swinish—horrible. Most of all I longed to escape from all that! I couldn't. I wonder if anyone ever has or can? We are made as we are made... . Yes, I longed to escape from it; but my very made-up story of escape was a disguised romance. Jimmy was to be the gentle Galahad who would some day rescue me. He had done battle for me once already—with Joe Gonfarone. But some day he would come in white, shining armor and take me far away from all the mud and sweat of Birch Street to blue distant hills. Artemis was all mixed up in it, too; she was to be our special goddess; our free, swift, cool-eyed protector. There was to be no heartsick shame, no stuffiness in my life any more forever! But it wasn't Jimmy who rescued me, Ambo. You did.

Only, when we've lived in a dream, wholly, for months and months and months, it doesn't vanish, Ambo; it never vanishes altogether; it's part of us— part of our lives. Isn't it? Gertrude was once your dream, dear; and the dream-Gertrude has never really vanished from your life, and never will. Ah, don't I know!

Well, then you rescued me; and you and Phil and Maltby and Sister and books and Hillhouse Avenue and France and Italy and England, and my Magic Circle—*everything*—crowded upon me and changed me and made me what I am; if I'm anything at all! But Birch Street had made me first; and my dreams... .

Ambo, I can never make you know what you've been to me, never! Cinderella's prince was nothing beside you, and my Galahad-Jimmy a pale phantom! I shan't try. And I can never make you know what a wild confusion of storm you sent whirling through me when I first felt the difference in you —felt your man's need of me, of *me*, body and soul! You meant me not to feel that, Ambo; but I did. I was only seventeen. And my first reaction was all passionate joy, a turbulent desire to give, give, give—and damn the consequences! It was, Ambo. I loved you.

But given you and me, Ambo, that couldn't last long. You're too moral— and I'm too complicated. My inner pattern's a labyrinth, full of queer magic; simple emotions soon get lost in me, lost and transformed. And please don't keep forgetting how young I was, and still am; how little I could understand of all I was conceited enough to think I understood! Well, dear, I saw you struggling to suppress your love for me as something wrong, unworthy; something that could only harm us both. And then all that first, swift, instinctive joy went out of me, and my old fear and distrust of what men call love seized me again. "Stuffiness, stuffiness everywhere—it leads to nothing but stuffiness!" I said. "I hate it. I won't let it rule my life. The great thing is to keep clear of it, clean of it, aloof and free!" The old Artemis-motive swept through me again like a hill-wind—but it came in gusts; and there were days —weeks, Ambo—when I simply wanted to be yours. And one night I threw myself into your arms... .

But the next day I was afraid again. The phrase "passion's slave" got into my head and plagued me. Then you came to me and said, "It's the end of the road, dear. We can't go on." That changed everything once more, Ambo, in a flash. That was my crisis. From that moment, I was madly jealous of Gertrude; knew I always had been, from the first. My telegram to her was a challenge to battle. It was, dear—and I lost. She came back; she was wonderful, too—her way—and the old Gertrude-dream stirred in you again; just stirred, but that was enough. You said to yourself, didn't you? that perhaps after all the best solution for our wretched difficulties was for Gertrude to return to her home. At least, that would end things. But you couldn't have said that to yourself if Gertrude had been really repulsive to you. The old dream had fluttered its tired wings, once, Ambo; you know it had!

And so I flopped again, dear! I was sick of love; I hated love! I said to myself, "I won't have this stupid, brutal, instinctive thing pushing and pulling me about like this! I'll rule my own life, thanks—my own thoughts and dreams! *Freedom's* the thing—the only good thing in life. I'll be free! Ambo, too, must learn to be free. We can only share what's honestly best in both of us when at last we are free!"

My Galahad-Jimmy had turned up again, too. Perhaps that had something to do with my final fiercest revolt against you. I don't know. He was all I had wanted him to be, Ambo; simple and straightforward and clean. Oh, he had his white, shining armor on, bless him! But I didn't want him to rescue me, for all that; not in the old way. I was just glad my dream-boy had come a little true; that's all. You were jealous of him, weren't you? Confess! You needn't have been.

But here in New York, with Sister, things happened that made a difference... .

First of all, dear, I discovered all I had lost in losing you; discovered I *couldn't* be free. All I could do was to make some kind of a life of it; for Sister, chiefly. And I tried; oh, I did try! Then those whispered scandals about us began. But it wasn't the scandal itself that did for me; it was something added to it—by Mrs. Arthur, I suppose—something *true*, Ambo, that I'd never honestly faced. Suddenly my father rose from the dead! Suddenly I was forced to feel that never, never under any conditions, would it have been possible for me to be yours—bear you children... . Suddenly I felt, saw—as I should have seen long ago—that the strain of evil, perhaps of madness, in my father—the strain that made his life a hell of black passions—must end with me!

Here's where Jimmy comes back, Ambo—and it's the worst of all I have to confess. My anxiety was all for you now: not for myself, I happened to love you that way. "Suppose," I kept thinking, "suppose something should unexpectedly make it possible for Ambo to ask me to be his wife? Suppose Gertrude should fall in love herself and insist on divorce? Or suppose she should die? Ambo would be certain to come to me. And if he did? Should I have the moral courage to send him away? As I must—I must!"

Dear, from that time on a sort of demon in me kept suggesting: "Jimmy— Jimmy's the solution! He's almost in love with you now; all he needs is a little encouragement. You could manage it, Susan. You could engage yourself to Jimmy; and then you could string him along! You could make it an interminable engagement, years and years of it, and break it off when Ambo was thoroughly discouraged or cured; you're clever enough for that. And Jimmy's ingenuousness itself. You could manage Jimmy." Oh, please don't think I ever really listened to my demon, was ever tempted by him! But I hated myself for the mere fact that such thoughts could even occur to me! They did, though, more than once; and each time I had to banish them, thrust them down into their native darkness.

But they didn't die there, Ambo; they lived there, a hideous secret life, lying in wait to betray me. They never will betray me, of course; I loathe them. But they can still stir in their darkness, make themselves known. That's what the references to Jimmy mean, Ambo, in those pages I scribbled in my trance; and that's *all* they mean. For I don't love him; I love you.

But I can't marry you, ever. I can't. That black strain concentrated in my father—oh, it must die out with me! Just as Sister's line ended with her... . She ran away from the one love of her life, Ambo—just as I must run away from you. You never knew that about Sister. But I knew it. Sonia told me. Sister told *her*, the week before Sonia married. Sister felt then that Sonia ought to run away from all that, as she had. But Sonia wouldn't listen to her... .

"Good for Sonia!" I might then have cried out. "God bless her! Hasn't she made her husband happy? Aren't her children his pride? Why in heaven's name should she have denied herself the right to live! And for a mere possibility of evil! As if the blood of any human family on earth were wholly sound, wholly blameless! Sonia was selfish, but right, dear; and Miss Goucher was brave, but wrong! So are you wrong! Actually inherited feeble-mindedness, or insanity, or disease—that's one thing; but a dread of mere future possibilities, of mere supposed tendencies! Good Lord! The human race might as well commit suicide *en bloc!* It's you I love—*you*—just as you are. And you say you love me. Well, that settles it!"

But who knows? It might have settled it and it might not—could any such imaginary conversation conceivably have taken place. It did not take place. We are dealing, worse luck, with history.

VIII

Perhaps six weeks after Miss Goucher's death one little conversation, just skirting these hidden matters, did take place between us; but how different was its atmosphere, and how drearily different its conclusion! You will understand it better now that—like a theater audience, or like God—you are in full possession of Susan's facts and of mine; but I fear it will interest you less. To know all may sometimes be to forgive all; but more often, alas, it is to be bored by everything.... .

[Firmly inserted note, by Susan: "Rubbish! It's only when we *think* we know it all, and don't really, that we are bored."]

I had taken Susan for dinner that night to a quiet hotel uptown where I knew the dining-room, mercifully lacking an orchestra and a cabaret, was not well patronized, though the cooking was exceptionally good. At this hotel, by a proper manipulation of the head waiter, it is often possible to get a table a little apart from the other diners—an advantage, if one desires to talk intimately without the annoyance of being overheard. It troubled me to find Susan's appetite practically nonexistent; I had ordered one or two special dishes to tempt her, but I saw that she took no pleasure in them, merely forcing herself to eat so as not to disquiet me. She was looking badly, too, all gleamless shadow, and fighting off a physical and mental languor by a stubborn effort which she might have concealed from another, but not from me. It was only too plain to me that her wish was to keep the conversation safely away from whatever was busying and saddening her private thoughts. In this, till the coffee was placed before us, I thought best to humor her, and we had discussed at great length the proper format for her first book of poems, which was to appear within the next month. Also, we had discussed Heywood Sampson's now rapidly maturing plans for his new critical review.

"He really wants me on his staff, Ambo, and I really want to be on it—just for the pleasure of working with him. It's an absolutely unbelievable chance for me! And yet——"

"And yet——? Is there any reason why you shouldn't accept?"

"At least two reasons, yes. I'm afraid both of them will surprise you."

"I wonder."

"Won't they? If not, Ambo, you must suppose you've guessed them. What are they?"

Susan rather had me here. I had not guessed them, but wasn't willing to admit even to myself that I could not if I tried. I puckered my brows, judicially.

"Well," I hesitated, "you may very naturally feel that 'Dax' is too plump a bird in the hand to be sacrificed for Heywood's slim bluebird in the bush. Any new publication's a gamble, of course. On the other hand, Heywood isn't the kind to leave his associates high and dry. Even if the review should fail, he'll stand by you somehow. He has a comfy fortune, you know; he could carry on the review as a personal hobby if he cares to, even if it never cleared a penny."

Susan smiled, gravely shaking her head: "Cold, dear; stone cold. I'm pretty mercenary these days, but I'm not quite so mercenary as that. Now that I've discovered I can make a living, I'm not nearly so interested in it; hardly at all. It's the stupid side of life, always; I shouldn't like it to make much difference to me now, when it comes to real decisions. I did want a nice home for Sister, though. As for me, any old room most anywhere will do. It will, Ambo; don't laugh; I'm in earnest. But what's your second guess?" she added quickly.

"You've some writing you want to do—a book, maybe? You're afraid the review will interfere?"

"Ah, now you're a tiny bit warmer! I am afraid it will interfere, but in a much deeper way than that; interfere with *me*."

"I don't quite follow that, do I!"

"Good gracious, no—since you ask. It's simple enough, though—and pretty vague. Only it feels important—here." For an instant her hand just touched her breast. "I hate so to be roped in, Ambo, have things staked out for me—spiritually, I mean. Mr. Sampson's a darling; I love him! But he's a great believer in ropes and stakes and fences—even barbed wire. I'm beginning to see that the whole idea of his review is a scheme for mending political and moral and social fences, stopping up gaps in them made by irresponsible idealists—anarchists, revolutionary socialists—people like that. People like me, really!—There! Now you do look surprised."

I was; but I smiled.

"You've turned *Red*, Susan? How long since? Overnight?"

"Not red," answered Susan, with bravely forced gayety; "pinkish, say! I haven't fixed on my special shade till I'm sure it becomes me."

"It's certain to do that, dear."

She bobbed me a little bow across the cloth, much in the old happy style— alas, not quite. "But I never did like washed-out colors," she threw in for good measure.

"You *are* irresponsible, then! Suppose Phil could hear you—or Jimmy. Jimmy'd say your Greenwich Village friends were corrupting you. Perhaps they are?"

"Perhaps they are," echoed Susan, "but I think not. I'm afraid it goes farther back, Ambo. It's left-over Birch Street; that's what it is. So much of me's that. All of me, I sometimes believe."

"Not quite. You'll never escape Hillhouse, either, Susan. You've had both."

"Yes, I've had both," she echoed again, almost on a sigh, pushing her untasted *demi-tasse* from her.

Suddenly her elbows were planted on the cloth before her, her face—shadowed and too finely drawn—dropped between her hands, her eyes sought and held mine. They dizzied me, her eyes....

"Ambo," she said earnestly, "I suppose I'm a dreadful egotist, but more and more I'm feeling the real me isn't a true child of this world! I love this world—and I hate it. I don't know whether I love it most or hate it most. I bless it and damn it every day of my life—in the same breath often. But sometimes I feel I hate it most—hate it for its cold dullness of head and heart! Why can't we care more to make it worth living in, this beautiful, frightful world! What's the matter with us? Why are we what we are? Half angels—and half pigs or goats or saber-toothed tigers or snakes! Each and every one of us, by and large! And oh, how we do distrust our three-quarters angels—while they're living, anyway! Dreamers—mad visionaries—social rebels—outcasts! Crucify them, crucify them! Time enough to worship them—ages of to-be-wasted time enough—when they're dead!" She paused, still holding my eyes, and drawing in a slow breath, a breath that caught midway and was almost a sob; then her eyes left mine.

"There—that's over. Saying things like that doesn't help us a bit; it's—silly.... And half the idealists *are* mad, no doubt, and have plenty of pig and snake in them, too. I've simply coils and coils of unregenerate serpent in me—and worse. Oh, Ambo dear—but I've a dream in me beyond all that, and a great longing to help it come true! But it doesn't—it won't. I'm afraid it never will—here. Will it *there*, Ambo? Is there a *there?* . . . Have we got all of Sister that clean fire couldn't take, shut up in that tiny vase?"

"We can hope not, at least," I replied.

"Hope isn't enough," said Susan. "Why don't you say you *know* we haven't! I know we haven't. I do know it. It's the only thing I—*know!*"

A nervous waiter sidled up to us and softly slipped a small metal tray before me; it held my bill, carefully turned face downward.

"Anything more, sir?" he murmured.

"A liqueur?" I suggested to Susan. She sat upright in her chair again, with a slight impatient shake of the head.

I ordered a cigar and a *fine champagne*. The waiter, still nervously fearful of having approached us at a moment when he suspected some intimate question of the heart had grown critically tense, faded from us with the slightest, discreetest cough of reassurance. He was not one, he would have us know, to obtrude material considerations when they were out of place.

"No; I can't go with Mr. Sampson," Susan was saying; "and he'll be hurt —he won't be able to see why. But I'm not made to be an editor—of anything. Editors have to weigh other people's words. I can't even weigh my own. And I talk of nothing but myself. Ugh!"

"You're tired out, overwrought," I stupidly began.

"Don't tell me so!" cried Susan. "If I should believe you, I'd be lost."

"But," I blundered on, "it's only common sense to let down a little, at such a time. If you'd only take a real rest——"

"There is no such thing," said Susan. "We just struggle on and on. It's rather awful, isn't it?" And presently, very quietly, as if to herself, she said over those words, surely among the saddest and loveliest ever written by mortal man:

> From too much love of living,
> From hope and fear set free,
> We thank with brief thanksgiving
> Whatever gods may be
>
> That no life lives forever,
> That dead men rise up never;
> That even the weariest river
> Winds somewhere safe to sea.

"To sea," she repeated; "to sea... . As if the sea itself knew rest!—Now please pay your big fat bill from your nice fat pocketbook, Ambo; and take me home."

"If I only could!" was my despairing thought; and I astounded the coat-room boy, as I tipped him, by muttering aloud, "Oh, damn Jimmy Kane!"

"Yes, sir—thank you, sir—I will, sir," grinned the coat-room boy.

On our way downtown in the taxi Susan withdrew until we reached her West Tenth Street door. "Good-night, Ambo," she then said; "don't come with me; and thank you for everything—always." I crossed the pavement with her to the loutish brownstone front-stoop of the boarding house; there she turned to dismiss me.

"You didn't ask my second reason for not going on the review, Ambo. You must know it though, sooner or later. I can't *write* any more—not well, I mean. Even my Dax paragraphs are falling off; Hadow Bury mentioned it yesterday. But nothing comes. I'm sterile, Ambo. I'm written out at twenty. Bless you. Good-night."

"Susan," I cried, "come back here at once!" But she just turned in the doorway to smile back at me, waved her hand, and was gone.

I was of two minds whether to follow her or stay. Then, "A whim," I thought; "the whim of a tired child. And I've often felt that way myself—all writers do. But she must take a vacation of some kind—she must!"

She did.

IX

I woke up the next morning, broad awake before seven o'clock, a full hour earlier than my habit. I woke to find myself greatly troubled by Susan's parting words of the night before, and lay in bed for perhaps twenty minutes turning them over fretfully in my mind. Then I could stand it no longer and rose, bathed, dressed and ate my breakfast in self-exasperating haste, yet with no very clear idea of why I was hurrying or what was to follow. I had an appointment with my lawyer for eleven; I was to lunch with Heywood Sampson at one; after lunch—my immediate business in town being completed—I had purposed to return to New Haven.

Susan would be expecting me for my daily morning call at half-past nine. That call was a fixed custom between us when I was stopping in New York. It seldom lasted over twenty minutes and was really just an opportunity to say good-morning and arrange conveniently for any further plans for the day or evening. But it was now only a few minutes past eight. No matter, Susan was both a nighthawk and a lark, retiring always too late and rising too early—though it must be said she seemed to need little sleep; and I felt that I must see her at once and try somehow to encourage her about her work and bring her back to a more reasonable and normal point of view. "Overstrain," I kept mumbling to myself, idiotically enough, as I charged rather than walked down Fifth Avenue from my hotel: "Overstrain—overstrain... ."

However, the brisk physical exertion of my walk gradually quieted my nerves, and as I turned west on Tenth Street I was beginning to feel a little ashamed of my unreasonable anxiety, was even beginning to poke a little fun at myself and preparing to amuse Susan if I could by a whimsical account of my morning brainstorm. I had now persuaded myself that I should find her quietly at work, as I so usually did, and quite prepared to talk things over more calmly. I meant this time to make a supreme effort, and really hoped to persuade her to do two sensible things: First, to accept Heywood Sampson's offer; second, to give up all other work for the present, and get a complete rest and change of scene until her services were needed for the review. That would not be for six or eight weeks at the very least.

And I at last had a plan for her. You may or may not remember that Ashton Parker was a famous man thirty years ago; they called him "Hyena Parker" in Wall Street, and no doubt he deserved it; yet he faded gently out with consumption like any spring poet, having turned theosophist toward the end and made his peace with the Cosmic Urge. Mrs. Ashton Parker is an aunt of mine, long a widow, and a most delightful, easy-going, wide-awake, and sympathetic old lady, who has made her home in Santa Barbara ever since her husband's death there. Her Spanish villa and gardens are famous, and her always kindly eccentricities scarcely less famous than they. I could imagine no one more certain to captivate Susan or to be instantly captivated by her; and though I had not seen Aunt Belle for more than ten years, I knew I could count on her in advance to fall in with my plan. Her hospitality is notorious and would long since have beggared anyone with an income less absurd. Susan should go there at once, for a month at least; the whole thing could be arranged by telegraph. Why in heaven's name hadn't I thought of and insisted upon this plan before!

Miss O'Neill, in person, opened the front door for me.

"Oh, Mr. Hunt!" she wailed. "Thanks to goodness you're here early. I can't do nothing with Togo. He won't eat no breakfast, and he won't let nobody touch him. He's sitting up there like a—I don't know what, with his precious tail uncurled and his head sort of hanging down—it'll break your heart to look at him! I can't bear to myself, though I'd never no use for the beast, neither liking nor disliking! He's above his station, I say. But what with all—— And I've got to get that room cleared and redone by twelve, feelings or no feelings, and Gawd knows feelings *will* enter in! Not half Miss Susan's class either, the new party just now applied, and right beside my own room, too, though well recommended, so I can't complain!"

I broke through her dusty web of words with an impatient, "What on earth are you talking about, Miss O'Neill?"

"You don't know?" she gasped. "You don't——"

"I most certainly do not. Where's Miss Susan?"

"Oh, Mr. Hunt! If I'd-a knowed she hadn't even spoke to you! And you with her all evening—treating to dinner and all! But thank Gawd it's a reel lady she went away with! Miss Leslie, in her big limousine, that's often been here! *That* I can swear to you with my own eyes!"

Susan was gone, and gone beyond hope of an immediate return. There is no need to labor the details of her flight. A letter, left for me with Miss O'Neill, gives all the surface facts essential.

"*Dear Ambo:* Try not to be angry with me; or too hurt. When I left you last night I decided to seize an opportunity which had to be seized instantly, or not at all. Mona Leslie has been planning for a long European sojourn all winter, and for the past two weeks has been trying to persuade me to go with her as a sort of overpaid companion and private secretary. She has dangled a salary before me out of all proportion to my possible value to her, but—never feeling very sympathetic toward her sudden whims and moods—that hasn't tempted me.

"Now, at the eleventh hour, literally, this chance for a complete break with my whole past and probable future has tempted me, and I've flopped. You've been urging my need for rest and change; if that's what I do need this will supply it, the change at least—with no sacrifice of my hard-fought-for financial independence. It was the abysmal prospect, as I came in, of having to go straight to my room—with no Sister waiting for me—and beat my poor typewriter and poorer brains for some sparks of wit—when I knew in advance there wasn't a spark left in me—that sent me to the telephone.

"Now I'm packed—in half an hour—and waiting for Mona. The boat sails about three A.M.; I don't even know her name: we'll be on her by midnight. Poor Miss O'Neill is flabbergasted—and so I'm afraid will you be, and Phil and Jimmy. I know it isn't kind of me simply to vanish like this; but try to feel that I don't mean to be unkind. Not even to Togo, though my treachery to him is villainous. It will be a black mark against me in Peter's book forever. But I can't take him, Ambo; I just can't. Please, please—will *you?* You see, dear, I can't help being a nuisance to you always, after all. And I can't even promise you Togo will learn to love you, any more than Tumps—though I hope he may. He'll grieve himself thin at first. He knows something's in the air and he's grieving beside me now. His eyes—— If Mona doesn't come soon, I may collapse at his paws and promise him to stay.

"Mona talks of a year over there, from darkest Russia to lightest France; possibly two. Her plans are characteristically indefinite. She knows heaps of

172

people all over, of course. I'll write often. Please tell Hadow and Mr. Sampson I'm a physical wreck—or mental, if it sounds more convincing. I'm neither; but I'm tired—tired—*tired.*

"If you can possibly help Phil and Jimmy to understand——

"Here's Mona now. Good-by, dear.

"Your ashamed, utterly grateful

"SUSAN.

"P. S. I'm wearing your furs."

THE SIXTH CHAPTER

I

S O Togo and I went home. My misery craving company, I rode with him all the way up in the baggage-car, on the self-deceptive theory that he needed an everpresent friend. It is true, however, that he did; and it gratified me and a little cheered me that he seemed really to appreciate my attentions. I sat on a trunk, lighting each cigarette from the end of the last, and he sat at my feet, leaned wearily against the calf of my right leg and permitted me to fondle his ears... .

II

"Spring, the sweet spring!" Then birds do sing, hey-ding-a-ding—and so on... . Sweet lovers love the spring... . Jimmy, Phil and I saw little of each other those days. Jimmy clouded his sunny brow and started in working overtime. Phil plunged headlong into what was to have proved his philosophical *magnum opus*—"The Pluralistic Fallacy; a Critical Study of Pragmatism." I also plunged headlong into a series of interpretative essays for Heywood Sampson's forthcoming review. My first essay was to be on Tolstoy; my second, on Nietzsche; my third, on Anatole France; my fourth, on Samuel Butler and Bernard Shaw; my fifth, on Thomas Hardy; and my sixth and last, on Walt Whitman. From the works of these writers it was my purpose to illustrate and clarify for the semicultured the more significant intellectual and spiritual tendencies of our enlightened and humane civilization. It is characteristic that I supposed myself well equipped for this task. But I never got beyond my detached, urbane appreciation of Nietzsche; just as I had concluded it—our enlightened and humane civilization suddenly blew to atoms with a *cliché*-shattering report and a vile stench as of too-long-imprisoned gas... .

III

During those first months of Susan's absence, which for more than four years were to prove the last months of almost world-wide and wholly world-deceptive peace, several things occurred of more or less importance to the present history. They marked, for one thing, the auspicious sprouting and rapid initial growth of Susan's literary reputation. Her poems appeared little more than a month after she had left us, a well-printed volume of less than a hundred pages, in a sober green cover. I had taken a lonely sort of joy in reading and rereading the proof; and if even a split letter escaped me, it has not yet been brought to my attention. These poems were issued under a quiet title and an unobtrusive pen-name, slipping into the market-place without any preliminary puffing, and I feared they were of too fine a texture to attract the notice that I felt they deserved. But in some respects, at least, Susan was born under a lucky star. An unforeseen combination of events suddenly focused public attention—just long enough to send it into a third edition—upon this inconspicuous little book.

Concurrently with its publication, *The Puppet Booth* opened its doors—its door, rather—on Macdougal Street; an artistic venture quite as marked, you would say, for early oblivion as Susan's own. The cocoon of *The Puppet Booth* was a small stable where a few Italian venders of fruit and vegetables had kept their scarecrow horses and shabby carts and handcarts. From this drab cocoon issued a mailed and militant dragon-fly; vivid, flashing, erratic; both ugly and beautiful—and wholly alive! For there were in Greenwich Village—as there are, it would seem, in all lesser villages, from Florida to Oregon—certain mourners over and enthusiasts for the art called Drama, which they believed to be virtually extinct. Shows, it is true, hundreds of them, were each season produced on Broadway, and some of these delighted hosts of the affluent, sentimental, and child-like American *bourgeoisie*. Fortunate managers, playsmiths and actors, endowed with sympathy for the crude tastes of this *bourgeoisie*, a sympathy partly instinctive and partly developed by commercial acumen, waxed fat with a prosperity for which the Village could not wearily enough express its contempt.

None of these creatures, said the Village—no, not one—was a genuine artist! The Theater, they affirmed, had been raped by the Philistines and prostituted to sophomoric merrymakers by cynical greed. The Theater! Why, it should be a temple, inviolably dedicated to its peculiar god. Since the death of religion, it was perhaps the one temple worthy of pious preservation. Only in a Theater, sincerely consecrated to the great god, Art, could the enlightened, the sophisticated, the free—unite to worship. There only, they implied, could something adumbrating a sacred ritual and a spiritual consolation be preserved.

Luckily for Susan, and indeed for us all—for we have all been gainers from the spontaneous generation of "little theaters" all over America, a phenomenon at its height just previous to the war—one village enthusiast, Isidore Stalinski—by vocation an accompanist, by avocation a vorticist, by race and nature a publicist—had succeeded in mildly infecting Mona Leslie—

who took everything in the air, though nothing severely—with offhand zeal for his cause. The importance of her rather casual conversion lay in the fact that her purse strings were perpetually untied. Stalinski well knew that you cannot run even a tiny temple for a handful of worshippers without vain oblations on the side to the false gods of this world, and these imply—oh, Art's desire!—a donor. And of all possible varieties of donor, that most to be desired is the absentee donor—the donor who donates as God sends rain, unseen.

At precisely the right moment Stalinski whispered to Mona Leslie that *entre them*—though he didn't care to be quoted—he preferred her interpretation of Faure's *Clair de Lune* to that of ——, the particular *diva* he had just been accompanying through a long, rapturously advertised concert tour; and Mona Leslie, about to be off on her European flight, became the absentee donor to *The Puppet Booth*.

The small stable was leased and cleansed and sufficiently reshaped to live up to its anxiously chosen name. Much of the reshaping and all of the decorating was done, after business hours, by the clever and pious hands of the villagers. Then four one-act plays were selected from among some hundreds poured forth by village genius to its rehabilitated god. The clever and pious hands flew faster than ever, busying themselves with scenery and costumes and properties and color and lighting—all blended toward the creation of a thoroughly uncommercial atmosphere. And the four plays were staged, directed, acted, and finally attended by the Village. It was a perfectly lovely party and the pleasantest of times was had by all.

And it only remains to drop this tone of patronizing persiflage and admit, with humblest honesty, that the first night at *The Puppet Booth* was that very rare thing, a complete success; what Broadway calls a "knockout." Within a fortnight seats for *The Puppet Booth* were at a ruinous premium in all the ticket agencies on or near Times Square.

I happened to be there on that ecstatic opening night. Susan, in her first letter, from Liverpool, had enjoined me to attend and report; Mona would be glad to learn from an unprejudiced outsider how the affair went off. But Susan did not mention the fact that one of the four selected plays had been written by herself.

Jimmy was with me. Phil, who saw more of him than I did, thought he was going stale from overwork, so I had made a point of hunting him up and dragging him off with me for a night in town. He hadn't wanted to go; said frankly, he wasn't in the mood. I'm convinced it was the first time he had ever used the word "mood" in connection with himself or anybody else. Jimmy and moods of any kind simply didn't belong together.

We had a good man's dinner at a good man's chop-house that night, and, once I got Jimmy to work on it, his normal appetite revived and he engulfed oysters and steak and a deep-dish apple pie and a mug or so of ale, with mounting gusto. We talked, of course, of Susan.

Jimmy, inclined to a rosier view by comfortable repletion, now maintained that perhaps after all Susan had done the natural and sensible thing in joining Miss Leslie. He emphasized all the obvious advantages—complete change of environment, freedom from financial worry, and so on; then he paused... .

"And there's another point, Mr. Hunt," he began again, doubtfully this time: "Prof. Farmer and I were talking about it only the other day. We were wondering whether we oughtn't to speak to you. But it's not the easiest thing to speak of—it's so sort of vague—kind of a feeling in the air."

I knew at once what he referred to, and nodded my head. "So you and Phil have noticed it too!"

"Oh, you're *on* then? I'm glad of that, sir. You've never mentioned anything, so Prof. Farmer and I couldn't be sure. But it's got under our skins that it might make a lot of trouble and something ought to be done about it. It's hard to see what."

"Very," I agreed. "Fire ahead, Jimmy. Tell me exactly what has come to you—to you, personally, I mean."

"Well," said Jimmy, leaning across the table to me and lowering his voice, "it was all of three weeks ago. I went to a dance at the Lawn Club. I don't dance very well, but I figure a fellow ought to know how if he ever has to, so I've slipped in a few lessons. I can keep off my partner's feet, anyway. Well, Steve Putnam took me round that night and introduced me to some girls. I guess if they'd known my mother was living in New Haven and married to a grocer, they wouldn't have had anything to do with me. Maybe I ought to advertise the fact, but I don't—simply because I can't stand for my stepfather, and so mother won't stand for me. Mother and I never could get on, though; and it's funny, too—as a general rule I can get on with 'most everybody. I told Prof. Farmer the other night there must be something wrong with a fellow who can't get on with his own mother—but he only laughed. Of course, Mr. Hunt, I'm not exactly sailing under false pretenses, either; if any girl wanted to make real friends with me—I'd tell her all about myself first."

"Of course," I murmured.

"And the same with men. Steve, for instance. He knows all about me, and his father has a lot of money, but he made it in soap—and Steve's from the West, anyway, and don't care. Gee, I'm wandering—it's the ale, I guess, Mr.

Hunt; I'm not used to it. The point is. Steve introduced me round, and I like girls all right, but Susan's kind of spoiled me for the way most of them gabble. I can't do that easy, quick-talk very good yet; Steve's a bear at it. Well —I sat out a dance with one of the girls, a Miss Simmons; pretty, too; but she's only a kid. It was her idea, sitting out the dance in a corner—I thought she didn't like the way I handled myself. But that wasn't it. Mr. Hunt, she wanted to pump me; went right at it, too.

"'You know Mr. Hunt awfully well, don't you?' she asked; and after I'd said yes, and we'd sort of sparred round a little, she suddenly got confidential, and a kind of thrilled look came into her eyes, and then she asked me straight out: 'Have you ever heard there was something—*mysterious*—about poor Mrs. Hunt's death?'

"'No,' I said.

"'Haven't you!' she said, as much as to tell me she knew, all the same, I must have. 'Why, Mr. Kane, it's all over town. Nobody knows anything, but it's terribly exciting! Some people think she committed suicide, all because of that queer Miss Blake.... She must be—*you* know! And now she's run away to Europe! I believe she was just afraid to stay over here, afraid she might be found out or arrested—or something!'

"That's the way she went on, Mr. Hunt; and, well—naturally, I pooh-poohed it and steered her off, and then she lost interest in me right away. But she's right, Mr. Hunt. There's a lot of that kind of whispered stuff in the air, and I'm mighty glad Susan's off for a year or two where she can't run into it. It'll all die out before she's back again, of course."

"I hope so," was my reply; "but the source of these rumors is very persistent—and very discreet. They start from Mrs. Arthur; they must. But it's impossible to trace them back to her. Jimmy, she means to make New Haven impossible for me, and I've an idea she's likely to succeed. Already, three or four old acquaintances have—well, avoided me, and the general atmosphere's cooling pretty rapidly toward zero. So far as I'm concerned, it doesn't much matter; but it does matter for Susan. She may return to find her whole future clouded by a settled impression that in some way—indirectly—or even, directly—she was responsible for my wife's sudden death."

"It's a damned outrage!" exclaimed Jimmy. "I don't know Mrs. Arthur, but I'd like to wring her neck!"

"So would I, Jimmy; and she knows it. That's why she's finding life these days so supremely worth living."

Jimmy pondered this. "Gee, I hate to think that badly of any woman," he finally achieved; "but I guess it doesn't do to be a fool and think they're all angels—like Susan. Mother's not."

"No, Jimmy, it doesn't do," I responded. "Still, the price for that kind of wisdom is always much higher than it's worth."

"Women," began Jimmy—— But his aphorism somehow escaped him; he decided to light a cigarette instead... .

And on this wave of cynicism I floated him off with me to *The Puppet Booth*.

IV

From the point of view of eccentric effectiveness and *réclame* wonders had been wrought with the small, ancient, brick stable on Macdougal Street; but very little had been or could be done for the comfort of its guests. The flat exterior wall had been stuccoed and brilliantly frescoed to suggest the entrance to some probably questionable side-show at a French village fair; and a gay clown with a drum, an adept at amusing local patter, had been stationed before the door to emphasize the *funambulesque* illusion. Within, this atmosphere—as of something gaudy and transitory, the mere lath-and-canvas pitch of a vagabond *banquiste*—had been cleverly carried out. The cramped little theater itself struck one as mere scenery, which was precisely the intention. There was clean sawdust on the floor, and the spectators—one hundred of them suffocatingly filled the hall—were provided only with wooden benches, painted a vivid Paris green. These benches had been thoughtfully selected, however, and were less excruciating to sit on than you would suppose. There was, naturally, no balcony; a false pitch-roof had been constructed of rough stable beams, from which hung bannerets in a crying, carefully studied dissonance of strong color, worthy of the barbaric Bakst. The proscenium arch was necessarily a toylike affair, copied, you would say, from the *Guinol* in the Tuileries Gardens; and the curtain, for a final touch, looked authentic—had almost certainly been acquired, at some expenditure of thought and trouble, from a traveling Elks' Carnival. There was even a false set of footlights to complete the masquerade; a row of oil lamps with tin reflectors. It was all very restless and amusing—and extravagantly make-believe... .

Jimmy and I arrived just in time to squeeze down the single narrow side-aisle and into our places in the fourth row. We had no opportunity to glance about us or consult our broad-sheet programs, none to acquire the proper mood of tense expectancy we later succumbed to, before the lights were lowered and the curtain was rolled up in the true antique style. "Gee!"

muttered Jimmy, on my left, with involuntary dislike. "Ah!" breathed a maiden, on my right, with entirely voluntary rapture. Someone in the front row giggled, probably a cub reporter doing duty that evening as a dramatic critic; but he was silenced by a sharp hiss from the rear.

The cause for these significant reactions was the *mise en scène* of the tiny vacant stage. It consisted of three dead-black walls, a dead-black ceiling, and a dead-black floor-cloth. In the back wall there was a high, narrow crimson door with a black knob. A tall straight-legged table and one straight high-backed chair, both lacquered in crimson, were the only furniture, except for a slender crimson-lacquered perch, down right, to which was chained a yellow, green and crimson macaw. And through the crimson door presently entered— undulated, rather—a personable though poisonous young woman in a trailing robe of vivid yellow and green.

The play that followed, happily a brief one, was called—as Jimmy and I learned from our programs at its conclusion—"Polly." It consisted of a monologue delivered by the poisonous young woman to the macaw, occasionally varied by *ad lib.* screams and chuckles from that evil white-eyed bird. From the staccato remarks of the poisonous young woman, we, the audience, were to deduce the erratic eroticism of an *âme damnée*. It was not particularly difficult to do so, nor was it particularly entertaining. As a little adventure in supercynicism, "Polly," in short, was not particularly successful. It needed, and had not been able to obtain, the boulevard wit of a Sacha Guitry to carry it off. But the poisonous young woman had an exquisitely proportioned figure, and her arms, bare to the slight shoulder-straps, were quite faultless. Minor effects of this kind have, even on Broadway, been known to save more than one bad quarter hour from complete collapse... . No, it was not the author's lines that carried us safely through this first fifteen minutes of diluted Strindberg-Schnitzler! And the too deliberately bizarre *mise en scène*, though for a moment it piqued curiosity, had soon proved wearisome, and we were glad—at least, Jimmy and I were—to have it veiled from our eyes.

The curtain rolled down, nevertheless, to ecstatic cries and stubbornly sustained applause. Raised lights revealed an excited, chattering band of the faithful. The poisonous young woman took four curtain calls and would seemingly, from her parting gesture, have drawn us collectively to her fine bosom with those faultless, unreluctant arms. And the maiden on my right shuddered forth to her escort, "I'm thrilled, darling! Feel them—feel my hands—they're *moon-cold!* They always are, you know, when I'm thrilled!"

"You can't beat this much, Mr. Hunt," whispered Jimmy, on my left. "It's bughouse."

In a sense, it was; in a truer sense, it was not. A careful analysis of the audience would, I was quickly convinced, have disclosed not merely a saving remnant, but a saving majority of honest workmen in the arts—men and women too solidly endowed with brains and humor for any self-conscious posing or public exhibition of temperament. The genuine freaks among us were a scant handful; but it is the special talent and purpose of your freak to—in Whitman's phrase—"positively appear." Ten able freaks to the hundred can turn any public gathering into a side show; and the freaks of the Village, particularly the females of the species, are nothing if not able. Minna Freund, for example, who was sitting just in front of Jimmy; it would be difficult for any assembly to obliterate Minna Freund! She was, that night, exceptionally repulsive in a sort of yellow silk wrapper, with her sparrow's nest of bobbed Henner hair, and her long, bare, olive-green neck, that so obviously needed to be scrubbed!

Having strung certain entirely unrelated words together and called them "Portents," she had in those days acquired a minor notoriety, and Susan—impishly enjoying my consequent embarrassment—had once introduced me to her as an admirer of her work, at an exhibition of Cubist sculpture. Minna was standing at the time, I recalled, before Pannino's "Study of a Morbid Complex," and she at once informed me that the morbid complex in question had been studied from the life. She had posed her own destiny for Pannino, so she assured me, at three separate moments of psychic crisis, and the inevitable result had been a masterpiece. "How it writhes!" she had exclaimed: but to my uninstructed eyes Pannino's Study did anything but writhe; it was stolidly passive; it looked precisely as an ostrich egg on a pedestal would look if viewed in a slightly convex mirror.... How far away all that stupid nonsense seems!

And, suddenly, Jimmy leaped on the bench beside me as if punctured by a pin: "Oh, good Lord, Mr. Hunt!" he groaned. "Look here!"

He had thrust his program before me and was pointing to the third play of the series with an unsteady finger.

"It's the same name," he whispered hoarsely; "the one she's used for her book. Do you think——"

"I'll soon find out," was my answer. "We must know what we're in for, Jimmy!" And just as the lights were lowered for the second play I rose, defying audible unpopularity, and squeezed my way out to the door. That is why I cannot describe for you the second play, a harsh little tragedy of the sweatshops—"Horrible," Jimmy affirmed, "but it kind of *got* me!"—written by an impecunious young man with expensive tastes, who has since won the means of gratifying them along Broadway by concocting for that golden glade his innocently naughty librettos—"*Tra-la, Thérèse!*" and "*Oh, Mercy, Modestine!*"

Having sought and interviewed Stalinski—I found him huddled in the tiny box-office, perspiring unpleasantly from nervousness and many soaring emotions—I was back in my seat, more unpopular than ever, in good time for Susan's—it was unquestionably Susan's—play.

But most of you have read, or have seen, or have read about, Susan's play... .

It was the sensation of the evening, of many subsequent evenings; and I have often wondered precisely why—for there is in it nothing sensational. Its atmosphere is delicately fantastic; remote, you would say, from the sympathies of a matter-of-fact world, particularly as its fantasy is not the highly sentimentalized make-believe of some popular fairy tale. This fantasy of Susan's is ironic and grave; simple in movement, too—just a few subtle modulations on a single poignant theme. And I ask myself wherein lies its throat-tightening quality, its irresistible appeal? And I find but one answer; an answer which I had always supposed, in my long intellectual snobbery, an undeserved compliment to the human race; a compliment no critic, who was not either dishonest or a fool, could pay mankind.

But what other explanation can be given for the success of Susan's play, both here and in England, than its sheer *beauty?* Beauty of substance, of mood, of form, of quiet, heart-searching phrase! It is not called "The Magic Circle," but it might have been; for its magic is genuine, distilled from the depths of Nature, and it casts an unescapable spell—on poets and bankers, on publicans and prostitutes and priests, on all and sundry, equally and alike. It even casts its spell on those who act in it, and no truer triumph can come to an author. I have never seen it really badly played. Susan has never seen it played at all.

On the first wave of this astonishing triumph, Susan's pen-name was swept into the newspapers and critical journals of America and England, and a piquant point for gossip was added by the revelation that "Dax," who for several months had so wittily enlivened the columns of *Whim*, was one and the same person. Moreover, it was soon bruited about that the author was a slip of a girl—radiantly beautiful, of course; or why romance concerning her! —and that there was something mysterious, even sinister, in her history.

"A child of the underworld," said one metropolitan journal, in its review of her poems. Popular legend presently connected her, though vaguely, with the criminal classes. I have heard an overdressed woman in a theater lobby earnestly assuring another that she knew for a fact that —— (Susan) had been born in a brothel—"one of those houses, my dear"—and brought up—like Oliver Twist, though the comparison escaped her—to be a thief.

And so it was that the public eye lighted for a little hour on Susan's shy poems. Poetry was said to be looking up in those days; and influential critics in their influential, uninfluenced way suddenly boomed these, saying mostly the wrong things about them, but saying them over and over with energy and persistence. The first edition vanished overnight; a larger second edition was printed and sold out within a week or two; a still larger third edition was launched and disposed of more slowly. Then came the war.... .

V

If I can say anything good of the war, it is this: Since seemingly it must have come anyway, sooner or later, so far as Susan is concerned it came just in time. A letter from Phil to Susan, received toward the close of July, 1914, at the château of the Comtesse de Bligny, near Brussels, will tell you why.

"*Dear Susan:* If the two or three notes I've sent you previously have been brief and dull, I knew you would make the inevitable allowances and forgive me. In the first place, God didn't create me to scintillate, as you've long had reason to know; and since you left us I've been buried in a Sahara of work, living so retired a life in my desert that little news comes my way. But Jimmy breaks in on me, always welcomely, with an occasional bulletin, and last night Hunt came over and we had a long evening together. He's worried, Susan, not without great cause, I fear; he looks tired and ill; and after mulling things over, with my usual plodding caution—I've thought best to explain the situation to you.

"It can be put in very few words. The deserved success of your play and the poems, following a natural law that one too helplessly wishes otherwise, has led to a crisis in the gossip—malicious in origin, certainly—which has fastened upon you and Hunt; and this gossip lately has taken a more sinister turn. More and more openly it is being said that the circumstances surrounding Mrs. Hunt's death ought to be probed—'probed' is just now the popular word in this connection. The feeling is widespread that you were in some way responsible for it.

"I must use brutal phrases to lay the truth before you. You are not, seemingly, suspected of murder. You are suspected of having killed Mrs. Hunt during a sudden access of mental irresponsibility. It is whispered that Hunt, improperly, in some devious way, got the matter hushed up and the affair reported as an accident. As a result of these absurd and terrible rumors, Hunt finds himself a pariah—many of his oldest acquaintances no longer recognize him when they meet. It is a thoroughly distressing situation, and it's difficult to see how the mad injustice of it can be easily righted.

"The danger is, of course, that some misguided person will get the whole matter into the newspapers; it is really a miracle that it has not already been seized on by some yellow sheet, the opportunity for a sensational story is so obviously ripe. Happily"—oh, Phil! oh, philosopher!—"the present curious tension in European politics is for the moment turning journalistic eyes far from home. But as all such diplomatic flurries do, this one will pass, leaving the flatness of the silly season upon us. This is what Hunt most fears; and when you next see him you will find him grayer and older because of this anxiety.

"He dreads, for you, a sudden journalistic demand for a public investigation, and feels—though in this I can hardly agree with him—that such a demand could end only in a public trial, in view of the peculiar nature of all the circumstances involved—a veritable *cause célèbre.*

"How shocking all this must be to you. The sense of the mental anguish I'm causing you is a horror to me. Nothing could have induced me to write in this way but the compulsion of my love for Hunt and you. It seems to me imperative that your names should be publicly cleared, in advance of any public outcry.

"So I urge you, Susan—fully conscious of my personal responsibility in doing so—to return at once and to join with Hunt and your true friends in quashing finally and fully these damnable lies. It is my strong conviction that this is your duty to yourself, to Hunt, and to us all. If you and Hunt, together or separately, make a public statement, in view of the rumors now current, and yourselves demand the fullest public investigation of the facts, there can be but one issue. Your good names will be cleared; the truth will prevail. Dreadful as this prospect must be for you both, it now seems to me—and let me add, to Jimmy—the one wise course for you to take. But only you, if you agree with me, can persuade Hunt to such a course…."

It is unnecessary to quote the remaining paragraphs of Phil's so characteristic letter.

———————————

No doubt Susan would have returned immediately if she could, but, less than a week after the receipt of Phil's letter, the diplomatic flurry in Europe had taken a German army through Luxemburg and into Belgium, and within less than two weeks Susan and Mona Leslie and the Comtesse de Bligny were in uniform, working a little less than twenty-four hours a day with the Belgian Red Cross… .

It is no purpose of mine to attempt any description of Susan's war experience or service. Those first corroding weeks and months of the war have left ineffaceable scars on the consciousness of the present generation. I was not a part of them, and can add nothing to them by talking about them at second hand. It might, however, repay you to read—if you have not already done so—a small anonymous volume which has passed through some twenty or thirty editions, entitled *Stupidity Triumphant*, and containing the brief, sharply etched personal impressions of a Red Cross nurse in Flanders during the early days of Belgium's long agony. It is now an open secret that this little book was written by Susan; and among the countless documents on frightfulness this one, surely, by reason of its simplicity and restraint, its entire absence of merely hysterical outcry, is not the least damning and not—I venture to believe—the least permanent.

There is one short paragraph in this book of detached pictures, marginal notes, and condensed reflections that brought home to me, personally, *war*, the veritable thing itself, as no other written lines were able to do—as nothing was able to do until I had seen the beast with my own eyes. It is not an especially striking paragraph, and just why it should have done so I am unable to say. Certain extracts from the book have been widely quoted—one even, I am told, was read out in Parliament by Arthur Henderson—but I have never seen this one quoted anywhere; so I am rather at a loss to explain its peculiar influence on me. Entirely individual reactions to the printed word are always a little mysterious. I know, for example, one usually enlightened and catholic critic who stubbornly maintains that a very commonplace distich by Lord De Tabley is the most magical moment in all English verse. But here is my paragraph—or Susan's—for what it is worth:

"This Pomeranian prisoner was a blond boy-giant; pitifully shattered; it was necessary to remove his left leg to the knee. The operation was rapidly but skillfully performed. He was then placed on a pallet, close beside the cot of a wounded German officer. After coming out of the ether his fever mounted and he grew delirious. The German officer commanded him to be silent. He might just as well have commanded the sun to stand still, and he must, however muzzily, have known that. Yet he was outraged by this unconscious act of insubordination. Thrice he repeated his absurd command—then raised himself with a groan, leaned across, and struck the delirious boy in the face with a weakly clenched fist. It was not a heavy blow; the officer's strength did not equal his intention. '*Idiot!*' I cried out; and thrust him back on his cot, half-fainting from the pain of his futile effort at discipline. 'Idiot' was, after all, the one appropriate word. It was constantly, I found, the one appropriate word. The beast was a stupid beast."

THE LAST CHAPTER

I

PHIL FARMER and Jimmy Kane stayed on in New Haven that summer of 1914; Phil to be near his precious sources in the Yale library; Jimmy to be near his new job. As soon as his examinations were over he had gone to work in a factory in a very humble capacity; but he was not destined to remain there long in any capacity, nor was it written in the stars that he was to complete his education at Yale.

My own reasons for clinging to New Haven were less definite. Sheer physical inertia had something to do with it, no doubt; but chiefly I stayed because New Haven in midsummer is a social desert; and in those days my most urgent desire was to be alone. Apart from all else, the breaking out of almost world-wide war had drastically, as if by an operation for spiritual cataract, opened my inner eye, no longer a bliss in solitude, to much that was trivial and self-satisfied and ridiculous in one Ambrose Hunt, Esq. That Susan should be in the smoke of that spreading horror brought it swiftly and vividly before me. I lived the war from the first.

For years, with no felt discomfort to myself, I had been a pacifist. I was a contributing member of several peace societies, and in one of my slightly better-known essays I had expounded with enthusiasm Tolstoy's doctrine—which, in spite of much passionate argument to the contrary these troublous times, was assuredly Christ's—of nonresistance to evil. I was, in fact, though in a theoretical, parlor sense a proclaimed Tolstoyan, a Christian anarchist—lacking, however, the essential groundwork for Tolstoy's doctrine: faith. Faith in God as a person, as a father, I could not confess to; but the higher anarchist vision of humanity freed from all control save that of its own sweet reasonableness, of men turned unfailingly gentle, mutually helpful, content to live simply if need be, but never with unuplifted hearts—well, I could and did confess publicly that no other vision had so strong an attraction for me!

I liked to dwell in the idea of such a world, to think of it as a possibility—less remote, perhaps, than mankind in general supposed. Having lived through the Spanish War, the Boer War, and Russia's war with Japan; and in a world constantly strained to the breaking point by national rivalries, commercial expansion, and competition for markets; by class struggles everywhere apparent; by the harsh, discordant energies of its predatory desires—I, nevertheless, had been able to persuade myself that the darkest days of our dust-speck planet were done with and recorded; Earth and its graceless seed of Adam were at last, to quote Jimmy, "on their way"—well on their way, I assured myself, toward some inevitable region of abiding and beneficent light!

Pouf! . . . And then?

Stricken in solitude, I went down into dark places and fumbled like a starved beggar amid the detritus of my dreams. Dust and shadow... . Was there anything real there, anything worth the pain of spiritual salvage? Had I been, all my life, merely one more romanticist, one more sentimental trifler in a universe whose ways were not those of pleasantness, nor its paths those of peace? Surely, yes; for my heart convicted me at once of having wasted all my days hitherto in a fool's paradise. The rough fabric of human life was not spun from moonshine. So much at least was certain. And nothing else was left me. Hurled from my private, make-believe Eden, I must somehow begin anew.

"Brief beauty, and much weariness... ."

Susan's line haunted me throughout the first desperate isolation of those hours. I saw no light. I was broken in spirit. I was afraid.

Morbidity, you will say. Why, yes; why not? To be brainsick and heartsick in a cruel and unfamiliar world is to be morbid. I quite agree. Below the too-thin crust of a *dilettante's* culture lies always that hungry morass. A world had been shaken; the too-thin crust beneath my feet had crumbled; I must slither now in slime, and either sink there finally, be swallowed up in that sucking blackness, or by some miracle of effort win beyond, set my feet on stiff granite, and so survive.

It is most probable that I should never have reached solid ground unaided. It was Jimmy, of all people, who stretched forth a vigorous, impatient hand.

Shortly after the First Battle of the Marne had dammed—we knew not how precariously, or how completely—the deluge pouring through Belgium and Luxemburg and Northern France, Jimmy burst in on me one evening. He had just received a brief letter from Susan. She was stationed then at Furnes; Mona Leslie was with her; but their former hostess, the young pleasure-loving Comtesse de Bligny, was dead. The cause of her death Susan did not even stop to explain.

"Mona," she hurried on, "is magnificent. Only a few months ago I pitied her, almost despised her; now I could kiss her feet. How life had wasted her! She doesn't know fear or fatigue, and she has just put her entire fortune unreservedly at the service of the Belgian Government—to found field hospitals, ambulances, and so on. The king has decorated her. Not that she cares—has time to think about it, I mean. In a sense it irritated her; she spoke of it all to me as an unnecessary gesture. Oh, Jimmy, come over—we need you here! Bring all America over with you—if you can! *Setebos* invented neutrality; I recognize his workmanship! Bring Ambo—bring Phil! Don't stop to think about it—*come!*"

"I'm going of course," said Jimmy. "So's Prof. Farmer. How about you, sir?"

"Phil's going?"

"Sure. Just as soon as he can arrange it."

"His book's finished?"

"What the hell has that——" began Jimmy; then stopped dead, blushing. "Excuse me, Mr. Hunt; but books, somehow—just now—they don't seem so important as—*see?*"

"Not quite, Jimmy. After all, the real struggle's always between ideas, isn't it? We can't perfect the world with guns and ambulances, Jimmy."

"Maybe not," said Jimmy dryly.

"It's quite possible," I insisted, "that Phil's book might accomplish more for humanity, in the long run, than anything he could do at his age in Flanders."

"Susan could come home and write plays," said Jimmy; "good ones, too. But she won't. You can bet on that, sir."

"I've never believed in war, Jimmy; never believed it could possibly help us onward."

"Maybe it can't," interrupted Jimmy. "I've never believed in cancer, either; it's very painful and kills a lot of people. You'd better come with us, sir. You'll be sorry you didn't—if you don't."

"Why? You know my ideas on nonresistance, Jimmy."

"Oh, ideas!" grunted Jimmy. "I know you're a white man, Mr. Hunt. That's enough for me. I'm not worrying much about your ideas."

"But whatever we do, Jimmy, there's an *idea* behind it; there must be."

"Nachur'ly," said Jimmy. "Those are the only ones that count! I can't see you letting Susan risk her life day in an' out to help people who are being wronged, while you sit over here and worry about what's going to happen in a thousand years or so—after we're all good and dead! Not much I can't! The

189

point is, there's the rotten mess—and Susan's in it, trying to make it better—and we're not. Prof. Farmer got it all in a flash! He'll be round presently to make plans. Well—how about it, sir?"

Granite! Granite at last, unshakable, beneath my feet!

Then, too, Susan was over there, and Jimmy and Phil were going, without a moment's hesitation, at her behest! But I have always hoped, and I do honestly believe, that it was not entirely that.

No; romanticist or not, I will not submit to the assumption that of two possible motives for any decently human action, it is always the lower motive that turns the trick. La Rochefoucauld to the contrary, self-interest is not the inevitable mainspring of man; though, sadly I admit, it seems to be an indispensable cog-wheel in his complicated works.... .

II

And now, properly apprehensive reader—whom, in the interests of objectivity, which has never interested me, I should never openly address—are you not unhappy in the prospect of another little tour through trench and hospital, of one more harrowing account of how the Great War made a Great Man of him at last?

Be comforted! One air raid I cannot spare you; but I can spare you much. To begin with, I can spare you, or all but spare you, a month or so over three whole years.

You may think it incredible, but it is merely true, that I had been in Europe for more than three years—and I had not as yet seen Susan. Phil had seen her, just once; Jimmy had seen her many times; and I had run into them—singly, never together—off and on, here and there, during those slow-swift days of unremitting labor. If to labor desperately in a heartfelt cause be really to pray, the ear of Heaven has been besieged! But, in common humanity, there was always more crying to be done than mortal brains or hands or accumulated wealth could compass. Once plunged into that glorious losing struggle against the appalling hosts of Misery, one could only fight grimly on—on—on—to the last hoarded ounce of strength and determination.

But the odds were hopeless, fantastic! Those Titan forces of human suffering and degradation, so half-wittedly let loose throughout Europe, grew ever vaster, more terrible in maleficent power. They have ravaged the world; they have ravaged the soul. An armistice has been signed, a peace treaty is being drafted, a League of Nations is being formed—or deformed—but those Titan forces still mock our poor efforts with calamitous laughter. They are still

190

in fiercely, stubbornly disputed, but unquestionable possession of the field—insolent conquerors to this hour. The real war, the essential war, the war against the unconsciously self-willed annihilation of earth's tragic egoist, Man, has barely begun. Its issue is ever uncertain; and it will not be ended in our days... .

Phil and Jimmy had gone over on the same boat, *via* England, about the middle of October, 1914. At that time organized American relief-work in Europe was really nonexistent, and in order to obtain some freedom of movement on the other side, and a chance to study out possible opportunities for effective service, Phil had persuaded Heywood Sampson to appoint him continental correspondent for the new review; and Jimmy went with him, ostensibly as his private secretary.

It was all the merest excuse for obtaining passports and permission to enter Belgium, if that should prove immediately advisable after reaching London. It did not. Once in London, Phil had very soon found himself up to the eyes in work. Through Mr. Page, the American Ambassador—so lately dead—he was introduced to Mr. Herbert C. Hoover, and after a scant twenty minutes of conversation was seized by Mr. Hoover and plunged, with barely a gasp for breath, into that boiling sea of troubles—the organization of the Commission for Relief in Belgium. It does not take Mr. Hoover very long to size up the worth and stability of any man; but in Phil he had found—and he knew he had found—a peculiar treasure. Phil's unfailing patience, his thoroughness and courtesy, quickly endeared him to all his colleagues and did much to make possible the successful launching of the vastest and most difficult project for relief ever undertaken by mortal men. Thus, almost overnight, Jimmy's private secretaryship became anything but a sinecure. For nearly three months their labors held them in London; then they were sent—not unadventurously—to Brussels; there to arrange certain details of distribution with Mr. Whitlock, the American Minister, and with the directors of the Belgian *Comité National*.

But from Brussels their paths presently diverged. Jimmy, craving activity, threw himself into the actual work of food distribution in the stricken eastern districts; while Phil passed gravely on to Herculean labors at the shipping station of the "C. R. B." in Rotterdam. He remained in Rotterdam for upward of a year. Susan, meanwhile, had been driven with the Belgian Army from Furnes, and was now attached to the operating-room of a small field or receiving-hospital, which squatted amphibiously in a waterlogged fragment of village not far from the Yser and the flooded German lines. It was a post of danger, constantly under fire; and she was the one woman who clung to it—who insisted upon being permitted to cling to it, and carried her point; and, under conditions fit neither for man nor beast, unflinchingly carried on. Mona Leslie was no longer beside her. She had retired to Dunkirk to aid in the organization of relief for ever-increasing hordes of civilian refugees.

And where, meanwhile, was one Ambrose Hunt, sometime *dilettante* at large?

It had proved impossible for me to sail with Phil and Jimmy. Just as the preliminary arrangements were being made, Aunt Belle was stricken down by apoplexy, while walking among the roses of her famous Spanish gardens in Santa Barbara, and so died, characteristically intestate, and, to my astonishment, I found that I had become the sole inheritor of her estate; all of "Hyena Parker's" tainted millions had suddenly poured their burdensome tide of responsibilities—needlessly and unwelcomely—upon me. There was nothing for it. Out to California, willy-nilly, I must go, and waste precious weeks there with lawyers and house agents and other tiresome human necessities.

The one cheering thought in all this annoying pother was—and it was a thought that grew rapidly in significance to me as I journeyed westward—that fate had now made it possible for me to purify Hyena Parker's millions by putting them to work for mankind.—Well, they have since done their part, to the last dollar; they have spent themselves in the losing battle against Misery, and are no more. Nothing became their lives like the ending of them. But for all that, the world, you see, is as it is—and the battle goes on.

Phil kept in touch with me from the other side, in spite of his difficulties— as did Jimmy and Susan—and he had prepared the way for me when at length I could free myself and sail. I was instructed to go to Paris, direct, and fulfill certain duties there in connection with the ever-increasing burdens and exasperations of the "C. R. B." I did so. Six months later my activities were transferred to Berne; and—not to trace in detail the evolution of my career, such as it was; for though useful, I hope, it was never, like Phil's, exceptionally brilliant—I had become, about the period of America's entry into the war, a modest captain in the Red Cross, stationed at Evian, in connection with the endless, heartbreaking task of repatriating refugees from the invaded districts. And there my job rooted me until January of that dark winter of our unspeakable depression, 1918.

With the beginning of America's entry into the war Phil had gone to Petrograd for the American Red Cross, his commission being to save the lives of as many Russian babies as possible by the distribution of canned milk. Then, one evening—early in September, 1917, it must have been—he started alone for Moscow, to lay certain wider plans for disinterested relief-work before the sinister, the almost mythical Lenine. That is the last that has ever been seen of him, and no word has ever come forth directly from him out of the chaos men still call Russia. The Red Cross and the American and French Governments have done their utmost to discover his whereabouts, without avail. There are reasons for believing he is not dead, nor even a prisoner. The dictators of the soviet autocracy have been unable to find a trace of him, so they affirm; and there are reasons also for believing that this is true.

As for Jimmy, you will not be surprised to learn that Jimmy had not long been content with relief-work of any kind. He was young; and he had *seen* things—there, in the eastern districts. By midsummer of 1915 he had resigned from the "C. R. B.," had made a difficult way to Paris, via Holland and England, had enlisted in the Foreign Legion, and had succeeded in getting himself transferred to the French Flying Corps. Thus, months before we had officially abandoned our absurd neutrality, he was flying over the lines—bless him! If Jimmy never became a world-famous ace, well—there was a reason for that, too; the best of reasons. He was never assigned to a combat squadron, for no one brought home such photographs as Jimmy; taken tranquilly, methodically, at no great elevation, and often far back of the German lines. His quiet daring was the admiration of his comrades; anti-aircraft batteries had no terrors for him; his luck was proverbial, and he grew to trust it implicitly, seeming to bear a charmed life.

But Susan's luck had failed her, at last. On Thanksgiving Day of 1917 she was wounded in the left thigh by a fragment of shrapnel, a painful wound whose effects were permanent. She will always walk slowly, with a slight limp, hereafter. Mona Leslie got her down as far as Paris by January 20, 1918, meaning to take her on to Mentone, where she had rented a small villa for three months of long-overdue rest and recuperation for them both. But on reaching Paris, Susan collapsed; the accumulated strain of the past years struck her down. She was taken to the comfortable little Red Cross hospital for civilians at Neuilly and put to bed. A week of dangerous exhaustion and persistent insomnia followed.

I knew nothing of it directly, at the moment. I knew only that on a certain day Miss Leslie had planned to start with Susan from Dunkirk for Mentone; I was waiting eagerly for word of their safe arrival in that haven of rest and beauty; and I was scheming like a junior clerk for my first vacation, for two weeks off, perhaps even three, that I might run down to them there. But no word came. Throughout that first week in Paris, Miss Leslie in her hourly anxiety neglected to drop me a line.

And then one night, as I sat vacantly on the edge of my bed in my hotel room at Evian, almost too weary to begin the tedious sequence of undressing and tumbling into it, came the second of my psychic reels, my peculiar visions; briefer, this one, than my first; but no less authentic in impression, and no less clear.

III

I saw, this time, the interior of a small white room, almost bare of furniture, evidently a private room in some thoroughly appointed modern hospital. The patient beneath the white coverlet of the single white-enamelled iron bed was Susan—or the wraith of Susan, so wasted was she, so still. My breath stopped: I thought it had been given me to see her at the moment of death; or already dead. Then the door of the small white room opened, and Jimmy—in his smart horizon-blue uniform with its coveted shoulder loop, the green-and-red *fouragère* that bespoke the bravery of his entire *esquadrille*— came in, treading carefully on the balls of his feet. As he approached the bedside Susan opened her eyes—great shadows, gleamless soot-smudges in her pitifully haggard face. It seemed that she was too weak even to greet him or smile; her eyes closed again, and Jimmy bent down to her slowly and kissed her. Then Susan lifted her right hand from the coverlet—I could feel the effort it cost her—and touched Jimmy's hair. There was no strength in her to prolong the caress. The hand slipped from him to her breast... . And my vision ended.

Its close found me on my knees on the tiled floor of my bedroom, as if I too had tried to go nearer, to bring myself close to her bedside, perhaps to bury my face in my hands against the white coverlet, her shroud; to weep there... .

I sprang up, wildly enough now, with a harsh shudder, the terrified gasp of a brute suddenly stricken from ambush, aware only of rooted claws and a last crushing fury of deep-set fangs.

Susan was dying. I knew not where. I could not reach her. But Jimmy had reached her. He had been summoned. He had not been too late.

There are moments of blind anguish not to be reproduced for others. Chaos is everything—and nothing. It cannot be described.

There was nothing really useful I could do that night, not even sleep. In those days, it was impossible to move anywhere on the railroads of France without the proper passes and registrations of intention with the military authorities and the local police. I could, of course, suffer—that is always a human possibility—and I could attempt, muzzily enough, to think, to make plans. Where was it most likely that Susan would be? Was the hospital room that I had seen in Dunkirk, or in Nice, or at some point between—perhaps at

194

Paris? It could hardly, I decided, be at Dunkirk; that stricken city, whose inhabitants were forced to dive like rats into burrows at any hour of the day or night. There was nothing to suggest the atmosphere of Dunkirk in that quiet, white-enamelled room. Nice, then—or Mentone? Hardly, I again reasoned; for Jimmy could not easily have reached them there. A day's leave; a flight from the lines, so comfortlessly close to Paris—that was always possible to the air-men, who were in a sense privileged characters, being for the most part strung with taut nerves that chafed and snapped under too strict a discipline. And in Paris there must be many such quiet, white-enamelled rooms. I decided for Paris.

Then I threw five or six articles and a bar of chocolate into my *musette*, a small water-proof pouch to sling over the shoulder—three years had taught me at least the needlessness of almost all Hillhouse necessities—and waited for dawn. It came, as all dawns come at last—even in January, even in France. And with it came a gulp of black coffee in the little deserted café down-stairs —and a telegram. I dared not open the telegram. It lay beside my plate while I stained the cloth before me and scalded my throat and furred my tongue. It was from Paris. So my decision was justified, and now quite worthless... . I have no memory of the interval; but I had got with it somehow back to my room—that accursed blue envelope! Well——

"Susan at Red Cross hospital for civilians, Neuilly. All in, but no cause for real worry. Is sleeping now for first time in nearly a week. I must leave by afternoon. Come up to her if you possibly can. She needs you.

"JIMMY."

Four hours later all my exasperatingly complicated arrangements for a two-weeks' absence were made—the requisite motions had been the purest somnambulism—and by the ample margin of fifty seconds I had caught an express—to do it that courtesy—moving with dignity, at decent intervals, toward all that I lived by and despaired of and held inviolably dear. But the irony of Jimmy's last three words went always with me, a monotonous ache blurring every impulse toward hope and joy. Susan was not dead, was not dying! "No cause for real worry." Jimmy would not have said that if he had feared the worst. It was not his way to shuffle with facts; he was by nature direct and sincere. No; Susan would recover—thank God for it! Thank—and then, under all, through all, over and over, that aching monotony: "She needs you. Jimmy. She needs you. Jimmy."

"Needs me!" I groaned aloud.

"*Plaît-il?*" politely murmured the harassed-looking little French captain, my vis-à-vis.

"Mille pardons, monsieur," I murmured back. *"On a quelquefois des griefs particuliers, vous savez."*

"Ah dame, oui!" he sighed. *"Par le temps qui court!"*

"Et ce pachyderme de train qui ne court jamais!" I smiled.

"Ah, pour ça—ça repose!" murmured the little French captain, and shut his eyes.

"She needs you. Jimmy. She needs you. Jimmy. She needs——"

Then, miraculously, for two blotted hours I slept. But I woke again, utterly unrefreshed, to the old refrain: *She needs you—needs you—needs you... .*

The little French captain was still asleep, snoring now—but softly—in his corner. Ah, lucky little French captain! *Ça repose!*

IV

One afternoon, five or six days later, I was seated by the white-enamelled iron bed in the small white room. Susan had had a long, quiet, normal nap, and her brisk sparrow-eyed Norman nurse, in her pretty costume of the French Red Cross, had come to me in the little reception-room of the hospital, where I had been sitting for an hour stupidly thumbing over tattered copies of ancient American magazines, and had informed me—with rather an ambiguous twinkle of those sparrow eyes—that her patient had asked to see me as soon as she had waked, was evidently feeling stronger, and that it was to be hoped *M. le Capitaine* would be discreet and say nothing to excite or fatigue the poor little one. *"Je me sauve, m'sieu,"* she had added, mischievously grave; *"on ne peut avoir l'œil à tout, mais—je compte sur vous."*

So innocently delighted had she been by her pleasant suspicions, it was impossible to let her feel how sharply her raillery had pained me. But I could not reply in kind. I had merely bowed, put down the magazine in my hand, and so left her—to inevitable reflections, I presume, upon the afflicting reticence of these otherwise so agreeable allies *d'outre mer.* Their education was evidently deplorable. One never knew when they would miss step, inconveniently, and so disarrange the entire social rhythm of a conversation.

"Ambo," said Susan, putting her hand in mine, "do you know at all how terribly I've missed you?" She turned her head weakly on her pillow and looked at me. "You're older, dear. You've changed. I like your face better now than I ever did."

I wrinkled my nose at her. "Is that saying much?" I grimaced.

"Heaps!" She attempted to smile back at me, but her lower lip quivered. "Yours has always been my favorite face, you know, Ambo. Phil's is wiser—somehow, and stronger, too; and Jimmy's is sunnier, healthier, and—yes, handsomer, dear! Nobody could call you handsome, could they? But you're not ugly, either. Sister was adorably ugly. It was a daily miracle to see the lamp in her suddenly glow through and glorify everything. I used to wait for it. It's the only thing that has ever made me feel—humble; I never feel that way with you. I just feel satisfied, content."

"Like putting on an old pair of slippers," I ventured.

"That's it," sighed Susan happily, and closed her eyes.

"That's it!" echoed my familiar demon, "but no one but Susan would have admitted it."

As usual, I found it wiser to cut him dead.

"Well, dear," I said to Susan, "there's one good thing: you'll be able to use the old pair of slippers any time you need them now. I'm to be held in Paris, I find, for a three-months' job."

She opened her eyes again; disapprovingly, I felt.

"You shouldn't have done that, Ambo! You're needed at Evian; I know you are. It's bad enough to be out of things myself, but I won't drag you out of them! How could you imagine that would please me?"

"I hoped it would, a little," I replied, "but it hasn't any of it been my doing —Chatworth's wife's expecting a baby in a few weeks, and he wants to run home to welcome it; I'm to take on his executive work till he gets back. God knows he needs a rest!"

"As if you didn't, too!" protested Susan, inconsistently enough. Her eyes fell shut again; her hands slipped from mine. "Ambo," she asked presently, in a thread of voice that I had to lean down to her to hear, "have they told you I can never have a baby now? . . . Wasn't it lucky if that had to happen to some woman—it happened to me?"

No, they had not told me; and for the moment I could not answer her.

"Jimmy's wife is going to have a baby soon," added Susan. "Jimmy's—

what!" I shrieked. Yes, shrieked—for, to my horror, I heard my voice crack and soar, strident, incredulous.

Susan was staring at me, wide-eyed, her face aquiver with excitement; two deep spots of color flaming on her thin cheeks.

"Didn't you *know?*"

The white door opened as she spoke, and Susan's Norman nurse hurried in, her sparrow eyes transformed to stiletto points of indignation. "*Ah, m'sieu— c'est trop fort!* When I told you expressly to do nothing to excite the poor little one!" I rose, self-convicted, before her.

"*Tais-toi, Annette!*" exclaimed Susan sharply, her eyes too gleaming with indignation. "It is not your place to speak so to m'sieu, a man old enough to be your father—and more than a father to me! For shame! His surprise was unavoidable! I have just given him a shock—unexpected news! Good news, however, I am glad to say. Now leave us!"

"On the contrary," replied Nurse Annette, four feet eleven of uncompromising and awful dignity, "I am in charge here, and it is m'sieu who will leave—*tout court!* But I regret my *vivacité, m'sieu!*"

"It is nothing, mademoiselle. You have acted as you should. It is for me to offer my regrets. But—when may I return?"

"To-morrow, m'sieu," said Nurse Annette.

"Naturally," said Susan. "Now sit down, please, Ambo, and listen to me."

For an instant the stiletto points glinted dangerously; then Nurse Annette giggled. That is precisely what Nurse Annette did; she giggled. Then she twirled about on her toes and left us—very quietly, yet not without a certain malicious ostentation, closing the door.

The French are a brave people, an intelligent and industrious people; but they exhibit at times a levity almost childlike in the descendants of so ancient and so deeply civilized a race... .

"I knew nothing about it myself, Ambo," Susan was saying, "until I was beginning to feel a little stronger, after my operations at Dunkirk. Then Mona brought me letters—three from you, dear, and one long one from Jimmy. But no letter from Phil. I'd hoped, foolishly I suppose, for that. Jimmy's was the dearest, funniest letter I've ever read; it made me laugh and cry all at once. It wasn't a bit good for me, Ambo. It used me all up! And I kept wondering what you must be thinking. You see, he said in it he had written you."

"I've had no letter from Jimmy for at least five or six months," I replied.

"So many letters start bravely off over here," sighed Susan, "and then just vanish—like Phil. How many heartbreaks they must have caused, all those vanished letters—and men. And how silly of me to think about it! There must be some fatal connection, Ambo, between being sick and being sentimental. I suppose sentimentality's always one symptom of weakness. I've never been so disgustingly maudlin as these past weeks—never!"

"So Jimmy's married," I repeated stupidly, for at least the third time.

"Yes," smiled Susan, "to little Jeanne-Marie Valérie Josephine Aulard. I haven't seen her, of course, but I feel as if I knew her well. They've been married now almost a year." She paused again. "Why don't you look gladder, Ambo? Why don't you ask questions? You must be dying to know why Jimmy kept it a secret from us so long."

I had not dared to ask questions, for I believed I could guess why Jimmy had kept it a secret from us so long. For the first time in his life, I thought, Jimmy had been a craven. He had been afraid to tell Susan of an event which he must know would be like a knife in her heart.

"I suppose I'm foolishly hurt about it," I mumbled.

How bravely she was taking it all, in spite of her physical exhaustion! Poor child, poor child! But in God's name what then was the meaning of my vision back there in the hotel room at Evian? Jimmy entering this room where I now sat, tiptoeing to this very bedside, stooping down and kissing Susan—and her hand lifted, overcoming an almost mortal weakness, to touch his hair... .

"You mustn't be hurt at all," Susan gently rebuked me. "Jimmy kept his marriage a secret from us for a very Jimmyesque reason. There was nothing specially exciting or romantic about the courtship itself, though. Little Jeanne-Marie's father—he was a notary of Soissons who had made a nice, comfy little fortune for those parts—died just before the war. So the Widow Aulard retired with Jeanne-Marie to a brand-spandy-new, very ugly little country house—south of the Aisne, Ambo, not far from Soissons; the canny old notary had just completed it as a haven for his declining years when he up and died. Well then, during the first German rush, Widow Aulard—being a good extra-stubborn *bourgeoise*—refused to leave her home—refused, Jeanne-Marie told Jimmy, even to believe the Boches would ever really be permitted to come so far. That was foolish, of course—but doesn't it make you like her, and *see* her—mustache and all?

"But the deluge was too much, even for her. One morning, after a night of terror, she found herself compulsory housekeeper, and little Jeanne-Marie compulsory servant, to a kennel of Bavarian officers. Then, three weeks or so later, the orderly of one of these officers, an Alsatian, was discovered to be a spy and was shot—and the Widow Aulard was shot, too, for having unwittingly harbored him. Jeanne-Marie wasn't shot, though; the kennel liked her cooking. So, like the true daughter of a French notary, she used her wits, made herself indispensable to the comfort of the officers, preserved her dignity under incredible insults, and her virtue under conditions I needn't tell you about, Ambo—and bided her time.

"It nearly killed her; but she lived through it, and finally the French returned and helped her patch up and clean up what was left of the kennel. And a month or so later Jimmy's *esquadrille* made Jeanne-Marie's battered little house their headquarters and treated its mistress like the staunch little heroine she is. Of course, Jimmy wasn't attached to the *esquadrille* then; it was more than a year later that he arrived on the scene; but it didn't take him long after getting there to decide on an international alliance. Bless him! he says Jeanne-Marie isn't very pretty, he guesses; she's just—wonderful! She couldn't make up her mind to the international alliance, though. She loved Jimmy, but the match didn't strike her as prudent. An orphan must consider these things. Her property had been swept away, and Jimmy admitted he had nothing. And being her father's daughter, Jeanne-Marie very wisely pointed out that he was in hourly peril of being killed or crippled for life. To marry under such circumstances would be to make her father turn in his grave. How can anything so sad be so funny, Ambo? Well, anyway, Jimmy, being Jimmy, saw the point, agreed with her completely, and seems to have felt thoroughly ashamed of himself for trying to persuade her into so crazy a match!

"Then little Jeanne-Marie came down with typhoid; her life was despaired of, a priest was summoned. In the presence of death, she managed to tell the priest that it would seem less lonely and terrible to her if she could meet it as the wife 'M'sieu Jee-mee.' So the good priest managed somehow to slash through yards of official red tape in no time—you know how hard it is to get married in France, Ambo!—and the sacrament of marriage preceded the last rites; and then, dear, Jeanne-Marie faced the Valley of Shadow clinging to M'sieu Jee-mee's hand. The whole *esquadrille* was unstrung—naturally; even their famous ace, Boisrobert. Jimmy says he absolutely refused to fly for three days." Tears were pouring from Susan's eyes.

"Oh, what a fool I am!" she protested, mopping at them with a corner of the top sheet. "She didn't die, of course. She rallied at the last moment and got well—and found herself safely married after all, and quite ready to take her chances of living happily with M'sieu Jee-mee ever afterward! There—isn't that a nice story, Ambo? Don't you like pretty-pie fairy tales when they happen to be true?"

That she could ask me this with her heart breaking! Again I could not trust myself to speak calmly, and I saw that she was worn out with the effort she had made to overcome her weakness, and what I believed to be a living pain in her breast. I rose.

"Ambo!" she exclaimed, wide-eyed, "still you don't ask me why Jimmy didn't tell us! How stupid of you to take it all like this!"

"I've stayed too long, dear," I mumbled; "far too long. I've let you talk too much. Why, it's almost dark! To-morrow——"

"No, *now*," she insisted, with a little frown of displeasure. "I won't have you thinking meanly of Jimmy! It's too absurdly unfair! I'm ashamed of you, Ambo."

How she idealized him! How she had always idealized that normal, likable, essentially commonplace Irish boy—pouring out, wasting for him treasures of unswerving loyalty! It was damnable. But these things were the final mysteries of life, these instinctive bonds, yielding no clue to reason. One could only accept them, bitterly, with a curse or a groan withheld. Accept them—since one must... .

"Well, dear," broke from me with a touch, almost, of impatience, "I confess I'm more interested in your health than in Jimmy's psychology! But I see you won't sleep a wink if you don't tell me!"

"I've never known you to be so horrid," she said faintly, all the weariness of body and soul returning upon her for a moment, till she fought it back. She did so, to my amazement, with an entirely unexpected chuckle, a true sharp, clear Birch Street gleam. "You don't deserve it, Ambo, but I'm going to make you smile a little, whether you feel like it or not! The reason Jimmy didn't tell us was because—after Jeanne-Marie got well—he spent weeks trying to persuade her that a marriage made exclusively for eternity oughtn't to be considered binding on this side! She had been entirely certain, he kept pointing out to her, that she ought not to marry him in this world, and she had only done so when she thought she was being taken from it." Susan chuckled again. "Can't you hear him, Ambo—and her? Jimmy, feeling he had won something precious through an unfair advantage and so refusing his good fortune—or trying to; and practical Jeanne-Marie simply nonplussed by his sudden lack of all common sense! Besides which, wasn't marriage a sacrament, and wasn't M'sieu Jee-mee a good Catholic? Was he going back on his faith—or asking her to trifle with hers? And, anyway, they were married—that was the end of it! And of course, Ambo, it was—really. There! I knew sooner or later you'd have to smile!"

"Did he give in gracefully?" I asked.

"Oh, things soon settled themselves, I imagine, when Jeanne-Marie was well enough to leave. Naturally, she had to as soon as she could. A soldier's wife can't live with him at the Front, you know—even to keep house for his *esquadrille*. She's living here now, in Paris, with a distant cousin, an old lady who runs a tiny shop near St.-Sulpice—sells pious pamphlets and pink-and-blue plaster Virgins—you know the sort of thing, Ambo. You must call on her at once in due form, dear. You must. I'm so eager to—when I can." She paused on a breath, then added slowly, her eyes closing, "The baby's expected in February—Jimmy's baby."

The look on her face had puzzled me as I left her; a look of quiet happiness, I must have said—if I had not known.

And my vision at Evian——?

I walked back toward the barrier down endless darkening avenues of suburban Neuilly; walked by instinct, though quite unconscious of direction, straight to the Porte Maillot, through the emotional nightmare of what my old childhood nurse, Maggie, used always to call "a great state of mind."

V

And that night—it was, I think, the thirtieth of January, or was it the thirty-first?—fifty or sixty Boche aëroplanes came by detached squadrons over Paris and, for the first time since the Zeppelins of 1916, dropped a shower of bombs on the *agglomération Parisienne*. It was an entirely successful raid, destructive of property and life; for the German flyers in their powerful Gothas had caught Paris napping, impotently unprepared.

I had dined that evening with an old acquaintance, doing six-months' time, as it amused him to put it, with the purchasing department of the Red Cross; a man who had long since turned the silver spoon he was born with to solid gold, and who could see no reason why, just because for the first time in his life he was giving something for nothing, he should deprive himself while doing so of the very high degree of creature comfort he had always enjoyed. He was stationed in Paris, and it was his invariable custom to dine sumptuously at one of the more expensive restaurants.

This odd combination of service and sybaritism was not much to my liking, seeming to indicate a curious lack of imaginative sympathy with the victims of that triumphing Misery he was enlisted to combat; nevertheless, I had properly appreciated my dinner. It is impossible not to appreciate a well-ordered dinner, *chez* Durant, where wartime limitations seemed never to weigh very heavily upon the delicately imagined good cheer. True, the cost of this good cheer was fantastic, and I shuddered a little as certain memories of refugee hordes at Evian intruded themselves between our golden mouthfuls; but the bouquet of a fine mellowed Burgundy was in my nostrils and soon proved anæsthetic to conscience. And Arthur Dalton is a good table companion; his easy flow of conversation quite as mellow often as the wine he knows so well how to select. But that night, though I did my poor best to emulate him, I fear he did not find an equal combination of the soothing and the stimulating in me.

Perhaps it was because I had bored him that I was destined before we parted to catch a rather startling glimpse of a new Arthur Dalton, new at least to me; a person wholly different from the amusing man of the world I had long, but so casually, known.

"Hunt," he said unexpectedly, over a final glass of old yellow Chartreuse, a liquor almost unobtainable at any price, "you've changed a lot since our days here together." We had seen something of each other once in Paris, years before, during a fine month of spring weather; it was the year after my wife had left me. "A lot," he repeated; "and I wish I could say for the better. You've aged, man, before you're old. You've let life, somehow, get on your nerves, depress you. Suffered your genial spirits to rot, as the poet says. That's foolish. It's a kind of defeat—acceptance of defeat. Now my philosophy is always to stay on top—where the cream lies. Somebody's going to get it if you and I don't, eh? Well, I'm having my share. I don't want more and I'm damned if I'll take less. Anything wrong with that point of view, old man? I'd be willing to swear it used to be yours!"

"Never quite, I think," was my answer; "at least I never formulated it that way. I took things pretty easily as they came, Dalt, and didn't worry about reasons. I've never been a philosophical person, never lived up to any consciously organized plan. If I had any God in those days I suppose I named him 'Culture'; or worse still 'Good Taste.' Not much of a god for these times," I added.

"Oh, I don't know," Dalton struck in; "I'm not so sure of that! I can't see that these times differ much from any others. There's a big war on, yes; but that's nothing new, is it? Looks to me pretty much like the same old planet, right now. Never was much of a planet for the great majority; never will be. A few of us get all the prizes—always have. Some of us partly deserve 'em, but most of us just happen to be lucky. I don't see anything that's likely to change that arrangement. Do you?"

"They've changed it in Russia," I suggested.

"Not a bit!" exclaimed Dalton. "Some different people have taken their big chance and climbed on top, that's all! I doubt if they stay there long; still, they may. That fellow Lenine, now; he has a kind of well-up-in-the-saddle feel to him. Quite a boy, I've no doubt; and if he sticks, I congratulate him! It's the one really amusing place to be."

"You sound like a Junker war-lord," I smiled. "Fortunately, I know your bark, and I've never seen you bite."

"My dear Hunt," said Dalton, lowering his voice, "my teeth are perfectly sound, I assure you; and I've always used 'em when I had to, believe *me*. It's the law of life, as I read it. And just here between ourselves, eh—cutting out all the nonsense we've learned to babble—do you see any difference between a Junker war-lord and a British Tory peer—or an American capitalist? Any real difference, I mean? I'm all for licking Germany if we can, because if we don't she'll control the cream supply of the world. But I can't blame her for wanting to, and if she gets away with it—which the devil forbid!—we'll all mighty soon forget all the nasty things we've been saying about her and begin trying to lick her Prussian boots instead of her armies! That's so, and you know it! Why, the most sickening thing about this war, Hunt, isn't the loss of life—that may be a benefit to us all in the end; no sir, it's the moral buncombe it's let loose! That man Wilson simply sweats the stuff day and night, drenches us with it—till we stink like a church of Easter lilies. Come now! Doesn't it all, way down in your tummy somewhere, give you a good honest griping pain?"

I stared at him. Yes; the man was evidently in earnest; was even, I could see, expecting me to smile—however deprecatingly, for form's sake—and in the main agree with him, as became my situation in life; my class. I had supposed myself incapable of moral shock, but found now that the sincerity of his cynicism had unquestionably shocked me; I felt suddenly embarrassed, awkward, ashamed.

"Dalt," I finally managed, pretty lamely, "it's absurd, I admit; but if I try to answer you, I shall lose my temper. I mean it. And as I've dined wonderfully at your expense, that's something I don't care to do."

It was his turn to stare at me.

"Do you mean to say, Hunt, you've been caught by all this sentimental parson's palaver? Brotherhood, peace on earth, all the rest of it?"

My nerves snapped. "If you insist on a straight answer," I said, "you can have it: I've no use for a world that spiritually starves its poets and saints, and physically fattens its hyenas and hogs! And if that isn't sentimental enough for you, I can go farther!"

"Oh, that'll do," he laughed, uncomfortably however. "I'm always forgetting you're a scribbler, of sorts. You scribblers are all alike—emotionally diseased. If you'd only stick to your real job of amusing the rest of us, it wouldn't matter. It's when you try to reform us that I draw the line; have to. I can't afford to grow brainsick—abnormal. Well," he added, pushing back his chair, "come along anyway! We've just time to get over to the Casino and have a look at the only Gaby. Been there? It's a cheap show, after

Broadway, but it does well enough to pass the time."

From this unalluring suggestion I begged off, justly pleading a hard day of work ahead. "And if you don't mind, Dalt, I'll walk home."

"Oh, all right," he agreed; "I'll walk along with you, if you'll take it easy. I'm not much for exercise, you know. But it's a perfect night."

I had hoped ardently to be rid of him, but I managed to accept his company with apparent good grace, and we strolled down the Avenue Victor Hugo toward the Triumphal Arch, bathed now in clearest moonlight, standing forth to all Paris as a cruelly ironic symbol of Hope, never relinquished, but endlessly deferred. Turning there, the Champs-Élysées, all but deserted at that hour in wartime Paris, stretched on before us down a gentle slope, half dusky, half glimmering, and wholly silent except for our lonesome-sounding footfalls and the distant faint plopping of a lame cab-horse's stumbling heels.

"Not much like the old town we knew once, eh, Hunt?" asked Dalton.

But conversation soon faded out between us, as we made our way through etched mysteries of black and silver under thickset leafless branches. An occasional light beckoned us from far ahead down our pavement vista; for Paris had not yet fully become that city—not of dreadful—but of majestic and beautiful night we were later to know, and to love with so changed and grave a passion.

It was just after we had crossed the Rond-Point that the first seven or eight bombs in swift even succession shatteringly fell. They were not near enough to us to do more than root us to the spot with amazement.

"What the *hell?*" muttered Dalton, holding my eyes.... .

Then, very far off, a curious thin wailing noise began, increasing rapidly, rising to an eerie scream which doubled and redoubled in volume as it was taken up in other quarters and came to us in intricately rhythmic waves.

"Sirens," said Dalton. "The *pompiers* are out. I guess they've come, damn them, eh?"

"Seems so," I answered. "Yes; there go the lights. I must get to Neuilly at once—a sick friend. So long, old man."

"Hold on!" he called after me. "Don't be an ass!"

To my impatient annoyance, for they impeded my progress, knots of people had sprung everywhere from the darkness and were standing now in open spots, in the full moonlight, murmuring together, as they stared with backward-craned necks up into the spotless sky.... .

So, with crashing, sinister, unresolved chords, began the Straussian overture to the great Boche symphony, *Gott Strafe Paris*, played to its impotent conclusion throughout those bitter spring months of the year of our wonderment, 1918! Ninety-one bombs were dropped that night within the old fortifications; more than two hundred were showered on the *banlieue*. No subsequent raid was to prove equally destructive of property or life, and it was disturbingly evident that, for the time being at least, the shadowy air lanes to Paris lay broadly open to the foe.

Yet, for some reason unexplained, the Gothas did not immediately or soon return. Followed a hush of rather more than a month, during which Paris worked breathlessly to improve its air defenses and protect its more precious monuments. Comically ugly little sausage-balloons—gorged caterpillars, they seemed, raw yellow with pale green articulations and loathsome, floppy appendages—were moored in the squares and public gardens; mountains of sand bags were heaped about the Triumphal Arch and before the portals of Notre Dame; spies were hunted out, proclamations issued, the entrance ways to deep cellars were placarded; and Night, that long-exiled princess, came back to us, royally, in full mourning robes. In her honor all windows were doubly curtained, all street lamps extinguished, or dimmed with paint to a heavy blue. We invoked the august amplitude of darkness and would gladly have banished the trivial prying moon, seeing her at last in true colors for the sinister corpse light of heaven which she is. No one, I think, was deceived by this lengthening interval of calm. Why the Gothas did not at once return, what restrained them from following up their easy triumph, we could not guess; but we knew they would come again, would come many times.....

Meanwhile, for most of us who dwelt there, life went on as before, busily enough; but for one of us—as for how many another—this no longer mattered.

Brave little Jeanne-Marie Valérie Josephine Aulard, on that night of anguish, died in giving premature birth to Jimmy's son, James Aulard Kane— as Susan later named him: for this wizened, unready morsel of man's flesh, in spite of every disadvantage attending his début and first motherless weeks on earth, clung with the characteristic tenacity of his parents to his one obvious line of duty, which was merely to keep alive in despite of fortune: a duty he somehow finally accomplished to his own entire satisfaction and to the blessed relief of Susan and of me. But I shall never forget my first pitiful introduction to James Aulard Kane.

After leaving Dalton, that night, I had finally made my way to Susan's hospital on foot, which I had soon found to be the one practicable means of locomotion. It was a long walk, and it brought me in due course into the

Avenue de la Grande Armée, just in time to receive the full stampeding effect of the three bombs which fell there, the nearest of them not four hundred yards distant from me. I am by no means instinctively intrepid; quite the contrary; I shy like a skittish horse in the presence of danger, and my first authentic impulse is always to cut and run. On this occasion, by the time I had mastered this impulse, I had placed a good six hundred yards between me and that ill-fated building, whose stone-faced upper floors had been riven and hurled down to the broad avenue below. Then, shamefacedly enough, I turned and forced myself back toward that smoking ruin.

Our American ambulances from Neuilly were already arriving—the *pompiers* came later—and the police lines were being drawn. A civilian spectator, even though a captain of the Red Cross, could render no real assistance; so much, after certain futile efforts on my part, was made clear to me, profanely, in a Middle Western accent, by a young stretcher-bearer whose course I had clumsily impeded. Clouds of lung-choking dust, milk-white as the moon's full rays played upon them, rolled over us—the subdued crowd that gathered slowly, oblivious of further danger. The air was full of whispered rumor—throughout Paris hundreds—thousands, said some—had already died. We were keyed to believe the wildest exaggerations, to accept the worst that excited imaginations could invent for us. Yet there was no panic; no one gave way to hysterical outcry; and the fall of more distant bombs brought only a deep common groan, compounded of growling imprecations—a groan truly of defiance and loathing, into which neither fear nor pity for the victims of this frightfulness could find room to enter. I cursed with the rest, instinctively, from the pit of my stomach, and turned raging away; my whole being ached, was congested with rage. For the first time in my life I then felt in its full hell-born fury that passion so often named, but so seldom experienced by civilized—or what we call civilized—man: the passion of *hate*.

By the time I had reached the hospital the raid was over; the air was droning from the bronze vibrations of hundreds of bells, all the church-bells of Paris, full-throated, calling forth their immediate surface messages of cheer, their deeper message of courage and constancy.

Though it was very late, I found a silent group of four nurses standing in the heavily shadowed street before the shut doors of this small civilian hospital; they were still staring up fixedly at the silver-bright sky. They proved to be day-nurses off duty, and among them was Mademoiselle Annette. She greeted me now as an old friend, and brushing rules and regulations aside like a true Frenchwoman took me at once to Susan. I found that Susan had risen from bed and was seated at her window, which looked out across the winter-bare hospital garden.

"Ambo," she exclaimed impatiently, "why did you come here! I'm so used to all this. But Jeanne-Marie, Ambo—in her condition! I've been hoping so you would think of her—go to her!"

Then what fatuous devil—was it my old familiar demon?—put it into my heart to say: "So you haven't been worrying, dear, about me?"

"About you!" she cried. "Good God, no! What does it matter about you— or me! This generation's done for, Ambo. Only the children count now—the children. We must save them—all of them—somehow. It's up to them—to Jimmy's son with the rest! They've got to wipe us out, clear the slate of us and all our insanities! They've got to pass over the wreck of us and rebuild a happy, intelligible world!"

She rose, seized my arm, and summoning all her strength thrust me from her toward the door... .

VI

It was well on toward three o'clock in the morning when at last I stood before the black, close-shuttered shop-front of the Vve. Guyot. I was desperately weary, having of necessity walked all the way. It was, as I had fully realized while almost stumbling along toward my goal, a crazy errand. I should find a dark, silent house, and I should then stumble back through dark, silent streets to my dark, silent hotel. The shop of the Widow Guyot was a very little shop on a very narrow street, a mere slit between high, ancient buildings—a slit filled now with the dense river-mist that shrouds from the experience of Parisians all the renewing wonders of clear-eyed dawn. The moon had set, or else hung too veiled and low for this pestilent alley; in spite of a thick military overcoat I shivered with cold; the flat, sour smell of ill-flushed gutters caught at my throat. To this abomination of desolation I had, with no little difficulty, found my way. Thank God I could turn now, with a good conscience, and fumble back to the warm oblivion of bed.

I paused a moment, however, to draw up the collar of my overcoat to my ears and fasten it securely; and, doing so, I was aware of the scrape and clink of metal on metal; then the shop-door right before me was shaken and jarred open from within. The fluttering rays of a candle, tremulously held, surprised and for an instant blinded me; faintly luminous green and red balloons wheeled swiftly in contracting circles, then coalesced to a flickering point of light. The candle was held by an old, stout woman with a loose-jowled, bruised-looking face; a face somehow sensual and hard in spite of its bloated antiquity. A shrunken, thin-bearded man in a long black coat stood beside her, holding a black hand-bag. The two were conversing in tones deliberately muted, but broke off and stared outward as the candle-light discovered me in the narrow street.

"Ah, M'sieu, one sees, is American; he has perhaps lost his way?" piped the thin-bearded man, pretty sharply. He, too, was old.

"But no," I replied; "I am here precisely on behalf of my friend, Lieutenant Kane."

At this name the old woman began, only to check, a half-startled squawk, lifting her candle as she did so and peering more intently at me. "At this hour, m'sieu?" she demanded huskily. "What could bring you at such an hour?"

"Do I address the Widow Guyot?" I was quick to respond.

"*Oui, m'sieu.*"

"Then, permit me to explain." As briefly as possible I told her who I was; that I had but very recently learned of the presence of Jimmy's wife in Paris, with a relative—learned that she was awaiting the birth of her first child at the house of this excellent woman. "It was my intention to call soon, madame, in any case, and make myself known—feeling there might prove to be many little services a friend would be only too happy to render. But, after this terrible raid, I found it impossible to retire with an easy mind—at least, until I had assured myself that all was well with you here."

On this there came a pause, and the thin-bearded man cleared his throat diligently several times.

"The truth is, m'sieu," he finally hazarded, "that your apprehension was only too just. You arrive at a house of mourning, m'sieu. You arrive, as I did, alas—too late! This poor Madame Kane you would inquire for is dead. The child, on the contrary, still lives."

"Enter, m'sieu," said the Widow Guyot. "We can discuss these things more commodiously within. Doubtless, otherwise, we shall receive attentions from the police; they are nervous to-night. Naturally." She seemed, I thought—in the utter blank depression which had seized me with the doctor's words— offensively calm. Whether, had a doctor been more quickly obtainable, or a more skillful practitioner at last obtained, little Jeanne-Marie's life might have been spared, I am unable to say. I feel certain, however, that the Widow Guyot —under difficult, not to say terrifying circumstances—had kept a cool head, done her best. I exonerate her from all blame. But I add this: Never in my life have I met elsewhere a woman who seemed to me to possess such cold-blooded possibilities for evil. Yet, so far as I know to this hour, her life has always been and now continues industrious and thrifty; harmless before the law. I have absolutely "nothing on her"—nothing but an impression I shall never be rid of, which even now returns to chill me in nights of insomnia: a sense of having met in life one woman whose eyes may now and then have watered from dust or wind, but could never under any circumstances conceivably human have known tears. Other women, too many of them, have bored or exasperated me with maudlin or trivial tears; but never before or since have I met a woman who *could* not weep. It is a fixed idea with me that the Widow Guyot could not; and the idea haunts and troubles me strangely—though why it should, I am too casual a psychologist even to guess.

At her heels, I crossed a small cluttered shop, following the tremulous flame of the candle through a fantastic shadow dance; Doctor Pollain—who had given me his name with the deprecating cough of one who knows himself either unpleasantly notorious or hopelessly obscure—shuffled behind us. Madame Guyot opened an inner door. Light from the room beyond tempered a little the vagueness about me and ghostily revealed a huddle of ecclesiastical trumpery—rows of thin, pale-yellow tapers; small crucifixes of plaster or base-metal gilded; a stand of picture post-cards; a table littered with lesser gimcracks. The direct rays from Madame Guyot's candle, as she turned a moment in the doorway, wanly illuminated the blue-coiffed, vapid face of a bisque Virgin; gave for that instant a half-flicker, as of just-stirring life, to her mannered, meaningless smile.

The room beyond proved to be a good-sized bedroom, its one window muffled by heavy stuff-curtains of a dull magenta red. A choking, composite odor—I detected the sick pungency of chloroform—emerged from it. I plunged to enter, and for a second instinctively held my breath. On the great walnut double-bed lay a still figure covered with a sheet; the proper candles twinkled at head and foot. But it is needless to describe these things... .

It was in a smaller room beyond, a combined living-and-dining room, stodgily ugly, but comfortable enough as well, that I first made the acquaintance of James Aulard Kane. What I saw was a great roll of blankets in a deep boxlike cradle, and in the depths of a deeply dented feather pillow a tiny, wrinkled monkey-face, a miniature grotesque. The small knife-slit that served him for mouth opened and shut slowly and continuously, as if feebly gasping for difficult breath. He gave not even one faint encouraging cry. I turned to Doctor Pollain, shaking my head.

"But no!" he exclaimed. "For an eight-months child, look you—he has vigor! I am sure he will live."

"Then, for his father's sake," I replied, "we must take no chances! Isn't there a maternity hospital in the neighborhood where he can receive the close attention that you, madame, at your age, with your responsibilities, ought not to be expected to give? I make myself fully responsible for any and all charges involved. Understand me, madame, and you, M. le Médecin, I insist that no stone shall be left unturned!"

These words produced, at once a grateful change in the atmosphere—hitherto, I had felt, ever so slightly hostile. It is unnecessary to follow our further negotiations to their entirely amicable close. Half an hour later I left the shop of the Widow Guyot, satisfied that Doctor Pollain would assist her to make all needful arrangements, and promising to get into communication as soon as it could be managed with "M. Jee-mee." I should return, I told them, certainly, before noon.

But for Jimmy's sake, on leaving, I raised a corner of the sheet covering the face of Jeanne-Marie. It was a peaceful face. If she had lately suffered, death now had quietly smoothed from her all but a lasting restfulness. A good little woman, I mused, of the best type provincial France offers; sensible, yet ardent; practical, yet kind. As I looked down at her, the meaningless smile of the bisque Madonna in the shop without returned to me, simpered for a half-second before me... . The symbols men made—and sold—commercial symbols! The Mother of Sorrows, a Chinese toy! Well... .

"One thing troubles me," said the Widow Guyot at my elbow, in her husky, passionless voice: "She did not receive the last rites, m'sieu. When the bad turn came, it was not possible for us to leave her. You will understand that. There was a new life, was there not? Assuredly, though, I am troubled; I regret that this should have happened to *me*. It will be a great cause for scandal, m'sieu—when you consider my connections—the nature of my little affairs. But, name of God, that will pass; one explains these things with a certain success, and my age favors me. I bear, God be praised, a good name; and in the proper quarters, m'sieu. But—the poor little one! Observe m'sieu, that she clasps a crucifix on her breast. Be so good as to remember that I placed it in her hands—an instant before she died."

VII

It is an artistic fault in real life that it deals so frequently in coincidence, to the casting of suspicion upon those who report it veraciously. On the very night that Jeanne-Marie died, probably within the very hour that she died, Jimmy was shot down, while taking part in a bombing expedition; the plane he was conducting was seen, by crews of the two other bombing-planes in the formation, to burst into flames after a direct hit from an anti-aircraft battery, which had been firing persistently, though necessarily at haphazard, up toward the bumble-bee hum of French motors—so betrayingly unlike the irregular guttural growl of the German machines.

Throughout the following morning I had been attempting, with the indispensable aid of my old friend, Colonel ——, of the French war office, to get into telegraphic communication with the commander of Jimmy's *esquadrille;* but it was noon, or very nearly, before this unexpected word came to us. And when it came, I found myself unable to believe it.

In the very spirit of Assessor Brack, "Things don't happen like that!" I kept insisting. "It's too improbable. I must wait for further verification. We shall see, colonel, there's been an error in names; some mistake." I was stubborn about it. Simply, for Susan's sake, I could not admit the possibility that Jimmy was dead.

During the midday pause I hurriedly made my way to the Widow Guyot's little shop. The baby had already been taken to the Hospice de la Maternité—the old Convent of Port Royal, near the cemetery of Montparnasse. He had stood the trip well, Madame Guyot assured me, and would undoubtedly win through to a ripe old age. A priest was present. I told Madame Guyot to arrange with him for a proper funeral and interment for Jeanne-Marie, and was at once informed that the skilled assistants of a local director of *pompes funébres* were even then at work, embalming her mortal remains.

"So much, at least, m'sieu," said Madame Guyot, "I knew her husband would desire; and I relied on your suggestion that no expense need be spared. I have stipulated for a funeral of the first class"—a specific thing in France; so many carriages with black horses, so many plumes of such a quality, and so on—"it only remains to acquire a site for the poor little one's grave. This, too, M'sieu le Capitaine, you may safely leave to my discretion; but we must together fix on a day and hour for the ceremonies. Is it yet known when this poor Lieutenant Kane will arrive in Paris?"

No, it was not yet known; I should be able to inform her, I hazarded, before nightfall; and I thanked her for the pains she was taking, and again assured her that the financial question was of no importance. As I said this, the priest, a dry wisp of manhood, softly drew nearer and slightly moistened his thin-set lips; but he did not speak. Possibly Madame Guyot spoke for him.

"At such times, m'sieu," she replied, "one does what one can. But naturally—that is understood. One is not an only relative for nothing, m'sieu. The heart speaks. True, I have hitherto been put to certain expenses for which the poor little one had promised to reimburse me——"

I hastened to assure her that she had only to present this account to me in full, and we parted with mutual though secret contempt, and with every sanctified expression of esteem. Then I returned to the cabinet of my friend, Colonel ——.

By three o'clock in the afternoon a brief telegram from Jimmy's commander was brought to us; it removed every possibility of doubt, even from my obdurate mind. Jimmy had "gone West" once for all, and this time "West" was not even a geographical expression... . I sat silent for perhaps five slowly passing minutes in the presence of Colonel ——, until I was aware of a somewhat amazed scrutiny from tired, heavily pouched blue eyes.

"You feel this deeply," he observed, "and I—I feel nothing, except a vague sympathy for you, *mon ami*. Accept, without phrases, I beg you, all that a sad old man has left to give."

I rose, thanked him warmly for the trouble he had taken on my behalf, and left him to his endless, disheartening labors. France was in danger; he knew that France was in danger. What to him, in those days, was one young life more or less? He himself had lost three sons in the war... .

But how was I to let fall this one blow more, this heaviest blow of all, upon Susan? It was that which had held me silent in my chair, inhibiting all will to rise and begin the next needful step. Yes, it was that; I was thinking of Susan, not of Jimmy. For me in those days, I fear, the world consisted of Susan, and of certain negligible phantoms—the remainder of the human race. It is not an *état d'âme* that Susan admires, or that I much admire; but in those days it was certainly mine. And this is the worst of a lonely passion: the more one loves in secret, without fulfillment—and however unselfishly—the more one excludes. Life contracts to a vivid, hypnotizing point; all else is shadow. In the name of our common humanity, there is a good deal to be said for those who are fickle or frankly pagan, who love more lightly, and more easily forget. But enough of all this! Phil with his steady wisdom might philosophize it to some purpose; not I.

In my uncertainty of mind, then, the first step that I took was an absurdly false one. There was just one thing for me to do, and I did not do it. I should have gone straight to Susan and told her about Jimmy and Jeanne-Marie; above all, about James Aulard Kane. Even if Susan, as I then supposed, loved Jimmy, and had always loved him—knowing her as I did, loving her as I did, I should have felt instinctively that this was the one wise and kind, the one possible thing to do. Yet a sudden weakness, born of innate cowardice, betrayed me.

I went, instead, direct to the Hotel Crillon and sent up my card to Miss Leslie; it struck me as fortunate that I found her just returned to her rooms from a visit to Susan. It was really a calamity. I had seen her several times there, at the hospital; I liked her; and I knew that Susan had now no more devoted friend. She received me cordially, and I at once laid all the facts before her and—with an entirely sincere humbleness—asked her advice. But God, in the infinite variety of his creations, had never intended Mona Leslie to shine by reason of insight or common sense; she had other qualities! And this, too, I should easily have discerned. Why I did not, can only be explained by a sort of prostration of all my faculties, which had come upon me with the events of the night and morning just past. I was inert, body and soul; I could not think; I felt like a child in the sweep of dark forces it cannot struggle against and does not understand; in effect, I was for the time being a stricken, credulous child. Perhaps no grown man, not definitely insane, has ever touched a lower stratum of spiritual debility than I then sank to—resting there, grateful, fatuously content, as if on firm ground. In short, I was a plain and self-damned fool.

It seemed to me, I remember, during our hour's talk together, that Miss Leslie was one of the two or three wisest, most understanding, and sympathetic persons I had ever met. Sympathetic, she genuinely was; very gracious and interestingly melancholy, in her Belgian nurse's costume, with King Albert's decoration pinned to her breast. It seemed to me that she divined my thoughts before I uttered them; as perhaps she did—for to call them thoughts is to dignify vague sensations with a misleading name. Miss Leslie had had always, I am now aware, an instinctive response for vague sensations; she had always vibrated to them like a harp, thus surrounding herself with an odd, whispering music. A strange woman; not without nobility and force when the appropriate vague sensations played upon her. The sufferings of war had already wrung from her a wild, æolian masterpiece, more moving perhaps than a consciously ordered symphony. And Susan, though she had never so much as guessed at Susan, was one of her passions! Susan played on us both that day: though the mawkish music we made would have disgusted her—did disgust her in its final effects, as it has finally disgusted me.

What these effects were can be briefly told, but not briefly enough to comfort me. There is no second page of this record I should be so happy not to write.

Miss Leslie had long suspected, she told me, that Susan—like Viola's hypothetical sister—was pining in thought for a secret, unkind lover, and she at once accepted as a certainty my suggestion that so gallant a young aviator as Jimmy had been what "glorious Jane" always calls her "object."

"This must be kept from her, Mr. Hunt, at all costs—for the next few weeks, I mean! She's simply not strong enough yet, not poised enough, to bear it—with all the rest! It would be cruelty to tell her now, and might prove murderous. Oh, believe me, Mr. Hunt—I *know!*"

Her cocksure intensity could not fail to impress me in my present state of deadness; I listened as if to oracles. Then we conspired together.

"My lease of the villa at Mentone runs on till May," said Miss Leslie. "Susan's physically able for the journey now, I think; we must take that risk anyway. I'll get the doctors to order her down there with me, at once. She needs the change, the peace; above all—the *beauty* of it. She's starved for beauty, poor soul! And there's the possibility of further raids, too; she mustn't in her condition be exposed to that. When she's stronger, Mr. Hunt—after she's had a few happy weeks—then I'll tell her everything, in my own way. Women can do these things, you know; they have an instinct for the right moment, the right words."

"You are proving that now," I said. Every word she had spoken was balm to me. Everything could be put off—put off... . To put things off indefinitely, hide them out of sight, dodge them somehow! Why, she was voicing the one weary cry of my soul!

And so, within three days, this supreme folly was accomplished. Mona Leslie and I stole across the river in secret to little Jeanne-Marie's meagerly attended "funeral of the first class," and with Madame Guyot, Doctor Pollain, and a few casual neighbors, we followed her coffin from the vast drafty dreariness of St. Sulpice to the wintry, crowded alleys of the cemetery of Montparnasse.—That very evening Susan left with Miss Leslie for Mentone.

She was glad enough to go, she said, for a week or two. "But Ambo—what shall I say to Jimmy? Will he ever forgive me for not having been able to make friends, first, with Jeanne-Marie? And it's all your fault, dear; you must tell him that—say you've been downright cross with me about it. I wish now I hadn't listened to you; I feel perfectly well to-night; I've no business to be starting on a holiday. But I shan't stay long, Ambo. I'll be back in Paris before little Jimmy arrives; I promise you that. And here's a letter to post, dear; I've said so in it to Jeanne-Marie."

A dark train drew out of a dark station. With it went Hope, the shadow, silently, from my heart... .

VIII

The days passed. Mentone, Miss Leslie wrote me, was doing everything for Susan that we had desired. "But she is determined," she added, "to be back in Paris by the last week of February—when the baby was expected. She begins to be bothered that you write so scrappily and vaguely, and that she hears nothing directly from Lieutenant Kane or Jeanne-Marie. I shall have to tell her soon now, in any case. It seems more difficult as I come nearer to it, but I still feel sure we have done the right thing. I'm certain now that Susan will be able to face and bear it. Already she's full of plans for the future— wonderful! Possibly, if an opportunity offers, I shall tell her to-night."

The next afternoon my telephone rang. When I answered it, Susan spoke to me. "Ambo," she said, "I'm at the France-et-Choiseul. Please come over at once, no matter how busy you are. You owe that much to me, I think." She had hung up the receiver before I could stammer a reply.

But nothing more was necessary. I went to her as a criminal goes to confession, knowing at last how hideously in her eyes I had sinned.

"You *meant* well, Ambo," she said with a gentleness that yielded nothing —"you and Mona. Meaning well's what I feel now I can never quite forgive you. *You*, Ambo. Poor Mona doesn't count in this. But you—I thought I was safe with you. No matter."

Later she said: "I've seen Madame Guyot—a horrible woman; and the baby. He's a nice baby. You did just right about him, Ambo. Thank you for that." She mused a moment. "I suppose it's absurd to think he looks like Jimmy? But to me he does. I'm going to adopt him, Ambo. You see"—her smile was wistful—"I *am* going to have a baby of my own, after all."

"I'd thought of adopting him, myself," I babbled; "but of course——"

"Of course," said Susan.

In so many subtle ways she had made it clear to me. I had disappointed her; revealed a blindness, a weakness, she would never be able to forget. In my hotel room that night I faced it out and accepted my punishment as just. Just—but terrible... . There is nothing in life so terrible as to know oneself utterly and finally alone.

IX

On the night of the eighth of March the Gothas, so long expected, returned; to be met this time by a persistent *barrage* fire from massed 75's, which proved, however, little more than the good beginnings of a really competent defense. Many bombs fell within the fortifications, and we who dwelt there needed no other proof that the problem of the defense of Paris against air raids had not yet successfully been solved.

There were thickening rumors, too, of an imminent German attack in force. Things were not going well at the Front. It was common gossip that there was division among the Allies; the British and French commands were pulling at cross purposes; Italy seemed impotent; Russia had collapsed; the Americans were unknown factors, and slow to arrive. It began to seem possible—to the disaffected or naturally pessimistic, more than possible—that the Prussian mountebank might make good his anachronistic boast to wear down and conquer the world.

Even the weather seemed to fight for his pinchbeck empire; it was continuously dry, and for the season in Northern France extraordinarily clear. By its painful contrast with our common anxieties, the unseasonable beauty of those March days and nights weighted as if with lead the sense of threat, of impending calamity, that pressed upon us and chilled us and made desperate our hearts.

I saw Susan daily. She did not avoid me and was never unkind, but I felt that she took little comfort or pleasure from my society. Mona Leslie, rather huffed than chastened, I fear, by Susan's quiet aloofness, had returned to her duties at Dunkirk. I was glad to have her go, to be rid of the embarrassment of her explanations and counsel—to be rid, above all, of the pointedly sympathetic and pitying pressure of her hand. Except for a slight limp, Susan now got about freely and was busily engaged with our Red Cross directors on plans for a nursing-home for the children of repatriated refugees—a home where these little victims of frightfulness and malnutrition could be built up again into happy soundness of body and mind, into the vigorous life-stuff needed for the future of France and of the world. A too-medieval château at ——, in Provence, had been offered; and plans for its immediate alteration and modernization were being drawn.

The whole thing, from the first, had been Susan's idea, and she was to have charge of it all—once the required plant was ready—as became its creator. But indeed, in the interim, she had simply taken charge of our Red Cross architects and buyers and builders and engineers, and was sweeping things forward with a tactful but exceedingly high hand. She meant that the interim should be, if possible, brief.

"I want results," said Susan; "we can discuss the rules we've broken afterward. The children are fading out *now*, and some of them will be dead or hopelessly withered before we can aid them. Let's get some kind of home and get it running; with a couple of good doctors, an orthopedist, a dental expert, and the right nurses—and I'll pick *them*, please!—we can make out somehow, 'most anywhere."

There was no standing against her. It was presently plain to all of us in the Paris headquarters that this nursing home was to be put through, in record time, Germans or no Germans, and no matter who fell by the wayside! And, in spite of my natural anxiety, I was soon convinced that whoever fell, it would not be Susan—not, at least, till the clear flame of her spirit had burned out the oil of her energy to its last granted drop.

In the rare intervals of these labors, she was arranging for the legal adoption of James Aulard Kane. No step of this kind is easily arranged in bureaucratic France. It is a difficult land to be legally born in or married in, or to die in—if one wishes to do these things, at least, with a certain decency, *en règle*.

Susan complained to me of this, wittily scornful, as we left the Red Cross headquarters together on the evening of March eleventh, and started toward her hotel down the dusky colonnade of the Rue de Rivoli.

"I'm worn out with them all!" she exclaimed. "All I want is to take care of Jimmy's baby, and you'd think I was plotting to upset the government. I shall, too, if some of these French officials don't presently exhibit more common sense. It *ought* to be upset—and simplified. Oh, I wish I lived in a woman's republic, Ambo! Things would happen there, even if they were wrong! No woman has patience enough to be bureaucratic."

"True," I chimed; "and you're right about men, all round. We're hopeless incompetents at statecraft and such things, at running a reasonable world—but we *can* cook! And what you need for a change from all this is a good dinner —a real dinner! It will renew your faith in the eternal masculine—and we haven't had a bat, Susan, or talked nonsense, for years and years! Come on, dear! Let's have a perfectly shameless bat to-night and damn the consequences! What do you say?"

"I say—damn the consequences, Ambo! Let's! Why, I'd forgotten there was such a thing as a bat left in the world!"

"But there is! Look—there's even a taxi to begin on!"

I hailed it; I even secured it; and we were presently clanking and grinding on our way—in what must have been an authentic relic from the First Battle of the Marne—toward the one restaurant in Paris. Unto each man, native or alien, who knows his Paris, God grants but one, though it is never the same. Well, I make no secret about it; my passion is deep and openly proclaimed. For me, the one restaurant in Paris is *Lapérouse;* I am long past discussing the claims of rivals. It is—simply and finally—*Lapérouse.* . . .

We descended before an ancient, dingy building on the Quai des Grands-Augustins, passed through a cramped doorway into a tiny, ill-lit foyer, climbed a steep narrow stairs, and were presently installed in a corner of the small corner dining-room, with our backs neighborly against the wall. In this room there happened that night to be but one other diner; a small, bloated, bullet-headed civilian, with prominent staring eyes; a man of uncertain age, but nearing fifty at a guess. We paid little attention to him at first, though it soon became evident to us that he was enjoying a Pantagruelian banquet in lonely state, deliberately gorging himself with the richest and most incongruously varied food. *Comme boissons,* he had always before him two bottles, one of *Château Yquem* and one of *Fine Champagne;* and he alternated gulps of thick yellow sweetness with drams of neat brandy. Neither seemed to produce upon him any perceptible effect, though he emitted from time to time moist porcine snufflings of fleshy satisfaction. Rather a disgusting little man, we decided; and so dismissed him... .

To the ordering of our own dinner I gave a finicky care which greatly amused Susan, for whom food, I regret to say, has always remained an indifferent matter; it is the one æsthetic flaw in her otherwise so delicately organized being. In spite of every effort on my part to educate her palate, five or six nibbles at almost anything edible remains her idea of a banquet— provided the incidental talk prove sufficiently companionable or stimulating.

That night, however, do what we would, our talk together was neither precisely the one nor the other. We both, rather desperately, I think, made a supreme effort to approximate the free affectionate chatter of old days; but such things never come of premeditation, and there were ghosts at the table with us. It would not work.

"Oh, what's the use, Ambo!" Susan finally exclaimed, with a weary sigh. "We can't do it this way! Sister's here, and Jeanne-Marie—as close to me as if I had seen her and known her always; and maybe—Phil. But Jimmy's here most of all! There's no use pretending we're forgetting, when we're not. You and I aren't built for forgetting, Ambo. We'll never forget."

"No, dear; we'll never forget."

"Let's *remember*, then," said Susan; "remember all we can."

For a long hour thereafter we rather mused together than conversed. Constraint slipped from us, as those we had best loved came back to us, warm and near and living in our thoughts of them. No taint of false sentiment, of sorrow willfully indulged, marred these memories. Trying to be happy we had failed; now, strangely, we came near to joy.

"We haven't lost them!" exclaimed Susan. "Not any part of them; we never can."

"They haven't lost us, then?"

"No"—she pondered it—"they haven't lost us."

"You mean it, Susan—literally? You believe they still live—*out there?*"

"And you?"

"I don't know."

"Poor Ambo," murmured Susan; then, with a quick, dancing gleam: "But as Jimmy'd say, dear, you can just take it from *me!*"

She spoke of him as if present beside her. A silence fell between us and deepened.

The small, bullet-headed man had just paid his extravagant bill, distributed his largesse, and was about to depart. He was being helped into a sumptuous overcoat, with a deep collar of what I took to be genuine Russian sables. There was nothing in his officiously tended leave-taking to stir my interest; my eyes rested on him idly for a moment, that was all. The head waiter, two under-waiters, and a solemn little buttons followed him out to the stair-head, with every expression of gratitude and esteem. Passing from sight, he passed from my thoughts, leaving with me only a vague physical repulsion that barely outlasted his departure.

"Do you know what I think Phil has done?" Susan was asking.

"Phil?" The name had startled me back to attention.

"I believe he's made himself one of them—the peasants, I mean—in some remote, dirty, half-starved Russian village."

"Why? That's an odd fancy, dear. And it isn't much like him. Phil's too clear-headed, or stiff-headed, for such mysticism."

"How little you really know him, then," she replied. "He's been steering since birth, I feel, toward some great final renunciation. I believe he's made it, now. You'll see, Ambo. Some day we'll hear of a new prophet, away there in the East—where all our living dreams come from! You'll see!"

"'In Vishnu-land what Avatar?'" I quoted, smiling sadly enough; and Susan's smile wistfully echoed mine, even while she raised a warning finger at me.

"Oh, you of little faith!" she said quite simply.

X

We had barely stepped out from the narrow doorway of the restaurant into a tenuous, moon-saturated mist, a low-lying diaphaneity that left the upper air-lanes openly clear, when the sirens were wailing again from every quarter of the city... .

"They're coming early to-night!" I exclaimed. "Well, that ends all hope for a taxi home! We must find an *abri*."

"Nonsense! We'll walk quietly back along the river. Unless"—she teased me—"you really *are* afraid, Ambo?"

I tucked her arm firmly into mine. "So you won't stumble, *Mlle. la Réformée!*"

"But it is a nuisance to be lame!" she protested: "I do envy you your two good legs, *M. le Capitaine.*"

We made our way slowly along the embankment, passing the Pont des Arts, and two shadowy lovers paced on before us, blotted together, oblivious of the long, eerie rise and fall of the sirens; every twenty yards or so they stopped in their tracks, as by a common impulsion, and were momentarily lost to time in a passionate embrace.

Neither Susan nor I spoke of these lovers, who turned aside to pass under the black arches of the Institute, into the Rue de Seine... .

As we neared the Pont du Carrousel the *barrage* began, at first distant and muffled—the outer guns; then suddenly and grimly nearer. An incessant twinkle of tiny star-white points—the bursts of high-explosive shells—drifted toward us from the north. So light was the mist, it did not obscure them; it barely dimmed the moon.

"Hold on!" I said, checking Susan; "this is something new! They're firing to-night straight across Paris." The glitter of star-points seemed in a moment to fill all the northern sky; the noise of the *barrage* trebled, trebled again.

"Why, it's drum fire!" cried Susan. "Oh, how beautiful!"

"Yes; but we'll get on faster, all the same! I'll help you! Come!"

I put my arm firmly about her waist and almost lifted her along with me. By the time we had reached the Pont Royal, the high-explosive bursts were directly over us; the air rocked with them. I detected, too, at intervals, another more ominous sound—that deep, pulsing growl which no one having once heard it could ever mistake.

"Gothas," I growled back at them, "flying low. They've ducked under the guns!"

And instantly I swung Susan across the open *quai* to the left and plunged with her up an inky defile, the Rue du Bac.

"Where are you taking me?" she demanded, half breathless, dragging against my arm.

"To the first available *abri*," I cried at her, under the sky's reckless tumult. "Don't stop to argue about it!"

But she halted me right by the corner of the Rue de Lille. "If it's going to be a bad raid, Ambo, I must get to Jimmy's baby—I *must!*"

"Impossible! It's at least two miles—and this isn't going to be a picnic, Susan! You're coming with *me!*" I tightened my arm about her; every instant now I expected the shattering climax of the bombs.

Then, just as we crossed the Rue de Lille, something halted me in my turn. About a hundred yards at my right, down toward the Gare D'Orsay, and from the very middle of the black street-chasm, a keen, bladelike ray of light flashed once and again—sharp, vertical rapier-thrusts—straight up through the thin mist-veil into the treacherous sky. Followed, doubtless from a darkened upper window, a woman's frantic shriek: "*Espion—espion!*"

Pistol shots next—and rough cries—and a pounding charge of feet... . Right into my arms he floundered, and I tackled him and fell with him to the cobbles and fought him there blindly, feeling for his throat. This lasted but a moment. Gendarmes tore us apart, in a brief crossing flash of electric-torches —and I caught just one glimpse of a bare bullet-head, of a bloated, discolored face, of prominent staring eyes, maddened by fear. There could be no mistake. It was our little man of the Pantagruelian banquet. We had watched him eating his last fabulous meal—his farewell to Egypt.

And that is all I just then clearly remember... . I am told that nine bombs fell in a sweeping circle throughout this district; one of them, in the very courtyard of the War Office; one of them—of 300 kilos—perhaps a square from where we stood. There was a rush past of hurtling fragments—glass, chimney-tiles, chips of masonry, *que sais-je?*—and even this I report only because I have been credibly so informed.

What next I experienced was pain, unlocalized at first, yet somehow damnably concentrated: pure, white-hot essence of pain. And through the stiff hell of it I was, and was not, aware of someone—some one—some *one*—murmuring love and pity and mortal anguish... .

"Ambo—you wouldn't leave me—not you! Not you, Ambo—not alone... ."

The pain dimmed off from me in an ebbing, dull-red wave; great coils of palpable darkness swirled down upon me to smother me; I struggled to rise from beneath them—fling them off... . From an infinite distance, a woman's cry threaded through them, like a needle through mufflings of wool, and pricked me to an instant, a single instant, of clear consciousness. I opened my eyes on Susan's; I strove to answer them, tell her I understood. Susan says that I did answer them—that I even smiled. But I can feel back now only to a vast sinking away, depth under depth under depth, down—down—down—down... .

XI

The rest, however, I thank God, is not yet silence; though it is high time to make an end of this long and all too faulty record.

They did various things to me at the hospital, from time to time; they removed hard substances from me that were distinctly out of place in my interior; they also removed certain portions of my authentic anatomy—three fingers of my left hand, among others, and my left leg to the knee. This was not in itself agreeable, and I shall always regret their loss; yet those weeks of progressive operation and tardy recuperation were, up to that period, the happiest, the most fulfilled weeks of my life. And surely egotism can go no farther! For these weeks of my triumphant happiness were altogether the darkest, saddest, cruellest weeks of the war. In a world without light, my heart sang in my breast, sang hallelujahs, and would not be cast down. Susan loved me—*me*—had always loved me! Rheims soon might fall, Amiens might fall, the channel ports, Paris, London, the Seven Seas—the World! What did it matter! Susan loved me—loved me!

And even now—though Susan is ashamed for me that I can say it—though I feel that I ought to be ashamed that I can say it—though I wonder that I am not—though I try to be—well, I am *not* ashamed!

Final Note, by Susan—*insisted upon:* "But all the same, secretly, he is ashamed. For there's nobody in the world like Ambo, whether for dearness or general absurdity. Why shouldn't he have been a little happy, if he could manage it, throughout those interminable weeks of physical pain? He suffered day and night, preferring not to be kept under morphine too constantly. I won't say he was a hero; he *was*, but there's nothing to be puffed up about nowadays in that. If the war has proved anything, it is that in nearly every man, when his particular form of Zero Hour sounds for him, some kind of a self-despising hero is waiting, and ready to act or endure or be broken and cast away. We all know that now. It's the cornerstone for a possible Utopia: no, it's more than that—it's the whole foundation. But I didn't mean to say so when I started this note.

"All I meant to say was that you must never take Ambo *au pied de la lettre*. I'm not in the least as he's hymned me—but that, surely, you've guessed between the lines. What is much more important is that he's not in the least as he has painted himself. But unless I were to rewrite his whole book for him—which wouldn't be tactful in an otherwise spoiled and contented wife—I could never make this clear, or do my strange, too sensitive man the full justice he deserves. He's—oh, but what's the use! There isn't anybody in the world like Ambo."

XII

More than a year has already passed since those dark-bright days, the spring of 1918. Down here in quiet, silvery Provence, at our nursing-home for children—I call it ours—the last of the cherry blossoms are falling now in our walled orchard close. As I write, James Aulard Kane sits—none too steadily —among a snow of petals, and sweeps them together in miniature drifts with two very grubby little hands. He is a likely infant and knows definitely what he wants from life, which is mostly food. He talks nothing but French—that is, he emits the usual baby grunts and snortings in a funny harsh accent caught from his Marseillaise nurse. Susan is far too busy to improve this accent as she would like to do: perhaps it would be simpler to say that she is far too busy. She is the queen-bee of this country hive; and I—I am a harmless enough drone. They let me dawdle about here and do this and that; but the sun grows more powerful daily, and I sleep a good deal now through the warmer hours. I am haunted by fewer mysterious twinges, here and there, when I sleep... .

Meanwhile, the world-cauldron bubbles, and the bubbles keep bursting, and I read of their bursting and shake my head. When a man begins shaking his head over the news of the day, he is done for; a back number. Susan never shakes her head; and it's rather hard on her, I think, to be the wife of a back number. But she's far too thoughtful of me ever to seem to mind.

Only yesterday I quoted some lines to her, from Coventry Patmore. Susan doesn't like Coventry Patmore; the mystical Unknown Eros he celebrates strikes her as—well, perhaps I had better not go into that. But the lines I quoted—they had been much in my mind lately—were these:

> *For want of me the world's course will not fail;*
> *When all its work is done the lie shall rot;*
> *The truth is great and shall prevail*
> *When none cares whether it prevail or not.*

"Stuff! We do care!" said Susan. "And it won't prevail, either, unless we make it. Who's working harder than you to make it prevail, I should like to know!"

You see how she includes me... . So this book is my poor tribute to her thoughtfulness, this Book of Susan.

But sometimes I sit and wonder. Shall we ever, I wonder, go back to my ancestral mansion on Hillhouse Avenue and quietly settle down there to the old securities, the old, slightly disdainful calm? I doubt it. Tumps, ancient valetudinarian, softened by age; Togo, rheumatic, but steeped in his deeply racial, his Oriental indifferentism—they are the inheritors of that august tradition, and they become it worthily. For them it exists and is enough; for us it is shattered. Phil, a later Waring, is lost in Russia. Jimmy is gone. But Susan will do, I know, more than one woman's part to help in creating a more livable world for his son, and I shall gain some little strength for that coming labor, spending it as I can. It will be an interesting world for those who survive; a dusk chaos just paling eastward. I shall hardly see even the beginnings of dawn. But—with Susan beside me—I shall have lived.

Farewell, then, Hillhouse Avenue! . . . Make way for Birch Street!

(THE END)

CPSIA information can be obtained
at www.ICGtesting.com
Printed in the USA
LVHW010046080820
662304LV00004B/721